PROLOGUE

SALVATORE

I COULD KILL THE RAT.

I could remind the other three men in the room exactly how I've earned the name whispered behind closed doors.

But the rat's just pissed all over his pants, so I'm not overly eager to touch him.

Dom shoots me a shit-eating grin from behind Barbara and Red. He's either laughing at the grown man with piss on his pants or reveling in how much I hate to get dirty. Probably both.

I shift my attention back to Virgilio.

"You thought it was a good idea to break omertà?" I don't bother to raise my voice. He's not listening.

"*I'm sorry I'm sorry I'm sorry. Please please oh god make it stop...*"

The acid eating away at his left hand doesn't listen either.

Barbara watches with his arms crossed over his hefty belly, wiry eyebrows drawn low. For a man who's always shuffling to the nearest armchair, grumbling about back pain, he stands tall now, as unyielding as stone.

His weaselly nephew Red stops posturing long enough to turn and spit on my concrete floor. Fucking disgusting. Behind him, Dom shakes with suppressed laughter. Dick.

Virgilio's steel chair rattles as he trembles. Staccato clacking joins his choked sobs.

"Maybe you could have been forgiven, Vio, but you ratted on family. Your own family. And they're not happy with you. Your good cousin Serafina"—at this, Dom's smile turns grimace—"she's been sent off to Aldo. Your brother and your uncle, they have to clean up your mess. And it's a big fucking mess."

Virgilio cries harder, tears mixing with blood, snot, and spit.

I'll need two scalding-hot showers after this, but I school my expression as I pick up a set of slip-joint pliers. Tradition demands I start with his tongue.

My phone pings.

Frowning, I straighten my back and check my phone. Distantly, Virgilio sobs in relief.

WORM

She got in.

I let the pliers clatter to the tray and swipe to the app for my security system, circling Vigilio with measured footsteps so no one can see my screen.

It'll be a false alarm. Nothing to get excited about.

Through the camera, Marisol springs up from her computer chair and pumps her fists in the air. A slice of soft belly winks from under the hem of her shirt and—*fuck me*—no bra. She plucks a lime-green flash drive from her computer tower, kisses it, and dashes out of the camera's range.

THE DEVIL'S WIFE

A DARK MAFIA ROMANCE

EVE CIRIC

To my husband,
who always gives me a shoulder to cry on and a mustache to ride

The insignia for Luporini Enterprises is dimly visible on her second computer monitor.

Pride and anticipation swell inside me.

WORM

> Looks like she's going to a friend's house.
> Want me to send someone to intercept her?

I consider this to the slow rhythm of Vigilio's labored breathing. She'll need a deliberate touch—too light and she won't take the threat seriously, too serious and she'll take it as a challenge.

No one knows Marisol better than I do. I move toward the exit. It's best I handle this myself.

"Boss," Dom calls out after me. "Where are you going?"

I nearly forgot about the other people in the room. My part's done here anyway.

"I'm tracking down the hacker."

Don exhales and scrubs his jaw, but doesn't argue. "And dumbass here?"

I'm already halfway out the door.

"Oh, him? Red can kill him."

1

MARISOL

GRANT'S GOING to lose his shit.

I squeal and bounce on the balls of my feet, catching myself at the last second when I slip in the soapy water. *Okay, focus.*

Seventy-two hours ago, two hackers entered the virtual Thunderdome, and only one left victorious. My eyes are drier than stale cereal, and my back might have permanently fused into a cooked-shrimp position, but I finally caught the slippery bastard who's been hacking into Grant's company for months.

Nello Marino, hacker name Beta, has been a busy boy. He's got his fingers not only in Grant's company Snap Close but also in Knossos Hospital, PRT Tech, Luporini Enterprises, a smattering of real estate firms, and way more I haven't had the chance to sink my teeth into. The details I *did* manage to download onto my flash drive would put Mr. Beta in a world of trouble.

My stomach swoops in delicious anticipation like I've just shuddered to a stop at the peak of a rollercoaster. Beta might be an actual idiot—storing passwords in plain text should be punished with a loss of your two least favorite fingers—but he wasn't working alone.

He's in the *Mafia*.

Uncovering Beta feels like snagging my prized fish only to glimpse a colossal squid lurking below in the depths.

I scour my hair, in part due to excitement, and in part because my apartment's water heater is broken *again*. I sent out a repair request, but I'll have to see about bumping us ahead in line later. Thank god I had the sense to install a virtual backdoor to the apartment's maintenance system months ago.

I manage to get my teeth to stop chattering once I've tugged on some clothes. Grant loves this long skirt with a blue daisy print—he says it makes me look like a sweet girl-next-door—although the last couple of times I've worn it, he didn't get to see because he was at work or staying out late with a friend. The thought makes me shove my headband through my wet hair with a little too much force.

I'm not entirely stupid. I know why Grant's been spending so much time at Jeremy and Lilah's place. I've seen the way Lilah laughs at his jokes and how Grant wears the new clothes *I* buy him when he goes to see her. Like every other man-child in the world, he thinks a hot new girl will solve all of his problems.

Obviously, that's crazy.

Because *I'm* going to solve all his problems—starting with his high-pressure work assignment.

I make my way to the kitchen and groan as I open the fridge door. I probably should stop by the grocery store soon. The contents of our fridge have been whittled down to a container of old deli ham, two bottles of hot sauce, and a dead fly. The ham is only a little shiny, so I stuff that into my purse along with The Flash Drive.

When I turn, I lock eyes with Buck. He glares at me from the kitchen counter, his tail lashing along the laminate.

"What?"

I run through my checklist. He has food and water, and his cat litter's pristine—the only chore I manage to actually stay on top of. Does he want... affection? He never let Kristin leave the house without saying goodbye.

I suck in a breath and offer my fingers to him. He maintains his death glare but he hasn't bolted yet, so I throw caution to the wind and creep my hand toward his neck. Before I can even touch his fur, he whips his head around to bite my hand then sails off the counter and scrabbles down the hall.

"Okay, *thanks!*" I call after him before slamming the front door. That's on me for expecting anything other than violence from that orange douche.

Despite my heels, I strike out toward the train stop for a little exercise. For the hundredth time this year, I swear I'll get into a regular exercise routine that doesn't involve the path from my desk to the bed. At thirty-two, with fantastic tits and a deep love of sitting down in air-conditioned spaces, back pain is a freeloader who's been crashing on my couch for way too long. I add "personal trainer" right along with "personal chef" and "house cleaner" to my never-gonna-happen dream team.

At the train station, I arch until my back cracks and sit on an empty bench to tear into my deli meat dinner, ignoring the side-eyes from the other people waiting around me. I could care less. In the middle of the city, this hardly ranks as the weirdest thing they'll see today. The train hisses as it pulls to a stop, and my reflection beams back at me in the glass before the doors open.

I can feel in my *bones* that Grant's going to get the

promotion to senior cybersecurity engineer from this. I mean, no one else in all of Snap Close was able to do what I did. He'll at least get a raise. We're so close to being able to pull the trigger on a house and then maybe he'll be ready for what he calls "the M-word talk".

Just because both our parents got divorced doesn't mean marriage is a bad word. We could still make it work. I can make it work.

The proof is in my purse.

Grant's boss Terrence gave him a "special" assignment to uncover who's been siphoning millions of dollars from Snap Close and swore in private meetings that the honest-to-god *Mafia* was responsible.

After months of failing to catch anything conclusive, I walked Grant through putting a subtle, possibly illegal, tracker on Terrence's employee login and when "Terrence" logged into work this Friday to look through our contracts, I tunneled back through the connection to find the real culprit. Beta was stealing details of all our proposals to give to our competitors. Turns out Tinhat Terrence was on to something.

I step off the train station and head toward Jeremy's apartment. It's unseasonably chilly today, but that's not why my arms are prickling with goosebumps. This whole time, I'd thought Terrence was just a weirdo. I mean, he believes in Bigfoot and is always talking about microscopic recording devices. But if he was right, and he knew what Beta was doing with Snap Close, why did he still need evidence to prove it? Was there something he wasn't telling us? Or was this a case of blind luck from a man who'll believe anything?

A shiver passes through me as I stop in front of Jeremy's door. There's also the matter of how easily I found Beta. Yeah, it took me months, but relatively speaking, I'm still a noob. If this guy's such a pro—and he is, judging by the number of systems he's infiltrated—then why was it so easy to catch him? I can't shake the feeling that I'm missing something important.

I knock, my nerves giving way to heady anticipation. For tonight at least, none of that matters. All I care about is Grant's reaction to the news.

He'll be so overwhelmed with relief and gratitude that he'll pin me up against the wall, make out with me on the spot, and take us home to break our forty-nine-day dry spell. And if he doesn't dick me to within an inch of my life, I'm going to the nearest sex shop to buy out their entire stock and then to the grocery store for several pints of dairy-free ice cream. I'll put on Sexy Hot Couples: Island Edition and have a totally normal crying-eating-and-violent-masturbating session.

No one comes to the door. I glance at my phone. It's seven-thirty. Maybe all the guys have gone down to the bar. I send another text to Grant asking where he's at.

While I wait for a reply, I gouge my heel into a divot in the concrete. Jeremy's next-door neighbor gives me the stink eye as she lets herself into her apartment. I can already smell the weed seeping through the door, so it's not exactly a mystery why the neighbors don't love him.

Grant still hasn't responded, and after another light knock on Jeremy's door, I jiggle the handle, hoping it's locked... and it opens immediately—*damn*.

It's been ages since I've had a proper excuse to use my lockpicks, but just in case, I still take them everywhere. Seeing as how they're not exactly, *strictly* legal to carry around without a license, they stay tucked away in my pink pouch labeled *TAMPONS*. I'm not about to let something as silly as the law stand between a girl and her hobby.

As I step inside, the living room belches a miasma of weed directly into my face. A glass bong that's halfway through the alchemical process of transmuting into a bong-shaped piece of resin sits in its place of honor on the coffee table. The carpet crunches under my shoes. Yick.

At least Jeremy and Lilah share one *very* redeeming quality—they both love to cook. I swim through the weed haze toward the scent of Jeremy's triple-fudge brownies as my stomach claws at itself. I'm either still hungry or that deli ham was more suspect than I'd thought.

Sadly, the baking dish on top of the stove is scraped clean. I blow out a sigh of disappointment. No brownies for Marisol.

I check my phone again. Nothing. Grant *did* say he was going over to Jeremy's for a guys' night, right? I was so fixated on the hacker lead that I hadn't paid close attention to what he'd said.

The sound of a muffled bump comes from Jeremy's room, probably his senile pug knocking something over.

The TV's on, queued to Demon Blaster, and it stings a little to see. I know it's important Grant gets guy time, but it still hurts that he's playing my favorite game with his buddies and not inviting me. Especially when Lilah gets to play with them.

Jeremy's dog thuds into the bedroom wall again. And again. Poor guy. I go to let him out of the bedroom but stop dead when I hear the unmistakable sound of a *smack* and a woman's moan.

A wild grin spreads across my face. Did I just stumble onto Jeremy and Lilah having sex?

Lilah's voice rings through the door, "Don't stop! I'm almost there!"

I clap a hand over my mouth to suppress a giggle and

back up slowly to wait outside the apartment until they're done.

Then another voice joins Lilah's—and it's not Jeremy's.

"Fuck, Lilah, I'm fucking coming!"

Icy horror wraps around my spine, freezing me to the spot. Was that *Grant's* voice?

I shake my head. No. No, no, *no*. I misheard that. Jeremy and Grant's voices are similar enough—I have to be wrong.

"Grant! Grant!"

Okay, there's no mistaking *that*.

That lying, cheating sack of shit! My skin prickles with burning rage as I stomp to Jeremy's door and yank it wide open.

The scene in front of me would've been funny in any other context.

Grant's balls and ass swing backward before he pumps one last shuddering load into Lilah.

"What the *fuck*!" I scream.

Grant throws himself off Lilah as they both flip around to face me. Lilah covers her tits and shaved pussy immediately, her cheeks flushed pink. Grant's dick bobs, and *he's not even wearing a fucking condom*. Both of their eyes are wide in horror.

I want to kill. I want to turn into a fucking tornado and tear everything in this room to shreds. My stupid face heats and tears prick my eyes. How could he do this? After everything I've done for him?

You knew, some horrible voice whispers in my head. *You knew, and you were too desperate and pathetic to leave.*

"Baby," Grant says, holding his arms open in supplication.

I step back, clenching my fists.

"Don't you *fucking dare*," I snarl as tears break loose. "We are so fucking done."

"Baby, I didn't mean it."

Lilah's mouth drops open as she stares in shock at him. He swipes a pillow off Jeremy's bed to cover himself and stumbles toward me.

My brain finally connects with my feet. I have to get out of here. I slam the door shut and storm away.

Grant opens it back up to trail after me.

"Mari, please," he calls, "it was just a mistake. I'm so sorry. Please, I'll meet you at home, and we can talk about it. I promise."

As I swing open Jeremy's front door, a chill breeze lashes against my face. I'm a bomb, and I'm going to explode and level this entire apartment complex if I don't get out of here *right now*.

I turn to Grant. The image of him standing there with a pillow across his wet dick, while Lilah watches us in the background, sears into my mind for eternity. My stomach roils with the knowledge that no amount of alcohol or therapy or time will erase this memory.

I gather all my anger and shame and utter loneliness and whittle it into a knife.

"There's nothing left to talk about," I tell Grant in a cool voice even as tears stream down my face. "We're done."

I should've left then, head held high, but a small, shitty part of me couldn't help but gloat.

"And by the way," I call over my shoulder, "I solved your hacker problem."

2

MARISOL

I THINK I'm going to throw up.

I shove away from the door and stumble toward the sidewalk. I need to stay moving. Get to the road.

Once the apartments are behind me, I take a moment to gather my bearings. Toward the left is the train station. Toward the right is the bar.

I storm off to the right.

By the time I leave the bar, it's nighttime, and I'm in a foul mood.

For the small price of listening to an entire drunken speech about the purpose of life from an old guy with a mullet named Bill—*it's, like, human connection, you know?*—I'm able to suck on a cheap cigarette as I weave down the sidewalk.

Several drinks ago, Grant's fortieth text message came through to explain how he was helping Lilah with her anxiety but things just got out of hand and *would you please not tell Jeremy?*, so I sent Jeremy a detailed message of what I saw and powered off my phone.

I have no other reason to leave it on.

I could message my gamer friends, but I don't want to overload them with more than two emotions at once. We pretty much just quote sci-fi movies at each other and talk trash about our latest matches. I don't even know their real names.

I could call Mom. But she would let me talk for all of thirty seconds before she forced the conversation back to any new updates on Dad or complaining about her coworkers.

And Dad changed his number years ago without telling me.

I lurch onto a bench, banging my tailbone on the hard metal.

"*Fuck.*"

The man sitting next to me takes one look in my direction and moves to the other side of the train station. He's missing out. I could have told him the meaning of life.

I brace my elbows on my open knees in a very ladylike fashion and suck down one more drag of my cigarette before the train arrives.

To be completely honest, once the initial shock and blinding rage swirled down a toilet bowl's amount of margaritas, I was a tiny bit relieved.

Grant and I only made it as long as we did because I was willing to do most of the work, and he liked blowjobs. We both knew I was really dating him for his mom anyway. And now that Kristin's gone, this kind of ending for Grant and me was inevitable.

Still sucks though.

In front of me, the train glides to a stop.

I put out the cigarette underfoot, flick it into a trashcan, and step inside. God, I could use another drink now. Maybe I'll stop at a second bar on the way home.

Riding a train in Chicago at night, drunk, is an enormously stupid decision, but two giant margaritas and three vending machine chocolate bars are not agreeing with me, and I'd rather throw up in the train than in some poor Uber driver's car... wait... actually, four margaritas. I drank *four* giant margaritas.

Two men in hard hats and florescent yellow safety vests watch me from the opposite end of the train. I arrange myself into a straight line and try to look less sloshed, but blinking in coordination is tricky right now, so instead, I turn to watch the city pass by in a glowing neon blur. Clutching the safety pole with two hands, I sway with the movements of the train.

I love the city at night. Everything looks so cool and cyberpunk and infinite. When Mom moved us here more than fifteen years ago as a "surprise" for Dad, being in a city like Chicago gave me endless possibilities. I didn't have to be the poor, fat girl with a crazy mom. I could be invisible, anonymous. I wasn't greedy—that was enough for me.

Then in high school, I met Grant's mom Kristin during a group study night at his house, and she saw something in me. She invited me over and celebrated my school grades and fed me spaghetti and tuna casserole and meatloaf and like any other stray dog, I fell head-over-heels in love with her.

Now that she's gone, and Grant and I are over, I'll have to ration out the scraps of her love more carefully. They'll need to last me the rest of my life because no one is ever going to make me feel that special again.

After a stop, the train zips forward, and I catch myself on the bar at the last minute. The two construction workers burst into laughter at a video on the bigger guy's phone. The smaller guy claps his friend's back as they grin together. It's kind of cute. I'm definitely not jealous.

I glance down and startle at the sight of an attractive man sitting near me. When did he get on?

Heat diffuses over my cheeks as I stare at him.

He's dressed simply in boots, jeans, and a black hoodie. A hawk's head tattoo covers the back of one hand. Long, elegant fingers interlace as he leans forward, elbows resting on muscular thighs. His dark hair falls in soft waves, framing bold eyebrows and a nose almost too big for his face.

I bet men and women throw themselves at him all day long. He looks like he'd refuse to wear a condom, jackrabbit you for all of thirty seconds, and not call you the next day. He's probably a complete jerk because he's hot enough to never have needed to develop a personality.

I could kill a man right now to find out what he smells like.

Unfortunately, while my body is having a near-religious experience at the sight of this beautiful stranger, he doesn't seem to have noticed me. For some reason, he's ignoring the weird drunk lady and staring straight ahead through the window behind me.

The alcohol must've burned off what little shame I have because I'm seriously considering finding out what he thinks about my forty-nine-day dry spell.

I glance behind me and catch him staring at me through the reflection.

His gaze lingers on me for half a second longer than necessary, a frown slashed across his face. Is he... *disappointed*? Before I can figure it out, he looks over to the side, bored. He's probably written me off as a hot mess of a drunk. Which... *fair*.

I need to get home, pack my shit, and get a hotel for a few days while I think about my next steps. My roommate from college might still be living alone. I could check with her about moving in. And then I need to find a job, like, yesterday.

Thinking about my next steps sucks.

And it's hard to focus when I'm still pissed.

I mean, I *solved* it. *I* found out who's pulling Snap Close's contracts out from under them, and now that secret's going to die with me because I'm sure as *hell* not giving The Flash Drive to Grant now.

I guess I could bring it to the police, although that seems like a lot of work, and who knows if they'd even take me seriously.

I could bring it to Terrence.

The thought stokes desire through my body like a lover's whisper.

What if I did? I know where Terrence lives. He's only a few stops past my apartment. I could ride the train until I got close, hunt down some fast food to sober up, then catch an Uber to his house. Terrence always liked me—or at least pretended he did—during the company dinners and events where we'd crossed paths. And I liked the thrill of talking to him while his company secrets buzzed around my head like a swarm of honeybees.

The construction workers get off the train, and a dozen more people step on. Most of them are worn-out men and women in suits who disperse to their seats without talking, sliding earbuds into place.

I sneak another glance at the man in front of me. How long is he going to ride?

A few thick silver rings—one set with a square, black onyx—accent his fingers, but there's no wedding band. For the first time in years, I'm single, and the perfect male specimen for rebound sex sits before me, but I don't make a move. Even in my drunken state, alarm bells are ringing in my head. The man shifts to recline in his chair, lithe limbs spread out, but he's not relaxed. He sits too still, like a coiled spring. This guy's trouble—and not the fun kind.

The train stops, and I glance up at the map.

"Oh, shit," I blurt out.

Fuck, I was so busy ogling that guy, I missed my stop. Whatever, I'll get off here and eat the extra Uber cost.

The stranger lifts himself in one fluid movement as I step off the train. The back of my neck tingles with intense awareness as he follows me, close as a shadow.

On the platform, I whirl to tell him off, but he's not even looking at me. He's watching the train as the doors slide close, focused unblinkingly on another man inside.

The other man's wearing jeans and boots too, but his hair's shorn short. He looks so similar to the stranger next to me that they could be brothers or cousins.

In the seconds before the train departs, the man inside the train turns and spots us with a harsh scowl. Next to me, the stranger shifts his weight ever-so-slightly so that he stands between me and the train man.

The train man's attention flits to me. I shrink behind the stranger's back.

There's something *dangerous* in the way the man on the train looks at me—like he'd love to sink his teeth into my soft belly just to hear me scream. As the train departs, the man inside wiggles his fingers toward us, a movement strangely reminiscent of a dying spider's twitching legs.

"Do you know him?" the stranger asks, turning to face me. His rich, soft voice strokes between my legs with a featherlight touch.

"No, I thought you did!"

We both laugh. The tension fades from my body.

"I'm Salvatore."

I look up at him, feeling shy and daring at the same time. Maybe he doesn't think I'm a hot mess after all—or he doesn't mind. His eyes are a curious shade of amber that reflects the warm glow of the streetlights.

"Natalie," I say, giving my go-to name for strange men.

We stand there for a moment in silence while Salvatore watches me without expression, and I memorize his face to fantasize about later.

"Can I walk you where you're headed?" he asks.

I hum thoughtfully. Normally, I'd say no, no matter how attractive he was, but the way train guy acted gave me the creeps. On the other hand, even though Salvatore says they didn't know each other, my gut says they definitely did.

The other passengers have all walked away already, leaving the station completely empty. I cross my arms over my chest to ward off the night chill. My instincts stagger, faceplant, and finally kick in. *This guy's trouble, remember?*

"No, thank you," I say politely. Better not piss off the strange man. My heart rate picks up. "My *boyfriend's* picking me up."

I turn and strike toward the street, already feeling a little silly for my worrying.

"I'll walk you there," Salvatore says from behind.

Panic shoots up my spine at his silent presence beside my elbow. He's going to get mad when he sees the Uber and not my "boyfriend". That's if he doesn't force me into an alley on the way there first and steal my wallet... or worse. I drop my purse from my shoulder to my hand. Maybe I can buy myself time if I throw it at him.

"Actually, I just remembered, I'm meeting him one stop down. I have to get back on the train."

I turn again, and he's *there*.

The illusion of civility drops like a guillotine.

"You're not getting back on that train," Salvatore says in a low voice. His arms hang loose at his side, and his hard, yellow eyes pierce me with cold indifference.

My lungs seize. Why is there not a single other soul in this damn station?

I take a step back, and he takes one perfectly spaced step forward, and then I spin and burst into a sprint, screaming at the top of my lungs.

My scream sticks in my throat as Salvatore hauls me against his solid chest, knocking the air out of me. He clamps a rough hand over my mouth and pins me against his body as I thrash desperately against him.

He leans down to grunt in my ear, "I can't knock you out, you're drunk. I'm going to set you down, and then you're going to walk with me to my hotel."

Fuck no!

Images of my face plastered across lost posters flash in my mind. *Fight! Fight, you idiot!*

I flail even more recklessly, doing whatever I can to escape or hurt him. My arm slips free enough to elbow him sharply in the ribs, and I scrape his shin with my heel.

"Marisol!" he shouts and squeezes my arm so hard that I freeze and whimper into his palm.

How does he know my real name?

I inhale raggedly through my nostrils, willing myself not to throw up. He knows my name. This is bad. Really, really bad.

"I'm going to let you go now. And you are *not* going to

scream. You are *not* going to run. Do we have an under-standing?"

I nod against his hand. First chance I get, I'm absolutely screaming and running.

Salvatore sets me down but grips my hand in his own like a vice. I shut my eyes for a moment, my belly churning with dread and nausea, and swallow the saliva pooling in the back of my mouth. I can't throw up. I need to focus.

"I'm going to take you to my hotel," he says, and I wince. Hotels are where girls get taken off the street and don't come back. "That other man on the train? He's going to hurt you if he catches you alone. And right now he's on the first train back."

He doesn't wait for a response, and I stumble and nearly eat shit as he begins to tow me down the sidewalk at a brisk clip. He hauls me upright and, instead of slowing down, he steadies me with a flat palm to my back that makes my skin crawl.

"Why are you doing this?" I demand, my anger undercut by how out of breath I sound. If I get out of this alive, I swear I'll go running every day of my life.

Salvatore ignores me. I try a few more times and then resign myself to observing our surroundings. Maybe some-thing will come in handy later.

This time of night, only a few cars whisper down the street beside us. We pass a few closed fashion boutiques, the headless display mannequins forced into poses in the dark-ness. One older couple is out on a stroll, but they're deep in conversation and don't notice my wide, panicked eyes. Down the street, a group of young men starts our way but veer down a side street before they get close. With each step, my breathing cuts shorter and shorter until I feel like I'm sucking air through a straw.

When we stop in front of a hotel, I blink dumbly at the gold-lettered sign in front.

"The Coquatrix?" I ask, voice pitching high.

"*Coquatrix*," he murmurs, pronouncing it correctly. *Snob.* I shoot a glare at him, and he meets my gaze evenly. "Don't make a face like you did with that couple back there. Don't mistake my calm for kindness. If you make a scene when we go inside, I *will* hurt you."

I meet his eyes for as long as I can before dropping my gaze. He nods to himself and then arranges us so he's clutching my limp hand.

Together, we enter the most expensive hotel this side of Chicago.

3

SALVATORE

I'm going to kill Aldo. He needs to answer my text so I can relax about a single thing tonight.

I'm practically naked, carrying only my knife, jammer, and a pair of handcuffs. I haven't done any pre-surveillance in this hotel, and it's making me twitchy.

This wasn't supposed to be the plan. I was going to follow Marisol to her apartment and convince her to stay away until I could bait her into working for me. But seeing Junior on the train threw a wrench into all of that. He knows about Marisol, and now everything's changed.

"Sit here," I tell her, pointing to a chair in the lobby that faces the exit.

She might try to run, but at least she won't get us in trouble by facing the concierge and mouthing *help me*. She hesitates until I lay a heavy hand on her shoulder that has her sinking into the soft leather with a pout. I lean down, looking for all the world like a husband who's kissing his wife or a lover whispering a secret. My lips brush against her cheek, and I inhale the scent of lime and alcohol. Her breath hitches.

"If you try to run, *I will catch you*."

I don't touch her dark, wavy hair. I don't linger.

I approach the hotel counter, feeling her sear a hostile look into my back. She can hate me all she wants. Better to be angry and at my side than drunk and defenseless on the train. She's not a stupid girl, so why the fuck would she put herself at risk the way she did?

A pale man with a flimsy combover greets me with a well-practiced smile.

"How can I help you?" he asks in a chipper tone.

I lean back against the counter so I can keep an eye on my little prisoner. I rarely get the chance to drink in her profile like this. She's got a sweet, round face with a button nose that masks her in an air of innocence, even now as she's scheming about the exits. Her white floral headband and long skirt suggest "pastor's daughter", although I know her to be anything but. She steals a glance at me, and when she sees me looking, whips herself forward and stiffens her shoulders. So tense. Tonight wasn't supposed to play out like this.

"Sir?"

"I'll take whatever your most expensive room is. One night."

"Absolutely! Let me get that processed for you."

The clerk needs to hurry up so I can be within arm's reach of her again. My body's wound up too tight, and I don't like how close I feel to snapping at any moment. There can't be any more fuck-ups tonight.

I would've punished one of my men for letting things go so off the rails the way I did. For letting Junior get as close to her as I did. He must've been waiting at the train stop, hoping to catch her getting off. It was pure luck that she willingly stepped off before Junior saw us, although I was ready to carry her out the moment I spotted him.

He's going to double back and sniff around that station, and then he'll call Dom and ask after me. Dom will try to keep him in the dark, but Junior won't wait long to call Papà Aldo next and needle him for my girl. We'll be two dogs tearing at the same steak until Aldo lets one of us keep her.

Until I have Aldo's word, I don't want anyone else putting eyes on Marisol. With Barbara and Red still in my basement, the Coquatrix is our best option for the night.

It's logical. And yet, I can't trust my own decisions when my state of mind is such a mess. She shouldn't have been in danger like that. She shouldn't be so drunk.

Tonight, I'll have her all to myself.

Once I get the keycard, I fetch Marisol and take her to the elevators. I hold her hand in mine, marveling at the delicate feel of the bones in her fingers. I've only ever seen her at her desk and through the occasional public camera, so I know she's not one for much physical effort, but she surprised me with that little escape attempt of hers. I'll need to keep a close eye on her. Well, *closer*.

When we get to our room, I use both locks on the door and wedge a chair under the handle. It's not perfect, but nothing short of a battering ram will break in. Or a small bomb. Or a fire. Or a screwdriver.

I wasn't planning on sleeping tonight anyway.

I expect to see Marisol wide-eyed as she takes in the opulence of the room or shivering in a chair, but instead, she's rummaging through the mini-fridge, completely ignoring the glittering Chicago skyline stretching out through the floor-to-ceiling windows behind her.

"More drinking?" I ask. It was an oversight not to ask the clerk to have all the alcohol removed from the room.

"Just water. I'm trying not to throw up right now. Do you have anything to eat?"

"No. We're not calling room service, and we're not leaving until tomorrow, so you'll have to wait."

She throws me an exasperated look, slamming the mini fridge shut and balancing three half-sized water bottles in one hand. She dumps herself into a nearby chair and then, glancing at me, assembles herself into a straight-backed posture at the edge of the seat before she gulps down the contents of the first bottle.

"Where are you taking me?" she asks, after finishing the bottle.

"My place."

She looks a little green at the thought. "Why?"

"Because that's where you'll be safest."

"From the guy on the train?"

"That's something we'll discuss at my place." I have my jammer in case the hotel room is bugged, but I don't want to explain to her what's going on while she's drunk. She needs a full night's sleep before I break the news that she's not going back to her old life.

She opens her mouth to reply, but instead, she shoots out her arm toward the little hotel trashcan and retches inside. From the sounds of it, it's mostly liquid. I should've grabbed her before she got to that bar instead of indulging myself and watching her for so long. This is my fault.

I consider offering to hold her hair back, but she probably wouldn't appreciate me touching her.

"Fuck," she moans into the trashcan. She wipes her face with the back of her hand and grimaces at a sticky lock of her hair. With a groan, she toes off her heels, drops her purse to the ground, and carries her trashcan toward the bathroom. She starts to close the door, but I kick a boot out.

"Phone," I say, extending my hand. She slipped her phone into her skirt pocket while she was puking.

"It's in my purse."

"Liar."

She glares at me and passes over her phone before shutting the door and locking it.

Normally, I wouldn't let her leave my sight, but judging by the sounds of dry heaving coming from inside the bathroom, she's not going anywhere soon.

Her phone's already off. Odd. I turn it on, note the fifty missed calls and texts from Grant, and turn it back off. Boyfriend troubles?

I sit on the bed to wait, but a moment later I'm pacing around the room. I make another useless call to Aldo while I wait by the bathroom door and listen to Marisol throwing up. She's not normally a drinker and the fact that something —*someone*—has driven her to suck down all those margaritas makes me grind my teeth together.

After a half hour, the shower faucet squeals, and the water kicks on. I perk up and cycle closer to the door. Fabric hits the tiled floor with a whisper, and then the rhythm of the water changes as she steps inside. Desire surges through me, sick and hot. I can't go into the bathroom with her. She wouldn't like that. But I need to touch something of hers. I cast my gaze over the room, and it lands on her heels and purse, discarded to the side. I walk over.

I kneel on the ground to pick up one of her heels and rub my palm along the inner sole of her shoe, imagining I can still feel residual warmth inside. The bottoms of the shoes are badly scuffed, especially the point of the heel. She's a destructive little thing.

My phone buzzes.

DOM
Junior's asking after you.

I shake my head. What a predictable asshole.

Tell him you can't get ahold of me.

DOM
Will do. Don't creep out Marisol too much.

I glance at the shoe in my hand before arranging her heels in a neat row near the door.

She steps out of the bathroom a moment later, fresh-faced and rosy-cheeked. Her hair's wet and braided back, and she's already redressed. The top of her white t-shirt is nearly transparent from the water, but it's hard to see anything when she's tucking her arms over her chest. I've never seen her look this uncertain and vulnerable. Another fresh wave of lust threatens to drag me under.

"Uh, sorry about all that," she says, after an awkward moment of silence.

"You shouldn't drink so much."

"I had a good reason."

She retrieves one of her water bottles and breaks open the seal. As the bottle touches her lips, she spots her shoes next to the door. Her eyes narrow and flick to me in suspicion. *Don't creep her out.*

"I caught my boyfriend balls deep in another woman."

I choke back a broken laugh.

"Yep, and then he told me he 'didn't mean it'. Even the other woman was shocked."

"Sounds like he didn't deserve you."

"Well, I seem to attract men that are bad for me." She regards me for a moment. "Are you going to rape me?"

"No."

"But you've kidnapped me."

"Yes."

"You should know I have no money."

"I know."

At this, her frown deepens. "How do you know my name?"

"I've been watching you."

"Stalking me," she spits back.

"Yes."

Marisol throws her hands up, exposing that swatch of wet fabric suctioned to her pillowy breasts. "What do you want from me?"

"I want you." I advance on her. Her eyes widen, and she backs up with her purse in hand. "To go to sleep. You'll need your rest for tomorrow."

Normally, she'd be in bed hours ago, and she's going to be exhausted tomorrow if I keep her up much longer.

"I'm not tired," she protests.

I smile and stop a breath away from her wet breasts. I keep my hands relaxed, but I'm dying to touch her. I wish she'd bolt again so I'd have an excuse to heave her against me.

"I'll tell you what you want to know when we're in a safe area. You just have to be a little more patient."

She braces herself against the bedside table and holds her head high, but her movements are jittery, nervous.

"When will I get my phone back?"

"Get on the bed."

"You said you wouldn't hurt me."

"I won't. But you'll need to obey me."

Her eyes flash with some unnamed emotion, and I think she might run, but after a moment, she lowers herself onto the edge of the bed. I pull out my handcuffs, and she balks.

"*Fuck*, no."

I extend my hand toward her right wrist. "Are you going to listen?"

Fury flashes over her face like a strike of lightning. "You haven't said a damn thing."

"Set your purse down and then give me your hand."

"I'm on my period," she says suddenly, and I blink at the sudden change in topic.

"You're early."

She normally doesn't start for another two weeks.

"*How*..." Her eyebrows shoot up before she shakes her head. "Actually, I don't want to know. Can I *please* keep my tampons? I don't have any other clothes, and I don't want to bleed through these."

Odd. She's usually eating jars of peanut butter once a month like clockwork, but she hasn't touched the stuff in two weeks.

"Keep them. But give me the rest of your things and your wrist."

She pulls out a pink pouch of tampons before thrusting her purse at me and offering her wrist. She hides the tampons in the folds of her skirts

I resist the urge to taunt her. Over the years, I've overseen the torture of dozens of men, and she thinks a tampon is going to offend me?

I cinch one handcuff around her wrist, letting my thumb linger over the soft skin there, and drop the other bracelet. Her anger melts into curiosity as I move to the bathroom, leaving the door wide open so we can see each other. I make no attempt to hide myself while I piss, and a thrill surges through me when her gaze drops down to my cock. By the time I'm done, I'm shoving a half-erection back into my jeans.

Marisol's figured it out once I'm back and sliding on top of the bed fully dressed. Her arm rises limply so I can cuff my left wrist with the empty bracelet. The second it clicks shut, she scoffs, "I just drank twenty-four ounces of water and had like four margaritas before that. I hope you hate sleep because I'm going to need to get up to pee *a lot*."

Being a Luporini man has its many perks, but soundly sleeping at night is not one of them. I shrug and flick off the lights with the remote. "That's fine. I'm a light sleeper anyway. I hope you like an audience."

She huffs at that.

I prop myself up with my pillow and try not to think too hard about the hotel's cleaning standards. I'm completely dressed, even wearing my boots in case of an emergency, and I've never slept well with another person before. I fully expect to spend the night watching the clock on the opposite wall and waiting for Aldo to get back to me. Vegas has got to be pretty fucking amazing if he can't be bothered to check his phone for an entire day.

Marisol's dressed too. All the little dips in the mattress from her slipping under the covers make the hairs on my arm stand up. I wish she was asleep already so I could watch her.

Marisol rolls over on her side to face me.

"Goodnight, I guess," she says.

I keep my face trained forward. "Go to sleep."

She mutters something under her breath that sounds suspiciously like "*asshole*", and I smirk a little. I lie there for a long time, feeling her shift in bed and listening to her exhales and the clink of the metal handcuffs as she tries to get comfortable. Finally, her breathing deepens into a gentle snore. She's asleep. I take my first real look at her in the dim light.

After watching her through a hidden camera opposite her desk for months, I thought I'd memorized every detail about her, but seeing her up close is a completely foreign experience. I'm more intimately familiar with the cowlick on the back of her head than I am with her face. Her eyelashes are long and dark against her cheek, and her mouth parts a little as she sleeps. A tiny scar I haven't noticed before cuts across her eyebrow. A light smattering of freckles dusts her nose. Even though she's almost completely covered by the sheets, my cock gives an interested jerk. I turn away from her to stare back up at the clock. It's going to be a long night.

"HEY. Wake up. I have to pee."

I lurch up, wrenching against something trapping my wrist. I rear back, ready to shove it off of me, but a scream stops me.

"Fuck! Stop it! You're going to break my hand!"

Consciousness slams into me. I'm at the Coquatrix. I have Marisol Vasquez handcuffed to me. She drank an entire mini fridge of water. I glance at the clock. It's barely past midnight. *I fell asleep?* Normally, I lie in bed for hours if I try to go to sleep this early.

"Hey," Marisol stage-whispers. "You here? I really need to pee."

I grunt and scrub my hand over my face before following her into the bathroom. She covers herself with her long skirt and sets the world record for longest pee while she stares in the opposite direction from me. As she's washing her hands, I note the heavy blush covering her cheeks. Even through all of my surveillance, I've never seen her blush, and I don't stop staring even when she scowls at me.

When we return to bed, she quickly passes back out. It was dangerous for me to fall asleep like that. I stare up at the clock and listen to her snoring, resolving to stay awake for the rest of the night.

SCRITCH. *Scritch.*

I wake and lie there on my side for a moment, collecting my thoughts with my eyes closed. *I fell asleep again?* If she'd had the opportunity, I would've suspected she'd drugged me. Through my eyelids, I can sense that there's light out. I slept through the night.

Click.

I inhale, and Marisol stiffens on the bed next to me. I let my breathing return to normal, and after a long pause, she shifts away from me. She holds her breath each time the bed creaks.

I snap my eyes open. She freezes. She's got a lockpick —*where the fuck did she get* that—in her mouth and has one foot off the bed.

While I watch, she gives me a sheepish grin through the metal pick in her teeth.

This woman is going to fucking kill me.

4

MARISOL

I spit the lockpick out of my mouth and take a step out of hitting range.

"I didn't want to disturb your sleep?"

It even sounds lame to me. He's going to throw me out the window.

Salvatore sits up with a frown. He produces a key from his back pocket and unlocks his handcuff.

"Give me that," he says, and I pass the pick to him. "And the rest?"

I hand him my pouch of "tampons". He glances inside the bag of loose lockpicks.

He levels a cold look at me, his frown deepening. Suddenly I'm back in school again, being chewed out by the principal for skipping class.

"What was your plan with these?"

I cough delicately. "Uh. I hadn't really gotten to step two."

He points to a chair opposite the bed. "Sit."

I consider disobeying for a half second before I remember we're on the thirtieth floor.

He gives me a disappointed shake of his head, and I wilt in my chair.

Personally, he can shove his disappointment next to the stick up his butt, but for the time being, my life is in his hands, and I'd rather not find out how easily my neck can break.

Salvatore goes to the bathroom and pees with the door wide open so he can watch me through the mirror the entire time. I glimpse the top of his firm ass before averting my eyes. *Don't piss him off and don't try to fuck him.* Two good rules for staying alive and keeping my wits about me, but it's not so easy when he's been engaging in chemical warfare all night, steeping me in his clean masculine scent. I'm now at day fifty of my dry spell and haven't masturbated in days. Things are about to get weird.

After washing his hands and arms with the thoroughness of a doctor preparing for surgery, he returns to sit on the bed. He checks his phone and exhales deeply, scrubbing his jaw and neck with his hand. I don't think about how the movement makes his forearm muscles stand out. I need to get out of here.

My nerves build in the silence that follows. "What?" I finally blurt out.

"My boss got back to me. He says you're under my protection until he gets back from his trip."

"And how long is that?"

Salvatore stretches out. His triceps tighten and the bottom of his shirt lifts to expose a glimpse of taut stomach and a trail of dark hair. I swallow dryly. "Two weeks. At least."

"Two weeks?" I spring to my feet. "What am I supposed to do for two whole weeks?"

"Sit," Salvatore demands, and my body obeys before my brain can object.

He lifts from the bed to loom over me in a single step, and I shrink back. He places his hands on either side of the chair, caging me in, dark hair falling forward to frame his face. His scent washes over me again, and I hold my breath to keep from breathing it in. His five o'clock shadow darkened overnight, and it's all I can do not to be sucked into his amber eyes, nearly golden like a cat's. I bow my head so I'm not looking directly into the sun, but even now, the heat emanating from him threatens to melt me.

"You must have not understood me properly. There's no going back for you. You shouldn't have gotten mixed up in our dealings, Marisol Vasquez, but you did, and now you are completely and utterly *fucked*. You are, officially, my property. And if you had any sense in that pretty head of yours, you'd fall to your knees and beg for a chance to thank me, because I am the *best*-case scenario for you."

Salvatore wraps his fingers around my jaw to pivot my face toward his. I can't help the way my eyelashes flutter when I make eye contact with him. Evil men are supposed to be vile and disgusting, not breathtakingly handsome, and I'm only human.

"Do you understand me?" Salvatore says, hypnotizing me with his strange eyes.

I nod against his hand.

"The next time you disobey me or you try to escape me, you will be *punished*. Understand?"

Heat pools between my legs, and I swallow again. "Yes," I whisper.

Salvatore's gaze flicks down to my mouth once, and I have the ridiculous thought that he's going to kiss me, but he releases me and stands. I stomp down the traitorous ripple of disappointment that follows.

"Come. We'll eat breakfast here, and then my men will take us to my place."

In the hotel dining room, I consider swiping a knife from the table, but every time I glance at Salvatore, he's watching me. I'm starting to think the man doesn't blink. Eventually, my hangover takes over, and I inhale two plates of pancakes with extra syrup while Salvatore sips coffee and orange juice and charmingly tells me to hurry up.

As we step out of the hotel, I squint against the sunlight shining on the shops and streets before us. We pause so a family of four can push their stroller along the sidewalk. This is wrong. It's *supposed* to be dark and gloomy after my life gets completely fucked over, not sunshine and rainbows. Just to rub it in, a little boy and his mom across the street are blowing bubbles and giggling. *Super.*

Salvatore grabs my hand and steers me to a black SUV waiting on the street. He opens the door for me. I hesitate. The interior is clean and dark, and there's no second hostage bound and gagged inside, but this is another door that's taking me further and further from my life and into whatever he has planned for me.

Salvatore leans down to whisper in my ear, "I will help you in or I will throw you in."

I knew I should've grabbed that knife. Salvatore holds my hand like the gentleman he's *not,* and I slide inside. He steps in behind me, sealing the door to the outside world.

The driver, a young man with dark hair, glasses, and a crisp white collar peeking out of his navy sweater, starts driving without a word. He looks like a schoolboy Salvatore's kidnapped to work for him. He probably is.

I start to shiver and rub my arms in the cold bite of the

car's AC. Soft strains of opera music bleed in through the speakers. I chose the seat furthest from Salvatore in protest, but he doesn't seem to care as he buckles himself in and pulls out his phone.

I miss my phone. I need something to even the playing field.

This isn't your standard kidnapping job. He knew I was on the train, he knew my name, *hell*, he knew I was early for my period. *I* don't even know when my next period is. He admitted to stalking me, but wouldn't I have noticed something like that? I don't recall any missing underwear. I haven't received any notes with cut-up magazine letters saying "YoUr BLooD SmElls NiCe". If this is about me discovering Beta, wouldn't I be sleeping with the fishes already? Nothing Salvatore's said has added up.

I flatten myself against the window and door. Whatever he wants, he's going to have to drag me in kicking and screaming.

My fingers glance over the door handle. Maybe when the car rolls to a stop, I can jump out into a crowd.

"There's a kid lock on that door," Salvatore says, without looking up from his phone.

My hand drops as if slapped.

As we pass by Knossos Hospital, the drive starts to take on a familiar route.

"Where are we going?" I ask.

"We need to grab your computer and any other notes you took."

Just my computer? Maybe... is this all to scare me? *We know where you live and what you did. Be smart about this.* A slap on the wrist.

"I don't have a notebook or anything," I offer, wide-eyed. "I swear. You can look through my stuff."

Obviously, I'll bide my time, get a new computer, and search for Beta again. Salvatore must be hiding something really juicy if he's going through all these lengths to scare me.

"You'll also have ten minutes to pack your things," he adds, slipping his phone into his pocket.

"B-but..."

I glance past Salvatore. We've parked right in front of my apartment complex.

Salvatore steps out of the car and extends a hand out to me, watching me wordlessly. I drop down without his help and glare at the concrete under my heels. Undeterred, Salvatore clamps his hand over my shoulder and leads us through the apartment lobby like he's been here a thousand times. Which he probably has.

A middle-aged woman and her white-haired mom shuffle through the lobby, but neither of them catches my eye.

I should scream or beg them to call the police, but I'm guessing Salvatore would just drag me back to the car. And *punish* me, he said in a tone that promised a bed would be involved. The memory makes my stomach dip. *Ugh. Chill out. He means he'll cut off my hand, not make me come.*

Once we're trapped in the elevator, and he presses level nine—without asking me—I try to jerk my shoulder out of his grip, but he only tightens his hold on me.

"Why don't you take my computer and go?" I ask dully.

"Would you promise me you wouldn't go digging around my systems again?"

I pivot toward him, flashing my best doe-eyed look and splaying a hand over my boobs. This little move has got me out of *two* shoplifting arrests. I take it a step further and skim my other hand down his firm bicep.

"*Of course!* Of course, I promise."

Salvatore watches all of this with mild amusement. His hand shifts from my shoulder to cup the back of my neck. The elevator heats up a hundred degrees as he draws me in.

His mouth brushes against my ear, and I suck in a breath.

"I don't believe you."

A little voice in my head suggests maybe *don't* instigate anything stupid with this dangerous man. But Stupid's my middle name, and I live for danger, so I tilt my face up until his hair tickles my cheek. "Cross my heart."

Salvatore's fingers stiffen around my neck.

The elevator door springs open and my neighbor Trenton jerks to a stop at the threshold, a stack of books in his arms nearly spilling over.

"Hey... Mari," Trenton says.

My heart pounds, and my face heats. *This isn't what it looks like,* I want to blurt out. Or maybe, *call the cops!*

Before I can think of anything to say, Salvatore guides me out of the elevator by the scruff of my neck.

Once Trenton steps inside, he adds in a carefully neutral tone, "Say hi to Grant for me."

"S-sure," I splutter.

Salvatore gives me no time to soak in my shame as he leads me red-faced to my apartment door. I left my key in my purse back in the car, but that's not a problem, because Salvatore has his own personal key. He lets us inside and locks the door behind him.

I shove his hand off my neck—which I should've done in the elevator—and rub the skin there as if checking for an injury. He barely touched me, but it feels like my skin's been branded with his handprint.

"How many times have you been in my apartment?" I ask, to distract myself.

"This is the first."

He looks ridiculously out of place in here. With his dark hoodie, hair, and tattoos, he swallows all the light in the apartment like a black hole. His gaze sweeps over the kitchen, the bookcase, and my desk before landing on the couch where a tattered beige bra hangs over the armrest. He glances back at me with a hint of teasing playing at his mouth.

I ignore the ridiculous urge to swipe my bra out of sight and cross my arms instead.

"So you've never been here before, but you have a personal copy of my apartment key?"

He nods.

"You understand I'm finding it hard to believe you right now?"

"I understand."

I throw my arms out. "You gonna expand on that?"

"No."

"Why. Not."

"It's something we can discuss at a more appropriate time. You need to pack your things so we can leave."

I don't move an inch except to jerk my chin in the direction of my desk. "My computer's right there. You already have my flash drive. You can just take my stuff and my phone. I won't tell Grant or the police or anyone."

The corner of Salvatore's mouth tips up. My life is just one big, fat joke to him. "You have ten minutes to pack. Take Buck too."

He knows my cat's name.

I wish the knives in my kitchen were sharp enough to do

any damage. And that I had a chance to use them without risk of stabbing myself.

"I don't like being kept in the dark. If you tell me what I'm packing for, I'll get started."

Salvatore looks around the apartment again, and his gaze lights on my bookcase where I keep all my DVDs of old sci-fi shows.

"Earth to Sal—"

Salvatore raises a finger to his lips. He pulls out a black box barely bigger than a deck of cards and presses a button on its side. A recording of a crowd of people chatting pours out of the box. He turns it to full volume and places it on the kitchen counter next to us.

"Do you know who I am?"

An electric charge of anticipation passes through me. *Finally.*

I have to lean in to hear him over his noise box, but I answer eagerly, "You're with the Mafia."

I know I'm right, and it *still* makes me feel silly to say it. It's way more likely the man in front of me is some sicko who's developed an obsession with me, rather than I've stumbled into a shadow organization of underworld criminals.

"Only outsiders use that word. We're called the Cosa Nostra. And in Chicago, we just call it the Outfit. Do you know what you did to piss off the Outfit?" He speaks as patiently as if he were explaining to a five-year-old why they shouldn't touch a hot stove.

"I discovered Beta," I say slowly, still trying to figure out how they found me. Did I leave some trace? I didn't touch any of Beta's accounts, only tracked him. It should have been impossible to detect me.

Salvatore's voice drops lower, and I have to lean in so close I can feel the heat coming off him.

"You uncovered secrets you weren't supposed to. And if you had taken that little flash drive to your ex-boyfriend or to the police, my organization would be looking at losses in the *millions*. You've scared quite a few people, Marisol. People that normally don't scare so easily." He lets that sink in for a moment, studying my face. "But luckily for you, you've also caught my eye. Because while every person that knows about you wants to see you dead or silenced, I want to help you."

"...by kidnapping me?"

"Remember that man on the train? His name is Junior. And as soon as you had my attention, you had his. If he had caught you last night instead of me, you would have been wishing you were dead right now. He's not a nice man."

So my instincts were right about the train guy—Junior, I guess, although that's a funny name for a gangster. I knew he creeped me out. Something tells me even if Salvatore's lying about everything else, that's one thing he's telling the truth about.

I exhale. I'm way too hungover to be parsing through this all right now.

"So how are you supposed to be helping me?"

Something bright and hungry sparks in Salvatore's eyes. "I staked ownership over you. No one will touch you while you're with me."

I focus very hard on not getting turned on by that *insane* statement.

"And what do you get out of this?"

"I get you."

Frustration bubbles in me and thankfully rises over whatever lust I'm experiencing. "Can you just speak clearly?

What do you want with me? You said you weren't going to rape me, and I'm not going to sleep with a *criminal*."

Salvatore's gaze drops to my mouth before flicking back up to my eyes. He rests a hand on the kitchen counter behind me, trapping me in on one side. "Carrying around lockpicks is a *felony*, Marisol. Shoplifting, a misdemeanor. How much money have you earned cheating in your little video game competitions?"

My throat goes dry. *How does he know about all that? I was careful. No one knew.*

"So maybe it's a little hypocritical that you wouldn't sleep with a criminal," he continues. "Which I'm not, by the way. Just like you're not. Being a criminal means being caught committing a crime, and people like you and me, Marisol, we don't get caught."

A shiver passes through me. "I'm not going to sleep with you," I whisper to myself.

"Okay, Marisol. You don't have to," he says in an amused tone. The heat rolling off his body is baking me through all my layers of clothes. Too cold, too hot. I need space. I can't move. "But you still have to come with me. If you stay here, you'll die. Very slowly and very painfully. But since you're coming with me, you'll be treated as a guest until I decide I can trust you, and then I want you to work for me."

"As what, a prostitute?"

Salvatore smirks. "Always sex with you, Marisol. Do you need something taken care of?"

I seal my mouth shut, and he continues in that smug tone of his, "The Outfit doesn't deal in prostitution. I want you on my cyber team."

Of all the things he could've said, that takes me most by surprise. "You want to give me a computer and let me hack into computer systems?" Maybe he's dumber than I thought, and I can get out of this whole situation without even breaking a sweat.

Salvatore laughs—even the way he laughs is rich and velvety. He'd make a killing as a voice actor. "Not for a long time. Like I said, I have to trust you first."

"So how do I earn your trust?"

"By doing what you're told." My breath hitches, and Salvatore leans in close enough that I could count each one of his dark eyelashes. "Now run along, you have five minutes left to pack your things."

I consider laughing in his face. I also fantasize about stomping on his foot or sneering or any number of things. I don't think about kissing him. I dart out from under him and race to my room.

Whatever I do, I'm certain he's going to hold me to that five-minute limit, and I have a lot of things I want to pack.

I waste an entire minute while Salvatore loiters in the living room to change into leggings, an oversized t-shirt, and some blessedly fresh underwear. I pull out my and Grant's suitcases from under our bed and stuff my clothes inside while Salvatore comes to watch from the doorframe. Buck trots out and sizes up the stranger in his home. I side-eye them as I throw my toiletries in Grant's suitcase, praying nothing spills. I hope Buck bites him.

Buck approaches Salvatore, sniffs his shoe, and then *winds through his legs.*

I fully stop what I'm doing and stare with my mouth dropped open.

Salvatore reaches down and strokes the top of Buck's head as he leans into the touch. The last person Buck let touch him was Kristin, and now this complete asshole waltzes in and has the nerve to pet *my* cat, and Buck just *lets* him.

I have more—more things, more clothes, but I don't care right now. I swipe tears out of my eyes as I zip up the suitcases and shove past Salvatore to roll them to the front door.

"I'm ready," I mutter. I stare at the door so I don't have to look at Salvatore or Buck.

Salvatore comes to stand behind me.

"Marisol—" he starts but we both freeze at the sound of footsteps stopping outside the front door.

I glance back, and Salvatore already has a knife out —*where the fuck did he get that*—and he grabs my forearm to drag me behind him.

Keys jangle outside the door. They clatter to the ground, and Grant mutters a curse.

"*It's Grant!*" I mouth silently to Salvatore.

He holds up his knife with a little smile as if to say, *Oh, I know*.

I want nothing more than to fuck with Grant, but I don't want to see him dead. At least for his mom's sake.

"I'll make him leave, I promise," I whisper. "Please, go hide. *Please.*"

Salvatore shrugs and makes a show of ambling to my bedroom while I hover at his heels. I desperately want to push him, but I don't want to piss him off. As the front door opens behind us, my fear of getting caught overcomes my fear of getting stabbed. My palms connect with solid muscle, and Salvatore lets me shove him forward. I nearly have the door to my bedroom shut when I hear Grant's voice from the end of the hallway.

"Mari?"

5

MARISOL

GRANT ROUNDS THE CORNER, and I freeze, my hand lingering on the half-closed door. Next to me, Salvatore is hidden, holding his knife loosely at his side and watching me. The threat is clear. *One wrong move and I'll gut you.*

I want to slam the door in Grant's face, but I don't want to him try to force it open and find out what's on the other side.

I put on my best ice queen face. "What do you want?"

Internally, I wince. I don't sound tough, I sound heart-broken. Grant's face softens with sympathy.

"I've been thinking..." Grant says.

"Don't."

He raises a hand. "Let me finish. I've been thinking, and what I did was a horrible, shitty, cowardly thing to do."

You think?

Sweat prickles along my hairline. It's taking serious mental energy to maintain eye contact with Grant and not look at the other man behind the door. Maybe I can signal to him somehow that I'm in trouble and get him to call the police. Too bad we always sucked at charades.

"But I think we both know we should've broken up a long time ago."

My sudden clenched fist makes the door tremble. "You don't know that," I say. "We could still get married."

Grant sighs and crosses his arms. "Mari, it's just you and me here. We can be honest with ourselves. Getting married would've been a huge mistake. You don't like me. We don't like doing any of the same things."

"Like what? Smoking weed with Jeremy and getting drunk and playing video games? You know, I think I could've liked those things *just* fine if you ever invited me over. But you didn't want me there, because you were too busy fucking Lilah!"

"*God*, Mari!" The tips of his ears redden. I used to think it made him look cute, but now he looks oafish. "No one wants to invite you over. You're too much! If we're playing video games, you have to win *every* time. If we're smoking weed, you'll get the *most* high. We can't even have sex without you begging me to spank you and choke you. It's fucking annoying to be around! Not everything has to be this insane competition with you!"

My heart pounds in my ears. "I win every game because I *like* to win," I spit. "People can like different things. So you weren't interested in doing what *I* wanted in bed? You sure *liked* all the blow jobs I gave you. You *liked* when I did all your assignments for you. Relationships are *work,* which is probably why you didn't want to bother with ours."

Grant jerks his hands through his hair and sucks down two deep breaths. "Mari, baby," he says in a patronizing voice, "I *need* you to send me what you found. There's a criminal out there stealing money from Snap Close. This is a matter of right and wrong—"

I roll my eyes. "For cripes sakes—"

"*That!*" Grant jabs a finger at me. "I hate when you do that shit. I hate how you remind me of her *constantly*."

"Oh! Should I brush her under the rug? Should we pretend she's *not* your mom?"

"You'd love that. I get it. If anyone's going to love my mom the most, it's gonna be you too? Even love is another fucking thing to win."

I step forward to get in his face, but Salvatore's hand wraps around my wrist behind the door. I start to look at him and then jerk my gaze downward so I'm not being so obvious.

Oh, fuck me. Buck is rubbing his head against Salvatore's pant legs.

"Mari, is there someone with you?"

I inhale. Salvatore's grip tightens. I level my gaze at Grant. "It's time for you to leave. Now. Before you get hurt."

Grant stares at me for several long seconds, unaware of death looming on the other side of the door.

Finally, he exhales, long and slow. "Lilah was right. You *are* a bitch."

The bedroom door swings open.

I barely catch the horror and shock on Grant's face before I turn to Salvatore. I'm nearly too afraid to touch him, but I do, placing my free hand on his firm chest. He hasn't let go of my wrist and tugs me to his side. At least his knife is tucked in the back of his jeans. He studies Grant with a totally flat expression except for the displeased twist of his mouth.

"Salvatore, please," I say. His name tastes strange on my tongue. "He's not worth it."

"You need to leave," Salvatore says to Grant, without raising his voice at all. He lets go of my wrist to wrap his arm around my waist. I drop my hand from his chest as if burned. Buck can't catch a hint and places his paws on Salvatore's pant leg, looking for pets while my life falls apart.

Grant's eyes dart between us. "Mari, who the *fuck* is this? Have you been cheating on me?"

I swallow a laugh. Somehow cheating feels so much smaller than what I'm going through right now. *No, he's here because of what I did for you, babe.*

At six feet tall, Grant's got Salvatore by a couple of inches, but it doesn't make a difference. The promise of violence rolls off of Salvatore in waves.

I need to get a sign to Grant. I don't want him to fight Salvatore, just to help me.

"Give me ten minutes, and then I'll be gone. Forever," I say. Salvatore squeezes me to his side, and I suck in a deep breath. The heat of his body sears along the length of mine. If he doesn't let me go, I'm going to have a panic attack. I need to get away from him. I open my eyes wide and blink rapidly at Grant. *Help me.*

Grant clenches his hands into fists. "Couldn't lose this either? Had to be the best cheater."

Before I can reply, Salvatore cuts in, "Get out. Now."

Grant's shoulders slump forward as he takes in Salvatore's appearance.

"Just so you know, Mari, I was only with you because Mom asked me to take care of you. I never really wanted to date you—you're a fucking psycho." One last jab as he ignores my pleading expression and storms out of the apartment.

Salvatore turns toward me. His face is calm. The worst day of my life is any ol' Monday morning for him. "Time is up. Let's go."

I'm surrounded by men who take from me and give nothing in return.

I swipe at my eyes and sniffle.

"Get your computer," he says.

Dick. I jerk my body from his grip and stomp to my desk. I drop down to yank my power cable out of the outlet, and when I stand, I crack my skull against the underside of the desk.

"Fuck," I mutter, touching the knot on the back of my head. For a moment I crouch there and try not to cry. Grant's abandoning me. Salvatore's taking me somewhere I don't want to go. Even Buck's betrayed me.

Sometimes I'd lay my head on Kristin's lap and clutch her blanket and sob at how unfair it was that she was leaving. She'd stroke my hair and tell me, *"One day at a time."*

I inhale deeply and force myself to stand. I just need to get through today.

Once I'm up, Salvatore grips my arm and wrenches me toward him.

What the—

He probes the back of my head, looking me over as impassively as a buyer in a livestock auction.

"You need to be more careful," he says.

I slap his hand away and twist my arm out of his grip. I want to scream or cry, but instead, I march over to my suitcases and grab the handles.

Salvatore couldn't care less about my tantrum. "Go get Buck."

Right, my treasonous cat and Salvatore's new best friend. I'm half-tempted to leave him here, but... but Grant hates Buck and Lilah's allergic, and I'm the biggest fucking sap in existence because I'm already moving to the bedroom to find the cat carrier.

While I pull out the plastic carrier from the top of my closet, I can hear Salvatore rustling around in the kitchen. I can't find it in me to care about what he's doing. Hopefully eating something expired out of the fridge or tripping and falling on a knife.

Buck's on top of the bed, but the second I look at him with the carrier in hand, his sixth sense kicks in, and he rockets out of the room.

I take one moment to stare at the ceiling, blinking back tears, and then pull myself together for the hundredth time today and follow him.

When I return to the living room, Salvatore holds out a bag of frozen corn to me.

I blink at him.

"Put this on your head." He presses the bag into my hand and then slips the cat carrier from my grasp.

He approaches Buck who's perched at the top of his cat tower. Buck eyes him suspiciously but doesn't move. He lets Salvatore lift him and slide him into the cat carrier like it's nothing. *How...?*

Salvatore ignores the shock on my face and opens the apartment door. He nods toward the hallway.

"Let's go."

6

SALVATORE

I DIDN'T LIKE LEAVING Davide to watch over Marisol in the car. Only a made man for a year, he's still too green. But I hadn't lied to Marisol about not having been in her apartment. This would be the last time we came back here, and I wasn't going to waste the opportunity.

I left Davide with a cold warning to keep his eyes forward and not to talk to my captive.

Prigioniera, I said, although she doesn't have to be one for long. She'll see I'm doing this for her own good, and then I won't need to keep such a tight leash on her. She'll come around.

I savor a slow perusal of her living room. For so long, the only part of her life I could see was a square around her desk, but now, I have her whole world exposed to me.

She's got a DVD player near her TV to complement the massive collection of old sci-fi shows and films. Star Wars, Star Trek, Dr. Who, The Twilight Zone, Stargate... the list goes on. I don't make time to watch TV, and not for the first time, I ask myself why *this* woman has a stranglehold on my attention unlike any other.

Then I flick open a wooden box on her bookcase. A handful of locks have been thrown inside, along with a metal file and a few keys. There's my answer. She loves a good challenge and doesn't respect rules and judging by her longtime attachment to her loser boyfriend, she's loyal—or clingy—not that it matters to me. An unfamiliar wave of urgency crests over me. I don't want to be forced to wait for her to accept she's staying with me. I want her to understand it *now* and let us skip to the good parts. Resisting the urge to take something for myself, I let the box fall shut.

She couldn't have known how close I was to sawing off her ex's fingers until he squealed like a pig. I didn't intend to show my face to him, but after hearing the way he insulted her... he's lucky he left fully intact. Not for the first time, I question the wisdom in bringing Marisol into my life. First Junior, then her ex. Something about her pulls me into snap decisions.

Once she gets back to the house, and she's safely tucked away, I'll keep my distance until I can control myself around her.

I reach out for one of Grant's model airplanes. Six of them take up a shelf, free of dust thanks to Marisol. I don't know which one is his favorite, but I know they were expensive and took painstaking effort to build, so I snap the wing off of each model. It's a good start.

Her fridge is empty, save for a few bottles of hot sauce with images of skulls and ghosts on them. No wonder she ate like a starved animal this morning. As soon as we get home, she'll get three square meals a day—four, if my chef Conchetta has anything to say about it.

Her bedroom is simple and, for the sheer indulgence of it, I lay down next to where I imagine she sleeps. I grab her pillow and press it to my nose, inhaling deeply. Cherry blossom. My dick jerks up like a dog who's heard the dinner bell. I give it an idle stroke and lean over the mattress to tug open her bedside table.

Why didn't she take these? She left her giant pink dildo, fuzzy handcuffs, and nipple clamps on top of a small pile of lingerie. She's going to get so needy without all her toys.

I take the soft garments out and rub them against my face without an ounce of shame. They smell overwhelmingly of Marisol. My mouth waters. My cock is begging to be released and stroked against all of the decadence here, but I simply shift it in my jeans and return her things. I'll order her new toys and lingerie once she's ready. And once I've regained control of myself and can think clearly around her, I'll see if she'll wear them for me.

I don't take any souvenirs. Now that I have Marisol all to myself, I don't need to.

When I place her computer tower into the back of the SUV and slide into the backseat, Marisol narrows her eyes at me like she has a few strong guesses as to what I was up to. Davide clears his throat and draws his hand back from the cat carrier in the passenger seat.

He passes me the blackout hood. Marisol studies it without recognition, but she still presses her pouty lips into a tight line when I crook a finger toward her. After a moment, she hesitantly inches toward me. Too slow. I grab her by her soft waist and slide her over the gap in the car seats until her plush thigh's pressed against mine.

I eat up her look of outrage as I slip the bag over her head and cinch the drawstring at the base, plunging her into darkness.

"Lay on my lap until we get there."

Again she balks, but once I wrap my fingers around her

delicate shoulder, she rushes to press her cheek against my thigh. This feels good. It feels right.

As Davide drives off, I pull her phone out.

"What's the password to your phone?"

She doesn't say anything until I squeeze her shoulder.

"Eight-zero-zero-eight."

"Boob?"

Davide coughs to cover up a laugh.

"I thought it was funny," she says, voice muffled by the bag.

I absentmindedly draw a pattern over her arm as I thumb through her text messages.

"You're a popular one, Miss Vasquez. Want me to read some of your ex's texts?"

She groans. "No, I'm good."

"Why not? Some of these are funny.

"*I didn't mean it. Lilah just lost her job, and I had to be there to comfort her because Jeremy's gone all the time.*

"*I'm sorry I'm such a fuckup. I screw everything up, and I don't deserve you.*

"*Baby, please send me the data at least. I have a meeting with Terrence on Tuesday.*

"*Who was that guy? How long have you been seeing him? He looks like a felon.*"

When she doesn't say anything, I continue, "Looks like your ex can't keep his mouth shut. Jeremy and Lilah are asking after you too. Why don't you help me write up some replies so they know they have nothing to worry about?"

"Tell Grant he can have that data over my dead body. And tell him I met you September 11th of last year."

"Hmm. Dead body? Nine-one-one? Not very subtle, Marisol. And you know he won't figure it out."

She exhales through the fabric. "At least tell him to fuck off."

Warmth spreads through my chest. "Much better."

I send out dry, boring texts to all of her friends, telling them she needs time alone. Her parents haven't texted her, and she has no other friends checking in on her.

I realize I'm squeezing her shoulder too tightly when she whimpers. I smooth over her arm with a flat palm. She deserves more than her shitty friends and parents. She's been kidnapped, and no one seems to notice. No wonder she was so attached to her ex. Was he the only person in her life who gave her affection?

My hand drifts to stroke her hair splayed over her shoulder and back. She's still and silent on my lap.

I can show her affection. She's already responding to my touch even as she fights it. Physical attraction is a good first step. I can work with that.

Once the car crawls up the length of gravel leading to my driveway, I breathe more easily. There's not a part of the house that isn't under surveillance through electronic or physical means. I won't have to push her so hard here. We can take our time.

"Davide, please take Miss Vasquez's things to my room." Marisol tenses on my thigh, and my cock twitches in response.

"Yes, boss."

I ease her up and take her hand. "With me."

I help her out of the car and down the concrete path to the front door. With the hood on, she's forced to grab onto me for balance, clutching at my forearm.

"You can take that off now," I say in a low voice once we're inside.

Marisol fumbles to tear the hood off and, once it's

removed, blinks several times in the bright light. She gets a good look at the honey-colored marble flooring and twinkling chandelier in the foyer and parts her mouth for a moment before slamming it shut.

I can't help but feel a little smug. "This is where you'll be staying for the next week. Welcome home."

"To *your* home," she says quickly.

"It'll feel like home to you too soon enough."

Giving her a tour of the house is a small treat before I have to bury myself in work, a duty I've never shied away from until now. All the emergencies and obligations of the family business couldn't be further away as Marisol examines a set of burgundy drapes in one of the guest rooms.

She examines every corner of the house like she's looking for the final piece of evidence in a brutal homicide. She casts her eye over all of the windows, the seams of the walls, the vents. I'd guess our door locks aren't up to snuff, because a faint, mocking smile tugs at her lips when she eyes them. I don't allow her to touch anything, although I'm sure she'd love the chance to rummage through the cabinets and dressers.

My little sparrow is already looking for her escape. I told myself I'd give her space and a measure of freedom while she stays here, but the way she studies the stone handrails on the second-floor balcony makes me want to lock her up. She's going to put herself in danger if she tries to run.

The housekeepers and the guards eye her warily as we tour the kitchen. They know to ignore any attempt for "friendship", but that otherwise, she can roam freely through the house. I have men guarding every exit. Even if she slips out, she won't get far.

"And this is your room."

Marisol takes a faltering step inside as if there's a trip wire she might trigger at any moment.

"Renovating?" she asks as she does her slow scan of the room.

"Not quite."

I had all of the furniture taken out of the room, except for a barely dressed mattress on the ground. Davide's already brought her things to my bedroom where they'll sit behind an *apparently* pointlessly-locked door.

I lay a hand on Marisol's shoulder from behind, and she stills. Will the two weeks before Aldo gets back be enough time for her to lose this fear of me? I haven't hurt her.

You've threatened her plenty.

I release Marisol just as quickly. I threatened her because I needed immediate compliance. I won't need to do that again.

"The room was fully furnished this morning," I say. "Can you guess why I had my housekeepers strip it down to the essentials?"

"Anything to do with my *tampons*?"

I smirk. "She learns. If you decide you want to stay put, I'll add in a bit of decor."

"I'll keep that in mind," she says dully. She glances at the adjoining bathroom. "Buck's going to need food and a litter box."

"I already have someone out shopping for him. He'll be set up tonight. And he'll be staying in a special room for the next several days while he adjusts."

"You mean while I *behave*?"

"You're a good girl, Marisol. I know you'll behave."

She flushes, but she doesn't lower her gaze. "And if I don't, you'll hurt him?"

I remember this isn't a game for her. My mouth twists

downward. "I'm not a monster. I won't hurt your cat. He's a guest."

"A guest..." She chews on the word as she looks over the room again, fiddling with the hem of her shirt. Stretching it. Picking at it. "I'd hate to see how you treat your prisoners."

"They don't normally get their own bed. They don't get hot meals and access to the house."

"Lucky me," she says, looking pointedly at the mattress on the floor. "So, as your *guest*, what are you going to make me do all day?"

"You can do whatever you'd like. You are not to touch any computers or other electronic devices, and the guards or house staff are advised not to speak with you. I have a small library and a gym and the other guest rooms have TVs. Someone will help you pick out something to watch."

"Can I leave the house?"

"No. It'll be best that you stay inside until you speak with Aldo."

She crosses her arms, but her fingers don't stop searching for something to touch. She absentmindedly flips the hem of her sleeve several times. "This is all for my protection? What if I told you I didn't want your protection?"

"You want it. You just don't know it yet."

"*You want it. You just don't know it yet,*" she mimics in a god-awful impression of me that almost makes me laugh. "Do you even hear how patronizing that is?"

"You can think of yourself as a guest or a prisoner, but the outcome will be the same. So I suggest you adapt quickly and maybe show a little gratitude to the person who decided you were better off alive than dead."

Her murderous expression suggests she'd rather crawl

through broken glass than tell me *thank you*. Fine. I don't need her permission to keep her alive.

I reach out and unroll the flipped hem of her shirt sleeve before smoothing over the fabric and her arm. Gentle, inoffensive, affectionate. She tolerates this with the barest twitch of her eyelashes.

"We don't have to fight. Enjoy your day, Marisol. And one last thing, I will have a female staff member performing a body search on you before you turn in for the night, so please resist the temptation to pick up any souvenirs."

7

MARISOL

I'VE SCRATCHED out four tally marks along the baseboard behind my bedroom door.

Four days ago, Salvatore gave me the grand tour and then disappeared. Another man with heavy scarring over his face and neck strolled in directly after and introduced himself as my guard.

Camillo's barely taller than I am, but he's nearly twice as wide and looks like he snorts protein powder and mortar mix for breakfast. The puckered burn marks over his once-handsome face seem to give him only the range of motion to scowl and look vaguely constipated.

After telling me his name, I've barely been able to get more than a grunt out of him, although he did pass me a cigarette when I asked for one on the balcony. He made me wait as he considered my request for a long moment and then handed it over without a word. His phone buzzed with a text immediately after, and when I asked for another an hour later, he said I wasn't allowed to smoke and lapsed back into silence despite my attempts to annoy him into saying *anything*.

Did that boss of yours text you?

Am I a guest or a prisoner?

Where'd you get all those scars?

Camillo responded to it all with stony silence.

No one serves me alcohol either. Most of the books in Salvatore's library are in Italian and the few that aren't heavy philosophical texts aren't something I could escape into, not that I'm much of a reader anyway. I've tried the TVs in the guest rooms, but after a few minutes of watching a random reality show, I get too restless, turn it off, and leave the room with a visibly disappointed Camillo.

A couple times a day, a loud, happy conversation will ring out from the kitchen or servant's dining room but when I turn the corner, the chatter abruptly stops, and everyone drifts away like dandelion seeds.

When I was a kid and Dad hadn't met his new wife yet, I'd visit him on the weekends. Sometimes I had nothing good to report when I got back, and Mom would give me the cold shoulder for days. It was especially bad during summer vacation when I didn't have school to break up the silence. But even then, I still had my computer or my phone.

Here, all the fun things are locked away and every time I try to touch something, Camillo snorts at me like an old bulldog.

I'm almost certain the passcode to Camillo's phone is four-eight-eight-eight, but unless I suddenly develop telekinesis, I'm not going to be able to pull his phone out of his stupidly-deep pockets. And I'm even less keen on swiping the house keys from Giordana, the hawk-eyed woman who frisks me each night.

So, my plans are pretty much shit right now.

In my pacing through the house, I've filed away the existence of four closed doors. I know the bottom two are locked

—I twisted their handles before Camillo took me by the upper arm and frog-marched me upstairs. The simple cylinder locks on every door practically wolf whistle in my direction when I pass by. *Heeey, beautiful, looking for an easy time?*

But it's the two smart locks, each on a single door downstairs and upstairs, that really get me hot under the collar. I've never tried my hand at locks like those, but smart *anything*—fridges, speakers, cars, whatever—are notoriously easy to hack. When you have the right tools, anyway.

I'm dying to see what's inside. Treasure? Advanced weapons? An embarrassing secret?

I'm going to find out soon. I've spent the last three days upstairs with my back propped up against a wall as I cultivate a bald patch in the fibers of an expensive hallway runner. My lookout spot is between one of the keycode doors and what I'm guessing is Salvatore's bedroom. After the first half hour of rubbing his calves, swinging his arms around, and grumbling in Italian, Camillo brings a chair over to sit and watch a soccer match on his phone.

With nothing else to do, my thoughts wander.

I find myself wondering what Grant might be up to and promptly shake myself by the imaginary shoulders. *Nope, not going there!*

I force myself to remember our other roommate—my piece-of-shit cat. I wish he were here, scowling at me or plotting ways to get me close enough to bite. If he really is with Salvatore, I hope he's pissing all over Salvatore's stuff and rubbing orange cat hair onto all of Salvatore's black, wannabe-rockstar outfits.

I *don't* miss Salvatore, but it's strange he's left me to my own devices for so long. Why did he pretend he was so interested in me only to ignore me for days after?

If he's playing at some kind of hot-and-cold psychological bullshit, this beautiful house of his is going up in flames. He's got to know I'm dying to get laid. Whatever he used to track me has definitely recorded me masturbating all over the apartment during Grant's many absences. Maybe he's trying to push me into such a horny, neglected state that I start rubbing myself on the carpet and yowling loud enough for the whole house to hear.

If he thinks I'm going to break that easily, he doesn't know who he's dealing with. In case he's got a camera in my room, I've sworn off touching myself just so I can deny him the satisfaction of watching—although, if this goes on for much longer, I may have to reconsider my strategy. I keep waking up in the middle of the night, gasping and covered in cold sweat with a slick wetness between my thighs and my pussy clenching around nothing.

The worst part is that I'm in a house surrounded by a dozen fit, well-dressed men. If I don't get out of here soon, I'll have to get naked and throw myself on the dining room table to see who wants to take the bait.

That guy from the train is supposedly after me too, and he was handsome enough, although, even in a fog of lust, he doesn't feature in any of my daytime or nighttime fantasies. He distinctly gave off the vibe that the only way he's going to have sex with someone is after he's given them a homemade frontal lobotomy.

The theory that Junior was some actor of Salvatore's gains more traction each day. If Junior's such a scary badass who'll stop at nothing to hunt me down, why has he been absent since I got here?

Which returns me to Salvatore. If he really wanted me on his cyber team, he could've put me in a shipping container with a computer and a couple of surly guards. So what does he really have planned, and why is it taking him so damn long to get there?

"Time for lunch," Camillo says, jerking me from my thoughts. He eases up from his chair with an old man grunt.

"I'll wait here. I had a big breakfast," I say casually.

Technically, it's true. I had six of these little fried balls filled with creamy rice and cheese and would've eaten more if my leggings hadn't started cutting into my belly. As annoying as everyone else is, I'd run away and elope with Salvatore's old Italian grandma chef in a heartbeat.

Camillo tucks his phone deep into his back pocket and side-eyes his impressive biceps as he flexes. "Don't make me carry you, I just did arms today."

I brush the carpet fibers off my leggings and stand to follow him.

In the kitchen, my frowning, grunting guard transforms into a rakish flirt. He shoots rapid-fire Italian at one of the kitchen staff, a woman who's a little taller than him with long chestnut hair tied back into a braid and brilliant green eyes. From Camillo, I've gathered her name is Nola—that or *amore mio bellissimo.*

Nola skittered away the first day I tried to approach her, so now I just perch at the end of the kitchen bar and wait for Camillo to bring me food. She doesn't seem to be bothered by his scars, because her cheeks burn bright red while he whispers into her ear. After several minutes of outrageous flirting where he steals a kiss from her cheek and she snaps him with a kitchen towel, Camillo brings me a plate with a sandwich.

A few of the other guards and house staff drift in and out of the kitchen. Some steal glances at me, others openly stare. I stare right back, doing what I can to memorize their faces. With such a big staff, there has to be *someone* who's against kidnapping and imprisonment.

I get halfway through the sandwich in my hands before the taste hits me. It's *delicious*. The bread's so soft and fresh, it had to be baked this morning. It's stuffed with deli meats and cheeses and pickled red onions inside. I'm going to have to get bigger leggings if I stay here much longer.

The head chef Conchetta enters the kitchen from the pantry area. Salvatore took me past so many people the first day that I wasn't able to remember them all, but I remember her. She's the oldest person on his staff and so short that she barely reaches *my* shoulder, but Salvatore still introduced her with a kind of reverence that stood out.

As I watch her, she smiles at me, reaches into a basket of pastries on the counter, and approaches me with one. She sets it on my plate.

"Cassetelle," she says.

We've been playing this game every day. Conchetta brings me a dessert. She makes me say it in Italian. I take a bite. I fall a little more in love with her.

Camillo and Nola watch from the other side of the kitchen. Camillo whispers something in Nola's ear, and she giggles. A pang of jealousy shoots through me. I bet Camillo would never cheat.

"Thank you," I say to Conchetta.

"*Grazie*," she corrects, and I repeat after her.

The pastry looks like an empanada, but when I bite in, it's filled with sweet cream and chocolate. *Fuck*. I groan.

"Grazie," I repeat.

Conchetta beams and pats my hand. "Turi is a good boy," she says in a heavy Italian accent. "He just pass too much time on the computer."

I file away the name Turi into a box labeled *Possible Salvatore Nuisances* and nod solemnly to Conchetta.

"I used to spend a lot of time on the computer too," I say clearly. "But after Turi *kidnapped* me, he won't let me use one."

"That's okay," Conchetta says blithely and piles another cassetelle onto my plate. *What's the word for kidnap in Italian?* "The screens are bad for you."

I resist the urge to roll my eyes. Conchetta's not going to star in an escape attempt anytime soon.

"Camillo," Giordana barks as she walks in. "Take our guest out of the kitchen now."

Camillo whispers a few more words to Nola who blushes furiously in response. Then he approaches me, his surly prison guard mask slipping back into place. I stuff the rest of the cassetelle into my mouth as we leave.

Once we're out of the kitchen, I dart ahead of Camillo so that I can lead us back upstairs to my post. He groans, but sits down in his chair and pulls out his phone.

After a few more hours, my ass is killing me from sitting on the ground for so long, but I'm finally rewarded when the electronic keypad to the mystery room beeps, and a huge man steps out.

I haven't seen this guy yet. He looks borderline feral with shaggy brown hair bound into a bun and tattoos covering his arms and peeking out of his shirt collar. His head swivels toward me, and he takes a few long strides to meet us.

Camillo snaps to attention, tucking his phone into his pocket. My muscles tense, and I shift my hand to cover the carpet's destruction. The man's eyes track my movement and narrow.

"Don't let her sit here all day. Make her walk around."

The man gives me a look like I'm dog shit he just found on the bottom of his shoe.

As far as looks of contempt go, I've seen worse.

"Yes, sir," Camillo says and goes to return his chair to its room.

The man seems satisfied and turns to leave, but I speak up quietly, "I'm a guest here."

When he turns back, he's showing off all his too-white teeth with a wolfish grin. He squats down to look me in the eye.

"And I'm Mother Teresa. You think you're being clever sitting here? Trying to figure out how you can escape? Don't be stupid. Why don't you be grateful Turi's protecting you and enjoy your vacation. Watch some TV."

The door beeps again, and Salvatore sweeps out.

"Domenico," he orders.

Still grinning, Domenico winks at me and then stands to join Salvatore.

"Let's go," Camillo says.

My legs have fallen numb, but I wobble onto my feet with whatever dignity I have left while I hold Salvatore's gaze. His expression is neutral until Camillo touches my shoulder, and a little frown crosses his face.

Don't like anyone playing with your toy?

Maybe don't leave it on the shelf all day, asshole.

He tracks me until Camillo leads me around the corner, and we're out of sight.

I WAKE UP ALONE. For several long breaths, I stare at the ceiling, wondering why my body decided to wake me up at the ass-crack of dawn. Since I've arrived, I've gotten shit sleep, but I refuse to accept being wide awake this early in the morning.

Groaning, I roll over and burrow deeper in the blankets, but I still can't get comfortable. I smack my dry lips a few times. I need water.

I shuffle to the adjoining bathroom in the darkness. While I'm lapping water out of the faucet, a man's distant scream shatters the silence.

I jerk my head and cut my lip against the faucet. "Ah, fuck."

I turn off the water and listen intently, holding my swollen lip.

A scream rings out again—from the first floor underneath me—and is abruptly cut off. This is bad.

I rush out the bedroom door, clutching my throbbing mouth, and nearly stumble over the man waiting outside.

I shriek. The man looks up.

"Did you have a nightmare?"

It's the driver. The one who took us to my apartment. Davide, Salvatore called him. He's sitting in a chair and doing a sudoku puzzle of all things, wearing horn-rimmed glasses that, on his baby face, make him look like a toddler dressed as a grandpa.

My brain finishes processing what he just said.

"I heard screaming."

"Oh. That." Davide returns to his puzzle. "Don't worry about it. You can go back to sleep."

"Who is he?"

Davide wrinkles his face and rubs the pencil eraser against his temple. It leaves a faint streak of pink shavings. "Some hacker, I think? I'm not sure to be honest. Dom just let everyone know they'd be bringing a 'guest' into the house around this time."

It doesn't escape me that I'm also supposed to be a "guest". And that this one's also a hacker. That's way too coincidental to be an accident. Is it the man I caught?

I watch Davide for a full minute, weaving my sleepy thoughts into something coherent. At this hour, they're mostly focused on the thought of a midnight snack. I could ask for a sandwich. But the possibility of finding a screaming man with some limb hacked off has me pausing.

"That's supposed to be a six," I say, pointing at one of Davide's cubes.

He squints at the paper. "Huh. Yeah."

"Can I sit out here for a little bit?"

He considers me. "Are you going to try to escape?"

"No."

"You cut your lip?"

I probe the tenderness with my tongue and nod. "Yeah, but I'm okay. I just cut it against the faucet while I was getting a drink."

He makes a sound of disgust. "Just come ask me for a bottled water next time." He waits, and when I don't go back to bed, he exhales. "Okay. You can sit here. But keep your eyes off my sudoku."

I lower myself to the ground, cross my legs, and settle against the doorframe. My eyelids drift shut while I strain my ears for any sound other than Davide's pencil skritching across his paper.

Something muffled and far-off catches my attention. More screaming? The image of a man being burned alive expands in my mind.

The terror gets the best of me, and I blurt out, "I want a sandwich."

The seven Davide's writing grows an errant tail. "Yeah, don't we all? And a root beer float."

A root beer float? Where did they find this guy?

I swallow and clench my hands. "No, I mean... Could we go downstairs? I just want to make a bite to eat. I'm starving. I... I could make you one too?"

He arches an eyebrow. "No fucking way, dude. If Dom or Sal see you down there, it's not gonna be pretty for any of us."

I inhale, ready to argue more, but my retort dies on my tongue when I hear heavy steps thud up the stairs.

I glance back to Davide. He's already standing. "Get back to bed," he says, without looking at me.

I can't go to my room without seeing whoever's coming upstairs. Moving slowly and deliberately, I push myself up to standing while Davide hovers over me.

The steps get closer, and at first, I don't recognize the man who appears at the end of the hallway—because he's covered in blood.

I stifle a scream and jump up. Davide snatches my arm to shove me toward my room.

It's Salvatore. He looks over at us. Even from here, I can see his black button-up shirt is soaked with dark stains. Tracks of blood run down his arms, neck, and face. How is he still standing with all those injuries?

"She had a nightmare, sir. She's going back to bed now," Davide calls out.

"Wait."

Salvatore approaches us with measured steps. Davide's hand falls from my arm, and he stands at attention next to me. My breath quickens.

Salvatore stops in front of us. His gaze ticks over me before he captures my jaw in his hand.

"Your lip's cut."

Any residual sleepiness zips out of me at his nearness. I inhale. He reeks of blood.

"It's fine," I say, but my voice comes out in a squeak.

"Get her an ice pack," Salvatore says, without looking away from my mouth.

"Yes, sir." Davide dashes down the hallway.

"Come with me," Salvatore says and turns.

For a moment, I consider disobeying him, just to remind him I'm not on his payroll, but the blood all over his body and face make anything other than speedy compliance suicidal, so I fall into step behind him. Some of my terror transforms into anticipation when I realize he's taking me to the mystery room next to mine.

With the lights off, only shadowy impressions are visible. A massive bed with dark sheets and two nightstands. A looming chandelier. We pass a big mirror leaning against the wall, and I make eye contact with a surprised-looking woman with blood on her mouth.

Despite the pain he must be in, his gait is as steady as ever as he leads us to the connected bathroom.

He flicks on a dim bathroom light, and I stop short. The bathroom door isn't made of the typical painted wood—it's a thick, heavy steel paired with a similarly reinforced doorframe. It's not just a bathroom—it's a panic room. I hesitate at the doorway, and I'm not sure if it's fear of being locked inside with Salvatore or being locked inside alone that roots me to the spot.

Salvatore doesn't notice—or pretends not to—as he crouches down to reach into the cabinet under his sink.

"Sit. On the bathtub."

I take a breath and cross over the threshold. Two more steps, and I'm lowering onto the bone-colored granite surrounding an impressive soaking tub. Somehow, it's hard to imagine Salvatore using this to take bubble baths, but when I glance behind me at his bath products, I spot an out-of-place pink bottle of bubble solution. It looks *just* like the bottle I use at home, but there's no way it's the exact same scent. I squint to read the label, but a sudden weight between my knees has me whipping my head forward.

Salvatore—hands and arms scrubbed clean of blood—holds out a white washcloth. He brings it to my mouth, and I rear back.

A faint crease appears between his eyebrows. "Hold still."

"It's really—I'm *fine*. Are you okay? Do... you... do you have a doctor you can call?"

Instead of answering, he slides one hand along my shoulder to grip the back of my head like he's steadying me for a kiss and lifts the washcloth to my mouth.

Warmth and moisture press up against my lips, and I instinctively squeeze my thighs together in an effort to suppress the echoing call of heat and wetness between them. My hands have nowhere to go, so I'm forced to fold them on my lap. I can't look at his face this close without doing something stupid, so I stare forward into the mirror behind him—*nope*—the image of a dark, bloody man bending between my knees gets filed away into a box labeled *Do Not Touch,* and I snap my eyes shut.

He's gentle as he wipes the smear of blood off my mouth, but I wish he wasn't, because I can't hold the concepts of "hated captor" and "kind of sweet" in my head at once.

Just when biting his hand seems like the only escape from my traitorous thoughts, he's done.

"It's not my blood."

"What?" I open my eyes. The washcloth has disappeared, but he has a small tube in his hand now.

"This isn't my blood. I'm not hurt."

"Oh." It's the other man's. What did Salvatore *do* to him?

Salvatore squeezes a dab of what looks like an antiseptic onto one clean finger, and I try to lean back again as he draws near, but his hand is still threaded into my hair—I'm trapped. I swear we can both hear my heartbeat pounding as he smears the substance onto my bottom lip. It's too late to close my eyes now. I'm locked in, forced to memorize his high cheekbones and dark lashes and bright eyes and the streak of dried blood up his temple that pushes his hair into a peak.

Please don't kiss me, I think, and then my stomach plummets with disappointment when he finishes his task and turns to wash his hands.

"How did you hurt yourself?" he asks over his shoulder.

"It was an accident. I bumped my mouth against the faucet while I was getting water."

He pauses in his ministrations. "Ask Davide for a water bottle next time."

I roll my eyes behind his back. For cripes sake, these guys are bossy.

"Where's the other man?" I ask when the silence stretches too long. "The one who was screaming?"

Salvatore finishes washing his hands and turns to me, leaning against the bathroom counter. Just like on the train and in the hotel, his air of quiet composure is a thin lie. His body's wound tight, like he's anticipating a bomb to go off at any moment. Maybe he is. The serene man I saw in the hotel bed, with his mouth parted open and hands loose, feels like a half-forgotten daydream. This predatory creature before me with blood smeared across his face in a visceral warning is the real Salvatore.

"He's in my basement," he says.

The problem is that I've never been so great at following warnings.

"Dead?"

He gives the slightest tilt of his head. I wait to feel a sense of horror or wrongness, but my moral compass isn't working. I don't feel anything other than the pull of more curiosity.

Would Kristin be upset in this situation? Probably, I realize with a delayed twinge of guilt.

"What did he do?"

"It's a long list."

I frown. "Start with a few things then."

Salvatore has deep circles under his eyes and for a moment, I think he's going to push me away so he can go to bed, but he still answers, "He failed at his job. And he was informing on you to Junior."

"So you killed him?" I ask incredulously.

"Yes."

I don't know what to say to that.

Davide knocks at the doorway to the bedroom. "I have the ice pack, boss."

Salvatore starts to unbutton his shirt like I'm not here, and I sit there, transfixed by my private peep show. More tattoos swirl over his chest.

"Run along, passerotta."

His nimble fingers continue down his shirt, and when he reaches his stomach, I feel an answering pull deep behind my own navel.

It's too much.

I dart out of the bathroom and let Davide lead me back to bed.

8

SALVATORE

"A<small>NDRÉS SAYS</small> his crew isn't too pleased with the new product. Might be a bit short. His bosses are looking into it, but they're worried you'll think they're trying to fuck you over."

"Are they?" I scan through the flickering images on the thirty computer monitors above my desk. Six are trained to the house cameras. One more than yesterday. Marisol walks out of frame of the kitchen camera with Camillo trailing a little too far behind. In a few seconds, they should reappear in the foyer camera or the cameras over the stairs. Three... two...

I scowl. *Where are they?*

"Maybe. Andrés says you have a nice ass."

I cast a disbelieving eye at Dom, his skin tinged greenish yellow in the monitors' glow. "Not with short product."

"Always figured you for a size queen." Dom grins and nods to the cameras leading up the stairs. "Looks like they're heading to the balcony."

My relief rises like a child's balloon at the sight of

Marisol's long, dark hair swaying with each step. Camillo follows, way too close this time. *Pop.*

"You gonna ride Camillo's ass some more?"

"I won't have to if he does his job right."

"And how's he supposed to do that?" Dom stretches a few fingers out to Buck who watches him with ears drawn back. The cat swipes at him before running off, and Dom laughs. "When he's not close enough, you complain and when he's too close, you're straight up pissy. Why don't you just put Mari in a cage and throw her up here with us? Then you could watch her all the time."

He's being sarcastic, but the thought of Marisol so nearby and safe feels *right.* She'd be furious, but she'd get over it eventually, wouldn't she?

A smile flickers over my mouth. I remember the woman with a lockpick between her teeth.

She'd escape a cage, given half a chance.

Better to give her this half freedom, where she can roam around the house as she pleases. Aldo's nearly back from Vegas and when he meets her, I can get his promise that Junior won't touch her and that she can work for me. This isn't rushed and underdone like on the train. I'm being patient. Giving her space. Last night was proof that this is working. She let me tend to her cut lip. It's killing me to wait this long, but in a day or two, I'll start joining her at the dining room table, and as she grows accustomed to me, she'll relax. This place will become home to her too.

"You know you're an asshole for considering it," Dom says.

What were we talking about?

Right, Marisol in a cage.

I scrub a hand over my face. "I don't want her in a cage. I want her to be safe. And I want her to make her own choices. But what she wants is a computer and a phone, and I might as well give her a loaded gun and let her loose in the house."

"Yeah, well, I'm sure she'll be real patient and understanding about that. She's a patient and understanding kind of woman, isn't she?" Dom says, smirking. He's seen nearly as much of Marisol as I have, a realization that always makes jealousy slither through my veins.

"No."

Marisol's impulsive and stubborn. And she doesn't like missing the full picture. She won't tolerate this forever.

"If I give her freedom, I need to keep her from lashing out."

"You could bring her over to Junior's. Let him throw a tantrum. *Show* her what's on the other side."

"I don't want any more of Junior's attention on her than necessary. This needs to blow over so he can fixate on something else."

Dom's skeptical look speaks volumes. Junior doesn't forgive, and he doesn't forget. There's no hiding Marisol behind my back and hoping he moves on.

"Have Worm pull up some of his warehouse videos," Dom suggests.

"That'll give her nightmares." Some of the things I've seen Junior do in his warehouse have given *me* nightmares.

"Good. Maybe she'll want someone to keep her safe at night," he says with a wink. "You know what that woman really needs? It's written all over her face. She could use a good—"

"*Don't.*"

Dom doesn't finish his statement, but he's wearing a smug, idiot grin. He might be a good head taller than me, but that just makes it easier to aim for his kneecaps. The mental image soothes me enough to compose my face into a neutral expression. Infuriatingly enough, it just makes Dom grin wider. Shithead.

"Let Worm know I want those videos of Junior. And make sure Andrés understands I'll do a *full* audit of his imports if anything's coming in short."

"Will do, boss." Dom gives me a lazy salute and saunters out of the room.

I slide into my computer chair to scan the house cameras again. The tightness in my chest eases a fraction as I spot her.

She's standing barefoot on the balcony near the handrails. Camillo sits in a lounge chair a little too far away, watching a soccer match on his phone.

For a few moments, I think she might finally be settling in and enjoying the view, but when I track her eyeline, I realize what she's looking at, and my hands curl into tight fists.

I lean toward the monitor showing her sweet, naïve face. Her lips are moving imperceptibly.

She's counting the seconds between the guards. She's looking for a gap in their patrol.

"If you try to fly away," I tell her image in a low voice, "I'll break your wings."

It's nighttime before I'm able to pull away from work.

All day long, my gaze kept slipping back to Marisol on the balcony and only the ping of an email or text to my phone would break the spell and force me to realize how much time I'd lost watching her.

I roll my shoulders as I push up from my chair.

Things need to change. My strategy of waiting for her to

come to terms with her situation on her own isn't working. She's not easing into her life here, she's just fucking scheming all day.

Worm already sent over the file with the videos of Junior. I'll show it to her tonight after dinner.

Maybe she'll want someone to keep her safe at night.

When she got here, I thought her nearness would soothe the constant itch to watch her, but it's only gotten worse. She wasn't supposed to take up so much mental space. How can I have a prisoner in my home and feel like I'm not the one in charge?

Because you're not. You've given her too many liberties. You're being weak and lazy, and you'll lose her for it.

I stride out of the watchtower and away from the voice that sounds like my dad. I just need to be patient. She's here now, and I have all the time in the world. Waiting and watching have rarely failed me in the past. I shouldn't be rash.

My phone vibrates in my pocket, and I pull it out, grateful for the distraction.

DOM

Guess who invited themselves over for dinner? Junior's in the dining room.

An invisible fist crushes my throat as red flashes over my vision.

Alone in the hallway, I stagger like I've been thrown onto a sinking ship. I slap the nearest wall to anchor myself while I fight to regain control of my heart rate. *Deep breaths, Sal.*

I swipe through my phone with jerky movements and exhale. Marisol's still on the balcony where she was twenty seconds ago.

GIORDANA

> Turi, hurry up. Junior wants to see you and Mari.

Fuck no.

I haven't caught my breath yet, but I stride through the hallway regardless, sending out rapid-fire texts to Dom and Giordana.

> Marisol won't be joining us for dinner.

> Let the staff know to be on high alert.

I give myself one moment to master my face and posture before I enter the dining room.

Junior sits at the head of the table in an impeccably tailored suit, gorging himself on an entire roasted chicken like a medieval king. Giordana watches him uneasily from the corner, along with Davide and Nola. One of Aldo's men stands at Junior's back. Mauro. He's got eyebrows like fat caterpillars and six kids he left in Sicily that he sends money to. I know for a fact he hates Junior. Good.

I sit at the opposite end of the table next to Dom and wait for Nola to load my plate. Dom doesn't even pretend to eat and instead plays with his knife while he shoots Mauro menacing looks across the table. Mauro stares forward at the wall, sweat shining on his forehead.

Junior exhales loudly and wipes his greasy fingers directly on the tablecloth. In the corner of my vision, Giordana's eye twitches.

"Thank you, Nola," I say as she brings a plate of food to me. It slips out of her hand, but I catch it smoothly. She cringes as she retreats back to the corner of the room. To Junior, I add, "To what do I owe the pleasure?"

"I love the way Conchetta roasts her chicken," Junior says in Italian. He grabs a platter of potatoes and pulls them toward him, picking one out and biting into it like an apple. "How does she get them so crispy? I keep telling you, Turi, one of these days, I'll poach her away from you, and then you'll have to come to *my* place to get some delicious roasted chicken."

He knows how much I *hate* when he uses my nickname, Turi.

"Do you have a kitchen now?" I answer in Italian as I slice through the chicken breast on my plate with a knife. Junior lives in a studio apartment above his warehouse in South Shore. He's got plenty of money, but he prefers to shit in a bucket and eat out of the garbage like a rat.

"Oh, yeah." Junior considers this as he picks out gristle from his teeth. "Well, you'd be surprised what a person can do when they're properly motivated."

How many men did Junior bring with him tonight? He's not going to take Marisol from me with anything less than a small army, but he might be able to scare her.

Camillo better have had the sense to bring her inside.

"You'll have to motivate someone else. I pay my staff well, you'd be hard-pressed to get them to leave."

"Sounds like I'll have to get a little more creative then, eh?"

That's one thing I won't deny. Junior certainly is very *creative*.

"Have you decided what you're going to do with the girl? Marisol, is it?" Junior asks. He knows full well what her name is. "I already asked Papà. He said once he gets back from his trip, he'll talk to you about her."

A thread of apprehension laces up my spine. I can guess Junior's complained enough that Aldo said he'll try to get her for him, reaching for the same kind of wanton generosity that gave Matteo his first car and me a full ride to UChicago.

But he can get Junior another strip club if he needs his balls scratched.

Marisol is a complete stranger, a civilian with no real criminal history, who's stumbled into our organization with a set of highly sought-after skills. How can Aldo not see any other use for her than letting his son have her?

Junior's only plan is to take her to that warehouse of his.

"Unfortunately," I say slowly, letting the word linger as I take a sip of water, "that's not a possibility."

"Why the fuck not?" Junior snaps, and I allow myself a small smile.

"Because she's my fiancée." Once I say it out loud, the puzzle pieces fall into place.

Marriage is the ultimate trump card, *especially* for Aldo who sends a dangerous man like me after his worst enemies, who still goes to church every Sunday, and who coveted Serafina for years but hasn't taken her because you *never* lay hands on another made man's wife or daughter.

It's tradition. It's backward and archaic—and I'm wondering why I didn't think of it sooner. I won't have to worry about Junior taking Marisol.

He can't take her, she's yours, says the voice in my head that sounds like my dad, but before my conscience can murmur its protest, Junior bursts into a crazed laugh. "You fucking liar! You just don't want me to have her, admit it!"

Dom leans to my side to show me a message on his phone.

CAMILLO

Marisol escaped. She's in the forest now,
but I have men after her.

"Let him know I'll handle it," I say to Dom.

Camillo will be punished for this.

So will Marisol. I warned her before that if she tried to run, I'd catch her. Now she's going to learn I'm the kind of man who keeps his word. Even with her head start, I've seen her run on the treadmill at her apartment gym—she won't get far.

I stand, letting my napkin fall over my plate. "Excuse me," I say. "Something came up. Dom will see you out."

A rare expression of canniness crosses over Junior's face. "Lady troubles, Turi? When you get tired of fucking her, be a pal and let me get a taste, huh?"

As I stride away, Junior's civil facade snaps, and he screams after me, "You better not be lying, Turi! Papà's gonna gut her like a fucking fish if you're lying!"

9

MARISOL

I THOUGHT if I could reach the forest, I'd be safe.

But now, terror and doubt suffocate me in the darkness.

The second I saw Junior step out of the black SUV that pulled up to the house, I knew.

Salvatore was giving me up. His boss was ordering him to give me to Junior, or he just got bored. Men lose interest so easily.

Junior saw me standing on the balcony. Blew me a kiss before he entered the house. Maybe it was his jerky movements or the look on his face, illuminated by the lights from the front door, but it struck a chord of horrible familiarity.

My mom was the same. Absolutely certain she deserved what she wanted. Even when the police were knocking at the door for another domestic dispute, she just *knew* Dad would see her side of things once the police left.

I'd been thinking about the ivy on the side of the house all day. It was a small drop from the stone balcony to the ground—less if I managed to fall onto one of the bushes.

I wasn't wearing shoes, but I could use my toes for traction.

One of the patrol guards had stationed himself at the front door.

I would never have a better chance.

My heart thundered in my chest as I watched Camillo's back. He hadn't turned around yet. Maybe we'd built up enough of a rapport that he trusted I'd stay nearby.

I'm sorry, I thought in Camillo's direction. *Good luck with Nola.*

I slung one leg over the balcony and smeared my sweaty, trembling palms against my jeans. The drop was so much taller now that I was at the edge. It wasn't until I was lowering myself along the other side of the stone railing that Camillo turned around.

"Mari!"

I slipped and lunged at the ivy. The roots tore away immediately with a burst of popping sounds that rang like gunfire as I clawed at the stone for purchase. I crash-landed onto a bush, a scream lodging in my throat. My brain hurt, my teeth felt loose, and something was stabbing my arm. I groaned. Camillo's silhouette appeared above me like a great bat. I threw myself off the bush, limping away as my whole body screamed in pain.

I had to get to the forest.

My lungs felt like they were going to explode as I sprinted across the well-manicured grass in my bare feet and prayed to all the gods that no one would shoot me in the terrifying openness of the lawn.

To my right, a man shot toward me like an arrow unleashed. He was fast—faster than me—and I put on another impossible burst of speed, fueled by wild panic.

Salvatore was going to be furious. He was going to shoot me in the back of the head and bury me in the forest.

I risked a glance back just in time to see Camillo

launching himself at the other man. They slammed to the ground in a tangle of limbs. The other man wasn't one of Salvatore's—he was Junior's.

"Don't!" Camillo shouted after me, but I was already at the tree line.

The trees didn't seem so packed together from the house, but now as I plow forward, the dense thicket of branches rakes at my face and hair, dragging me to a syrupy, nightmarish crawl. Not that I could go any faster when I'm forced to navigate by touch and shadows. Even with the half-moon glowing above, the web of tree limbs chokes out everything but a weak light. I've never had to move through darkness like this before, and a host of primal fears creep to the forefront of my mind. A soft patch of dirt buried between the jagged rocks and branches feels like a coiled snake. The dead leaves brushing over the tops of my feet paint swarms of biting ants and spiders on my skin. Some part of me, floating out of reach, urges me to breathe, to calm down, but I can't, I can't, *I can't*.

He has to know I'm gone by now—if not from Camillo, then by some uncanny intuition of his. He could already be racing against Junior, both of them hurtling after their stolen toy—not that they give a shit about catching me. They're just greedy monsters who want to make the other suffer.

They can find a different toy. I don't want to play their stupid game.

The sweat on my chest and neck turns frigid, leaving me shivering as I creep through the forest. I didn't think about the cold or the darkness. I didn't think about anything. I just ran. Mom always said I was too smart to be this stupid. Guess she was wrong—I'm just stupid. I huff out a shaky laugh, but it sounds like a sob.

When I fell, I ripped a gash into the back of my arm. I should be grateful it's the worst of my injuries, but blood's streaming in rivulets past my elbow, and the pain burns hotter with each step. I pluck at my soaked shirt sleeve. I need to take a look at it, but I don't dare stop now, and I wouldn't be able to see much in the darkness anyway. When my hand comes away, it's left slick and wet. How much blood loss can I handle? Maybe no one's after me, and I'll just collapse and bleed out on the forest floor, slowly buried under the autumn leaves.

Something snaps at the fringes of my hearing. I freeze like a startled rabbit, staring off into the darkness, straining my ears to hear something other than my own rapid breathing.

Snap.

There.

Fuck me.

I push myself harder. There's absolutely something or someone behind me. Not that far by the sound of it. I hadn't even considered the possibility of a wild animal in these woods. Or that Salvatore might have hunting dogs, somewhere deep in his house, locked in one of those secret rooms.

The thing behind me speeds up, and the heavy crashing sounds it makes as it barrels through the trees seize my chest with fear. Those are the sounds of a man—Salvatore or Junior?

He's going to get me. I'm so fucked. He's going to skin me alive and dip me in a vat of acid.

I can almost feel his hot breath on the back of my neck. I swat behind me, but my fingertips skate along empty air. *A clearing!* I break through into a little clearing and sprint to the other side.

I can't think about how fucked up my body is right now, or I'll break down. My hand touches the edge of the first tree, and then my entire world flips upside down as pain explodes in my ribs. I hit the ground *hard,* and my body crunches like a dry eggshell underneath me. For a moment, my panic reaches its climax.

I can't breathe!

Then the force that struck me lifts, and I suck in a deep lungful of air.

"*Marisol!*" a furious voice booms.

A strange sense of serenity washes over me as I look up into the face of my death.

In the clearing, moonlight bathes Salvatore's dark hair in silver. His face twists in savage rage as his hips and hands pin me down in a contorted position along the forest floor. He slams a fist down on the ground inches from my face, and it breaks my calm. I scream.

"Marisol!" Salvatore shouts again, gripping my shoulders and shaking them roughly. "What the *fuck* are you doing?"

"What does it look like I'm doing?" I cry out, my eyes squeezing shut because I'm too scared to look at his face. "I'm running!"

"*You can't do that!*" Salvatore shakes my shoulders again, harder and harder as his breath heaves over me. "I make the rules here, *not* you! And you are *mine*! You will never, *ever* leave!"

I open my eyes and shut them again just as quickly. Red. Blood all over him. I can't look at his face. "I can't stay here!" I shout back. "You're going to kill me! Please, *please* let me go!"

Salvatore hauls off of me, and I have the wild thought

that he's going to let me go, but instead, he jerks me upright and lifts me into his arms.

I stiffen my body to try to roll away from him, but Salvatore crushes my body to his, suffocating me against his chest. I open my eyes. He's not bleeding—that's *my* blood smeared across his cheek and forehead. He doesn't even look angry anymore.

"Don't," he says. Some of the sanity returns to his voice, though it's barely concealing a sharp edge. "You're done running. I'm taking you back to the house, and you'll only make it worse for yourself if you struggle."

I want to. I want to fight and claw his eyes out and scream, but I have nothing. No weapons, no strength left in me. He already caught me with such a long head start. Tears prick my eyes as the hopelessness of my situation weighs down on me.

Salvatore's chest presses up against me in intervals as his breathing returns to normal.

"Put your arms around my neck. It'll make it easier to carry you."

"No."

He gives me a wild, violent look, and I fling my arms up to obey him. There's nowhere for me to escape, to pull away from him. Every part of my body is pressed up against his.

You had it good, you dumb bitch. You were being fed and left alone, and you fucked it up.

Silent tears track down my cheeks as he walks me back through the forest, picking his path with ease. He doesn't complain, though he does set me down once to stretch his back and arms. I stare at the dark, leaf-choked ground, facing away from him and hugging myself. When he picks me up again, I wrap my arms around his neck without hesitation. It doesn't take long to break out of the forest onto his manicured lawn. I hadn't even been running in a straight line. I made it easy for him.

"I told you what would happen if you tried to escape again," he says quietly.

My body tenses, and I shake my head a little.

"I said I would punish you."

Fear, anticipation, and hot shame have me tucking my face into his chest as he brings me inside the house where Giordana and Domenico are waiting.

Salvatore gives them orders in Italian and carries me up the stairs, two steps at a time. He's bringing me back to my room. Is he going to lock me inside?

We don't get that far. He takes me to his room instead, all the way to his bathroom. Some of my terror returns here, knowing that he could lock me behind that thick steel door.

Salvatore stands me up on the cold tiles and perches himself on the edge of the bathtub, big enough to fit three people, to start the water.

"Strip," he says without looking at me.

A violent shiver wracks through me. "No," I whisper.

Salvatore looks up at me, and something inscrutable crosses his face. "If you listen to me, I won't touch you."

I stand there for a long time, waiting to see if he'll change his mind or if some other plan of escape strikes me.

"Now."

I turn from him and slowly undress.

Fuck you, Salvatore.

I tuck my body into itself, staring at a small imperfection in the light grey paint on the wall across me.

"Get in the tub."

I take a deep breath. He said he wouldn't touch me. With that flimsy hope, I turn, crossing my hands over my breasts.

He's leaned against the bathroom sink, tapping a message out on his phone. He doesn't look up at me.

Like he's some kind of fucking gentleman for not watching me get into the tub.

I ease into the lukewarm water.

"Do you need medical attention?" he asks, eyes locked to his phone.

I mentally scan over my body. I feel like one big bruise, but otherwise, I'm whole. The cut on the back of my arm had mostly coagulated, but it's opening back up in the warm water, tinging the bath pink.

"No."

"The cut on your arm?"

"No."

Salvatore shrugs. "You have five minutes. Clean up."

I sit there sullenly. I'm not going to get clean just so he can do whatever he pleases after.

His gaze flicks up. He looks bored. I wrap my arms around my knees, splashing the water.

"Either you bathe yourself, or I will."

He fixes his gaze on me until I reach for a washcloth, and then he returns to his phone. I work quickly, watching him the entire time. His shirt's torn in a few spots, I note with a tiny measure of satisfaction.

I hate you. I hate you. I hate you.

Salvatore reaches out of the room for a moment, and when his hand draws back in, he has a tidy pile of my clothes. He sets them on the edge of the sink without looking at me.

"You can't keep me here forever," I whisper. I don't know what stupid urge is overcoming me to poke at him now when I'm at my most vulnerable, but I just need some resolution. I've been tense, waiting for something Bad to happen for a week now, and I can't take any more uncertainty.

"Of course I can," he says, without looking at me.

I let the tub drain and stand up, a torrent of water pouring from the ends of my hair. I reach for a towel without covering myself, but Salvatore maintains his gaze on his phone.

"Clothes," I say, holding a hand out.

Salvatore passes them over to me. His gaze flits over me once, and his pupils swallow the honeyed color in his eyes as he takes me in. A thrill passes through me, and then he's back to his phone, but this time his thumbs aren't moving.

Once I'm dressed in leggings and a t-shirt, and my hair's towel-dried, he slides his phone into his pocket. He turns to grab a clear container from underneath the sink, the same as when I cut my lip.

"Sit," he says, nodding to the bathroom sink counter.

I don't move.

"Now, Marisol."

Reluctantly, I move to the counter and ease myself up onto the edge as Salvatore digs through the medical supplies in the box. He takes out a few bandaids.

With a featherlight touch, he rotates me enough to expose the back of my arm. He swipes a gel over the cut there, and I grit my teeth to keep from whimpering. He makes eye contact with me in the mirror for a split second before he refocuses on applying a bandaid. His gaze touches every part of me. He picks up another bandaid and places it on a small cut on my neck.

"What were you thinking?" he murmurs. "You could've been hurt."

I inhale sharply. Anger and arousal swirl through me at his touch.

"You were going to give me to Junior," I say, staring at him through the mirror.

Salvatore sweeps his gaze over me again. "No, passerotta. I was protecting you from him."

Oh.

More lies?

What does he want? It's unthinkable to consider he could be doing all of this for *me*.

"I can't live like this. You put me in limbo," I say, turning toward him. "I don't know what you want. I don't know where my life goes next."

Salvatore rests his hands on my arms. My spread knees skim along his stomach.

"I thought I've been clear with you," he says gently. "I want you, Marisol. I want you to stay with me."

I'm tired. I haven't masturbated in days and haven't had sex in weeks. I just want one kind touch from one kind person, and Salvatore's a close enough approximation that I have to resist leaning into him.

"You can't take my things and ignore me for days and expect me to fall into step for you."

Salvatore blinks. He tucks a strand of hair behind my ear. "I haven't been ignoring you. I've been watching you. Constantly. I can barely work, barely think, because all I do, all day long, is watch you."

My breath catches. Every part of me is screaming to stop fighting and just give in to him, but I can't do it.

"We can't have a relationship that exists just in your head."

"I know." Salvatore gathers me in his arms, and I relax against him, just a little. I'm tired of fighting.

I tense slightly as we pass his bed. Will he drop me there? Is that what I want?

But he doesn't stop. Instead, he takes us down the stairs. I'm starting to feel sleepy, but I revive at the sight of Domenico standing next to the door on the first floor. The one with the electronic lock.

Domenico has a hard look on his face that makes my blood run cold.

"You'll spend some time here until I have something better designed," Salvatore murmurs into my hair.

"Wait, what?"

Salvatore sets me down. Immediately, Domenico hauls me into the room by my arm, slamming the door shut behind me. Locks slide into place with two clicks.

I take in the room at a glance. One naked bulb screwed into the ceiling casts my surroundings in a sickly light. The floors and walls are bare concrete, perfumed faintly with bleach. Someone set my mattress and blankets in the center of the room with a stack of books next to the bed. There's a camping toilet in the corner.

A dungeon. He's locked me in a dungeon.

I whirl and pound on the door, screaming until my throat is raw, but no one comes.

10

SALVATORE

"Thanks for helping with that *rat* problem, Sal," Red says over his glass of whiskey.

I've lectured Red more than once about the dangers of talking business in public meeting places, but he thinks if he has a gun at his back and speaks in code, he's invincible. He's lucky Barbara has a soft spot for him because I would've let Dom run him out of town ages ago.

I nod at him as I cut into my steak. Next to me, Dom's nearly finished wolfing his down and is already eyeing the bread basket.

"You might be dealing with another infestation soon," I say, ignoring the crawling sensation over my skin. I just had this restaurant swept for bugs—I don't need to overthink it. What I need is to move this check-in along so I can get back to the house.

My phone buzzes. It's my special alert for movement in the basement. Marisol must've woken up from her nap.

Next to Red, his uncle Barbara puffs at a cigar. A breeze carries it directly to my face, and I make note to shower immediately after this. Technically, Medium-Rare doesn't allow cigars, but you wouldn't know it by the waiter's gleeful expression as he races to our table.

"More whiskey, gentlemen?" the waiter asks.

"No, Matty, we're good," Barbara says, rousing from his torpor. Red looks at his own empty glass and pouts. "How's your mom doing?"

"Great, thank you, Mr. Barbara."

"Stay in school, yeah?" Barbara flashes a few twenties as a tip, and Matty takes the money and runs. Barbara turns to me. "What sort of infestation?"

"Wild dogs," I say. "Running around your warehouses. Make sure they're locked down tight is all I'm saying."

The younger of the Boughan brothers Colin goes by Mad Dog—a fitting name for a man that makes Junior look like a Boy Scout. His older brother Gavin does what he can to reign in the younger but despite Gavin's efforts, Mad Dog's been mixing with a bad crowd. He wants to hit some of the warehouses the Barbaras' use for their prescription drug distribution. If he doesn't blow himself up, he's liable to start a war.

Barbara digests this as he accepts a fresh cigar from his nephew. "Thanks, Turi. We'll look into it."

As he pulls out his cigar cutter, I lean back in my chair. This is the same song and dance he always goes through when he's about to suggest something I might not like. Dom senses it too and yanks the bread basket toward him. My phone buzzes. My fingers twitch.

"Aldo still hasn't changed his mind about Rekhson?" Barbara asks once he's finally sucking on his new cigar.

Next to me, Dom snorts.

We had a good thing going with the former District Attorney Harrison. He stayed in his lane, helping protect the fine men and women of Chicago by passing all the laws that Aldo didn't veto.

When Rekhson took over last year, Aldo set himself to charming her as well, but she rejected him. She's completely clean and a little too popular. She ran her campaign on reducing gang crime within the city, and she just passed a law that punishes gang members harshly if they're caught with a gun. Such a simple and effective measure to keep us in line.

Aldo was spitting mad when it came out. She caught Barbara's nephew Virgilio with that one, and the idiot almost threw us all in hot water by making a plea deal with her. Luckily, Summit Construction is building a high rise over his remains as we speak.

"Maybe," is all I say.

Barbara's on board to scare Rekhson or bribe her, but as consigliere, he needs to keep what the other families want in consideration. And very few people other than Aldo want her dead. Better that Aldo goes to jail for a while than the entire Family takes the kind of heat that comes with killing a state official.

"Be careful with her," Barbara says. "We don't need any extra attention, capisce?"

Of course, I agree. But Aldo likes flaunting himself in front of God and everyone. And Rekhson doesn't like that it makes her look like a fool. She's made Aldo a special project of hers, and I can't say I blame her.

"Yeah."

Barbara sighs. "You're a good boy, Turi."

"One more thing," I add. "I'm getting married."

Red sputters on his water, but Barbara only raises one thick eyebrow.

"The e-girl?" Barbara asks, using the stupid fucking nickname Dom came up with for Marisol.

"Her name is Marisol Vasquez," I say at the same time Dom chimes in, "The very same."

"You got a picture of her?" Red asks, too-casually.

"Shut the fuck up, Red," Dom cuts in.

Red mutters something about wanting another whiskey and wanders off in search of the bar.

After a long pause, Barbara scratches the side of his neck with his fork like an orangutan with a stick.

"Good. This is good. Aldo know?"

"Not yet."

For a moment, Barbara is all cunning consigliere as he files that information away. Then he burps, and the impression fades. He lifts from the table with a groan, sounding every bit the old man he is.

"I better go pull Red outta that bartender's tits," he says. We shake hands, and he brings me into a tight hug. "You take care, Turi."

"You too."

Barbara reaches over to clasp Dom by the back of his head and presses their foreheads together. Dom has to fold himself over to meet Barbara, but he does so willingly.

"You take care, Dom. Come by soon. No one appreciates Debbie's arancini like you do."

Dom grins. "I will."

The second we're in the car, I whip out my phone to check on Marisol. She's been in the basement for two days and hasn't stopped pacing long loops around the perimeter. She's looking for another exit, I note with equal measures of disappointment and thrill.

I thought we were getting somewhere after she let me fix up her lip. She saw me covered in another man's blood, but she hadn't cared. We were finally ready for me to join her at dinner instead of watching her on my monitors all night. And then she ruined it by running.

She keeps reminding me she's not the girl behind the camera. That girl couldn't argue with me. She couldn't lie to me. She didn't know she could leave.

I run my thumb along the edge of my onyx ring and stare out the window. Now that I have the real Marisol, I'm fucking it up.

Mom told me all the ways Dad had hurt her. Matteo would cry and refuse to listen, but I couldn't turn away. I always had to know. A few days before we escaped New York, she slipped Dad's onyx ring onto my too-skinny finger. She made me look into her bruised face and swear I'd kill him one day. He was the first man I learned to hate.

I'm not him.

I'm not hurting Marisol. I want to protect her.

Even to myself, it tastes like a fucking lie.

"How's your prisoner?" Dom asks as he drives the car into the street.

"Restless."

He's been doing this all day, needling me with questions.

What's the captive doing? Is she crying? Did you break her yet?

He wants to call on my threadbare conscience, force me to reckon with my paradox. I have a woman—my fiancée—in my basement, and somehow, I still want her to walk out and tell me she'll stay with me and she won't ever try to leave again.

"I would be too. I don't think I'd *ever* forgive someone who put me in a cage like that. I'd certainly never marry them."

I meet Dom's bright eyes across the rearview mirror.

"Where was all this empathy while we were dipping Viriglio's fingers in a jar of acid?"

Of all the shit we've done over the years, keeping Marisol *safe* in my house with hot food, fresh water, and clean clothes has to be the mildest of my sins. I haven't forced her to do anything. I haven't hurt her.

"Same place as your foresight. Tucked *deep* away. You keep trying all this vinegar nonsense, but where's the honey? All you've shown this woman is that you're a grade-A asshole with control issues. There's not a single thing she could point to that would make her say, yeah, *that's* the guy I want pumping me full of babies."

I set aside the image of pumping Marisol full of my babies. "And now you're an expert on women?"

Dom scoffs. "Doesn't take an expert to know if you treat a woman like shit, she's gonna hate you for it. Especially *your* woman."

"I'd rather her hate me than get caught by Junior and tortured."

"Pretty fucking convenient the only solution you've come up with is keeping her under lock and key in your basement."

I grit my teeth. "What would you do if it was Annetta?"

His hands tighten on the wheel and then slacken just as quickly. "I'd let her make her own choices," he answers gruffly. "Even if I hated them."

All the building anger drives out of me like a punch to the gut.

We drive the rest of the way home in silence.

FALLING into work is the easiest thing in the world. It's as simple as turning on my computer and letting myself get dragged in any one of a hundred different directions.

But not today.

The only screen that draws my eye is Marisol's. She's taken the books I had left next to the mattress and torn the pages from them one by one.

She left them artfully arranged on the concrete floor in a pattern that spells "LETS TALK".

I'm surprised it doesn't say "FUCK U".

Let's talk.

Half of me wants to hear how the person with no options tries to bargain. The other half knows they'd be sweet, empty lies.

Dom, and likely the rest of my staff, think I'm a tyrant for doing this to her, but I haven't even put in a fraction of the effort I could into breaking her.

She broke the rules and now she can suffer the consequences. That's not tyrannical, it's fair. Expected. She had no reason to run when Junior came to my house. She was perfectly safe with Camillo.

I watch as she falls back on the mattress and stares at the ceiling, her arms extended like wings.

Better that she's bored than floating in pieces at the bottom of Lake Michigan.

Buck hops onto my desk and peers at the monitor with Marisol's image. He levels an accusatory gaze at me.

Giordana knocks at the door.

Besides Dom, Giordana's the only person who has the access code to my watchtower, and Dom doesn't knock. She lets herself in, dragging a vacuum and duster behind her. I swivel around in my chair as she makes a show of plugging the vacuum in. She's normally very efficient about cleaning my watchtower when I'm out, so there's only one reason she's here at this moment.

She cocks an eyebrow at me as she starts vacuuming and glances meaningfully at the duster.

In the old days, Mom and Giordana took us to work cleaning people's houses. Matteo would always pout and huff over a stove or bookcase for an hour, but I didn't mind the labor. I liked having the excuse to look through the clients' things.

I pick up the duster and work alongside her in silence. When she finishes, she doesn't slip me a cookie like she did when I was a kid. Instead, she gives me a sour look and folds her arms across her chest.

"Let's hear it," I say. Everyone's volunteering their opinions today.

"Are you *ready* to hear it?" Giordana asks. I nod, and she continues, "You're being an idiot."

I can practically hear Matteo muttering, "*Lecca-culo.*" *Ass licker.*

When Giordana was pissed, he'd always say her face puckered up like she'd just licked someone's dirty asshole.

"Care to expand on that?"

"You're torturing this poor girl. She doesn't want to be here, and you can't keep her locked up forever."

"I'm not locking her up forever. *She* escaped against my orders, and now she has to understand what the consequences of that look like. Anyone else in her shoes would have been cleaned up by the Janitor. The basement's hardly a punishment in comparison."

Impossibly, Giordana's mouth puckers further. "What did she eat for lunch?"

"Antipasto, chicken involtini, salad—"

"No kibbles?"

"Not to my knowledge."

"Just double-checking, because you are treating her like a *dog*. If you want one, get yourself a puppy and let her go."

"I'd love to treat her like a *guest*, but every time I give her another freedom, she tries to escape."

Giordana looks like she's making a concerted effort not to swat me with the feather duster. "Of course she does! I swear, Turi, if your mom could see you now..." She pauses, and we both let that sink in. "Marisol's a smart girl, right? She's going to see the danger in your life and go running in the opposite direction, as any person with common sense would. What do you have to offer her? Protection? How is she going to feel protected when you're suffocating her? The only thing you're going to get out of this is a broken girl or a woman who *hates* you."

"So I just let her go, knowing Junior will take her?"

"What would your dad do?"

I frown. My dad would do whatever he needed to get what he wanted.

He convinced my mom as an eighteen-year-old girl to abandon her family and get pregnant, knowing her weak-willed Don of a father wouldn't anger God—or the new connections my dad's family offered—by taking her back. And once he had his wife and his two heirs, he wanted complete obedience from us all. He beat my mom every time she forgot an associate's name, failed to show anything less than absolute adoration, or whenever baby Matteo or I pissed him off.

My kind, delicate mom, who'd grown up on canapés and champagne, withered into a bitter husk. Once her brother Aldo came to power, he sent for the stolen Mafia princess, but by then, it was too late. It'd been too late for years.

She worked cleaning jobs with Giordana, ate dinners

with Aldo, and watched movies with Matteo and me, but none of us could distract her from the letting go that drinking could offer. Even with all the love surrounding her, real life continued to poison her when my piece-of-shit dad —who already had a new, younger wife—sent Mom regular death threats because he couldn't stand the idea of her surviving without him. In the end, he got what he wanted when I came home from college to find Mom's body in the garage, surrounded by empty bottles and her pistol.

"If you love this woman so much," Giordana says, dragging me back to the present, "let her go. Be patient and watch out for her. If she decides she wants to come back to you, then trust her."

I swore I'd never be the kind of man my dad was. I want to guard and control Marisol, but I don't want to hurt her. I don't want to break her.

"If I let her go," I say, "Junior's going to hurt her."

"*You're* hurting her."

"I... don't want to do that." My shoulders drop on an exhale. "Thank you. Please help her bathe and change. I'll wait for her in the dining room."

"About time."

Giordana takes the cleaning supplies and leaves.

11

MARISOL

There's no escape.

I'm stuck inside a sealed concrete box with only a single door for an exit.

When the door opens, it's the same routine each time. Locks click. Light pours in. Giordana takes two steps into the room to remove the trash, set down my new plate of food, and leaves without answering any of my questions.

Judging by my meal timing, shortly after my first breakfast, a man with greying hair and owlish, round glasses stepped into the room with Domenico at his back.

He introduced himself as Dr. Macaluso and, without any inflection in his voice, asked if he could look at the injury on the back of my arm.

At first, I refused. If Salvatore wanted me fixed up, he could come down here and do it himself. But Domenico cheerily announced he'd bring some men in to hold me down for the doctor if I said no, so I just sat limply on the mattress while Dr. Macaluso checked me over.

I tried to lie. I watched the grin grow on Domenico's face as I whispered in Dr. Macaluso's ear all the horrible things

Salvatore had done to me and several things he hadn't. The good doctor didn't even blink. He said I didn't need stitches, and both men left.

I've had four meals since then.

I could try fashioning one of the plastic forks they give me into a shiv and rush Giordana the next time she comes inside, but she's about the same height and weight as me, and I haven't missed the threatening presence of the guard holding open the door for her.

And who am I kidding? I have all the viciousness of an angry kitten.

I could try to convince her to let me go. I'm an idiot for not trying to develop some kind of rapport with her earlier because now I've got a snowball's chance in hell. Maybe I could've had a better opportunity with Camillo—but he's conspicuously absent from my food drop-offs.

He was nice, even if he did grumble a lot. Salvatore better not have done anything too bad to him for letting me escape. Not that it would've kept me from trying or that I could make good on any threats from here.

Eventually, someone will have to come in to empty the camping toilet, and that'll probably be my best opportunity to run, though I'm way more likely to get shot or tackled than I am to miraculously escape.

Without a phone or my lockpicks, I'm dead in the water.

Someone thought they were pretty fucking funny leaving *Crime and Punishment*, *Les Misérables,* and what looks like a philosophical book on ethics... in *Italian* next to my mattress. I've already torn out all three hundred and thirty-six pages of the ethics book. At first, it was just to give me something to do, but now I want to test if Salvatore's watching me.

I've laid the pages out on the ground like a castaway

trying to catch the attention of passing aircraft. I haven't found any evidence of a camera in here, but Salvatore seems paranoid enough that I think there's a good chance there's one embedded in the shadowy corners of the ceiling.

My message spells out, "LETS TALK PLEASE".

I added the PLEASE a few minutes ago, as much as it grinds against my sense of dignity. I don't want to have to debase myself to this asshole, but I'm not going to leave any rock unturned, and astoundingly, I think Salvatore still wants me to like him. At the very least, he wants me to be compliant, so if he gives me the chance to talk, I'll show him how obedient I can be.

I'm working on adding a "PRETTY PLEASE" now. The last of my dignity astral projected from my body the first time I had to poop in the camping toilet. Hell, I'd throw in a *pretty, pretty please with a cherry on top* if I thought it'd get results.

As I adjust the "Y", my fingers skim a dark stain set in the cold concrete. A shiver passes through me, and I sit back on my haunches to press the heels of my hands into my eye sockets.

I'm *not* going to feel sorry for myself.

I'm still healthy and strong...ish. I'm not giving up to self-pity today.

I inhale and continue adjusting the letters. I'm going to keep trying anything I can think of until someone—Domenico probably—comes and shoots me in the head.

If I get another chance, I'll play it smarter. So what if Salvatore wants me docile? I've been pretending to be just that for thirty-two years. What's another few months? And when he *least* expects it, I'm going to leave and cover my tracks so well, he'll never find me again.

What do I have in Chicago anyway? No one would miss

me if I disappeared. It would take months—probably a year—before anyone thought to call the police.

I squeeze my eyes shut.

The *worst* part was how attracted I let myself be to him. His soft voice and the way he could be so tender... what kind of sociopath pets you with one hand while he strangles you with the other?

A tear slips down my cheek, and I scrub at it with my palm.

Only an idiot, a complete fool of the highest order, someone truly *pathetic* would take the scraps Salvatore's offered and spin a relationship out of it. Just like I did with Grant. And my Dad. And my Mom.

I sigh shakily.

I'm going to leave this place, and I won't mess up next time. I'm not going to be a doormat for people just so they like me. I'm going to demand that someone make space for me in their life and that they treasure me, or I'm going to leave.

The lock to the door clicks, and a sudden bright light pierces my eyes. Giordana's form takes shape in the doorway.

When she doesn't immediately walk in with dinner, I stand.

"Come with me," she says.

Is she... breaking me out?

I scurry over to her side and immediately recoil at the sight of the guard standing behind her.

"We're going upstairs. Come on," Giordana says.

I study her stern expression. This isn't a breakout. Maybe Salvatore got my message and wants to talk. In any case, it's showtime. I follow Giordana up the stairs, keeping my head bowed and movements slow. From now on, I'm going to show everyone how sweet and uninterested in escape I can be.

Giordana stops next to "my" bedroom, but it's barely recognizable inside. It's furnished with a full bed, night-stands, and a desk. There's even a vase with beautiful, blush-pink roses on the desk.

My favorite.

Salvatore's offering me a poisoned olive branch. If I accept the room and pretend to be thankful for it, he'll let me back into the light, and if I don't, it's back to the base-ment until I "learn".

That's fine. I'm a quick study.

"You can shower here. Your clothes are there and there," she says, pointing to a dresser and the closet. "Once you're finished, Salvatore will be expecting you in the dining room."

I'd prefer to stomp down now. Make him uncomfortable with my greasy hair and disheveled clothes. Or even to wait in my room all evening and ignore him.

But that's not the plan.

I grab Giordana's hand in both of mine.

"Thank you," I say earnestly.

She frowns a little, and I swallow back the uneasy suspi-cion that she doesn't believe me.

Once she leaves, I hurry to the bathroom to shower. Getting clean again feels *glorious*. I scrub off the grime from the past two days and then just stand there in the scalding hot water until all the bathroom mirrors fog up. As much as I'd like to decompress here for hours, I better not burn through Salvatore's newfound conscience.

I make my way to the walk-in closet. Someone's gone through all of my clothes and hung them neatly on hangers, organized by type and color. It's a nice upgrade from the clean pile of laundry on the floor that I usually pick through.

I brush my fingers against the elegant garnet dress I wore for Grant's brother's wedding. Is this the type of outfit Salvatore would want to see me in? I've only ever seen him in jeans and a t-shirt. He's practical, for himself at least. Maybe he prefers me to be some glamorous eye candy while he dresses down. Grant could hardly be bothered to wear anything other than basketball shorts and a tattered t-shirt, but he loved to see me in skirts and heels.

I end up choosing a pair of jeans, boots, and a white t-shirt that fits tightly around my boobs. Simple, flattering, and vaguely similar to Salvatore's daily outfit. I'm hoping it'll send some kind of subliminal message that I'm already siding with him. I suck at hiding my emotions, so I'll have to rely on all the props I can.

Right before I leave the room, I kick off my boots and socks. Maybe my bare feet will show an extra measure of vulnerability.

When I come into the dining room, Salvatore's already waiting at the head of the table, sipping a glass of water. Giordana stands in the corner of the room, hands clasped in front of her.

Another glass is placed two chairs away, presumably to say *you don't have to sit next to the mean man. Don't worry, you're safe*. A wide charcuterie board laden with cheeses and meats and a tray of sweet pastries cover the surface of the table. The pastries are already making my mouth water, but I resolve not to eat unless he does.

Docile, easy, weak, agreeable.

He's wearing a soft grey sweater that clings to his chest instead of his usual black tee. Did he dress to disarm as well?

I hate how little he's given me. How poorly I can read him. I wish I could've put *him* in that basement until he spilled all his secrets to me and then only let him out when *I* felt ready.

Instead, I offer a shy smile as I enter, and Salvatore's expression flickers. I ignore the suggested seating and sit near him. Fixing a doe-eyed, uncertain look on my face, I reach for the wine glass and hold it out to him like a child asking for a cup of grape juice. He pours me a perfect serving and returns the bottle to the table without pouring himself a glass.

I sip from it, letting the Merlot stain my lips a sensual red. Innocent but sexy—every man's impossible fantasy.

"Thank you for letting me out," I say.

I've always been told my round face looks innocent and un-threatening, and I play that up with a guileless expression. Salvatore leans back, frowning. He's suspicious. I glance down at my wine. *God, I'm fucking bad at this. Tone it down.*

"I... I shouldn't have done that," he says. *Yeah, no shit.* "I brought you here to apologize." *You're not on your knees, asshole.* "Do you... are you hungry?"

"No. I was very well-fed."

"Good. You should know that, after this dinner, you'll be free to leave."

12

MARISOL

YEAH, right.

I sip from my wine. "You'll let me go home?"

Salvatore exhales and scrubs his jaw. "Yes. If you want," he says reluctantly.

This messes heavily with my plans to make him think I'm meek enough that I can attempt another escape. Is he being sincere or is this a test to see if I need more Dungeon Fun Time?

"I put you in the basement," he continues, "because I thought I was protecting you. But I was wrong. I shouldn't try to control you. I only want you here if you want to be here."

"In your basement?" More poison drips into my voice than I intended. I drive my nails into my leg under the table. *Chill the fuck out.*

"No. You have my word. I'll never do that again. If you choose to stay, things will be different. You'll get access to a monitored computer and cell phone, but otherwise, you'll be free to come and go from the house as you please. I just ask that you bring a guard of your choosing."

I buy myself time to think by taking another sip of wine. Motionless as a snake, Salvatore watches me.

If he's giving me an out, of course I'll take it. I'm not going to stay here so his Highness can change his mind again and take my toys away. But if this is some ploy to test my loyalty, I'll fail if I seem too eager. I have to be patient.

Ugh. Not my strong suit.

"Why the sudden change of heart?" I ask when the silence has drawn on for too long.

"I... lost track of my goals. I was so concerned with how Junior might get to you, I thought the basement was the only surefire way to protect you—"

"You said—" I bite my tongue and drop my gaze.

Salvatore places his hand over mine. It makes my skin crawl. "It's okay. You can speak your mind. I want to hear what you have to say."

My mouth kicks in before my brain can. "You said the basement was to *punish* me."

Salvatore's eyes flash, and he squeezes my hand. "You escaped when I told you not to."

"You kidnapped me!"

"You're right," he says immediately.

It drives the anger out of me, leaving me empty. His thumb rubs over the back of my hand, and I blink in surprise.

He's changing tactics.

"I thought I was doing the right thing," he says. I raise an eyebrow, and he huffs a laugh. "Yes, I know. But you haven't seen what Junior's capable of. If you leave my house, he's going to hunt you down."

He's just trying to scare me, I tell myself even as Junior's manic eyes flash in my mind.

"What if I can stand up for myself?"

"Do you own a gun?"

"No."

He smirks. Smug asshole. His thumb continues its repetitive, distracting motion over my skin. I want to yank my hand away, but I don't want to piss him off.

"Junior regularly takes down other capable men and women. He's a bastard, but a competent one. I wouldn't send any of my men out alone to deal with him."

"Will you give me a gun then?" My docile mask is slipping off, but he seems sincere, and I want answers. If this is another trick, I just hope I won't end up worse off than where I started.

"Can you use one?"

"Point and shoot, right?" I've handled lots of guns in Demon Blaster, how different could it be?

"Those are the essentials, yes. I can arrange for you to have one. Is there anything else you need?"

"Money. Just enough to get established." It's an absolute stretch to ask for this, but he *is* offering. I twitch my fingers under his wrist.

The corner of his mouth tilts up. "I'll make sure you have enough. Anything else?"

My brain works double-time to consider what else I'd need and the potential ramifications of asking for them.

I'll be in debt to a gangster. Probably not a great idea.

"I won't be able to pay you back right away. I'll need some time to get a job."

His expression softens. "You don't owe me anything. Consider them gifts."

Who is this Jekyll and Hyde man who throws me in a basement and makes me shit in a bucket for two days and then turns around and gives me everything I ask for?

"If you run into any trouble at all, promise me you'll call. My number will be in your phone."

"Why should I call?" I say with more than a little sarcasm. "You'll be watching me, won't you?"

"I will."

I blame the sudden flush of heat on the wine and finally slip my hand out from under his to place it onto my lap.

God, I need to get my taste in men re-evaluated.

"Cameras, right? That's how you've been keeping track of me?"

"Yes."

"How many do you have in my apartment?"

"Just the one. In your—"

"Actually, I'd like to find it myself, if you haven't taken it out yet."

"I haven't." Salvatore drinks deeply from his water. He adds offhandedly, "Would you like a prize if you find it?"

I frown even as my heart rate picks up. "What kind of prize?"

"How does a hundred thousand dollars sound?"

It sounds like more money than I've ever had in my entire life.

"Yeah, okay," I say, trying to play it cool even as my voice pitches up.

I consider him for a few long moments. He's trying to buy me back. As far as strategies go, I like this one considerably more.

I reach over to take a sweet-looking twisted bread off a tray while Salvatore watches me approvingly. I bite into it, and the sugar and butter coat my tongue. It's *so* delicious—but the rich flavor rings out like an alarm, and I drop the rest of the pastry onto my plate and wipe my hands delicately on a napkin.

A few pastries and a smile are all it takes to convince me to do anything, just like with Kristin. I have to be stronger than this.

"Why are you really doing all this? I mean, with me. And don't say it's to give me a job. Tell me the truth—" I almost add a *please* at the end, but cut it off at the last minute. I can be civil, but I won't be sweet. Not if I don't have to.

Salvatore gives a short, husky laugh, and it's so genuine and unexpected that I almost smile with him.

"I think you know, Marisol."

I frown. More hot and cold then. "Why don't you say it out loud anyway? Just to make sure we're all clear."

Salvatore glances toward Giordana. "Could you give us the room?"

He waits until she leaves, and when he turns back to me, I have a sudden sense of dread at what he's about to say.

He doesn't waste a second.

"I'm obsessed with you."

"What?" The words tumble over in my brain without meaning. "*What?*"

"I'm obsessed. With you." Salvatore rakes a hand through his hair and shakes his head, staring at a spot on the wall behind me. "I couldn't tell you when it happened, I just know it has. I've been watching you daily for months—"

"Whoa, *what?*"

"And I can't stop. I thought if I took you home, it wouldn't be as bad. I had an honest intention of hiring you to work for me. The team you'd be on—you'd *love* it."

"How do you know what I'd love?" I clench the armrests of my chair like I'm about to pitch forward from the sharp edge of a skyscraper. Why would anyone be obsessed with some ill-adapted geek? With a psycho?

Salvatore shifts in his chair, picks up a knife from the

table absentmindedly, sets it back down, and flicks his gaze back to me. "That's what I do. I watch people. I find out every single desire and fear in their little black hearts, and I use it. I know you want thrill and a challenge, and you can't see a rule without dreaming up a hundred different ways to break it. You're impulsive and vindictive and stubborn. You'd love working for me. For most people, it takes blackmail, money, or a promise of power to work on my cyber team, but I know you well enough to be damn certain that you'd do it for free, just for kicks."

Salvatore becomes more animated as he speaks—as if the entire time I've known him, he was sleepwalking and only now he's waking up. I want to shut him down. Stuff the words back into his mouth.

"After you finally came home, I thought the *need* in me would lessen and finally let me breathe, but it's *so much worse.*"

My heart slams against my chest, and my breathing narrows to thin sips of air. Salvatore erupts from his chair, circles behind it, and grips the headrest with fingers like talons. He leans over to stare at me. "Since you've been here, I can barely work. I can barely think. I just watch you all day and wonder what you're doing and what you're planning. I've seen you pick apart every piece of furniture you touch, and I know about your tally marks on the bedroom wall."

This is a thousand times bigger than I imagined. I thought he was ignoring me all that time, but he was watching me? Like he's apparently been doing for months?

The bath bubble solution in Salvatore's bathroom? It *absolutely* is the same kind I have at home—cherry blossom. Some unnamed emotion settles low in my belly.

"So you're..." I'm about to say *in love with me*, but that's not what he said. He said *obsessed*. I try again even though I have to swallow to get my voice to work. "You're still going to let me go?"

"My preference is to keep you." Salvatore pauses and levels a stare at me to emphasize his point. I shake my head imperceptibly. "I would *very much* like to keep you. And I do believe it's in your best interest to stay with me. But I won't stop you from leaving. I'm taking steps so if you choose to leave my house, I can protect you, but it won't be as effective. There's only so much I can do. If you stay, I want to change things between us. We can go at your speed. Dinner, movies, walks on the beach... whatever you'd like. Anything you'd want."

My stomach dips with a woozy *rush*, and I jump up from my chair, nearly knocking it over.

What. The. *Fuck*.

The emotion in my belly? I finally recognize it as a kind of twisted excitement at being the center of *anyone's* attention, but especially Salvatore's.

Some cosmic entity is laughing their ass off right now. I helped my mom stalk my dad for years until I started living with Kristin, and I swore I'd never get near that level of crazy again.

How did I escape the orbit of my mom's obsession only to fall into the center of Salvatore's? What is *wrong* with me?

Dinner, movies... I want to laugh. We are so far past the realm of normal dating that we might as well be on the moon. And the way he described me—*impulsive, vindictive, stubborn*—that's not how you describe someone you like.

Salvatore doesn't move, just watches, as I step back and then forward. Farther, closer. I can't decide if I want to run or stab him.

"You're crazy," I say finally.

Salvatore laughs without conviction. "Maybe. Probably."

"How many other women have you *obsessed* over? Did you throw them in the basement too?"

"No. There's only you. I haven't been with another woman since I started watching you."

I scoff, even as my face burns. "I didn't even realize you were interested in that sort of thing. You've completely ignored me since you brought me here."

Salvatore circles closer to me as he talks. "I'd cut those jeans off and suffocate between your thighs right now if you'd let me. We could see how many fingers I could fit in you before you came. That ex of yours wouldn't, but I'd *love* to spank and choke you. I'm *very* interested in that sort of thing."

Burning, crackling heat sears through me. I should throw something at him. Be reckless. Suffocate him just like he's proposing. He's close enough to touch now. Close enough to see the intense amber of his eyes, the hard muscles shifting under his sweater, the impressive outline of his cock through his jeans.

I clench my jaw. "What's holding you back? You've already kidnapped me. Imprisoned me. You could take me too, couldn't you?"

He smirks. Suffocation sounds very tempting right now.

"I could justify kidnapping you because I was trying to protect you. I'm not going to fuck you until you are certain you're ready. You've managed to fascinate me with only the back of your head for six months. If you spread your legs for me and have a change of heart, it's going to kill me. I won't touch you until you're dripping wet and begging for it."

"*Jesus*, Salvatore." My blush only deepens when I remember how often I've masturbated in my computer chair. "You've seen me masturbate, haven't you?"

He's silent for a moment. Then, "Yes."

"What do you do?"

"I turn off the monitor for about ten minutes and delete that segment of the recording so that no one else will see." He pauses. "And then I use the cherry blossom lotion I had stolen from your apartment to jerk myself off."

I place a palm on the wall next to me so I don't slide down on shaky legs. All of the tension in my body gathers into a single point between my legs, pulsing, needy, frustrated.

I close my eyes for a moment to find an emotion inside me that's not just wanton desire. I can't use that right now. I haven't forgiven him. I'm still furious.

I take that spark of anger and coax it into something more substantial.

How *dare* he tell me all this after he threw me into a *literal fucking dungeon*?

He kidnapped me.

He stood up to Grant for me. Tended to my wounds—*no*. I watched as Mom tracked Dad down and obsessed over him for years. He hated her for it. This is wrong and unhealthy. I'm—I'm not my parents.

"Marisol."

I startle, my eyes flying open. He's right in front of me, looking down with an unfamiliar softness in his normally sharp gaze.

"Stay," he murmurs, as if his admission of truth was a minor moral failing like jaywalking or cheating at cards and not a huge, arousing—no, *infuriating*—violation of privacy. "I was wrong to try to control you. Stay, and I'll give you whatever you want."

Whatever I want sounds so good right now.

I want to be special. To be loved.

But he didn't say love.

I take a deep breath.

"You kidnapped me. Took my phone, my computer, and my cat. You imprisoned me." My body is thrumming with the desire to touch him, to force him to make good on all his teasing. Salvatore watches me carefully, his gaze darting between my eyes and my wine-stained lips.

"Tonight..." I let the word linger, tipping up to bring my face closer to his, stopping just before our lips touch. He cups my face in his hand, and I smile invitingly. "I'm going to sleep in my own bed, and then tomorrow you're going to take me home. Alone."

He needs to experience the tiniest fraction of suffering that he put me through. Even if I'm dying to be touched, I'll survive without him. God made vibrators for a reason.

But the lazy smile that crosses his face isn't sarcastic or angry or mean.

He looks proud. He tucks a strand of hair behind my ear, and I drop back onto my heels, surprised. He's supposed to be frustrated, not pleased, but as he takes in my little scowl, his face brightens even more. He frames my face with his hands and watches me for a few moments like I'm the most precious creature in the world.

"You are perfect, Marisol."

My eyelashes flutter. Lips part.

And then his hands drop to his sides, and it's like someone's flicked off all the light in the room.

With a feather-light touch, Salvatore rests his hand along the small of my back. "Let's go. I'll walk you to your room."

When I'm still not asleep hours later, lying alone in the most luxurious bed of my life and squeezing my thighs together with nothing in between, I think, *I am a giant, fucking idiot.*

13

SALVATORE

THE NEXT MORNING, I'm up before most of the staff to drag myself to the kitchen for an espresso. I wave off Nola who's already awake to bake the day's bread. She's annoyingly cheery most mornings, but not today. Her face is gaunt with worry, and she doesn't meet my eye as she flits through the kitchen. I have to snuff out a flicker of guilt as I prepare the espresso machine. After that royal fuck up, Camillo's lucky to be alive. Nola will have to deal with it.

I've downed a few espressos by the time the rest of the staff trickles through the kitchen. I like to let myself be seen down here every once in a while to prove to my employees that I'm calm and approachable, but today, with Nola holding back tears, I give the opposite impression—*don't disappoint me.*

That's also acceptable.

Dom slips in through the back door and slumps over the kitchen bar in typical man-baby fashion until Nola brings him a cup of coffee, American-style. Giordana makes her cup of tea and then sits away from the rest of us, eyes closed and soaking in the morning sun like a cat.

Hefting a box of shallots that has to weigh as much as her, Conchetta slams it down on the counter next to Nola who jumps with a shriek. Conchetta pats the back of her hand.

"Pull it together, cara mia. He's a strong man. He's doing just fine," Conchetta says in Italian, managing to make it sound more supportive than condescending. "I need twelve pounds of shallots for dinner. Cut thin."

When Marisol steps into the kitchen, everyone except Dom turns to look at her. She meets my gaze first, capturing it for a heartbeat, before turning away to ask Nola for coffee.

The red scratches and bandaids covering her arms and neck make my stomach churn with something like panic. I can't let her leave like this. She's even worse off than when I first found her. I have to keep her. Convince her to stay. I squeeze my fingers around my delicate espresso cup.

Nola helps Marisol find what she needs for her breakfast and retreats to a corner of the kitchen to cut her shallots. For a few moments, I'm able to observe Marisol without restraint.

Sunlight burnishes her hair to a rich sable and accents the stretch and drape of her t-shirt across her curves as she gently stirs eggs in a pan. Every part of her is meant to be devoured. How would it feel to dip my fingertips into her full thighs and crush her heavy breasts against my chest? To pull that ponytail of long, dark hair? To hear her moan my name?

Call this off. Make her stay.

Before I can follow that ruinous train of thought, Marisol brings her plate and coffee to the stool next to me. I'm already sporting a minor erection at watching her cook eggs. When her thigh brushes against mine, I'm wildly grateful that my lap's protected by the kitchen bar.

You are perfect, Marisol.

What I would give to read her mind right now. Or better yet, last night, when she looked very much like a woman who might be willing to drown me in her cunt for pleasure and spite.

Marisol scans the kitchen and meets my eye without a shred of timidity or fear. "Where's Camillo?"

From the corner, Nola chokes out a sob. I have to clench my teeth so that a wave of jealousy can pass through me like a storm passing over a wooden shack.

What a fucking mistake it was to give her a single guard. I thought Camillo would be too off-putting with all his scars, but I knew better, didn't I? Marisol's codependent, and in the absence of love, she's going to attach herself to the first person who shows her kindness.

That should've been you. You should've been nicer like Camillo was, you fucking asshole. You deserve this.

"He's in the woods," Dom answers from my other side while I seethe. His coffee finished, he goes to rummage through the refrigerator for leftovers like he didn't just drop a riddle into Marisol's lap.

"Why is he in the woods?" Marisol asks me with the barest hint of threat, and it'd be sexy if it wasn't because she was defending her crush. My wife shouldn't have crushes on other men. Camillo's about to find himself doing a lot of out-of-state assignments.

"He was supposed to protect you, but he let you get all the way into the woods by yourself."

"That's not his fault. He was watching Junior's men. He came after me and tackled the other guy who came after me. If it wasn't for Camillo, I'd probably be kidnapped. Again."

What is it she sees in Camillo? He's in love with Nola.

There's no way he'd flirted enough with Marisol enough to win her over. Is it because he saved her?

I saved her.

"He failed you," I say steadily, so she knows what I think of him. "Dom drove him a few hours north past Milwaukee. His punishment is to walk back. No phone. No supplies."

She glares at me. "That's not fair."

"Actions have consequences." And because I want to give her another chance even if it is just to work with me, I add in a low voice, "Will you stay here if I bring him back? Dom will go pick him up right now."

Marisol's eyes widen, and in my periphery, I note everyone else's reactions. Dom groans, Nola looks hopeful, and Giordana's posture goes rigid. Only Conchetta continues puttering about, mixing a huge bowl of dough.

Marisol has to notice too, but she holds my gaze. "You said it's just until tomorrow?" she ventures.

"Yes, but he's likely very thirsty. And there are coyotes in the woods." I don't mention the fact that I *know* Nola slipped him a bottle of water before he was exiled, and I have a tracker in his shoe. Dom suggested chopping off a finger, but I don't see the point in mutilating my own men if I can teach them a lesson instead. He should have been more vigilant. He'll learn that in the woods.

Marisol chews her plump lower lip for several long seconds. "No. I'm leaving."

That's my girl. Relief rushes over me. She doesn't love Camillo. Of course not.

Nola breaks into tears, and Conchetta waves her into the pantry, shouting, "Stop crying, silly girl! He'll be back soon."

. . .

MARISOL GRIPS her seatbelt with two fists when I open the SUV door and slide in, but instead of ripping her out of the car and laughing maniacally like I'm sure she's expecting, I sit next to her without a word. Davide pulls the car down the driveway.

Marisol looks between the two of us. "No blindfold this time?" she asks me in a poisonous voice.

"Would you prefer one?"

She pouts. Fuck me, she's so adorable.

"Why do you want me to see this time?"

"I want you to know how to get back."

Her eyes narrow. "I'm not coming back."

I knew she'd say that, but it still stirs displeasure in my gut. "Have you decided where you'll go instead?"

"Somewhere you won't find me." She crosses her arms and looks out the window, but the way her head drops against the headrest is loaded with exhaustion.

I've done this. Taken her from her home and pushed her into a state of fatigue. I know Junior would have done worse, but that was my fault too. I allowed him to learn about her because I wasn't honest with myself and hid my interest in her like I needed to. My dad had work, my mom had wine, and my brother wouldn't accept a job that wasn't laced with risk, and I still didn't recognize the claws of addiction until everyone else pointed it out to me first.

Marisol and I are trapped now. If I let go of her, Junior will go after her, and I can't go after Junior without Aldo—and likely the entire Commission—coming down on my neck.

And because I couldn't convince her of all this properly, now I have to throw this newborn foal into a den of wolves.

No, that's not right. She's not a foal. She's a fox. Cunning, but still weak. Her best bet is to escape without the notice of other predators.

Despite what she said about not coming back, she watches out the window a little too closely, and I pray it's to memorize the way back to my house. Her lips move subtly, as if she's reciting the Rosary under her breath.

I clench my hands over my knees so I don't reach out to drag her onto my lap.

Our time together ends too quickly when Davide rolls to a stop in front of her apartment complex.

She and I step out of the car in silence. I lift out her suitcases while she holds Buck's carrier.

In her apartment, I'm itching to do a sweep, but I resist. I've already seen Grant pick up his things through the camera, so she shouldn't be getting any visitors.

I set her suitcases down, nudging her front door shut behind me. Before she can object, I flick on my jammer and set it next to us on the kitchen counter. The sound of people talking fills the space.

"I would suggest leaving today," I say, and I can almost pretend I'm speaking to an associate and not this woman who I'd willingly swear myself to. "Junior will know you've left my house. Your apartment will be the first place he checks. I'd estimate you have a headstart of a few hours."

"How would he know?"

Good, she's already asking the right questions. "Because Junior thinks Dom is loyal to Aldo and Barbara. So in a few hours, Dom will tell him you've left. He'll throw Junior off the trail, but it won't take long for him to figure it out. That's if he doesn't already have cameras or one of his men watching the apartment. I have several trackers on him, but he's slippery. Trust me when I say I've been *very* invested in a reliable source of information on him."

"You seem really beat up by it."

Marisol, whose expression has been one of mild horror the entire time, gives me a crooked smile, and seeing *that* look on her face sets off fireworks of satisfaction in my brain. I want to make that happen often.

"I'm being calm so that you don't panic. I want you to succeed." And that... is true. I want a lot of things from her, but I also want her to succeed.

When her eyes flare with curiosity at that statement, I decide, no, *that's* what I want to see more of.

"What would you do if you were me? Hypothetically speaking, of course," she asks.

"Hypothetically, I'd leave within the hour and drive west away from all the major hubs of criminal activity. And then north. I'd take a train as far as I can, then a taxi, and then rent a car, returning it as far as I can from my final destination. Then I would start a new life in a small town I'd never heard of before. I'd use my computer skills to make money and figure out how to create a new identity. And I wouldn't talk to anyone from my old life ever again."

She blinks a few times. Maybe she didn't expect me to give her sound advice. Then she narrows her eyes at me.

"And you'd stop watching me after I did all that?"

She peers into my face like she can guess before I answer.

I almost want to laugh.

"No. I'll search for you. But this time, I'll keep you to myself. No one will know I've found you."

"That's *if* you find me."

I step toward her so that she has to look up into my face. "I'll find you." She swallows. I jerk my chin toward the couch. "Sit."

Without a word, she turns and sits on the edge of the

couch cushion, thighs pressing together, and watches me expectantly. As I approach her, she stiffens and her eyes darken. Her ponytail trails down one shoulder, thick as a rope.

I'd rather not ruin this, but she shouldn't go in blind. I sit next to her on the couch and pull out my phone.

14

SALVATORE

SHE'S HOOKED by the first four seconds of footage, completely pressed up against me as we watch Junior saw into the leg of a sobbing man in a cage. We also see several clips of him scooping out a person's eye while they scream. By the twelfth clip, I figure she's had enough. She'll understand now.

"You're not going to let him catch you, are you?" I ask carefully.

Marisol clutches my forearm while she stares straight ahead at the reflection of us on the dead TV. I have to resist the teenage urge to flex into her hands.

"Why haven't you shown this to the police?" she asks.

"There are hundreds of years of history to explain why the Family doesn't trust the police. And there's also the risk that if Junior were caught—by one of the very few officers that aren't in our pocket—he might rat us out. Some of our own men ordered him to do the things you saw. Others he did just because he wanted to. If there's a problem, we handle it internally. But seeing how Junior's the underboss *and* the only son of the don... no one's stuck their neck out yet." At the way she worries her bottom lip, I desperately want to tuck her into me and fill her ear with all the promises I could offer. I settle with taking her hand in mine. "There's one other thing I need to tell you."

"I'm not sure my heart can take any more of your show and tells," she says with a forced laugh that teases at the corners of my own mouth.

I wish there was a better time for this. A beach somewhere with a sunset and her warm, tanned legs stretched over mine. "The night you ran away, I told Junior I was going to marry you."

Marisol rips her hand out of mine and shoves me away from her as she throws herself off the couch. "*What* did you just say to me?"

"We're engaged."

"*No.*" Her ponytail whips across her back with the force of her negation. "We can't be engaged, because I *never* agreed to that. You can't just spring that on someone. What the *fuck,* Salvatore? Who says I even want to be married?"

"You were willing to marry that ex of yours. You want to be a wife. I want to be your husband. We would be good together—"

I move to stand, but she pushes me back into the couch. Or, tries to, and I let her manhandle me, because I'm so far gone for this woman that even her fury is a harsh light I could bask under.

She glares daggers at me and speaks in a low voice that pumps all the blood straight to my dick. "We are not going down that alley again. This is what's going to happen. You are going to figure out where Junior is, and you are going to tell him I'm *nothing* to you because if you don't, you've painted a giant red bullseye on my back."

"I'm not going to tell Junior that. If he touches you, then by code, I'll have the right to do the same to him."

Her jaw drops, and for a few moments, I can see the gears turning in her head. I brace myself for violence.

"You complete and utter *dickhead*." She pronounces each word with a lethal measure of venom. "Not only did you make me your *property* in this ass-backward world of yours, but your consolation prize for me is that you'll get to shoot Junior after he saws off my legs and gouges out my eyes. You..."—Marisol rubs her temples in quick, jerky movements—"*vile, pathetic* piece of shit. You did this so I couldn't leave. So I'd be forced to stay here and be your... shitty little way of getting under Junior's skin. Fuck and *I*... god, I'm such a fucking idiot."

She stomps to her front door and swings it wide open. "It's time you got the fuck out."

I stalk toward her, using the same cold expression that's made weaker men piss their pants and rat out their own mothers, but my Marisol hardly blinks. I remove her hand, which balls into a fist, and then gently close and lock the door. I keep hold of her wrist.

"I thought this would be the best way to protect you." My heart's pounding, but my voice is composed. At least I can control my body like this—a steady, calm tone while staring down the barrel of a gun—even as I'm starting to realize I can't control the majority of my reactions to her.

"*You*—" she starts, and her hand flexes while she takes a deep breath before continuing in an icy tone. "You found a solution that would benefit *you*. You'd get me—because of your 'obsession' for me, or whatever—or you'd get the chance to take down Junior, someone who you clearly have problems with."

"By code, I'm also not supposed to attack a higher-up, so

Junior hurting you doesn't give me a clear-cut path to killing him. It's just insurance."

"Insurance for your property."

"You are not property. I don't think anyone could hope to own you."

At that, her fist releases into a limp arrangement of fingers. Exhaustion shadows her face, and guilt stabs at my chest with a dull blade. I bring her hand up to my mouth to kiss the base of her wrist before releasing her. "Tell me how I can fix this for you."

Her sharp inhale tugs at my dick.

"How you can fix the mess you—and only you—made?"

She discovered Beta's identity in the first place, but I'm not about to mention that right now.

"Yes."

"I want a car. A clean, nondescript car that I can use. And cash. And I want you to find Junior and figure out some loophole in your stupid little code that lets you confine him for as long as you can so that I have the barest chance of escaping."

"Done." I take out my phone and send a text to Dom telling him everything Marisol's asked for while she reads over my shoulder. He responds immediately that he'll have the car and cash delivered to her apartment within the hour and that he's sending men out to search for Junior.

"And tell him to end Camillo's punishment and bring him back."

"That's not—"

"Salvatore."

I consider her for a long moment. There's no compromise in her sweet face. Fine. I could use the extra manpower anyway.

I type out another text. Dom responds immediately.

DOM

Someone's whipped. He'll be home asap.

Marisol hides a smirk.

"You're not going to argue about that?" she says, gesturing at my pocket.

"About what?" I circle her in one step.

"That you're *whipped*."

"What's there to argue?"

Marisol bumps her back against the door. We're close. I can smell *my* shampoo in her hair and *fuck*, if that doesn't make me feral. My cock's uncomfortably hard and straining in my jeans, but I don't want to adjust myself when she's *right there,* and all I can think about is touching her thick hair or her soft tits or her lovely face.

"If you're so whipped, why don't you do what I say?"

My chest brushes against hers. "What else do you want me to do?"

Her eyes flicker between mine. She could ask for anything at all right now, and I'd do it without question, without care to the consequences. Her mouth firms, and my gut sinks.

"Suffocate."

I freeze. Suffocate? What is she...

I'd cut those jeans off and suffocate between your thighs right now if you'd let me.

One of her eyebrows ticks up as if to say, *I knew you wouldn't. Coward.* "Don't turn saint on me now, Salvatore. It's been a long, long time since I've had someone's mouth on me—but you probably already knew that. I should go into this with a clear head, don't you think?"

Of course I agree with her. She shouldn't have any distractions whatsoever while she's on the road.

I drop to my knees with a heavy thud.

"Just say stop, and I will."

I scan her face for regret, but her eyes are bright and alive, and her rosy lips part on an exhale. One edge of her mouth tilts up, transforming her face from innocent to impish. My little succubus.

I hook two fingers into her waistband, dragging her leggings and panties down her rich curves. Her chest rises and falls in quick succession, and her eyelashes flutter like she's warring between keeping them open or squeezing them closed. I slip her shoes off, and it's a shock to be able to leave them on the floor like the castings they are because now I have Marisol, the *real* Marisol in between my fingers, and I can shuck her panties and leggings off as well, and there's no overwhelming, burning need to hoard them. Her shirt skims the top of her thighs, just barely covering her pussy and making it all the more tempting by suggesting sex, but not baring it.

I slip her shirt up to bare her to me anyway. My cock presses painfully into my jeans, but I don't dare stop touching her even for a second. I'm going to make this so good for her that she won't think twice about staying here with me.

"Take the rest off," I say in a husky voice before I crush my lips to her inner thigh and suck hard.

Marisol cries out and jerks in my arms, but I've got her. She won't fall. She works to get her shirt and bra off while I coat her inner thighs with kisses and nips and lovebites.

Distantly, I'm aware of her clothes falling to the floor with a rustle. I drag one fingertip along her seam to guide the collected nectar into my mouth. Her flavor explodes on my tongue, sharp and carnal, and I lick along her thigh to seek access against the dark curls there, groaning into her entrance while she writhes above me. She fists one hand into my hair, better than any dream or fantasy.

I cast my gaze over her heavy breasts and her supple belly, and then I'm snagged in her sharp-eyed look. She might be naked, trembling in my arms, but she's the one dissecting me, like a scientist about to cut into an amoeba.

"Is this what you wanted?" she asks. She manages to sound breathless and teasing at the same time.

"No," I groan. I rub my face into her thatch of curls and inhale shamelessly. "But it's a start."

Her playful laugh turns into a moan as I dig into her slit with my tongue. I turn her thighs out so that I can drive my face deeper, but it's not enough. I want more of her taste.

She squeals and balances on the balls of her feet, tugging my hair to a painful degree, and that's good too, because it's part of her punishment for me. She can do anything she wants to me as long as it's *her* doing it to *me*. I throw one of her thighs over my shoulder.

"Need more," I gasp out and throw her other leg around my shoulder and *there*. Her back strikes against the door with an obscene thud, and while I hope all her neighbors hear, she's past caring. Her heels dig into my back and her nails drive into my scalp and I have Marisol Vasquez balanced on my tongue.

Her sexy little moans and breathless *Salvatore, right there, yes, yes* drive me into a frenzy. There's nothing else in this moment—no jobs, no assignments, no rats, no schemes, no cameras, no leaving, just a woman and a man blending into the sublime.

I crawl a hand up her torso to squeeze one of her perfect tits. It's a greedy, selfish touch, but all the same, she rewards me with a gush of wetness that I lap up.

"Sal..." she chokes out, her thighs clenching around me.

My free hand snakes to her entrance and just manages to squeeze in two fingers. Fuck, she's tight. *How is she going to fit*—I can't worry about that now. I jerk my mouth away just as she begins to flutter around my fingers, and she cries out in frustration.

"Tell me," I start.

She bursts out with, "Yes, yes! Anything! I'm so *close*. P-please."

"Say you're mine." I pinch her nipple hard enough to make her gasp.

Her eyelids fly open, but her gaze is hazy and unfocused. "What? Sal—"

I force another finger into her and piston my arm underneath her. My biceps are burning, but I grit my teeth and don't stop. I need her to say it. She can't leave. She bounces up with each thrust, and her hips chase my mouth, but still, I deny her, and I hope it hurts as badly as the ache in my cock.

"*Say it.*"

"I'm *yours*, Sal."

I suck her clit into my mouth and pull hard and in seconds, she's chanting *I'm yours I'm yours I'm yours,* and I pray it sticks into her brain because it's searing into mine.

As she sags down the door, I ease her onto the ground and stand over her body.

It feels like the first time I killed a man. There was the weight of the knowledge that my old life was behind me, and I would never be able to return—except this time, I don't ever want to go back. My new life starts now.

As the seconds pass, Marisol seems to become conscious of her nakedness because she covers one breast and twists toward her t-shirt. Before she can reach it, I lift her back up in my arms.

"Sal," she starts warningly.

"It's okay."

She studies me as I walk the short distance down the hallway to ease her on her bed. In her bathroom, I find a rag to soak in warm water, wipe my face, and then return to Marisol so I can clean her.

Her gaze is cautious. "Sal."

"Let me take care of you," I say gently.

Despite her reluctance, she melts into my hand as I cup her through the rag. Once I'm finished, I toss it onto her dresser and sit with her on the bed, pulling her onto my lap. She's taken down her ponytail, letting her long hair spill over her shoulders, and with her post-sex glow, she looks like a goddess.

"Don't leave," I say, after a long pause. "Come back home with me. You can set the terms."

Marisol strokes my jaw with her hand and stretches up to kiss me, long and deep. When she pulls away—too quickly—she steps off of me in one fluid motion.

She walks out of the room.

I wait.

She doesn't come back.

A minute later, I find her in the living room, dressed, and considering the bookcase. She's searching for my camera.

Looking at her makes my chest hurt.

"If you can find it in ten minutes," I say, instead of a hundred other things. "I'll double your reward."

Her gaze flicks to me, dark eyes bright and delighted. "Start the timer."

15

MARISOL

THE CASSETELLES ARE GONE.

For the past nine hundred miles, I've been trying to resist Conchetta's cassetelles in an almost superhuman exertion of willpower. The lunch and dinner Salvatore had prepared for me are long gone.

And now everything's gone.

I should be angrier about the food. I held the styrofoam ice box of meals over a gas station trash can for several seconds until cursing and tossing it back inside the car. *Someone* picked out all my absolute favorites of Conchetta's dishes, everything unnameable to me except for the desserts Conchetta would bring me in the kitchen.

It would've been a sweet gesture if I didn't think Salvatore was trying to change my mind. He wanted to give me one last reminder of what I'm leaving behind.

I suck the powdered sugar off my fingertips. I've been surviving off of ramen and old deli ham for my entire life. A little home cooking isn't going to drag me back.

And neither is sex. He almost got me there at the end—I

nearly asked if I could stay after what I did. After what we did.

I probably shouldn't have told him to eat me out, but in my defense, I completely assumed his "obsession" with me had been an act, and that he'd try to drop some macho shit like, *I don't eat out women, but you can suck my cock*, and I was —still am—so sex-starved that there was a nonzero chance I would've done it just to feel a hard cock for the first time in months. Instead, I got the most hot, animalistic oral sex of my life. He ate me like a man starved, and for the rest of my life, the upper half of his face is going to be the star of all of my masturbation fantasies.

Bumpbumpbump.

I serve off the rumble strips and back onto the road. I've pulled over twice already to furiously rub one out, studying my rearview mirror for other cars on the highway. As soon as I find a hotel, I'm going to need to change my uncomfortably damp underwear.

The fact that he *made* me tell him I was *his*? Denying me an orgasm until I did it? That was some caveman behavior —I'm not some pet that he gets to label as his and then give orders to—

Bumpbumpbump.

I swerve back onto the road and ignore the throbbing between my legs to rub at my eyes.

In the privacy of my own thoughts? Okay, it was hot. Super fucking hot. And the whole thing gave me the strongest orgasm I've had in a long time.

Probably the last one you'll have for a while.

I thought when I finally got away from Salvatore, I would feel relief or maybe satisfaction at winning our little game, but mostly I feel frustrated and alone, and I'm doing my best not to analyze that too closely.

I peer through the windshield at a giant green sign that flashes SEDGWICK in my headlights.

I need to find somewhere to pull over, but every time I consider it, I imagine Junior standing at the edge of one of the pitch-black cornfields holding a rusty saw. A boning knife. Pliers.

And each time, a sudden burst of energy jolts me awake, I cram a handful of sour gummy worms in my mouth, and I white-knuckle another fifty miles.

But now I'm out of gummy worms and my ass hurts and I have a cramp in my foot from pressing down the pedal for so long because the cruise control in this junker doesn't work. Sedgwick it is. If Junior manages to hunt me down nine hundred miles away, at least I didn't make it easy on him.

I haven't used GPS for this entire trip, so I'm at the mercy of the street signs to get to a hotel. When I roll to a stop and peer up into a wooden sign that says *Budget Inn*, I've made it.

Some fucking luck to finally get my phone back and then have to leave it with Salvatore again. When he returned it to me, I stared at it for all of three seconds before handing it back to him. I don't need any reminders about my loser contacts list, and it would've been too easy to use to track me. The ancient, battered flip phone he gifted me as a "clean" replacement made me half-consider just turning myself into Junior then and there.

"Don't use it unless there's an emergency," Salvatore told me from outside the car. Then he'd stretched through the window to tug the seatbelt across me and click it into place. I could still smell my arousal on his face when he gave me a chaste kiss on the cheek and dropped his onyx ring into my lap. "Stay safe, passerotta. I'll see you soon."

I chucked the phone in a gas station bathroom somewhere in Iowa. But not before memorizing the single phone number in the contact list written as *Husband*.

And *whoo, boy,* does that do something dangerous to me.

"I'll be right back," I tell Buck in the passenger seat. I peek into the cat carrier to make sure he's still breathing, and yeah, he's good. He's been pouting the entire trip. It's another thing I'm trying not to think too hard about. My elderly cat was depressed and heartbroken after losing Kristin and only came out of his shell for stupid Salvatore and now he's being ripped away again and he doesn't understand why.

I reach under my seat for the duffel bag of cash to pull out a handful of twenties. Salvatore gave me all the money he promised and the extra reward for finding his hidden camera. There's enough with me to buy a small house in cash.

The camera was behind the bookcase, pointing straight toward my desk. Salvatore had hinted enough about its location that the bookcase was my first guest. I'd pulled all the books and trinkets off, checking them methodically and spotting a broken-off wooden B-17 airplane wing where Grant used to keep his planes. Salvatore said nothing when I glanced at him, but Grant treats his airplane models like babies, so I have my thoughts on the real culprit of that "accident". With all the decor gone, I'd run my hands down the wooden bookcase, nearly running out of time until I noticed the outlet on the wall. An undetectable camera would need a power source and with how much time Salvatore said he watched me, it couldn't run off of batteries alone. I stared at the outlet for a full minute until it struck me.

I told Salvatore the camera was inside the outlet, and

now I'm a hundred thousand dollars richer. I can buy a small house *and* groceries from the fancy grocery stores.

But first, that camera discovery taught me a lesson. If Salvatore can hide a tiny, nearly invisible camera inside an electrical outlet, he can hide one anywhere. After tonight, I need to work on getting rid of everything he's... *gifted* me. Getting rid of the cell phone was a good first step, but who knows what else he's slapped a tracker onto.

Budget Inn's just a single strip of doors and a front office in a parking lot. Two of the four street lamps in the area are broken, throwing the streets and fields beyond into inky darkness. I scurry across the sidewalk to the front doors, goosebumps rising on my arms.

When I burst in through the front doors, a man with neatly trimmed blond hair, a short beard, and a camo hoodie startles and nearly drops his book. We stare at each other.

"Do... you need a room?" he asks.

Right. Normal. "Yes, please," I say, laughing nervously and approaching as my heart rate returns to normal.

His gaze travels down me, touching inappropriate places, before he glances back to his monitor and says in a low rumble, "Let me take care of that for you."

I glance at his book. *Crime and Punishment.* Of fucking course it is.

"Do you have any pets?" he asks, giving me an easy, confident smile.

I cast about for a "no pets" sign and blurt out, "Uh—yes. A cat."

The man—name tag says Brandon—shakes his head and then leans forward like he's going to tell me a secret. "Let's just keep that between us then."

"Great. Thanks."

Brandon frowns a little before turning to the monitor, all business now. Normally, the manly, confident, intellectual thing would be working wonders, but I can't help but think he looks *off*. Hair too blond, eyes too blue, nose too precise. No smoke to the edge of his voice that makes me want to sink to my knees.

Brandon gives up on flirting after another impassive response which suits us both just fine.

Not long after, I have Buck locked into the bathroom with a litter box and water, and I'm lying on top of a thin mattress that smells of mildew. The overhead fan kicked off a snowstorm of dust when I turned it on, and I brushed off as much as I could from the sheets before lying down in full clothes. I miss the Coquatrix.

If I listen very closely, I can hear a woman crying a few doors down. Hopefully, someone just left their TV on too loud.

My whole body is exhausted, crushed under the weight of the stale hotel air. Even my eyelids are heavy and sticky. I want to sleep, but I need to make a plan for tomorrow. I should probably trade the car in for someone else's as soon as possible because Salvatore's definitely tracking that too.

And then I get to pick the place where I'm going to live in secrecy for the rest of my life.

Instead, my thoughts wonder to what Salvatore's doing. Has he caught Junior yet? Is he watching me right now?

I clutch his onyx ring where it rests on a gas station necklace chain between my breasts.

He made me say I was *his*. He said he wanted to marry me and that he was going to find me. He fucked up, but he's going to fix things.

I must be really love-starved because thinking about all

of those things fills me with a sense of warmth. Of belonging.

When I pick a place to settle down, I'm going to buy a computer with all that money Salvatore gave me. And then I'm going to figure out how to watch *him* through all *his* cameras.

Something tells me he wouldn't hate the idea.

16

MARISOL

My hands hurt.

No, it's my wrists. They're screaming out in white-hot pain. And my shoulders too.

Did I get drunk last night? I feel awful.

I need to find a toilet so I can throw up, but I can't move my arms.

"Someone's finally up."

I jolt, chains rattling as I look around, bleary-eyed. I'm in a garage. Two rusty, discolored cars with parts stripped off hunker down on either side of me. The air is warm and stagnant. Junior looms in front of me.

He snatches the front of my shirt, swinging me toward him.

"It's good you're awake. I was starting to get bored."

I glance up—*ow,* even my eyes hurt—and icy horror drips down my spine. He's tied my hands together with a rope and thrown me onto a giant grey hook that dangles from the ceiling by a thick chain. My bare toes skim along the dusty concrete, and even when I stretch, I can't get any purchase beneath me.

Junior's wearing dress shoes, grey trousers, and a crisp white button-up. It all looks so out of place in this grimy garage that for a split second, I wonder if this is a dream, but no, the pain is all too real. I look down, relieved to see I'm wearing my t-shirt and leggings, even if my shoes are missing. Did he drug me?

"How..." My throat is so dry that my voice comes out as a croak. I swallow and try again. "How did you find me?"

"It wasn't that hard. Turi's not nearly as clever as he thinks. I had a guy trail you, with a little heads-up from someone on the inside—and I don't mean Dom the Butcher. That oaf's too busy eating Turi's ass to actually be useful."

"Who?" I groan.

Junior leans in with a finger to his lips. "*Shh*, that one's a secret. Thirsty?"

Fuck, fuck, *fuck*. This is not good. I wriggle my hands as much as I can, but the rope binding my wrists is so tight that there's no space for movement, and my skin's already tender under the abrasive fibers. Pain pricks up and down my arms with every twitch. How long have I been up here?

"I wouldn't do that if I were you," Junior says, glancing up at my hands. "You're gonna rub your wrists raw, and it'll hurt worse."

He hauls me close and shoves a bottle of water into my mouth. I choke and sputter as he empties the entire water bottle over my face and then tosses the empty container onto the ground.

"What I want are simple answers to simple questions." He presses down on my neck so that even more weight is applied to my already strained shoulders and wrists, and I scream from the pain.

"Please! I'll tell you what you want to know!"

I have to get out of here, right now. My eyes dart around

the room, looking for anything I could possibly use. He has me facing away from the door, so all I can see are the cars next to me and the dusty brick wall. Everything smells like gasoline, and I can't hear any noise outside the shop, although the bright patches of sunlight leaking in from the ceiling tell me it's daytime.

Junior grabs my jaw and wrenches my face to his. His mouth reeks of meat, and he's got gasoline on his fingers. I gag.

"That's not very polite," he says with a frown, and his grip on my jaw tightens so much that I start to whimper.

"Wha—" I try to say with my jaw forced open.

Junior releases me, and I quickly spit out, "I'm sorry. I'm sorry. What do you want to know?"

I shouldn't be apologizing to this monster, but I'm not ready to die over my pride.

"That's better," he says and scratches at his chin absent-mindedly. There's puckering along the back of his hand that looks like an old burn. "Where was I? Oh yeah, why don't you tell me about your relationship with Salvatore Luporini?"

What?

That's what this is about? I wrack my muddled brain, looking for any insight into what Junior wants.

CRACK!

Pain explodes in my face as Junior backhands me.

"I told you I was getting bored. Start talking."

I speak before I even know what I'm saying. The pain is blinding. "He watched over me at his house. He took care of me. And then he let me go, and I ran. That's all."

Junior considers this. "When was the first time you met him?"

"On the train, same time I saw you." What is he getting

at? What is he looking for? I can barely think through the raw pain in my face and the rest of my body. Every cell in my body is suffering.

"And you fell in love with him, eh? In a week, you wanted to marry him?" His voice drips with sarcasm.

The bullseye on my back. I *told* Salvatore marrying me was only going to whet Junior's interest. Junior watches with a growing frown. His hand twitches. I have to tell him something, and I have no *fucking* idea what he's looking for here. I'm certain if I tell him *yes,* he's going to torture me to get at Salvatore. But if I tell him *no*, he's going to torture me and *then* kill me.

Junior jerks like he's about to hit me again, and I scream out an answer, "Yes! We're in love!"

"Oh, really?"

My heart sinks. I'm praying I can play the part of ditzy lover and make him think I'm not a threat. Maybe he'll underestimate me enough to give me an opportunity to escape.

"And then he just let you go scot-free? With a car and a fuckton of cash and Daddy Matassa's ring?" Junior fingers the necklace around my neck and draws it up out of my shirt. "His special little ring, you can just *have*?"

It's my *ring*, I think with a jealous flare. "I didn't know whose it was. He just gave it to me."

Junior barks out a laugh and jerks the ring so that the chain cuts into my neck. My whole body sways on the hook. "Has he told you what they call him?"

I say nothing.

"They call him *il Diavolo*," Junior says. "They say *I'm* fucking crazy, but the shit he's done out there is so fucking evil that he's got all the other families whispering about *il*

Diavolo when he comes around. You knew that? That you're in love with the fucking Devil?"

I don't have to pretend for a shiver to pass through my body.

"I didn't know," I whisper. "Please let me go."

Junior sucks in air through his teeth. "Nope, I don't think so. How about we show Turi I can be a scary guy too and send his ring back? Maybe with a little souvenir? He already has so much, so we'll have to be a little creative about what to give him. How about a finger? Or an eye?"

"Please," I beg as I hold back tears. I *know* Junior won't like me being pathetic—I have to keep it together—but I'm out of ideas. "I'll do whatever you want. Just let me go."

He cocks a smile at that. "Whatever I want, eh? I think I'd like that."

There's a banging sound outside, and I snap my head toward it eagerly, but Junior doesn't even look up. The way his gaze travels over my body makes me shiver, but I grit my teeth in determination. If he gives me an opening, I'll do whatever it takes to lower his guard. There's no shame in doing what I have to do to survive. I just need to get outside of this building and pray we're not in the center of some middle-of-fucking-nowhere cornfield.

I stick out my chest as much as I can, even as nausea roils through my stomach. "Anything."

Behind me, something metallic bangs again. My back tingles. Whoever it is, I hope they don't shoot. Junior looks up past me with a wary expression. I'm too scared to hope. I choke back a sob.

A huge swath of bright sunlight cuts across Junior's face as the sound of metal against metal rumbles behind me.

"*NO!*" Junior screams out against our intruders.

A deep voice calls behind me and—oh thank *god*—relief threatens to drown me. "Don't fucking touch her."

17

SALVATORE

Rage storms through me, splintering skin and bones until it feels like my fucking soul is going to shatter under the pressure.

He has her strung up on an engine hoist like a pig carcass.

You never should have let her go. Weak, pathetic, worthless.

Junior's miserable, sallow face twists in indignation, but he says nothing. He hunches over and watches me with a dead-eyed look.

I'm going to skin him alive, flay him piece by piece, and then stitch it back on. I'll bring rats and let them eat the raw flesh. I'll roast him alive in a Brazen Bull.

I can feel Dad's belt biting into my back.

Conquer or kill.

Kill or be conquered.

A heavy weight falls on my shoulder.

"Let me cut him up, boss," Dom hisses in my ear, loud enough for the others to hear.

He's buying me an out. Dom's the only one here who's

seen me lose myself to my true, sadistic nature. He's the only one who knows exactly what I'll do to Junior.

I take a step through the two cars as my men follow. Every footstep thunders like the beat of war drums.

No one's pulled out a gun yet. Good. I want Junior alive.

His gaze darts between all of us and the exit.

My skin is hot and feverish as I stop. Anger, turmoil, and grief swarm inside me, crushing my organs, swelling against my skin.

I'm not a man anymore. I am a tool, designed for suffering and pain.

"Sal."

I glance at Marisol. Her eyes are wide, and she mouths the word *please*.

Her t-shirt's soaked and plastered to her skin. *Blood?* Her wrists are raw. Her cheek is red, and her lip is cut.

Junior steps back from Marisol with jerky, tense movements. He's seething.

My hands clench. He'll be screaming soon.

But first, Marisol.

I lift her carefully from the hook, and her whimper needles into my chest as I ease her arms down. She needs a doctor. I didn't think to bring her a doctor.

Distantly, I'm aware of Junior breaking into a dash behind me and then wheezing as someone punches him.

My men will handle him. I have a different task. I pull my knife out to saw at the ropes binding my wife. Once she's free, she throws her arms clumsily around my waist. I touch the liquid on her shirt. Not blood. Water.

"Thank you, thank you," she murmurs against me, and the desperation in her voice squeezes my heart so hard it feels like it'll burst. I splay my hand over her back. I failed her.

"Marisol, go with Davide. You'll be safe with him."

She can rest while I begin Junior's punishment.

"Let me stay, *please*," she whispers against my neck.

No fucking way.

Then she rubs her cheek against my chest like a stray cat, and I remember myself. I can't lose it here. She's alive. She needs a doctor, and I have to take her to one. I have to be strong.

I bury my face in her hair and inhale deeply, her scent dragging me back to sanity.

I have to be a good husband and take her away from here, but I can't stop being a capo. Junior can't go unpunished. I know exactly what I'm going to do, but it'll require me to leash my bloodlust. I can't lash out right now. I need precision. I need control.

Marisol shouldn't see this, but I like knowing she'll be within arm's reach. And I told her we'd do things her way if she came back. If she wants to see her would-be murderer tortured, I won't stop her.

I jerk my chin forward. Dom and Eduardo wrestle Junior through the space between the cars until he faces me.

He bursts into renewed efforts to kick, bite, and scratch out of his restraints until Dom elbows him so hard that he dry heaves.

"How was I supposed to fucking know?" Junior finally shouts. His head hangs low as he drools onto the dusty concrete below. "She said you let her go!"

"That's between me and my wife," I say, pressing Marisol against me by the curve of her waist. I want to gauge her reaction, but right now, all my focus is on Junior.

"You fucking liar," Junior spits. "You're not married. You just didn't want me to have her! Papà—"

"Papà isn't here right now." I sigh, disappointed. "I am.

And while Papà's gone, I'll have to be the one who punishes you."

"Fuck you! *Fuck you! Fuckyoufuckyou—*"

"Gag him," I call out over Junior's incoherent screams.

Davide darts over to a pile of rags against a wall and tears one into strips. He stuffs one piece of filthy cloth into Junior's mouth and wraps another around his head. Junior howls against the fabric, every vein in his neck bulging out as my men hold him back.

I pull away gently from Marisol and step forward to drive a heavy fist into Junior's stomach.

He tries to lurch forward to retch, but I grab the back of his gag and haul him up to face me instead.

"We're going to start with you apologizing to my wife."

Finally, I look at Marisol. I expect any number of things —this isn't the first time I've had a witness nearby. Her eyes should be wide open and her hands squeezed together, although from what I know of her, I expect her to be studying Junior with grim satisfaction. Instead, I'm stunned.

I've never seen her look more alive.

Marisol flicks her bright, fascinated gaze between Junior and me. She doesn't turn away—she leans in, magnetized. Her little pink tongue darts out to swipe her lower lip, and her skin glows with the radiance of a sunrise filtered through stained glass.

She looks the exact same as when she spread her beautiful legs for me, and for a moment, I deeply regret bringing my men here with me. This is a sight for my eyes only.

I should've known better. My girl loves to win.

I smack Junior on the back of the head.

"Apologize." The rags stifle his screams. I lean in. "Again, Junior. I can't hear you."

He roars impotently. It sounds a lot like *fuck you*, but

Marisol doesn't seem to care. She hasn't blinked once. Would she be just as satisfied if *I'd* been the one caught and gagged—a taste of revenge for locking her in my basement? Am I just a tool to realize her will and be cast away once my job's finished? After all my observations of her, I can't answer with certainty.

In the end, it doesn't matter. I'll let her do whatever she likes to me once we're home—she's not the only one whose blood sings in the face of violence. She can punish me, and then after I can show her again how good I can make her feel.

"Passerotta, come here," I say, dropping Junior's head and extending my palm out to Marisol. She approaches me and places her hand in mine. I take full advantage of the moment to draw her close and tuck a strand of hair behind her ear. Her lips part as she directs a gaze toward me that's full of gentle adoration. If this is how she plans to manipulate me, she's going to find it's very effective. "Tell me, bella, what did this man threaten you with?"

Her gaze darts to Junior.

"Don't look at him. Look at me. Tell me," I admonish her gently, tilting her face back to me. In this room, I can be as familiar as I want with her. It's a performance. I'm playing the part of big bad capo, and Marisol's my delicate, innocent wife.

She leans into my hand as she considers my demands. There's not a thing I could deny her right now. "He told me he would send back your ring with a souvenir. A finger or an eye."

I skim my thumb along her cheek, and her eyelashes flutter. "How about I give *you* a souvenir? A wedding present. Your choice. A finger or an eye."

Next to me, Junior stills, as hooked on Marisol's next words as I am.

Aldo and the Outfit will more easily accept a finger as acceptable retribution, but I hope she picks an eye. It'll help me sleep at night, knowing Junior's out there suffering as much as possible before I'm able to hunt him down and finish him off.

Marisol kisses my fingertips and murmurs against them, "I want his eye."

Junior breaks into an explosion of frantic struggle. Davide joins Dom and Eduardo as they wrestle him in place.

My new wife's a bloodthirsty little thing. I lean down, daring to drop a kiss onto her full lips. Our first. "Anything for you," I tell her. Her breath hitches.

I turn to Junior, softness melting from me like flesh from bone. Junior glares up at me with every ounce of hate he can muster, but with my men securing him and dirty rags in his mouth, it's laughable. I brace myself. I've done this a few times before, but digging an eye out of a socket is a tricky thing. They're slippery, and I don't want to smash it too badly before giving it to Marisol.

I grip Junior's head in my hands and dip a thumb into the corner of his eye. Anticipation skitters down my spine. This, at least, I can do perfectly for her.

I push, digging in with calculated force as Junior thrashes against the men holding him. His eye shifts, smashing against the shell of his socket like a grape in a shot glass, and it takes me a couple of tries until it pops out, still connected by the optical nerves. I saw at the slippery fibers with my pocket knife until finally, I have my bloody prize.

Pressure eases from my chest. I exhale.

Junior looks like a fucking nightmare. His face is covered in blood as he screams and screams against his bonds.

Marisol holds her hand out to me, and I stifle my surprise as I place the eye in her hand. Is this for show too? She cups it like it were a baby bird that's fallen from its nest and rises on her toes to kiss my cheek.

"Thank you," she says. "I love it."

If any of my men thought she was a temptation before, they're likely to swear themselves off her now. Good.

She's just for me.

I lean toward Junior who's howling and crying and fighting against his restraints. "Next time I see you, I'll kill you."

With that, I sweep Marisol into my arms and call out over my shoulder, "Bind his hands and throw him on the hook."

18

MARISOL

Outside, Camillo takes Junior's eye from me. His scarred mouth twists into a grimace, but he says nothing.

"Hold on to that for her," Salvatore says, his voice rumbling through me like far-off thunder. "Let Dom and Giordana know I'm taking her home. And have Dr. Macaluso wait for us there."

"Yes, sir."

Camillo gives me the faintest smile before leaving. A pink hickey peeks out from under his collar. Looks like he made it back to Nola okay.

We pass by two other SUVs and an old beater that must be Junior's car. An eerie feeling drifts through me. I have no memory of the drive. Did he buckle me in the backseat or just throw me into the trunk like a set of old golf clubs? I tighten my grip on Salvatore's shirt.

His shoes crunch along the gravel lot until we're at the end of one of the SUVs. He pops open the trunk and, for one panicked moment, I wonder if he's going to toss me inside like Junior had. He must feel me tense up but doesn't say a word as he drags a big plastic dispenser of water to the edge.

He sets me down and presses a bar of soap in my hands. "Wash your hands."

Even with the sun out, by the time I'm done, I have goosebumps. I step back, flinging water droplets off me, but Salvatore snares me by the elbow and pulls me back. He washes my red wrists with a firm, clinical touch. When I'm suitably clean, he releases me, passes me a shop towel, and washes his own hands just as thoroughly.

I clench my teeth so they don't chatter and look out at the squat, desolate buildings opposite the garage. Where are we?

How did Junior find me?

I'd bet it was one of Salvatore's trackers—his ring or something in the food.

I don't fight when he picks me up again and takes me to the passenger seat. *My feet are fine*, I want to say, but I shut up for once in my life because Salvatore still hasn't said a word to me. A few muted thuds sound from the garage before Salvatore slams my car door shut.

The steering wheel squeaks under his grip as he drives us through the nearly abandoned rural town and back onto the highway.

So... the silent treatment? He's icing me out?

I guess it's not technically silent, because he has his cafe noise generator playing even now. Mustn't want the FBI listening in to him pouting.

I cross my arms and look out the window at the rolling yellow fields beyond the road. I get caught, almost tortured, and *he's* pissed off? I shiver. The AC's freezing me through my thin clothes, but I ignore the urge to rub my arms. My eyes prick with tears.

I should've expected this. I fought to leave, and I got *caught.* First day too, like a big idiot loser. And now he gets to drag me back to Chicago and say *I told you so* before he deals with the maelstrom of shit I just kicked up for him.

I bite the inside of my cheeks. I'm going to shut up and take whatever he wants to dish out because, whether he knows it or not, he bought my loyalty back there. I shiver, and this time it's not because of the cold. I watched him take out a man's eye, and I *liked* it.

He can be pissy all he wants. After what he did for me, he can do whatever he wants to me.

Salvatore turns the car heat on full blast.

I glance at him, but he's still wholly focused on the road. We pass by a sign for Iowa, *Fields of Opportunities.* I calculate how much further we have to drive and groan internally.

"What do you remember?" Salvatore asks, finally breaking the silence. His voice is eerily calm. He's probably holding himself back from strangling me right now.

"I went to sleep in a motel, and when I woke up, I was on that hook." When he doesn't do anything besides flex his hands menacingly on the wheel, I go on. "He said he wanted to know about us. Why I wanted to marry you. He wanted to send your dad's ring back with... my eye."

I don't repeat what Junior called him, although I'm burning to. "I'm sorry," I add.

Salvatore pins me to the seat with a single furious glance. I recoil, slamming my jaw firmly shut.

He blinks a few times, and the muscles in his arms relax. He extends a hand toward me, and for a moment, I think he's going to touch me, but it drops to the center console instead. His long fingers form a loose fist.

"Why would you be sorry?"

"Because I made you drive all this way to come get me. I didn't even"—my voice breaks and tears threaten to spill over—"I didn't even last a full day. I'm *sorry*, I did everything I could."

Salvatore guides the car to the shoulder and flicks the emergency lights on.

"Come here."

He unbuckles me and drags me over onto his lap, and I should be terrified, but I haven't been hugged in months and if he's going to strangle me after, then at least it felt like kindness.

He tilts my face up to his. Dark shadows circle his eyes.

Did he sleep at all while I was gone?

"You did well," he says.

I burst into tears. There's nowhere to go. I cram my face into his chest and sob.

Salvatore strokes my back and doesn't say a thing.

Every time I think about how badly I messed this up, it triggers a new wave of hot, shameful tears. I let Junior catch me, I had to be rescued like a runaway teenager, and now I'm forcing Salvatore soothe me through my meltdown.

Once I regain some level of emotional control and wipe my face on my shirt, I look up at Salvatore. Well, at his throat, because I'll start crying again if I look into his eyes.

"You threw out that phone, didn't you?" he asks.

The question surprises me enough that I dare to glance up. He's smiling.

I nod.

His eyes soften indulgently, and I'm suddenly aware of the swell of his chest under my hands.

"Good," he says. "I was tracking that. And your car. And your shoes. And my ring. And Buck's collar. You got much further than I would've expected from any of my men."

Buck's collar. I gasp. "Buck! I completely forgot! He's—"

"In your hotel, I know." Salvatore runs a soothing hand

down my arm, the tension bleeding out of my body with each stroke. "We have him and the rest of your things. Two-Fingers is driving him home now."

"Is he okay?"

"Two-Fingers is a little shaken, but he'll survive. Buck pissed all over his car."

"Oh... He used to piss in Grant's shoes all the time."

Salvatore snorts. I smile.

"I knew I liked that cat." His hand squeezes over my elbow, and I lean into the touch. Something big and hard presses into the underside of my thigh.

"You can still leave if you want to," he says in a low voice. "But first I'm taking you to Chicago to see my doctor. After... if you want to leave again, we'll need a better plan, but you can still go."

"So long as you can track me?" I say without much bite.

He hesitates. "My mom would drink herself sick if I didn't find all the hiding spots for her wine, and I had to monitor her every time she left the house. And I couldn't watch her and my brother at the same time when he kept sneaking out to go do reckless jobs for Aldo. It was on me to keep them safe. I need to know where you are. I need to know you're safe."

It's not a request. But it's not a demand. It's a soft plea. I should hold on to my anger. I want to be mad about him stoking Junior's interest in me and throwing me in his basement and not really letting me go.

But I'm too damn pleased he didn't really let me go.

"Canada. Will you help me get to Canada?" I ask, searching his face for the truth.

His eyes flash, but he nods. "I'll help you go wherever you'd like," he says even as his grip on my elbow tightens ever so slightly.

I close my eyes.

I don't want to be on the run. I'm tired of shuffling down the same worn path I've taken my entire life—alone and desperate for someone to love me.

I already have Salvatore here, underneath me, and he feels warm and solid and real. And he was right when he said I'd want to work for him. Being trained by someone with resources like him would be a dream.

And he came back for me. If this had really been about Junior, Salvatore would've been better off letting me die so he could've had the right to kill Junior, but he came back instead, and that's more than anyone's ever done for me.

And... Buck likes him, and that little asshole hates everyone.

I blink my eyes open.

"You're telling me things will be different," I say slowly. "I believe you. I'll stay with you."

Salvatore wraps his long fingers around my face and crushes my mouth to his, scattering my thoughts to the wind. His smell, his warm weight, the way he sucks against my lower lip, and the faint, possessive pressure of his fingers along my jaw all threaten to drown me in pleasure.

"Wait—" I choke out.

Salvatore pulls back immediately. "I'm sorry. I thought—"

I grab his wrist to anchor myself, to reassure him, and because even that small taste has my panties drenched and heightened my arousal to the point where, right now, it feels slutty and indulgent to touch his wrist. His stupidly sexy wrist, covered in tattoos and strong enough to lift my entire body.

How does he make me feel drunk like this in a matter of seconds?

I look out the window at the farmland surrounding us to tether my thoughts into place. In the distance, a hawk flies in slow, predatory circles.

"I have other conditions."

"Of course." Salvatore clears his throat and shifts, but his cock is trapped beneath me.

I focus very hard on resisting the urge to grind into him.

"I want my phone and my laptop," I say. "And I want to be able to leave the house. When I want to."

"Your phone's at the house. No laptop. I'll pay for a much better computer. And you can leave the house, but take a guard with you. You can pick who."

I don't say that it's unlikely I'll ever leave the house again after what just happened in that garage, but it doesn't hurt to have him think otherwise. And I do like the sound of a new computer.

"Were you serious about letting me work in your cyber team?"

I clench my thighs for the tiniest ounce of relief, and Salvatore's eyes sharpen as his fingers press into my thigh. Would he eat me out again if I asked?

"Absolutely. The lead still has a spot prepared for you."

I shift myself onto the center of his lap, and his hand rises to my hip. I'm not really grinding into him and he's not really squeezing my waist because we're talking and if I keep him talking, I don't have to admit to what I'm doing. Our shirts are both damp, mine from Junior's water bottle and Salvatore's from my tears. The air between us grows sticky and hot.

"Will I get my own income? That goes into *my* bank account?"

"You could. I have a legitimate company you'll be hired under. You'll get paid through them."

I squeeze his wrist and give a deliberate roll of my hips. A groan rumbles in his throat.

"Are they all going to hate me for being a nepo hire?"

His cool gaze tells me, *no one will hate you because I'll shoot them if they do.* "No. The lead wants you there."

The press of his cock against my cloth-covered pussy is making me delirious. I need him to *touch* me.

"You know I dropped out of college? I barely even finished high school. Hate reading books. Might not even be able to read—couldn't tell you the last time I tried."

His laugh vibrates through my chest.

"Trust me. Worm's been begging me to get you onto our team for a while now, regardless of my interest. You're a driven problem-solver and a skilled rule-breaker. You'll be perfect."

"Perfect, huh?" My heart gives a squeeze. "I thought I was impulsive and vindictive?"

"And stubborn. You are. And you're still perfect."

We're skating into dangerous territory now. The kind that has me trailing after a man for years as his bang-maid because he's offered me a steady stream of Love Lite.

He's answered almost all of my questions, but the last one has me cooling down.

I glance back out the window. The hawk spots its prey. It dives.

"Do we still have to get married?"

Why don't you want to marry me? I asked Grant. *I told you, I'm just not ready*, he said and left for Jeremy and Lilah's place while I finished folding his socks and tried not to cry.

Salvatore scrubs a hand over his jaw. "I'm not sure..."

My Marisol's-a-Pathetic-Idiot alarm bells are ringing. "That's fine, I just wanted to make sure."

I scramble to get off of him, but he pins me down to his

lap by my hips, and I suck in a breath so I don't moan at the sudden friction against my pussy.

"Sal—" I warn.

"I told you I'd marry you because I thought it could offer you protection. I still think it will. But I'm also biased because I'd marry you whether or not it helps you. I want you at my side. I want you as my wife. I love you, Marisol."

My thoughts crash into a brick wall. All I can hear is white noise.

Salvatore laughs, and it's just the tiniest bit unhinged, and *that* shouldn't be sexy, not when he has me trapped on his lap and his cock is digging into me.

"Junior's still alive and so is Aldo. The longer you're with me, the more dangerous it'll be for you to leave. But so long as you're with me, I'll protect you with everything I have... but there's one caveat."—My belly clenches—"I want divorce off the table. If you agree to this, I want you all in."

My shoulders twinge. I was running away from this man *yesterday*, I remind myself desperately, but I can't stop the champagne bubbles from fizzing and popping in my belly. I bite into my lower lip to stop a smile from forming.

No. Stop it, dummy. For cripes sake, when will I learn?

I want to turn off my brain. I don't want to think about this right now. I'm going to ask him to fuck me. I just want to feel good.

"Sal..." *Dammit.* I sigh. "Can you let me think about it?"

He searches my face for a moment and then nods before easing me back into the passenger seat. My pussy aches and my nipples hurt. *Stupid.*

He adjusts his cock and drives back onto the road. "We have a long trip ahead. Try to sleep."

I turn my face toward the window next to me, resolving to stay awake and think about what he's offering.

. . .

WHEN I WAKE UP, my entire body has rotated toward Salvatore like a sunflower toward the sun. He left his noise generator running, but his voice weaves in another low layer, speaking softly and urgently to someone in Italian. I peer up at him through my lashes.

The moon highlights his beautiful, fierce profile in the car's dark interior. He falls silent for a moment to listen, exhaling as he pinches the bridge of his nose. When he responds in a slow tone, I get the idea he's patiently explaining to a child how to cook toast—or whatever the Mafia equivalent is. How to recover a faulty loan debt or cheat at cards. As he talks, his hand falls to circle my forearm, carefully avoiding my raw wrist and impressing long fingers and calluses onto my skin.

I fall in and out of consciousness like that, lulled into dreamy relaxation by Salvatore's voice and kept on edge by the possessive grip of his hand.

Il Diavolo, Junior called him. And after seeing him in that garage, I believe it.

But what he did back there, he did for me.

Just before I drift off, I make my decision:

He's *never* getting rid of me.

19

SALVATORE

ONCE, when Mom was in rehab, Aldo took Matteo and me to our first baseball game. Said it was a crime we hadn't gone before and got us matching Sosa jerseys. Junior came too, sulking and throwing Matteo dark looks the entire time. They were always at each other's throats back then. After the fifth inning, Aldo left to take a piss.

Matteo threw his middle finger up at Junior, swiped Aldo's beer, and chugged the whole thing while I held Junior back by his skinny arms. I swore Aldo was going to give us the belt, but he just laughed and told Matteo to go grab another beer and the biggest bag of popcorn Matteo could carry so us boys would stay off his drinks. I kept waiting for Aldo to punish Matteo or teach him a lesson, but it never came. The Cubs won twenty to one. It's one of my happiest memories.

And now I've paid him back by taking his son's eye.

He still doesn't know yet. At the moment, he's eating steak at Celsius with Barbara and Serafina.

Junior's just managed to lower himself from the hook.

I've had plenty of time on the long drive back to identify

even the smallest shred of guilt, but there's none. Guilt implies regret, and the closest thing I feel to regret is wishing I'd taken his other eye so he'd never be able to look at Marisol again.

I do feel pity for the old man. If Junior dies out in that cornfield, Aldo will be devastated, even if he knows deep down what a piece of shit his son is. And I don't envy the choices he'll have to make after today—both as a father and a don. I won't blame him. I understand what it's like to be compelled to protect someone entirely set on your ruin.

Aldo hasn't fought his own battles for years, but he's been a good don. The other capos will stand by him—for now. I'll need time to win them over, and I'm prepared to do so, but I won't get that chance if Aldo decides to blacklist me before I set foot in Chicago. I'd have to take Marisol and run.

Each time dark apprehension tears at my insides like a carrion bird, I rub my thumb over the soft skin on the underside of Marisol's forearm, and the tension inside me untwists. She's been awake for over an hour, listening to me talk on the phone and pretending to be asleep, but she's not fooling me. She snores.

This is the longest I've been able to touch her without her pulling away. After she came on my mouth and *promised* me that she was mine, I thought I'd never have to lose her. And then she left anyway. I thought I knew what she wanted.

I always know what people want. It's a talent that's kept me on the right side of a gun for as long as I've been with the Outfit. Five years ago, Camillo wanted to quit. I hired Nola. Giordana was suddenly skittish at work. I offed her abusive ex-husband. Dom needed brotherhood and a sense of purpose after Matteo died. He's my right-hand man.

I can always reach into a bag and use a variation of money, power, love, or revenge to tether someone to me.

But Marisol?

I thought her carnal nature led her. She likes thrill and pleasure, and I gave that to her. But then she left without a second thought.

What did that milquetoast ex-boyfriend of hers offer that I don't? Stability? Normalcy? I didn't think she cared about those things.

Right now, I can't fucking afford to be uncertain with her. I need her completely and utterly loyal to me because I'm going to be putting everything on the line for her. I already have, wagering all my chips without even knowing what cards I have.

Dom says I've lost my fucking mind.

"Didn't I say you should've just let her fucking run?" Dom shouts in Italian. He made the rest of our men pile into a separate car so he could speak freely. "Aldo's never going to turn a blind eye to this. He's going to slaughter Marisol, and if you're lucky, that's all he'll do."

I trace aimless shapes over Marisol's arm. "You know how Junior is. Give him a finger and he takes an arm. He broke omertà. Aldo will respect the code."

"That girl will be your ruin."

I turn onto my driveway and release an exhale. We're home.

"He had her like Matteo," I say. Dom is the only other person who knows. Who was there. He helped me take my little brother's body down from that hook, even though there was almost nothing left to take down.

I've always suspected Junior had a part to play, but not a single one of those Columbians ratted him out while I razed my way through their gang.

He hoisted Marisol up in the exact same position and tied her hands with the exact same bowline knot that I released Matteo from all those years ago. If he didn't kill Matteo, he'd been there.

He was lucky to lose an eye.

Dom sighs deeply. "I know."

"I have to go. The doctor's here."

"Bye, Turi."

I park next to Dr. Macaluso's car and step out into the biting cold to open Marisol's door.

"We're here," I say in English.

She opens her big, dark eyes and offers a drowsy smile that wraps me in warmth. Then I see the bruising that's formed around her wrists, and anger and grief threaten to suffocate me.

Marisol moves to unbuckle herself, but I pick her up before she can get out, as much for my benefit as for hers. She seems to sense that I need this because she lays her head against my chest without a fight, calming me enough so I can think.

At this late hour, the household is silent. Macaluso's exactly where I expect he'll be—swirling a glass of whiskey in the kitchen.

He stands to attention once we enter.

Our arrangement is simple. Aldo paid for his medical school, and now he does house calls for our elites. Macaluso tried to leave once with a woman before I was inducted, but Aldo paid her to disappear, and he hasn't tried again. I've never understood how he could have let go of that woman so easily, but it's a rare thing to find someone who's truly willing to do *anything* to get what they want. Most simply give up first. I won't make that mistake with Marisol.

"Salvatore," he says by way of greeting. His gaze ticks to Marisol. "Are we doing this in the kitchen?"

"My bedroom." I make my way upstairs without waiting to see if he'll follow.

"Sal," Marisol murmurs as we cross the threshold. "He doesn't have to be here. I'm not hurt."

I set her on the edge of my bed. This is where I should've taken her the first day she arrived. "You were drugged and then hung from your hands for who knows how long." I touch her wrist and then her cheek. "You have bruises."

She gives me a questioning look. Probably wondering where the man who locked her in his basement is. I withdraw my hand. A moment later, Dr. Macaluso enters the room, and even though she must be exhausted and upset, she straightens her back and gives him a polite smile.

That's my girl.

Dr. Macaluso nods to her and sets up the contents of his bag on my dresser. He turns and holds out a plain, white hospital gown.

"I will need you to get undressed. You can change into this. Salvatore, if you would, you can wait just outside the room for some privacy."

I open my mouth to snap out a refusal, but Marisol interrupts as she rises to accept the gown, "He'll stay."

She strides to the walk-in closet while I fight between the urge to puff out my chest in pride and the need to snatch her back and demand an explanation.

Dr. Macaluso shrugs. In twenty years of knowing this man, I've never seen him crack a smile.

Marisol returns in the gown, her dusky nipples jutting out against the pale fabric. What I'd give to stuff my mouth with one of her beautiful tits. She catches me looking and smirks before sitting on the edge of the bed. I stand close to her shoulder while Dr. Macaluso rotates her arm at various angles. Wordlessly, she reaches for my hand, and I clasp her delicate fingers in mine.

Macaluso works efficiently. He might not like his role, but he plays it well, and he's smart enough to know not to linger longer than necessary with my wife.

"I have to draw blood," Dr. Macaluso warns us. He ties a rubber tourniquet around Marisol's arm. "You might want to look away."

Unsurprisingly, she observes every step of the process.

Afterward, she gets dressed while he cleans up his supplies.

"The good news," he tells Marisol as she sits back down on my bed, closer to me this time, "is that you weren't raped. As far as I can see, that's not a concern. When was the last time you had sex? Including oral and anal."

Marisol glances at me. "Oral was yesterday. Everything else has been more than two months."

Dr. Macaluso follows her gaze and assesses me coldly. "*Ah...* Well, in that case, you're STD-free. When I come back, I'll bring a list of physical rehabilitation exercises you can do for your shoulder. For now, you can start with these. Do them every day and call me if you have any sharp pain in your shoulders or wrists. Get lots of rest for the next few days. Any questions?"

"Can you preserve the eye and bring it back?"

Dr. Macaluso lifts an eyebrow at me.

"Wait downstairs. Camillo will give it to you when he arrives," I say.

"Congratulations on the engagement," Dr. Macaluso says without a hint of emotion and leaves the room, closing the door behind him.

"Where do you plan on putting that eye?" I ask.

Marisol looks up at me and scrunches her nose. "*Egh.* I'm not going to keep a gross old eye around. I just want to mess with Macaluso for not doing anything to help me while I was in your dungeon."

I sit next to her to unlace my boots. The side of her thigh presses into mine. "That's right. Dom mentioned a few of your claims. I didn't realize you were a pregnant Venezuelan cartel princess."

"Yeah, well, for all the good it did. The guy's made of stone." She leans back on the bed, totally without remorse.

I finish tugging off my boots and carry them to my closet.

"So," she calls after me, "where's my new computer?"

"What are you in a hurry for?" I cast an eye over the leather upper for scuffs, slip in cedar shoe trees, and return my boots to their shelf.

Her teasing voice drifts closer. "I want to see if you'll make good on your promise, or if I need to make another escape attempt."

I snap toward her, closing the space between us with a step. A smile flickers across her lips as she crosses her arms and rests her hip against the closet doorframe.

Blood rushes to my groin. Is she trying to test my restraint? She had me on my knees with a word. She should know by now how little it'll take for me to break. I brace my forearm against the doorframe, edging closer until she's pinned against the wood, and drag my gaze down her body, lingering on all my favorite places: her dark eyes, her elegant neck, her generous breasts, her wrists—beautiful, even when they're wrapped in white gauze. She holds herself completely still for my inspection, but I'm not fooled by her apparent harmlessness. She's both the hunter and the lure.

"I don't have a computer for you," I murmur. Her eyes narrow. "So you'll have to order a new setup. Make sure you spare no expense—I want my wife to have whatever her heart desires."

I'm playing with fire, calling her my wife before she's agreed, but the way hunger flashes across her face tells me I'm not the only one who likes the idea.

"Whatever I want?" she asks.

Can I hook her with gifts? It'd be so simple to spoil her with whatever she'd like.

"Anything."

She rises on her toes to bring her mouth to my ear, stoking desire down the length of my spine. I rest my hands gently around her waist, letting my fingers dip into the soft flesh there. Her body was made to be touched, to be pleasured, to be draped in silks and rubies. Whatever my little Aphrodite asks for, I'll give her seven times as much.

"I want..." A tiny, breathy moan, then, "my cell phone."

With a light shove that feels like a bucket of ice water, she pushes away from me and settles back on her heels.

"In the far nightstand, top drawer," I grit out, hands clenched at my sides.

She glances down with a private smile at the angry bulge in my jeans before walking over to the corner of the room.

I told myself I would let her torture me for kidnapping her and throwing her in the basement. This is the least she can do.

As she leans forward to open the nightstand, the soft curve of her hips stretches her pants taut, and her hair spills over her shoulders in a shadowy waterfall. Lust chokes my thoughts. Before, she was just a fantasy—as dangerous as a ghost—but now, I've tasted what's between her thighs and weighed the heft of her breasts in my palm, and I'm still forced to wait here like a beggar outside of heaven's gate.

I'll just ask her to shoot me and call it even.

She turns, holding out her phone and a small black velvet box. "There's more in the drawer," she says with a tilt of her head to where I've stored Mom's Bible and my lockbox.

"You can go through those later."

She won't be able to resist the lock. That's fine. I want her to see.

She makes a doubtful sound but redirects her attention to the box she's turning over in her hand. "And this?"

"Open it."

When she sees the diamond wedding ring and matching necklace inside, she inhales sharply and sinks onto the mattress. I didn't know what she'd like, so I asked for something extravagant. I could buy her matching earrings next, then a bracelet—fuck, a tiara if she wants. She'll never have to wear the same piece twice. I circle the bed eagerly to read her reaction.

She's frowning.

"You don't like them?" I ask, burying my disappointment. I should've known she wouldn't be so easy to crack.

She laces her fingers through the gold necklace and concentrates on the pendant, drawing it close to her face.

"There's a GPS tracker in this, isn't there?" she asks.

"Clever." I knew she'd figure it out eventually, but I didn't expect so quickly.

"I want a matching one for you."

The soft glow of the lamp casts her face in amber and obsidian.

I brush my fingers along her neck until I touch the necklace already there. She inhales and stiffens. For the first time since she's returned home, she looks terrified. I ease the chain holding my ring over her head, and she blows out an exhale once I'm finished. Her eyes raise to meet mine with a spark of defiance as I consider her. Did Junior touch her like this too?

I hate that I couldn't see what happened in that garage, but Junior would probably be dead if I had. In any case, he'll die soon enough.

I'd half-hoped she'd throw out the damn ring like she did her phone, but it's found its way back to me. I slide it back onto my finger and flex my hand.

"You already do. Pass me your phone." I show her how to use the tracking app I had designed for my ring years ago when it was retrofitted with GPS to monitor Matteo. It didn't help him, but at least it saved her. "You're the only person with access to this, and you're welcome to change the security settings to your liking. The charger for your necklace is in the box."

She bites into her lip and picks at her leggings, pulling at a stray thread as she studies the blip on the map that marks my location. She clicks her phone off, tosses it onto the bed, and then holds out her golden necklace as an offering, wordlessly sweeping her hair to the side.

I take the necklace, and my fingers kiss against her soft skin as I fasten it on her. I smooth my hands over her shoulders before dropping them to my sides.

She's shy when she looks at me again, her hand rising to touch the pendant. An overwhelming sense of peace fills me. I'll never have to lose her.

"And the ring?" she asks, a hint of teasing returning. "Is that also a tracker?"

"It's a normal ring. But when you say the word, I'll have an officiant come to the house to marry us."

She spins it in her hand, making the diamond glitter in the lamplight. "You're going to be in trouble for what I made you do to Junior, won't you?"

"In trouble" is an understatement. This isn't the type of thing that blows over with a slap on the wrist. It's more like the assassination of Archduke Ferdinand detonating into World War I.

Even knowing how deeply we are fucked, I still want to tell her of course, *of course* it wasn't her fault, and that I can protect her from this too. But there are too many moving parts for a guarantee like that, and I don't want to start our marriage on lies.

"Yes."

"And if we're married... that'll give you more credibility when you have to defend yourself."

"I believe so."

She considers the ring for a long moment and then, with the same finality as pulling the trigger of a gun, she jams it on her finger.

She's not doing this because she wants to. It's a necessary and practical evil for her. I know that, but I still have to shake the low, possessive satisfaction that rumbles through me.

"Sal?"

"Hm?"

"When was the last time you slept?"

"Last time you were here."

"That was almost two days ago."

I couldn't sleep, knowing we still hadn't caught Junior. "That's not so long to go without sleep. I'll survive."

I've been running off of espresso and fury since she's been gone. What I need now is a shower. I need Marisol's body wash in one hand and my cock in the other so I can burn off some of this excess energy. I need to get back to work so I can catch up on everything I've neglected while tracking down Junior. Marisol needs to rest.

I lean down to kiss her forehead and make my way to the bathroom.

"Where are you going?"

"To take a shower. Then work. Sleep in my bed, passerotta, I'll join you in a few hours."

"You said I could set the terms if I came back, right?" she says from behind.

I pause and half-turn to look at her. Technically, she didn't come back of her own volition...

She narrows her eyes as if she's reading my thoughts. "You said you'd give me whatever I wanted if I stayed. I put on the necklace and the ring, and I'm here. So is that true or not?"

I give her a brief nod.

She smiles like a cat that's caught a particularly fat bird, and I bite back a measure of amusement. She might play dirty, but I'll never get tired of watching her win.

She scoots herself back on the bed until she's leaning against the headboard and hooks the waistband of her leggings with her thumbs. I pivot my entire body toward her, more alert than if a gun had gone off. She slowly exposes lush bronze skin that looks like it'd bruise copper if I kissed it too hard and a set of simple black panties I could tear off with my teeth. A soft exhale draws me a step closer.

Maybe I do need sleep. Several of my dreams have started off like this.

She gives me a dazzling smile as she slips her legs under the sheets and pats the empty space next to her.

"You let me sleep in the car. It's my turn to keep watch," she says.

"The doctor said you should rest."

She wiggles her phone at me. "Nah. I have some computer parts to order. And when you wake up, you can show me how I can start my new job."

I want to argue, but a wave of exhaustion crashes into me. Maybe she's right. I sit on the side of the bed to take off my socks.

"You know," I say as I fold them together. "I normally sleep in my underwear."

Something rustles on the side of the bed.

"I normally sleep without a bra."

I catch a glimpse of the bra she's tossed to the side, more closely resembling a battered, beige military tank than a piece of lingerie.

"Something on your mind?" she asks. My attention snaps to the pillowy breasts she's smuggling under her t-shirt, and my thoughts go blank.

I finish folding the rest of my clothes and set them on my nightstand before sliding into the sheets with her. She's so warm and soft and inviting with that wicked little grin on her sweet face. And she's wearing my ring. Every night could be like this.

I drape an arm across the tops of her thighs, and she laces a hand through my hair. While the rest of my body's wiped out, my cock still hasn't caught the memo. I grind it once into the mattress. It'll have to wait a little longer.

I glance up into Marisol's expectant face. She raises an eyebrow.

"I was wondering how many generations back that bra goes."

Her laugh is brief and delighted. "It's actually a prized family heirloom."

"Great-great-grandmother?"

She leans in confidentially. "Rumor has it, she used it to strangle her ex-husband."

"Poor bastard never stood a chance."

She grazes her nails against my scalp, and a hum of relaxation ripples down my body. I haven't been touched like this in years. How have I gone so long without this? I bury my face into her thigh, and she gives a short gasp. I smile against her skin.

"Goodnight," I murmur.

"Go to sleep, Sal."

Something Dom said to me lingers at the back of my mind, but the only thought I form before I pass out is what I'll do to Marisol when I wake up.

20

MARISOL

UNKNOWN

I know who that guy is. You need to message me back ASAP

Calvin said he called you too. I'm gonna call the police if I don't hear from you by tomorrow

SALVATORE WIPED MY PHONE, but he didn't remove the SIM card, so I'm still receiving messages, all marked as "unknown". It's not hard to guess who they're from. Calvin and Jeremy sent me a couple of messages to see how I was doing, but Grant's bombarded me with nearly a hundred texts and calls over the past week.

For someone who couldn't figure out why I was upset when he forgot my birthday last year, he's sure showing a wide range of emotions now. Denial, anger, bargaining, regret...

I'd be flattered if it wasn't so blatantly clear that he's trying to save his ass at work *and* that he's jealous, even if he has no right to be. His newest strategy to provoke a response is threatening to reveal the criminal identity of my mysterious boyfriend. I'm half-tempted to log into his work email to see if Terrence left him an ultimatum to track down the hacker or get canned because I've never seen him this driven before.

Even though Grant's freaking out, I don't feel as warm and fuzzy as I'd expect. Instead, a little worm of guilt wiggles through my chest. I know it's ridiculous because Grant absolutely deserves to suffer after the way he treated me, but... I promised his mom I'd take care of him and letting him get fired is breaking that oath even if he *was* a god-awful boyfriend.

I turn off my phone and tuck it away, but the guilt lingers.

As if he senses my discomfort, Salvatore shifts and drags me closer to him. I run a hand through his wavy hair, and we both exhale at the same time.

Even when he sleeps, it's like he can't help but keep me tethered to his side. I can't say I hate it—I like feeling needed. And I like that each time my thoughts roam back to Junior or Grant, I can stroke a hand over Salvatore's strong body curled protectively around me, and I feel invincible.

He's slept for so long that I had plenty of time to pick out all the components for a bad-ass computer setup and catch a nap myself, tucked up against his bare chest and enjoying the pressure of his morning wood against my belly.

Dom came by once, peeking his head through the door. We made eye contact as I stroked Salvatore's sleeping head over my thighs. Dom raised an eyebrow but said nothing and locked the door before shutting it again. We haven't been disturbed since.

I trace over the long strips of scar tissue on his back, shrouded by dark tattoos. Talons, a cross and rosary, and something that might be a poem or a song in Italian. I thought I'd be able to decipher some of them while he slept, but instead, I'm left with more questions.

I'm a pro at becoming the type of woman my partners want me to be. I've been a cool girl who loved pizza and beer and hanging with the boys. An art snob who dissected foreign films and had long, boring discussions about aspect ratios. And with Grant, I was a mommy who cleaned, did his work, and comforted him when he had a rough day, while making sure never to weigh him down with my own problems.

And Salvatore? He seems to like it when I tease him and boss him around. Maybe he wants a feisty brat... but then he was incredibly protective of me yesterday. He might prefer a sweet damsel in distress.

After he confessed his obsession with me, and I defied him in the dining room, he said I was *perfect*. The memory sets off a swarm of butterflies in my belly.

In the car, he said he loved me.

My ring catches the daylight peeking in through the thick curtains behind us. It's more ostentatious than I would've picked for myself—which makes it perfect to receive as a gift. It's the type of ring that makes me want to write *Mrs. Marisol Luporini* all over my notebook with little hearts over the i's. It's the kind of ring that's coming off of me when it's pried out of my cold, dead hands.

I slip out from under Salvatore's arm and pad to the nightstand, pausing for a few breaths to see if he'll wake up.

Yesterday, I saw more items in the drawer underneath my gifts. An old Bible and a squat black box.

The box had a lock... which means it'll have some answers inside.

I pull out the Bible first and place it on the carpet without bothering to disguise the *thump*.

Years of observing my mom taught me the trick to doing something you're not supposed to is—if you get caught, you act as though you have zero shame.

When we moved into Dad's new neighborhood after he filed a restraining order against her, it was because she thought it was only *natural* that a father would want to be close to his daughter.

When I got caught stealing underwear because mine all had holes in them, no one was more surprised than I that they'd fallen into the bottom of my bag, and besides, who'd want undies so ugly in the first place?

If Salvatore wakes up to find me rifling through his things, I'll be shocked a husband would feel the need to hide anything from his wife. And anyway, he said I could go through them, even if he didn't explicitly give me permission to open the box.

I stifle a snicker when I see the simple combination lock. It has to be a joke. An actual child could break into this.

I start to turn the first dial, looking for a notch in the smooth metal behind the numbers that indicate their configuration.

Six.

Two.

Seven.

Click.

I shake my head with a smile. It's almost more attention-grabbing to use such an easy lock than not to use one at all.

Hmm.

I glance at Salvatore. From this angle on the floor, I can just make out his back rising and falling with each deep breath.

Did he leave this there for me? He knew I'd see it and be tempted.

Only now it crosses my mind that I could've just asked him for the code, and he probably would've given it to me. But since I already have it open, I'm taking a peek inside. I lift up the lid.

It's filled with trash. Very *familiar*-looking trash.

I remove each item and place it on the carpet in a row.

A pomegranate lip balm.

A rumpled stack of notepad paper with chicken-scratch notes I'd written about Grant's work problems.

A cheap pen I'd all but destroyed with my teeth.

A mini R2-D2 I crocheted a few months ago and assumed Buck had eaten or hidden.

The last item, a half-eaten bag of sour gummy worms, I keep in hand.

I look back over Salvatore's stolen treasures as I pull out a fistful of gummies and eat them. They're a little stiff but still delicious.

I pop off the lid of the lip balm and run my thumb over the top. He's used so much of it that there's only a sliver left. Has he ever threatened someone in one of his all-black outfits with pomegranate-scented lips?

It's a strangely... *attractive* thought. Like he so badly needs to feel close to me that he'll wear my lip balm and eat my candy.

I stuff another gummy worm into my mouth, return all of my things back to the box, and close the lid.

The exterior of the Bible doesn't tell me anything new. I split it open and shove my face in the center. Musty old pages followed by something faint... and floral... like perfume. I grimace.

Was this an old girlfriend of Salvatore's? His one true

love that got away, and now I'm here as the replacement? I glance back at my ring, the bright shine now mocking me. If that's true, then I'll uncover what he liked about her and become a better version.

I tear through the book's delicate pages, looking for more clues. A few elegantly written notes jump out at me, but they hardly make any sense. One page has several words circled: land, mountain, woody, trees, grapes... all words related to nature. I've only gone to church twice, but I'm pretty sure this wasn't something the priest asked of them. Some pages have seemingly random words crossed out while others have drawings that weave through the paragraphs. It's the pages with Italian words added in with the shaky penmanship of a child that make me pause. I trace over those with my fingertips.

The writing of a childhood friend? A sibling? He mentioned a brother, but not his name... I sigh. Salvatore's like a giant black box with no seams or entry points. How am I supposed to figure him out when he's so damn mysterious all the time?

With a snap, I close the Bible and set it back in the nightstand with the lockbox.

I steal another glance at Salvatore. Still asleep. I blow out a long stream of air and push myself into a standing position, my wrists and shoulders whining. I waver. I want to wake him up. I want to ask him about the lockbox and the Bible, and I really want to flash him my boobs, because we still haven't had sex, and it's making me nervous. How much willpower can one man have? It's unnatural.

I pace around the room until I'm nearly clawing the walls with anxious, bored energy. After a lifetime of moving and an unstable mom, I should be more comfortable with uncertainty, but it's maddening. I don't understand my role here, and my little perusal of his nightstand revealed nothing.

My stomach gives off a long, angry growl. I shove away thoughts of leaving the room. That's one thing I can do for him, even if it's laughable. I'll survive off gummy worms and lip balm if that's what it takes to stand guard over him. He came back for me. I won't leave him until he wakes up.

When he starts to stir, I've already decided what I'm going to do.

I'd hoped I'd be in the bathroom when he woke, but his amber eyes flick open and zero in on me without warning. For a moment, I'm snared. Then I wink at him and sway my hips as I walk to the bathroom, imagining the burn of his gaze on my back and ignoring the way the bathroom's imposing steel door feels like the lid of a coffin, ready to snap shut and lock me inside at any moment.

Even though he won't be able to see me from this angle, once I start the shower, I take my time slipping off my shirt and panties, warming to the thought of what I'm about to do.

I step inside, noting with mild amusement the presence of a cheap, pink bottle of cherry blossom body wash. I squirt a little into my palm. I wonder when I'll find the glass jar of my old toenail clippings and chewing gum.

I work down from my face, lingering as I rub the soap over my chest. In the corner of my eye, Salvatore enters the bathroom and stops.

I drop more body wash into my palm and take my time sudsing it up before rubbing it over my breasts in broad, generous strokes. My entire body relaxes into my touch. My eyes shutter closed, and I turn so I can lean against the cold tiles, just out of reach of the water spray.

"Enjoy yourself?"

"Very much so," I say, and stifle a moan as I press my breasts together.

His voice floats closer. "I meant with my things in the nightstand."

I chuckle and open my eyes. "You mean *my*—"

My mouth goes completely dry.

Salvatore stands there, close enough to touch if it weren't for the glass, watching me with a wry twist to his mouth. In just black boxers, his entire body is on full display. His dark, unkempt hair and the beginnings of a beard give him a predatory look. Shadowed tattoos weave over his muscular chest, bisected by the whitish sheen of more scars—but none long and meticulous like the ones on his back. He's so fucking beautiful. He makes me want to lick and suck and bite my way down his throat to his chest to his belly and end with burying my face against that bulge in his boxers.

I want to see if the way he ate me out was a one-time thing, or that's just how he is, a corruptive mixture of dominance and worship.

I reach for the glass door.

"Don't," he says quietly. "I want to watch."

My hand drops as if burned. I swallow and squirt more soap into my hands before bringing them up to my breasts. Before, with my eyes closed, I could pretend I was touching myself just for me, but now that Salvatore's watching me through the glass, I'm hyper-aware of my every movement. I squish the bubbles between my breasts and rub my thumbs back and forth over my nipples.

I feel like a piece of art or an exotic animal, stolen and put on display for him. I'm the woman he's purchased and trapped in a glass box, meant only for his pleasure. I'm his priceless secret.

My clit is pulsing and aching to be touched, but for once, I make myself wait, instead moving my hands freely over my belly, my breasts, and my neck.

Salvatore watches everything. His cock is rock-hard. It must be painful.

"I asked you a question," he continues. His hand flexes, but he doesn't touch himself. "Did you enjoy looking through my things?"

"*My* things," I correct. "And yes, I did. Saw you're running low on lip balm—need a refill? I can break it in for you first."

"No. The next time I taste you, I'll get it from the source."

I trail my hands down my belly, and Salvatore finally moves to adjust himself with a lingering touch.

"I also found an old Bible. Who did you steal *that* from?" I try to ask lightly, but it slips out with a jealous bite.

We watch each other for a moment.

Maybe I *won't* let him touch me. I grit my teeth as I swirl my clit. Maybe I'll make him watch me pleasure myself in his glass box, and I'll get my answers later another way.

"I didn't steal it. It was gifted to me by my mother."

His jaw softens, and his playful arrogance disappears. Something twists in my belly. The mother who drank herself sick. "Is she...?"

"She's dead."

Guilt prickles my skin. I shift uncomfortably, hands frozen between my legs like I've been caught mid-act. Should I comfort him? I don't think we're playing this game anymore.

"Keep going," Salvatore murmurs and draws closer. He places a palm on the glass door, the condensation blurring everything but his hand. "What else do you want to know?"

"The handwriting inside," I say before thinking. "That was yours?"

At this point, I would normally break out my vibrator or another toy, but my fingers feel so good right now, better than normal while I have my private audience, and he's spilling his secrets. Sparks spread through my body, and I slow down so I don't finish too quickly.

"Faster," Salvatore urges, his voice a broken whisper.

This is messed up. I should stop. But instead, I tighten the figure-eight pattern over my clit before dipping two fingers inside myself, moaning with relief at the full sensation and sliding a little further down the shower wall.

"It was. Or Matteo's. My mom played word games to entertain us at church for hours." Salvatore pauses. His voice takes on a bitter edge. "It was the only place we could go where my dad would give us a respite from his training."

I pump my fingers in and out and circle my clit with my other hand as I consider Salvatore through hooded eyes.

He wants to be seen—so maybe *that's* my role, to be the person in his life who'll pry his chest open and draw out the secrets inside.

I could be that woman for him—hell, I couldn't be a different woman if I tried.

Maybe we could be good for each other.

I'm so close to the edge now, I can feel the walls of my pussy clamping onto my fingers. I just need a little extra stimulation. I want him to break already and touch me.

"Are you satisfied?" he asks hoarsely, his face almost touching the glass.

"No," I murmur. I throw him a look of silent challenge.

Something almost like anger, or impatience maybe, crosses his face and he shoves his boxers to the ground—oh my *god*—and yanks the door open.

I stay rooted to my spot even as arousal and fear spike through me. I meet his burning intensity with a smirk. He came to me. I win.

Salvatore closes the distance between us in a single step before snaring my waist and hauling me against him so that my back is crushed against his chest and his cock is pinned against my ass. He cups his hand over mine and stuffs two of his fingers and one of mine inside me. The burning stretch is so *good*, but I can't help but rear back from the sudden intrusion. He's got me though, pressed steadily against his chest as his cock tries to drill a hole into my back. Just as suddenly, he pulls his fingers out and rubs over my clit, using my own hand like a tool to masturbate myself with.

He's not the watcher beyond the glass anymore. He's my provoked captor, taking his frustrations and desires out on me. I clench hard and then cry out as a wave of pleasure tears through me, but Salvatore doesn't stop. He keeps rubbing and circling over my hand on my clit until I'm bucking against him, forced to rub myself, wet bodies slipping together, and crying out *I can't I can't.*

When I finally slump against him, body spent, he releases me.

"Now?" he asks, warm voice caressing my cheek. "Are you satisfied now, passerotta?"

I smile lazily at the steam rising up in front of the wall of dark green tiles. "Yes."

Another brushing of a velvety murmur against my face. "The officiant is waiting downstairs. Are you going to marry me?"

I weave my fingers through his hair and tilt my head up to capture his mouth with my own. Soft lips—is that pomegranate?—meet mine before his wicked tongue flicks into my mouth. I open for him, tongue meeting tongue for a few delicious moments, letting the moment draw long enough that he might snap again. I break away.

"Yes. I'll marry you."

Water pours out in a soft *shush shush*. I don't remember what I came in here for, just what I want right now. I want him to fulfill his promises.

"Are you going to fuck me, Sal?"

Despite the thick, humid air wrapping me in a sleepy embrace, I'm all tight awareness as he stirs beneath me.

"Do you remember what I told you?" he rumbles. I search my memories but come up blank. It doesn't matter— he doesn't make me wait long. "I said I won't touch you until you're dripping wet and begging for it."

I'm at the top of a cliff, looking down while my stomach swooshes and a breeze curls against my back.

"You want me to beg?"

He adjusts his cock so that it slips between my legs, rubbing against my pussy, but not entering. He wraps his hand around the length of my hair and tugs until my neck is bared to the spray of warm water and my back arches against him. A flush of arousal runs through me as his teeth meet my exposed neck.

"I should make you wait," he says, half to himself. "Make you go through a fraction of what I've gone through having to watch you all this time."

"No," I murmur mindlessly. "Please."

I squirm, but between his grip on my hair and his arm barred across my belly, I'm locked against him. I push my ass back, forcing some kind of friction, but it's not enough.

"*Please* fuck me, Sal. I want... want your cock inside me."

He bites at my shoulder and groans, his cock dragging between my thighs.

"I want you to use me," I say. "I want your cum filling me up and running down my legs."

Salvatore jerks us to the side and lowers us onto the integrated stone bench. He leans back so the head of his cock teases my entrance, but he doesn't push in. He's still in control. He releases my hair so he can massage my breasts, and it's as much of a relief as it is torture.

What else is he looking for? I bear down to try to take him inside me, but he drops both hands to the underside of my thighs, forcing me up, just out of reach. I whine in frustration.

"Make me yours." I'm barely aware of what I'm saying, only the glide of his cock through my folds, but not *in* me. I need him *inside* me. "I... I want you to own me. *Please.*"

My awareness expands to the ten points of pain digging into my thighs. He's slipping. His cock catches against my entrance and notches there, pressing, pushing.

"Please, what?"

"Please, *sir.*"

He lets me drop.

His cock fills me up in a single stroke, and I cry out in surprise and pleasure and relief. I'm stretched wide over him, ecstasy radiating from our point of connection.

"Thank you. Thank you, sir," I moan.

Salvatore groans appreciatively underneath me.

"That's right. Good girl, using your manners. You can take a little more, can't you?"

My eyes fly open. What does he mean, *more*?

His hands grip my waist and steadily ease me down, forcing me to take more of his length, while I gasp and water droplets spray my face. Once he's seated fully inside me, he reaches forward to circle my clit. A small piece of tension I didn't realize I was holding melts away.

"This is where you belong, Marisol," he murmurs in my ear. "On top of your husband's cock, every night. Satisfied, filled up, used."

"Yes, Sal—sir. Please, sir, I want more."

I tremble in his arms. Raw need amps up in me again, even with him strumming my clit. I need to move. To feel him thrust into me, shaping one to the other.

He groans and snaps his hips upward once, twice.

"Next time you try to leave, I'm going to fuck you so hard you won't be able to walk."

A shiver wracks through me. He *means* it.

Salvatore seizes my waist and sets a punishing pace, driving himself into me over and over again, and he never stops rubbing me like he's as determined to force me to come as he is to fill me with his. To bind us together.

I'm close already. I want to feel him release inside me. I want to own him too. I clench around him. I hope it hurts.

"Who do you belong to?" he asks.

"You. S-Salvatore. I belong to you, *oh fuck*, sir." I'm about to...

"Don't come."

I suck in a breath. "Please, sir. I c-can't."

"You can. Hold it."

My pussy's already pulsing. Tears prick my eyes. I try to push his hand away, but he doesn't stop rubbing me. I grit my teeth and writhe in his arms. If he doesn't say it soon, I'm going to lose—

"Come."

My orgasm rushes through me like a fierce torrent breaking through a dam—overwhelming, powerful, inevitable. I shake and clutch at Salvatore's arms as he wrings out every drop of pleasure from me. He pumps into me one last time and crushes us together as his cock spurts stream after stream of cum into me, prolonging the after-shocks of my orgasm into a euphoric infinity.

As I float down from my high, Salvatore spins me around and kisses me gently.

"Satisfied?"

My laugh sounds dazed.

Am I satisfied?

I'm sore and spent. I still don't know what kind of *training* he did as a kid or what those scars on his back were from or what's behind his other locked doors.

But I know he likes it when I call him *sir*. And I know I can make him lose some of that control he likes to hold on to so tightly.

"Yes, sir," I say and grin when he tucks his face into my neck and groans.

"Let's go get married."

21

MARISOL

AFTER THE FLINCHING, sweaty-faced officiant took our signatures in front of Giordana and Domenico, Salvatore asked if I wanted to go see "Worm".

I wasn't gonna say no to that.

I can almost pretend we're on a date as Davide drives us into the city.

For once, I'm not wearing a shirt with Darth Vader on it or holes along the hemline. Salvatore's men brought all my things from the hotel and my apartment along with poor Buck who was too tired even to hiss at me. Salvatore whisked him away to eat while a pang of jealousy drove into my chest. I'm glad Buck trusts someone again, I just wish it'd been *me*.

The rest of my things were neatly packed and stored in one of the guest rooms. Someone even marked the boxes in tidy handwriting with labels like *Mrs. Luporini's DVDs*, *Mrs. Luporini's Shoes*, *Mrs. Luporini's Intimacy Products*—which I learned meant "Marisol's box of dildos".

I picked through everything until I pulled out one of my sweaters, a loose, cream-colored, cable knit with a high neckline that makes me look like a Sunday school teacher and sleeves long enough to hide the white gauze on my wrists. I must've already gained a few pounds from Conchetta's efforts because when I found my favorite jeans, they needed a few extra bounces to squeeze into. I paired it all with my thrifted leather boots and pulled my hair into a long ponytail.

When I met Salvatore downstairs, he gave me a once-over and said I looked *stunning* while Davide stood next to him, eyes cast downward and cheeks bright red.

The memory makes me steal a glance at Salvatore—and his amber eyes are already locked onto me. I turn back to the window, heart racing like I've been caught trying to swipe toothpaste from the drugstore.

I've never felt this nervous around a man before. I've always been able to do the dance. The squeeze-your-boobs-together, giggle-at-his-unfunny-jokes, give-great-head do-si-do. So long as I kept it up and didn't show what was behind my back, I'd have a warm bed. Things like stealing, lying, cheating—basically everything that gets you a stern talking-to from the principal—got shoved into a black box and packed away in my mind, guarded by a laser fence and automated turrets.

Grant was past my defenses before I realized I wanted to charm him. I realized if I could figure out how to marry him, I'd get the Hallmark Christmases with my own gingerbread house to decorate and care packages full of gummy worms and burnt-on-one-side sugar cookies. I should've realized we were doomed before the start.

Grant already had me figured out when I pinged around *his* house on the weekends he and his brother left to spend with their dad because it meant I had his mom Kristin all to myself. I'd already dropped out of college to care for Kristin before he even thought to ask because I'd given myself a backdoor to his and Calvin's text messages just in case. While he gifted Kristin another #1 Mom mug for her birthday, I made her cry with the porcelain baby from Lladró that she'd added to an online shopping cart months ago but decided was too expensive.

After she died, I worked twice as hard to keep him hooked. Half of his airplane models arrived in my purse with the tags ripped off. His parking ticket just... disappeared from the system. The coworker he didn't like got fired.

Helping him with work was supposed to give me the ultimate trump card. But everything I did for him just pushed him further and further away, and why wouldn't it? His mom raised a good boy.

This evening, I could've asked Salvatore to show me the contents of his lockbox, but a part of me wanted to see what he'd do if I didn't ask first. He was *supposed* to shake me by the scruff of my neck and tell me, "Don't ever do that again!" He wasn't supposed to fuck me to complete satisfaction and ask me *again* to marry him.

Salvatore takes my hand in his—*fuck*—I never sweat, and now's the time my palms decide to give it a try. With my other hand, I dig into the leather seat for something to pick at.

This late at night, the streets are soaked in flickering restaurant signs and red brake lights. Davide pulls to a stop and a cluster of friends burst out of the nearest bar, shrieking with laughter and stumbling over each other. The woman nearest to us grabs her girlfriend dressed in a matching puffy coat, and they kiss. When they break away, their faces are glowing with easy, relaxed smiles. The light turns green, and we drive off. Envy coils inside me.

"Have you guessed where we're going yet?"

My fingernail snags a tiny piece of thread in the seam of my seat—*jackpot*—and I get to work picking at it. I don't look at Salvatore. His thumb draws lazy circles over the back of my hand.

He made me come with my own hand. It was weird and hot, and now I can't look at him, because even though I thought I was the kind of girl who eats danger for breakfast, it turns out I'm just a huge coward. I want him to like me so badly that if I look at him and it's anything but utter adoration, I'll melt in shame. And if it is adoration, I won't know what to do—I'll just turn to stone so I don't mess it up.

His thumb stops moving.

Oh, yeah. I make a half-hearted guess. "Someone's apartment?"

"No."

That was on me. I map out what I know about this part of the city. We're about to cross over the bridge, probably heading to River North, so... something upscale?

"A restaurant?"

"No." He sounds amused—that barely perceivable lilt to his voice already plucking at my clit. "Do you give up?"

Ha. I'd play this game for hours if it meant I'd eventually make the correct guess. Infinite monkeys with typewriters and all that. I chew on my lower lip. We're meeting a hacker friend of Salvatore's. Davide seems to know where he's going since he's not using GPS. Maybe we'll pretend to be Cold War spies and meet at a random park to exchange manilla envelopes.

"A park?"

"No."

I fume. *Think.* It'd be smart to make your base of operations in the middle of the city where there are a lot of people who can hide your illegal activity with their own digital presence. A hotel would be perfect.

"A hotel?"

"No."

"A club."

"Yes."

With a triumphant grin, I whip my face toward him. A strip of searing white light flashes his look of mirrored satisfaction in the dark cabin.

"Which club?" I ask.

"Would you like to guess?"

Two tries later, I have my answer. Hightop. I've heard of it—there was a shooting in the club less than a year ago. Three people died.

Our game ends when the SUV pulls up next to a brick building. Salvatore steps out, offering me his hand. I force down a blush as his long, elegant fingers wrap around mine. Davide drives off, and then it's just the two of us on the empty street, standing under an awning as a light rain begins to mist around us. Faintly, bass thumps through the nearest brick wall. Time to go impress Salvatore's friends and prove I'm the prophesied dark queen for his criminal empire. No pressure. I tug my sweaty hand out of Salvatore's to wrap around my arm.

I'd rather be back in the car playing guessing games.

"Nervous?" he asks.

Ugh, not this kind of guessing game.

"No. I'm excited."

"You were nervous in the car."

I take a deep breath. I don't get nervous. I get ready. I jump straight in, eyes closed and screaming in delight the whole way down.

"I'm on birth control," I say instead, surprising even

myself. All of a sudden, I'd rather provoke him to anger than be honest about some reasonable nerves. What is wrong with me?

I glance up at him. He's completely unbothered by the conversational whiplash. He's mildly amused even—like he expected this from me, like he knows exactly what I'm doing.

"I know."

I don't have to ask. "You shouldn't go through people's medical records. That's illegal."

He raises an eyebrow at that. His mouth twitches. It's *not* funny.

"And I don't want kids," I add defiantly.

"That's not a problem."

"Really? You don't want an heir? Doesn't that mess with the whole Family thing?"

"I don't like kids. And it does, but I've never wanted to bring someone into this lifestyle."

"You brought me."

Salvatore pauses. I tug the ends of my sleeves over my knuckles and try to look tough instead of quivering and pathetic in the chilly night air. He shrugs off his coat without hesitation. I shake my head no, but he still wraps it over my shoulders, bathing me in warmth and his clean scent and tying my stomach in knots.

"You were miserable," he says and waits for me to deny it, but I don't. "You crushed yourself into a shape that didn't fit because you wanted someone to love you. And now you're nervous because, for the first time in your life, you're going to see what happens when you have no limits put on you. There's no need to be nervous. You're going to do well, and if you don't, you'll learn. You have nothing to worry about. I've got you."

The look in his eyes isn't adoration. It's not gentle. It's the same burning intensity that he always uses to look at me with—like I'm going to float away if he doesn't pin me down with the force of his attention. Like if he watches carefully enough, my face will reveal to him the secrets of the universe.

I press my lips into a shaking line. "Whoever you've built me up to be in your head? I'm not her."

Salvatore reaches forward to slip the end of my ponytail out from under his coat and then he cups his long fingers to the sides of my neck. Heat flushes through me, and my pussy—still sore from our shower—throbs.

His lips part as he observes me for a long moment. Without meaning to, I hold my breath.

"You are exactly who I knew you'd be." He inclines his head and gives me the softest, most chaste kiss of my life. At the same moment he pulls back, he releases his hold on my neck, but I can still feel his scalding touch on my throat and mouth. "Let's go, passerotta."

I have a little time to blink the tears out of my eyes as he leads me down the sidewalk. Bass music rumbles louder with each step until we round the corner where a man with a scorpion tattoo along his temple guards the doors from a river of waiting people. Most of the women and men hold purses or jackets over their heads to shield their hair from the rain, but instead of being miserable in the wet cold, they're all chatting animatedly with each other. Must be some club.

Salvatore takes us straight to the doors which Scorpion Face scrambles to open in time.

"Welcome back, Mr. Luporini." The man gives me a curious look but says nothing else. The doors slam shut behind us.

The bass is louder in here, thumping against the walls of a barely-lit hallway. At the end, the biggest man I've ever seen stands in front of another door. He recognizes Salvatore much faster and opens the door smoothly. Whatever he says drowns in the music.

I grit my teeth as bass thunders down into my bones. Salvatore wraps one arm around me, drawing me to his side. It feels like hundreds of people are stuffed into the room, dancing and grinding against each other as women in fancy underwear gyrate in cages suspended from the ceilings. Neon lights cast the dancers' skins in vivid shades of pink or purple. I couldn't be more out-of-place tonight in my dumpy sweater and now with Salvatore's coat hiding my body completely.

I fucking hate clubs, especially with a partner. Crowds like this always drench my natural competitiveness in gasoline and then flick in a match. I can't be the most sexy, the most mysterious, the most fun all at once, but I'm sure as hell gonna try. A few of the men and women stop to openly stare at Salvatore and, as an afterthought, at me. I glare back at them, cataloging the women's long eyelashes and toned bellies. Whatever Salvatore has planned for tonight, I won't be sharing.

THUMP. THUMP. Salvatore stops us, and his mouth moves.

"What?" I shout.

He leans in until his lips brush against my ear. The rough scruff along his jaw makes me shiver.

"Go inside." He points me to another door, his hand rising to cup the nape of my neck.

The next room is a shock of near-silence. Once the door shuts behind us, all I hear is my ears ringing and the barest hint of what's outside. Two men kiss and grind against each other on a long sage couch while a woman in black boots and underwear mixes a drink at a little bar in the corner. A dozen computer monitors along the farthest wall form a semi-circle in front of a crimson computer chair fashioned to look like a throne.

I lick my lips. *Hell yeah.* I hope I get to sit there.

"Worm," Salvatore growls.

One of the men detangles himself from the other and perks up with a grin. Standing from the couch, he spreads his arms wide, his button-up shirt falling open to reveal his tattooed chest underneath. His fingers and ears gleam with gold rings and his green eyes are lined with kohl.

The other man, dressed in a black button-up and trousers and sporting a *massive* erection, jumps to attention.

The woman leaves her drink to scurry behind us and slip out of the room.

"Sally!" the cat-eyed man calls out. He glances at me and flashes a roguish grin. A tooth glints gold under the light of the chandelier. "And *Mari.*"

"How many of my guards are you going to fuck, Worm?" Salvatore asks.

The guard glances at Worm with a hint of accusation.

"It's just you, babe," Worm says with a grin and kisses the guard's cheek. "Relax, Sally's already known for a while now. He likes to watch."

Salvatore's jaw ticks, but he says nothing. I burn the name *Sally* into my memory for later.

The guard looks like he's bracing to get shot at any moment. Worm pats his back and turns to me.

"Well, you gonna introduce us?"

"You know Marisol," Salvatore says. "My wife."

Worm approaches to hug me, but Salvatore shoves him

off. Worm stumbles back, laughing. "Nice to meet you, Marisol, my wife."

"Uh, you too... Worm?"

"Has your husband told you why you're here today?"

I glance at Salvatore. His glare flicks between the guard and Worm like he's deciding who he'll shoot first. The guard stares hard at the blank wall ahead of him.

"A little."

Worm *tsks*. "Come on then. Let me show you my throne."

Salvatore follows us, close as a shadow, pausing only to drag a green tufted armchair to face the wall of Worm's monitors.

The guard marches to stand in front of the door, clasping his hands over his bulge and staring straight forward.

One by one, I take in all the computer monitors in front of me. Two are open to candy-colored lines of code, a third plays a live gaming stream, and the other three are several pages deep into obscure computer forums.

"Sit," Worm says, motioning to his computer chair.

"Worm," Salvatore warns darkly from behind.

Worm rolls his eyes. "If you wouldn't terribly mind and are so inclined, I beg of you to consider sitting. My queen."

Salvatore doesn't say a word to that. I settle into the throne. A girl could get used to this.

"Anyway," Worm says. "What Sally didn't tell you is that tonight is an interview."

"An interview?" I scan over the two monitors showing code. One is in a language I don't recognize but the second looks like it might call to a database—an area I'm not especially skilled in. "My impression was that you'd be *training* me."

Worm laughs, not unkindly. "It's more of a placement exam. You'll be working with me no matter what because you're beautiful and talented, and I guess also because Sally demands it, but I want to see what you can do first."

"I've never done a coding interview, and I've only done one hackathon," I start in a mild panic, but Worm shushes me.

"*Worm,*" Salvatore growls.

"Don't worry," Worm continues, undeterred. "In fact, I did most of the work already."

He points to two of the computer monitors with his ring-studded forefinger and pinky. "*This* is a section of source code from the servers of a little Swedish bank called Framhärda, ever heard of it?"

"No."

Worm scoffs. "I hadn't either until a couple of months ago. Turns out that's where our not-so-good friends the Corsicans have been storing a metric fuckton of cash. Now, I've already exploited the vulnerability here and made them very angry as well as your husbie there very rich. Well, *richer*. I want you to find the same vulnerability I found and tell me how I exploited it."

I'm already squinting at the screen, trying to skim through it before Worm's finished speaking.

"How long do I have?" I call out over my shoulder as Worm walks away.

"As long as it takes."

22

SALVATORE

THE DOOR TO Worm's room opens with a blast of sound, and everyone except Marisol turns to look at the new arrival. For the past three hours, she's barely moved an inch and hasn't reacted to anything going on around her. It's a healthy reminder of how defenseless she is when she's in a flow state.

Dom strides in. For once, he's not smiling as he leans down to whisper to me in Italian, "Aldo knows."

I clench my fists, fighting to retain my composure as adrenaline shoots through my bloodstream.

I've never been this reactive to a piece of news before, but I know the difference today. She's sitting in her computer chair only a couple of feet away.

"He wants you to come meet him now," Dom adds.

Worm's standing in the corner of the room, watching Marisol and pretending he's not focusing intently on Dom and myself. I catch his eye.

"Where's Junior?" I ask. His Italian's shitty, but he can understand it well enough.

"About six hours out," Worm answers.

I glance at Dom, and he shakes his head almost imperceptibly. After working together for so long, we hardly need words to communicate, and right now, he's telling me shit I don't want to hear. Targeting Junior is still a suicidal mission. I need to try diplomacy first.

My gaze drops to his bulletproof vest. Not that diplomacy is significantly less suicidal.

"I have another in the car," he suggests.

Walking into Aldo's house looking like I'm preparing for a fight will only piss him off more. I shake my head before standing and approaching Marisol.

She's oblivious to what's going on, slowly twirling a piece of hair around her finger just like how she would in her apartment and in so many of my dreams. My racing heart slows. I have her. I can figure out the rest.

I kneel next to her, and she startles, a hand flying to her chest. She's so goddamn cute.

"Jesus, Sal," she laughs shakily. She takes in my expression and Dom standing behind me, and her smile crumples. "What's going on?"

"Junior's on his way back. Aldo knows, and he wants me to come meet him." Marisol gives a little desperate shake of her head. "I have to. It's a direct order."

"When are you coming back?"

"In a couple of hours. Aldo's not gonna shoot me. I'm like a son to him." And it almost sounds true when I say it out loud. She still looks doubtful. "You're going to stay here and finish what you're doing. If anything happens, this is your safe house, and Worm and Dom will know what to do."

"Turi..." Dom says behind me.

"Stay, Dom. I need someone here who actually knows how to shoot a gun."

"Hey!" Worm chimes in from where he's not supposed to be listening.

Marisol's voice drops to a whisper. "And if I told you I didn't want you to go?"

A tempting thought. We could run. Right now. I'd take her to Europe with bags of cash. We could lay low for years, sunbathing on the beach and existing in a world of two.

But then I'd be leaving behind Worm and Dom and Giordana and everyone else who counts on me to be the necessary evil that protects us from men like Junior. And my sweet Marisol would get bored.

"I'd ask if you were getting soft on me. Is that true, wife?"

"No," she says immediately, but her blush suggests otherwise.

As I lean in to kiss her soft lips, she wraps her arms around me. "Little liar," I whisper into her ear, and she shivers.

I kiss her again and leave.

As much as I'd love to burn through traffic like wildfire, I force myself to observe the speed limit. I can't risk catching the eye of some asshole cop tonight, not when I need everything to fall perfectly into place.

Things are good with Marisol right now. She found my lockbox of her things and Mom's old Bible and was completely undeterred. And now with her tight, hot cunt dripping with my cum and her vows made, this is more progress than I could've dreamed of in such a short time span. She's still flighty, not trusting fully what's between us, but I can eventually tease that out of her. I just need to make it through the next couple of hours alive first.

I lower the driver-side window to let in a biting wind that lashes against my face and inhale deeply. I need discomfort right now, something to sharpen my focus.

I can see Aldo in my mind's eye, whipping himself into a frenzy the longer he has to stew. That, and the fact that it's two in the morning are doing nothing to help my case. The man hates to miss his beauty sleep.

For as long as I've known him, he's been content to let Junior and me run the business, so long as it meant he can smoke cigars, play cards with his friends, fuck his mistress, and be in bed by eight p.m. Through the crystal ball of my microphones, I know he's been planning to retire to Trieste in the next few years with Barbara's slip of a daughter Serafina. I would've been the obvious choice as the next don. If only Marisol had found Beta *after* Aldo's retirement...

Well, no use fixating on what I can't change.

At Aldo's house, I park on the street. Two other SUVs I recognize as Barbara's and my own are in the driveway.

I breathe in and out as my car engine cools.

Aldo wants an audience. He's invited my men tonight because he wants me humiliated.

Good. If he wants me cowed, that'll play in my favor. Aldo's never had the imagination to understand that a man could be motivated by more than pride. If I can sell that I'm properly broken, he might take that as punishment enough.

I lean forward to slide my gun out of my pants and into the glovebox.

Don't bring a weapon when you're asking for a favor. One of Dad's many lessons.

Looking pale behind his glasses, Davide opens the door before I knock.

"Davide," I say.

"He's in the kitchen," Davide whispers and then falls into step behind me.

I step over the squeaky floorboard in the hallway as we pass a framed photo of Matteo, Mom, and me in Christmas finery and a photo of Junior as a solemn, skinny third grader. It wasn't until seventh grade that we all found out what he'd been doing to the neighborhood cats.

A sizzling sound comes from the kitchen. When I turn the corner, Aldo has his back to all of us as he cooks up what looks like guanciale. Camillo sits straight-backed at the kitchen table with both his elbows on the polished wood, and Barbara's snoring in a chair in the corner.

"Turi," Aldo says in Italian without turning. "Sit down. I'll be done with this in a minute."

"A minute" turns out to be forty. Barbara eventually wakes up from his nap and finds a cigar to chew on. Davide's developed a twitch in his left eye that he keeps rubbing with his fingertips. Camillo doesn't move, his scarred face blank.

Aldo passes out loaded plates of creamy white carbonara speckled with salty guanciale, and I'm hungry enough that my mouth waters. He pours out a glass of white wine for everyone.

"For Paola," Aldo says, meeting my eye. "A loyal sister and a loving mother. You were taken too soon."

Everyone mutters *for Paola* and I say *for Mom*, and we all take a sip. The wine tastes like venom, but I manage not to spit it out before sliding my glass to the side.

"Eat up!" Aldo shouts. Davide's seat scrapes as he startles at the sudden order.

We eat in complete silence. Once everyone's plate is cleared off, Aldo's ready to talk.

"You know, Turi," Aldo says, swirling his wine glass

thoughtfully. "Once we're done with the wedding, I don't think I'm gonna stick around here much longer. Might take Serafina to see the old country or go to one of my other properties. I'm getting old. And whenever I try to forget, my joints remind me otherwise. What I'm trying to say is, there'll be room for the two of you at the top. Junior, he's got guts. He's never shied away from a difficult decision or hard work. And you, Turi, you got the brains to keep the ship afloat. So tell me why, when I'm weeks away from the first real vacation I've had in years, you're starting shit?"

"He took my wife."

"He says she was a thousand miles away."

"He broke omertà."

Aldo drags a hand down his jaw. "So that's the kind of pussy shit I can expect from you now? You're gonna marry some random whore and send her to bumfuck nowhere just to instigate your cousin to violence?"

Pretty fucking hypocritical when Aldo's been married four times—once to his favorite prostitute. Barbara must really not give a shit about his daughter to let Aldo marry her, because Junior makes sure his stepmoms don't last long.

"I have the right to marry who I want."

"You see, that's where you're wrong! You should've come to me for permission first, and you didn't. So the way I see it, you owe me an eye and a marriage!" Aldo leans back in his chair and jabs a finger at me. "This is what's gonna happen. You're gonna take an eye out of that girl's head and send it off to Junior. And then you're gonna annul the marriage. You can keep her as a mistress, and I'll make Junior swear not to touch her. When we finally get you married to a nice *Italian* girl, you can put Mari up in a bougie apartment in West Loop. Or maybe you'll get over her a little faster with the one eye, eh? Either way, I want that eye tonight, Turi, and be fucking grateful I don't make you take two."

"I'll take care of Rekhson for you," I say quickly. I pause. "If you let me keep Marisol. And her eyes."

Barbara's gaze cuts over to me from the cigar in his hands, and he grunts in surprise. Aldo raises an eyebrow.

"How do you think you're gonna do that?" Aldo says. "The boys would gut you like a fish if you tried."

"The boys", being the Commission, the five elite families in New York that reign over all crime in North America. Aldo's right. The Commission's made it very clear we don't touch officials like Rekhson. If they catch even a whiff of what I'm offering, I'll find myself on a list, and then there's no hiding where I take Marisol.

"I'll talk to my dad." My back burns and my ribs ache, but I school my face into neutrality.

Aldo turns to make a spitting sound. "That bastard piece of shit. He doesn't know family. He'll shoot you sooner than help you."

"He won't. I clear it with him first, and then I'll handle Rekhson."

The Commission is supposed to be an oligarchy with no family having more power than another. But that's never how things shake out—power can't be shared. And Ottavio Matassa's been making deals and earning debts for years to make sure he has just a little more sway to his vote than the other bosses. He's a shit excuse for a dad and a husband, but he's a through-and-through businessman. If I come to the table with something good, he'll listen.

The problem is, I don't have a damn thing to offer him.

But Aldo and Barbara don't need to know that. They consider me for a long moment while my hands form fists under the table. Finally, Aldo looks back at Barbara who nods once deeply, and then he turns to me, standing.

"Alright, Turi," he says. "You got yourself a deal. You have three months—no, I don't wanna hear it. That's being generous, and you know it."

That's putting me on a time crunch to produce a miracle, and he knows it, but I don't say shit about it.

"And Junior?" I ask.

"He should've respected omertà. Everyone has to learn." Aldo levels a gaze at me. "And Turi, if you don't handle this in three months, she's gonna lose both eyes, and then I'm giving her to Junior. And if you *ever* lie to me again like this, it'll be *your* eyes. Now all of you, get the fuck out of my house."

A WOMAN with blown pupils and glittery tits stumbles into my path, smiling up at me. I weave past her and the mass of other bodies while the bass speakers drive a nail through my skull and my shoes get pulled to the floor by whatever's been spilled tonight.

Loud, dirty, crowded. I fucking hate Hightop.

I nod to my man stationed outside Worm's room and barge inside. Worm stumbles up from the couch, pulling a gun from his boot and pointing it at my head. From the wall, Renato is already lowering his weapon once he sees it's me. Dom gives me a lazy salute from the couch, his eyes fixed on his phone.

Worm lowers his gun with a shaky laugh. "Oh, hi, boss. Maybe knock next time, yeah?"

I ignore him and stalk over to Marisol who's completely absorbed by the contents of a screen. Déjà vu crashes through me. When will I stop being stunned by the sight of her in front of a computer? I've watched and jerked off to and obsessed over this specific image for so long that seeing her like this grabs me by the throat every time.

Marisol startles, hand over heart in that adorable gesture, and then throws herself into my arms.

"Sal!"

Just like that, the angry buzzing in my head mutes as her soft curves push up against me. My cock swells. God, the *shower*. Her perfect little sounds and her plush, soaked pussy.

Marisol takes a step back with a wicked glint to her eye. She holds me by my wrists and gives me a once-over, lingering on my erection. I'm such a fucking goner. She could lead me around the room by my wrists like this, and I wouldn't give her any resistance. My cock throbs, and my balls ache. I need to get her to my bedroom as soon as possible.

"You made it back in one piece," she says.

"I'm indestructible," I say, and she rolls her eyes. "It's time to go home, passerotta."

Marisol chews her lip and flicks her gaze back to the monitors. She should be exhausted. There's an open can of Red Bull on her desk and a pack of M&Ms—who brought her those? She never eats M&Ms.

"I want to stay. I'm getting close," she says. She's not asking for permission, but she's not poking at me for a response like she was outside the club.

I need to get her home, locked away in a room with me so I can get back to work. But I know this is important to her. And I promised her.

"Fine, but I'm staying until you're finished."

She blinks. "Of course," she says like it's the most

obvious thing in the world, and something hot and satisfied rumbles inside my chest.

Once she returns to her work, I drop onto the couch next to Dom and start to fill him in, but he raises his hand to stop me.

"I already heard it all," he says in Italian. "That little wife of yours eavesdropped on you at Aldo's the entire time. And she made Worm translate for her. I had Renato face the corner of the room."

A smile tugs at my mouth. *Good girl.*

"Keep an eye on Rekhson. I want to know her schedule like the palm of my hand, understand?"

Dom eases up from the couch with a groan. "I understand I'm about to be having a lot of sleepless nights," he says.

"We'll sleep when we're dead."

"Where we're going, I don't think there's gonna be a whole lot of sleeping. Maybe a little more weeping and gnashing of teeth."

"Real fucking cheerful, Dom. Thanks for that."

He grins like an asshole and disappears through the door.

For the next several hours, I alternate between pacing the length of the room and failing to focus on my phone. I keep finding myself returning to the armchair stationed behind Marisol so I can watch her and the door.

She doesn't seem to suffer from the same affliction. She's completely blind to what's going on around her as she parses through lines of code and computer forums and translation services. I have to draw my fists into my lap to keep from touching her whenever she pauses to stretch or yawn.

She's not my mom, I remind myself with an echoing

yawn. This is what she's meant to do. I'm not pushing her too hard. She won't crumble. She wants this.

When I wake up, she's not there.

I lurch to a standing position, reaching blindly for my gun as a blanket falls from my lap.

"Hey, hey!" Worm says, rushing over to me. "She's right there, chill out."

Marisol's asleep on the other couch with her head resting on the lap of Worm's go-go dancer friend Joselyn. I frown. Joselyn might be a woman, but if Marisol needs someone to sleep on, it'll be me.

"She did it," Worm leans in to whisper.

Joselyn catches my eye and blanches, raising her hands in a *don't shoot* position. Worm waves her off and takes my arm, pointing to the computer monitors.

"It took her a day," he says.

I have no frame of reference for this. I tilt my neck until it releases with a satisfying *pop*. "With some training, you can help her move faster next time."

Worm laughs and shakes his head. "No. It *only* took her a day. It took me *three*." He lets the shock of that statement sink in for a moment. "Now, granted, I was going through a breakup and had a lot on my mind at the time, and I didn't know there was a vulnerability to exploit, but yeah. She did fantastic. I'll start putting some assignments through to her immediately. But she needs sleep now. And food, 'cause she wouldn't eat anything other than candy."

"Thanks."

"Anytime, boss."

Ignoring Joselyn's whispered apologies for touching her, I slip Marisol into my arms and carry her outside where

Davide's waiting with the car. She stirs a little when I slide in with her, but she falls back asleep easily, clutching my waist.

I stroke her ponytail and her arms and over her hip like she'll stop breathing if I lose the rhythm of touching her.

In three months, I'll be preparing myself to move into position as the new don of the Chicago Outfit or huddling in the back of a shipping container on a boat.

I tighten my hold on the end of her ponytail. At least I'm certain of one thing—in either case, I'll have Marisol at my side.

23

MARISOL

I ROLL over on the bed and come into contact with something hard and warm. Eyes closed, my hand traces over Salvatore's chest, sifting through coarse hair and reading his raised scars like braille.

It feels good to lie like this. When he's asleep, I have zero worries. No expectations about doing or saying the right thing.

He shifts to sling an arm and a leg over me, trapping me against his chest. For a few blissful moments, his deep, steady breathing almost lulls me back to sleep. Then the ache in my shoulders grows too unbearable, and I have to slip out from under him.

Yesterday, I didn't need to think about sore shoulders and tender wrists and where I got them from.

I was flying. Kicking ass and taking names. Eating lightning and shitting thunder. Once I found the tricky little bug in one of Framhärda's libraries, it was just a matter of experimenting and developing a Trojan that would allow me to push malicious code to the bank's database and give us control. I smile at the memory of Worm's surprise. He'd burst out laughing when I suggested using the exploit in ransomware bots against other companies. He'd already done exactly that, and we nerded out for a couple of hours until he tore me away from the computer to sleep.

I twist to grab my phone from the nightstand, flicking it on so I can check for a message from Worm, and as I do so, my gaze snags on the fresh, white gauze covering my wrists.

My heart stutters.

I lean back to spread my fingers over Salvatore's chest, wishing I could wrap my entire self around him, but just like this, when he's asleep and not so... *much*. He put his reputation on the line for me last night. He prioritized my work. He took me to bed and bandaged my wrists.

So far, all I've done is get kidnapped and made him wait around all night so I could play at being a hacker.

I trace one of the tattoos on his chest, a wide-open eye in the center of a starburst pattern. At least this one's easy to understand. An all-seeing eye for my husband who sees everything, all the time.

My computer parts come in today. After I start with whatever Worm plans to assign me, I'm going to do a little research on District Attorney Rekhson. If Salvatore wants to know everything that goes on, I can help with that.

My phone buzzes violently against my side.

"Who is it?" Salvatore mumbles without opening his eyes.

The contact flashes *Unknown*, but it's an Appleton area code. "Grant." I want to hurl my phone at the wall.

"What does he want?"

I sigh. "To harass me. He keeps sending messages to warn me about you and threatening to call the police. I'm going to let it go to voicemail. He'll give up eventually."

Salvatore's smile is sleepy and self-satisfied. "Oh, really? Answer it. Let him know he's got nothing to worry about."

Maybe he's right. Better to tell Grant off than let him spiral further. I take a deep breath and shamelessly rub a hand along Salvatore's hard chest muscles before answering and setting the call to speaker.

"Mari!" Grant sounds breathless. "Are you okay? Where are you? I went by the apartment, but they said you closed the lease!"

I glance up at the ceiling like it'll hold an easy answer for me. Salvatore rolls over and rubs his face into my lap. I suck in a moan and arch my hips toward him. I could use the distraction.

"I'm great. I just wanted some distance after the breakup."

"Yeah... I'm sorry for all the mean stuff I said. That wasn't okay. Mom wouldn't have wanted us to end it like that. I still want to be friends, you know, after some time's passed. When we're ready."

"Friends?" I gasp. Salvatore just ground his jaw against my clit. He tugs at my underwear while Grant talks.

"I mean, you don't have to sound so surprised. We *both* cheated. But I still love you—as family. I think if I can move on, so could you."

Salvatore flings my underwear to the side of the bed and wrenches my thighs open while I squirm underneath him and try to focus on whatever dumb shit Grant's saying. I *never* cheated—

"Mmm," I strangle out as Salvatore shoves his face between my legs and digs his tongue into my pussy.

"Anyway, I wanted to say I'm still worried about you. You're... alone right?"

"Mm-hmm." Two of Salvatore's fingers replace his

tongue, stretching me out. Now that his mouth is free, he presses it to my inner thighs and sucks, sparking electricity up my spine. I grit my teeth to keep from groaning out loud.

"Terrence was going to fire me since you didn't want to give me that data." Grant pauses, as if to give me a chance to jump in and offer to rescue him with a cooed *poor baby*. Maybe old Marisol would've done that, but new Marisol—

Salvatore yanks me down the bed, and my head thumps against a pillow. My phone's lost to the sheets. He clamps a hand over my mouth before pistoning a third finger inside me as his mouth seeks my clit. *Fuck*. I am *drowning* in him.

Distantly, I hear Grant sigh and continue in a muffled voice, "But when I told him about how I was having a hard time, and I mentioned that *guy* I saw in your apartment, Terrence sounded like he recognized him. You know how he was always saying the Mafia was hacking him. Mari, that's what I've been trying to warn you about. I think that guy you're seeing is in the Mafia."

I don't say a single thing, because that Mafia man is currently finger-fucking me so hard I'm seeing stars. Salvatore presses his fingers against the seam of my mouth and when I open, he hooks two fingers inside, filling me up deliciously at both ends.

"Look, I know it sounds crazy, but the more I thought about it, the more it made sense. I don't know how long you've been seeing this guy, but I think he might be using you to get to me."

If I wasn't almost gagging on Salvatore's fingers right now, I'd laugh.

"I want to meet up. In person. I want to make sure you're okay, and if you haven't already, I really think you should run a background check on this guy…"

Grant's voice drones on as Salvatore licks and sucks

against my clit. Pleasure skitters up my belly and my spine until I'm tumbling, careening over the edge. My vision flashes white in an explosion of pleasure—I have to latch onto Salvatore's fingers so I don't cry out. Wave after wave of euphoria courses through me as I shudder and bow underneath him. I'm a passenger—no, the captain—and he's the sea, vast and mysterious and generous and cruel.

"Mari?"

For cripes' sake, what the hell was Grant saying?

Salvatore reaches over and hangs up the call.

"Sal!"

"You can call him back," Salvatore says evenly from between my legs. His jaw glistens with my arousal. "Invite him to dinner at Nahash, tonight at six. My treat."

I gape at Salvatore. Did coming fry my brain or did he really just suggest that? I can't fathom why he'd want to. My phone rings as Grant starts calling back.

A thought strikes me, and I narrow my eyes at Salvatore. "Are you going to hurt him?"

He rubs his hands over my breasts and kisses my hipbones, sending aftershocks of arousal through me. We both moan at the same time. "No, passerotta, I'm not going to hurt him. I'm going to help set his fears aside. I'll be very well-behaved, I promise."

Another thought. I'd been trying to get Grant to go with me to Nahash for months, but he'd either say it wasn't in the budget or that he didn't have the time. "Did you know I wanted to go there?"

Instead of an answer, Salvatore smiles with perfect innocence as he taps my phone.

"Mari? Did you hang up?" Grant asks.

"Sorry, I dropped my phone in water, and it's been acting weird since. We can meet for dinner at six. Let's do Nahash."

"Oh…" The hesitation in Grant's voice makes me grin. He recognizes the restaurant too. "Okay. We'll be there."

After I hang up, I realize he said *we*, meaning him and Lilah. My smile falls. *Awesome.*

Salvatore doesn't seem to care as he stirs between my legs and rises to kiss me, his arms boxing me in on either side. We're supposed to be focusing on Rekhson and Junior, so why would he want to have dinner with my ex? He dips his head down to lash his tongue into my mouth the way he did between my legs. Even as my pussy squeezes eagerly, my mind won't shut up, and I blurt out, "Are you worried about the cops?"

He smiles against my mouth. "What makes you say that?" he says in a low rumble.

"Is that why you invited Grant to dinner? Because he said he'd call the cops?"

"I'm not worried about the police."

"Oh." I frown. I should just shut up and get back to whatever treat Salvatore clearly has in mind, but I add, "So why…?"

He pulls back to meet my eyes, and the significance in his gaze makes me want to hide away. He scrubs his thumb along my cheek until his hand wraps fully around my jaw. "To claim you, passerotta."

My cheeks burn. "From Grant? You… you don't have anything to worry about there."

"Either he doesn't understand you're mine, and I'll correct that mistake tonight, or he does, and he'll learn to respect my wife's wishes."

I try to twist my face to the side, but he doesn't let go, and that little show of force sends a gush of wetness between my thighs. "You said you wouldn't hurt him."

"I won't need to hurt him to teach him a lesson."

My skin crawls as Salvatore's gaze travels over me, clinical and detached. Why is it that I'm flooded with desire, and he gets to keep his cool? I ride through an explosive urge to shove him off me. I want a real reaction from him.

"That's... petty."

His smile is small and hard. "Yes."

He kisses me again, this time pushing me into the bed with all of his weight and gripping my face with both hands. I buck up hard against him, but he doesn't let go, so I do the only thing I think to—I suck his lip into my mouth and *bite*. All that weight disappears from on top of me at once, and then it's just the two of us staring at each other and breathing heavily.

His tongue darts out to touch his swollen lower lip. His gaze is electric. Feral.

Trapped under his boxers, his cock is rock hard.

"You bit me," he says. It's not an accusation. It's a challenge.

I exhale a small puff of air. "Take those off." I nod to his boxers.

In an instant, he's naked before me, long, muscled, fierce, and judging by the flex of neck and abs, barely restraining himself.

I tug my shirt off and throw it to the side of the bed.

We're caught in a staring contest, or a trance, watching the other from across the bed, neither of us moving an inch. I don't know why, but I'm fucking terrified. Terrified that there might be no one else on Earth that makes me feel the way he makes me feel. Terrified I'll mess this up.

His breathing is ragged, but he's slowly straightening, like he's coming to his senses.

I let my leg fall open to the side, exposing myself.

Salvatore lunges.

He yanks me down the bed by my thighs and, with one hand around the base of his cock, shoves himself inside me. I'm so wet that it slides right in with a filling, burning stretch that has me arching up against him.

"Salvatore," I groan, pushing against his thighs with my fingertips. "You're too big—"

Slap.

I gasp. He just slapped me—hard enough to shock— across my inner thigh. He stops where he is, only moving with a barely-there rocking of his hips.

"Spread your legs." Even with his swollen lip, his voice is soft and in control. Always with his precious fucking control.

After a beat, I relax and let my knees fall to the sides.

"What do you call me?" Dark eyebrows, dark eyelashes, firm mouth. The picture of disappointment.

Fuck his disappointment.

"I call you sir—" I barely get the word out before he pushes deeper inside me at the same time his thumb strums over my clit, driving a choked gasp out of me.

"There's a good girl," he purrs as he shoots arcs of electricity through every cell of my body with every swipe of his thumb. "What did you want to tell me?"

Fuck, I love his praise.

My fingers spasm against his thighs. "You h-have to go s-slower. You're too big, sir. I... need a moment to adjust." I hastily add another "sir" at the end for good measure.

He smiles indulgently and then even wider as my pussy clenches hard around him at that. God, he's fucking beautiful. I'm putty in his hands.

"Good girl, asking for what you need." He grips me by the back of one knee and looms over me, close enough to kiss. He doesn't stop circling my clit. "Is this slow enough for you?"

"Yes, sir." I can feel every delicious spark of friction, but now he's too close. Too intimate. It's making me frantic. I squeeze my eyes shut and focus on breathing, on taking him all. If I can do that, the knot in my belly will loosen.

I exhale a low moan once he's fully seated inside me, skin-to-skin.

"Open your eyes."

I screw my eyes tighter and shake my head. If I look at him, I'll burst out crying. He's too much. Too intense, too possessive, too attentive.

I suck in a breath as his mouth finds my breast and kisses it, trailing up to my nipple where he circles it with his tongue and sucks it into his mouth. I squirm underneath him, heaving like I've just sprinted a mile. It's too much—the nervy sensation of his mouth on my breast, the incessant circling of my clit, and the heavy pressure of his thick cock inside me.

He lifts. "Open your eyes, Marisol."

My eyes snap open. Dark, wavy hair halos his face with shadow, but his amber eyes are fixed on me. Always on me.

"I'm going to fuck you now," he says gently. "Are you ready?"

Some of that wild emotion inside me reduces from a boil to a simmer. I want this. I nod.

"Use your words."

"Yes, sir. Fuck me, please."

His eyes flash. He drags out of me with excruciating slowness and pushes back in with a snap of his hips. For what feels like an eternity, he torments me with the rhythm of a long, slow emptying, and then an almost punishing filling.

I can barely keep my eyes open, barely think past the all-encompassing fullness of him inside me, past the immense pressure building just behind my navel, but I force myself to look. I watch him the entire time. I lose myself in him, gripping his thighs hard enough to leave crescent-moon marks. He says he knows me. Says he'll claim me.

I want that so badly. I want... I want...

My eyes are glued to his as heat races through me, coalescing in my core, and finally, I'm collapsing into myself like a dying star before exploding into pleasure as a powerful, raging orgasm roars through me. Salvatore thrusts his hips to mine and groans as he empties himself, his cock hardening and jerking inside me, and he's muttering my name like a curse.

I melt into the bed, boneless and smiling. My head is empty, my body is sated, and I'm floating on a white, fluffy cloud of nothingness.

Salvatore folds over to kiss me softly. He looks almost boyish right now, with a flush over his face and a smile playing at his lips.

"Let's shower. I have a surprise for you."

Turns out "showering" also included a trip to Salvatore's home gym downstairs where he compelled me through Dr. Macaluso's rehab exercises with barely-there touches and clipped commands. By the time he let me retreat to the treadmill, I was soaking wet again, and getting to watch him lift heavy weights and sprint next to me did nothing to help my poor underwear.

After we cleaned up, he takes me to my real surprise—his upstairs room with the electric lock. I bite back a grin. *About time.*

"Watch," he says softly and keys in four digits.

That's my phone passcode. I glance at him. Salvatore looks back at me with a glimmer in his eye.

The door opens with a soft click, and a multicolored glow flickers through the gap. He guides me inside, shutting the door behind us.

A massive desk spans nearly the entire length of one wall. Above the desk sits dozens of monitors, all perfectly spaced apart and tuned in to different images—an empty basement, a hairy man fucking a much younger woman in a pink apartment, a group of tattooed gangsters gossiping over a table in an empty warehouse. Amazingly, the room is comfortably cool. I can't imagine how much heat that must spew out to run this many monitors at once. But where's his computer tower? No way it'd be anything less than an absolute beast.

My gaze lights on the end of the room where a sand-colored cat paradise stretches across the wall. Two towers sit at opposite ends of a house, joined together by a series of bridges and shelves. Buck sits at the top of one of the towers like a little orange prince.

My heart gives a squeeze as I approach Buck and his cat kingdom. "Is this where you've been all this time? Fell in love with big, bad Salvatore?"

Buck narrows his eyes but doesn't hiss at me. Just as I'm considering reaching out to pet him, something brushes against my elbow, and I have to swallow a gasp. Salvatore's going to get a bell if he's going to be sneaking up on me like that.

I glance up at him. "Thank you," I say sincerely, "for taking care of him."

He smiles a little but doesn't say anything. Finally, I notice my surprise.

Oh my god.

A matching desk to Salvatore's sits against the opposite wall, with houseplants and a track of grow lights eating up two tremendous swathes. It's so close to the vision I had when I decorated my desk back at my apartment that it might as well have been ripped straight from my fantasies. I drift closer to rub my palms along the smooth wood. Six black monitors hang off the wall. *Six.* I collapse into the computer chair, and a giggle bursts out of me as I realize what I'm sitting on. A fucking Herman Miller? This chair costs more than... well, *anything* I own.

Except maybe my wedding ring.

Several boxes with my favorite brands sit neatly stacked by my feet. They're all the new computer parts I'd ordered.

"Sal..."

When I swivel around, he's right there. I take in his eye-level cock, swallow hard, and raise my gaze to meet his. His look of smug confidence sinks a pulse of arousal through me that pins my limbs to my new thousand-dollar chair. A fleeting moment of panic seizes my lungs.

Please just cut out my heart and eat it already. What else can I offer to repay this feeling of being seen? Is there any part of me he doesn't own yet?

"What do you think?" he murmurs, watching me with those bright eyes of his.

I think if he changed his mind and discarded me, I'd follow him around in despair forever, like a wraith without a body or a soul, longing for the sweet burn of his recognition.

I swallow past the emotion lodged in my throat. "Don't you think it's a little small?"

Salvatore strokes a hand over the top of my head. There's so much power at his fingertips, but he moves gently, for me. He does everything for me. "Does my wife need something bigger?"

A shiver passes through me at his touch. "N-no. I don't think I could handle any bigger," I say with a weak smile. "This is perfect. I love it."

"Good."

The computer monitors behind his back glitter and wink like a swarm of fireflies. His all-seeing eye tattoo flashes in my mind. Does he see the potential in me to be another piece in his chessboard? I saw enough to understand Worm is irreplaceable in Salvatore's team. I run my tongue over my bottom lip. *Irreplaceable.* I like the sound of that.

"How many cameras do you have?" I ask.

"One hundred and twelve active cameras. Almost two hundred microphones."

All that data has to be stored somewhere. *Fucking databases.* "How do you parse through it all?"

"I have alerts set up for specific words. Worm has a small team that sifts through the footage to see if there's anything useful."

"But you miss a lot."

He doesn't hesitate. "I do." And at least I know him well enough to recognize it has to sting, even if his voice doesn't betray him.

His face is cast in shadow from the backglow of the monitors.

"When did you start doing this?"

"When my brother died."

"Matteo?" I ask.

"Yes."

Dread settles over me. I imagine two little boys with dark hair and amber eyes who played word games in a church with their mom. Maybe across a wide distance, we were going through the same thing. Avoiding one parent and clinging to another.

I straighten up. At least now, I can better understand how I might fit into Salvatore's life. He has an entire family's lost love to offer, and I'm the recipient. I'll eagerly accept his need to control me, to keep me in one piece, to claim me, if it means I get to keep all that love and affection for myself, and I won't have to share with another living soul.

"When did that happen?" I ask.

"Thirteen years ago. At the time, we were feuding heavily with the Columbians. They tricked him into a meeting, strangled him with a garote, and then cut him up into dozens of pieces. He was twenty-one."

"And what did you do?"

"I laid out dozens of cameras and hunted down every man associated with Matteo's murder."

"Did it help?" I ask, but I already know the answer.

"No, passerotta. It didn't help."

24

MARISOL

Salvatore hasn't said a word to me in the hours we've been working at opposite ends of the room. I'd think he was angry I'd pried too deeply about his brother if it wasn't for the way he keeps glancing over at me.

There's no trace of the subtle flicker of resentment in his gaze. Instead, it's long and assessing, like he's running through some lengthy mental checklist to assure himself nothing's awry. It's the way you'd look at the crown jewel of your collection. Admiration laced with a sharp possessiveness, like he's suspicious I'll be stolen right from under his nose if he's not vigilant enough.

I snap each piece of RAM into place, taking care not to touch the gold-plated contact points of my new motherboard. The soft clicks are the only sound in the room aside from the whirring of the computer fans. Salvatore moves in complete silence. No annoying pen clicks or tapping noises or sighs. If some internal compass didn't keep me annoyingly attuned to his presence, I could forget he was here.

He sifts through emails while video clips of an older

woman in navy suits and a severe bob fill half of his monitors. District Attorney Rekhson.

She seems like a nice woman. She goes to dog shows with her bowtie-wearing husband and picks up her grandkids from daycare and works late hours in the office. She wants to clean up Chicago. I vaguely remember voting for her.

I don't want her to die.

But if it comes down to her or Salvatore, I already know where my loyalties lie.

"WHAT DID you think about Worm's first assignment?" Salvatore asks hours later, voice rumbling through me and dredging me back to the present where my cheek's pressed against his chest in the SUV. Classical music plays softly around us as Davide weaves through the evening traffic.

Salvatore's got to be talking about the mob work and not the basic assignments for his real-life company that I started knocking out as warmups. Worm's going to have me cut my teeth on hacking into CryptTalk, the encrypted network all the major gangs—not just the Italians—use for their cell phones. I'm still not convinced it isn't some joke of his to haze the newbie, like "go get me the left-handed screwdriver", because the idea that every major criminal organization relies on a single phone company, a single point of failure, for all of their illegal communication needs is staggering. That company must have the single best security system in the planet, or it's a house of cards waiting to topple over.

"I can't wait to get back to it," I say.

Salvatore's smile in the car's dark interior is victorious. "I thought you might enjoy it."

I don't just *enjoy* it. I'm a pint-sized sugar monster with an unlimited budget and no supervision in a candy store. The only thing I can see keeping me from learning about encrypted phone systems and ransomware and DOS attacks and everything else I plan on throwing myself into headfirst are basic physical functions like sleeping and eating. And mind-blowing sex with Salvatore.

I pluck at a frayed string on my champagne-colored wrap dress. I could've picked out that blue daisy print skirt that Grant loved, or even my black sheath dress for non-existent interviews so I'd match Salvatore, but I'd been saving this dress for a special occasion. It makes me feel like royalty—and I want every advantage to convince myself I belong at Salvatore's side. If anyone can fake it till they make it, it's me.

"Where'd you go?" Salvatore asks, capturing my fidgety fingers and pressing them to his lips.

My stomach flips, but I hold his gaze over my fingers until we're so close, that a tilt of the head would be enough to kiss. I skate my other hand over the front of his shirt, dipping into the smoldering heat inside his coat. I could touch this man for hours.

"I was thinking we could pop in, show Grant I'm doing *swell*, and head back home."

"Seems like a waste to finally get you out of something that isn't a t-shirt of a wrinkled green man just to put you right back in."

My laugh is breathless as he wraps long fingers against my lower back and tugs me up against him. I shove my breasts into him, praying he'll give me mercy and touch my aching nipples.

"But..." he continues in that soft, indulgent tone of his, "if you really want to go home, we could cut dinner short. You wouldn't even have to show."

"And what would you do?" I ask through a smile and then bite back a moan when his thumb skates over my bra. Maybe he can ask Davide to take a walk once we're parked.

His hands trace my body with methodical slowness as his breath burns the shell of my ear. "I'll take that ex of yours out back. Bring him up to speed. Why don't you stay in the car? Davide can wait outside. And when I get back, I want you to give me a number between one and four."

One and four? Of what? Spankings? Fingers?

My trapped moan slips free as Salvatore kisses against my neck. I bury my blushing face in his coat. Every brush of his body against mine is a filthy promise. The man is temptation incarnate.

We're installing dividers in all the SUVs as soon as possible.

"We're here, boss," Davide says.

My eyes flutter open to catch the neon-gold lettering outside the window that reads *Nahash*.

While Salvatore delivers a steady flow of commands in Italian to Davide, my brain slowly boots back online.

"One through four," he reminds me in a low voice and unbuckles himself.

"Wait." I clutch his coat, blinking. "What are you going to do with Grant?"

The dangerous look in his eye cuts through the last of my lusty haze.

"You said you weren't going to hurt him," I add firmly.

Salvatore's eyebrows crash down in disappointment. "Vai via."

Davide fumbles with his seatbelt before stepping out and shutting the door behind him. He jogs to the sidewalk a few feet away and pauses there, facing away from us.

"Do you still have feelings for him?" Salvatore asks.

I try to lean back, but he anchors me against him. "Sal," I warn.

"He was disloyal to you. Used you."

His arm is a steel bar against my back as I twist to look him in the eye. I resist the urge to laugh in his stern face. Disappointment's never gotten far with me.

"You couldn't pay me to go back to him, and if it were up to me, I would've already gotten him fired, poured sugar into his gasoline tank, and infected everything he owns with viruses." I take a breath and as I exhale, Salvatore's grip loosens. "But his mom Kristin has done more for me than anyone. She fed me, housed me, and loved me when I didn't deserve any of it and when I needed all of it so badly. If there's anything good in me, it's because she nurtured it. I promised to her that I would take care of Grant and Calvin and Buck, and while I don't owe Grant a *damn* thing, I'll never break my promises to Kristin." I search for understanding in Salvatore's eyes. He has that Bible in his nightstand. He understands devotion to a ghost. "And I need to know you won't break yours, either. Are you going to hurt him?"

In the span of one long breath, Salvatore's fingers tighten and then relax against my back. Like a screw loosening, everything in him releases a measure of tension. "No, passerotta."

Feeling like I've redirected a loaded sniper rifle at the last minute, I smile and stretch up to kiss him. "And I have another request."

A dark eyebrow rises in silent acquiescence.

"I want you to give him a job." Salvatore gives me one of those cute disappointed looks again, and I continue, "Something in his field with average pay that he couldn't mess up. If he's not fired yet, he will be, and I already had to push him to interview for the job he has. I don't want him to suffer if I can do something about it and this way... I can still keep an eye on him."

"I'm sure your Kristin would want her son to become strong. She wouldn't want him to be an impotent man-child."

I laugh. "I'm pretty sure he's an impotent man-child *because* of Kristin. When he didn't make varsity, she tucked him into bed with *Die Hard* and a plate of sugar cookies. If she could've child-proofed all the sharp edges in the world, she would've. I think she'd be proud knowing I got him a cushy job he couldn't be fired from."

Salvatore makes a non-committal humming noise. "So you know, your ex's old boss Terrence is also in the restaurant, hiding at one of the tables. I plan on talking to him as well. He wants to take pictures of me and concoct some blackmail scheme to keep me from bleeding his company dry."

My smile turns sharp. So Grant's concern for me really was a lie to save his own hide? God, he's such a sack of crap.

"Surely Kristin wouldn't be too upset if I cut off only a finger or two?" Salvatore offers at the change in my expression. "It could be just the thing he needs for some character growth."

The thought raises my mood considerably. "You'd better not," I say. "But we should get this over with before I change my mind."

A blast of cold cuts through my wimpy coat as we step out of the car. I fight a shiver as Salvatore calls out in Italian to Davide, reminding myself for the hundredth time that I need to pull my hideous brown winter coat out of storage instead of being vain and using my black peacoat. But when Salvatore shrugs his off and drops it over my shoulders, perfuming the air with his scent and body heat, I remember this is the far superior option.

"You don't have to give me your coat," I offer, but he captures my jaw and presses a hard kiss to my mouth, tongue flickering in to taste me.

"I want to," he murmurs, the words burning down my throat like a shot of whiskey. With a glint of satisfaction in his eye, he ushers me into the restaurant, his palm at my lower back.

"Reservation for Luporini," Salvatore says to the hostess as I scan the dining area for Grant or Terrence.

Vines and pothos plants hang from the ceiling, pops of living green against stains of dark, velvety russets and olive decor, placing us in a nighttime garden or a domesticated jungle. Months back, I saw a grand opening announcement about this restaurant and thought Grant would like the chicken schnitzel, but he was gone so often on the weekends that we never had the chance. Bitterness fills my mouth. I was so hungry for love that I stubbornly ignored every glaring red flag that came my way.

Grant and Lilah are already seated when the hostess takes us over to our table.

Before I have a chance to sit, Salvatore takes my chair and drags it right next to his. He holds it out for me and pushes me in, ignoring everyone else. Once he sits, he swipes the menu and drapes his other arm around the back of my chair, curling his fingers around the nape of my neck. His thumb sparks a burning path where he rubs lazily against my skin. My cheeks burn, but I meet Grant's look of distaste without blinking. Lilah is carefully focused on her own menu.

Barely any time has passed, but Grant looks terrible, I note with a small measure of glee. Now that we're broken up, everything about him is like a shoddy mirror version of what it used to be. His hair isn't cute, it's slovenly. The gap in his teeth looks oafish, and his eyes are too far apart, and his dimple, just like Kristin's... it's his one saving grace. He's lost a bit of weight, and he has bluish circles under his eyes. Guilt lodges itself under my ribs, and then annoyance flares. I can see the roadmap of his entire life—jumping from relationship to relationship because he'll always find a soft woman to land on. Salvatore's right. Grant will never learn.

Lilah looks beautiful in her blush pink dress and an elegant chignon that my thick hair could never be tamed into. She won't meet anyone's eye at the table. Strangely, all I feel for her is a trace of pity. Maybe she'll be smarter than I was and bail out of her relationship with Grant before it's too late.

"Salvatore, this is Grant and Lilah," I say after a long moment of awkward silence. "And this is Salvatore."

"Her husband," Salvatore adds, reaching forward to pour water into our cups from the pitcher on the table.

"H-husband!" Grant splutters. His gaze drops to my wedding ring. "When did you get married?"

"This week," I say, taking a sip from my water in affected casualness. *Guess I'm not so unwedable after all.*

"How long have you known each other?" Grant asks in a pouty voice. Something thumps under the table, and Grant winces. Lilah throws him a dirty look before burying her face in the dinner menu again.

"I've known Marisol for a long time," Salvatore says, brushing invisible lint from his coat on my shoulders. "I'd admired her on the train for months, and when I finally asked her on a date, she'd just recently become single. The timing couldn't have been more perfect."

"Yeah, that's interesting... timing," Grant says. He gives Salvatore a once-over. "What do you do for work?"

"I run a cyber security company called Black Shield Security," Salvatore says with a practiced air.

I swallow my water with some difficulty. I didn't know he owned Black Shield Security. They were a dream hire for me while I was in college. Grant probably doesn't even recognize the name, but the waiter saves him from coming up with an intelligent answer by approaching the table.

"Still looking at the menu?" the waiter asks.

"Seared black sea bass for me," I say. Salvatore orders the same in a bored voice.

When the waiter gets to Grant and Lilah, she orders for the two of them, "I'll take the lamb ribs, and he'll have the chicken schnitzel."

"Are you satisfied?" I ask Grant as the waiter hurries off. "I know it's sudden, but I'm certain. Salvatore makes me happy."

Happy and almost sick with terror that now I have something precious and irreplaceable that I'm supposed to guard for the rest of my life, and that the longer I'm with him, the worse it'll get. The loss of Kristin almost killed me with grief. What would happen if I let Salvatore die? How do normal people fall in love without going mad?

Grant snorts, oblivious as fucking always. "For what, a day? It doesn't strike you as odd that this guy proposed to you after barely knowing you? Did you do"—he glances at Salvatore—"the background check?"

I grit my teeth and claw Salvatore's thigh under the table. "You need to drop it."

Grant opens his mouth to speak, but Salvatore cuts in smooth and soft as a blade through mallow, "She said drop it."

Salvatore touches his knife on the table with the side of his pinky and fixes his gaze on Grant for the first time tonight.

Grant glances between the knife and Salvatore's face, animal instincts finally kicking in. He takes a breath and turns to me, compassion etched across his features. His little puppy-dog act always used to work, but this time I'm asking myself how in the world I found affection for something that constantly shits on my rug. "I just... I'm worried for you, Mari. This isn't like you. What would Mom say?"

Ding, ding, ding!

I close my eyes for a moment. He did it. The ultimate ace card he plays when he wants to win a fight for good.

It didn't matter what she'd say, just the thought that she'd say anything was always enough to make me fold.

I stand up, letting Salvatore's protective arm fall from my shoulders. "I have to go to the bathroom."

I march away from the table before Grant can lob another word. As soon as I've shoved through the swinging door, I scream through gritted teeth.

An older woman with a cane takes one look at me and hobbles out of the bathroom without drying her hands.

Grant's not here because he's worried about me. He's here because he wants to use me as a stinking bucket of chum to lure in Salvatore and please his stupid boss. And meanwhile, he can't help but remind me how utterly shocking it is that anyone would want to be with me— desperate, psycho Mari Vasquez.

I splash water on my cheeks and stare at myself in the mirror.

The woman in the mirror isn't Mari Vasquez anymore. Mary-of-the-Solitude lonely Mari with a deadbeat father's last name and a crazy mother's reputation.

I'm Marisol Luporini. Marisol, said with the full accent that turns my name from an awkward, ill-fitting thing into something dark and sensual, and Luporini, a name of promise and power.

I am... desirable.

Salvatore said he wants me, and he's *proven* it over and over again. I can just... accept that, instead of creating a bunch of reasons like Grant about why Salvatore would be lying about this.

My husband is currently playing nice with my ex-boyfriend because he wanted to show me off, and at a snap of my fingers, he'd do anything I ask. He got me a matching desk so we could be near each other while we work, he eats me out like a man starved, and he carved out his cousin's eye for me.

I laugh at myself, my chest suddenly filling with fizzy delight.

I'm going to find our waiter and get our food to go. Salvatore and I are going home, and then I'm going to rub my tits all over my husband's face while I come on his fat cock.

Plan formed, I leave the bathroom and scan the restaurant for our waiter.

My gaze snags on a familiar face. Terrence hunches over a corner table with a baseball cap low over his face like a paparazzi-harrassed celebrity as he snaps pictures with his phone of... *my* husband.

I take long strides back to our table. At least one idiot is getting put in his place tonight.

"Sal, we're leaving," I say, cutting off whatever dumb bullshit Grant was saying, and without a moment's hesitation, Salvatore stands in one fluid movement.

He reaches into his wallet, pulls out two hundred dollar bills, and tosses them on the table.

"Let's go, passerotta," he says without a hint of surprise or anger. His even tone of voice is a balm to my rage.

I turn on Grant with cool disdain.

"Did you invite your boss here?"

Grant glances down at the table without answer. Lilah gapes openly at him.

"Why would you..." she starts.

I clench my hands into fists. "Grant, I don't ever want to hear from you again."

And even as a mother's guilt shreds into my belly like broken glass, I don't back down. I'm not breaking her promise—I'll take care of Grant, but I'll do it from a distance. She wouldn't have asked me to sacrifice my sanity for Grant's comfort. She loved me too.

As Salvatore and I walk away, he takes my elbow and gently guides me toward Terrence.

Terrence spots us and turns away, finding sudden interest in the wall.

"Why don't we have this conversation outside?" Salvatore says once we're within earshot.

Terrence blanches, his already pale skin turning paper white. "I... I still have to pay."

Salvatore sighs, reaches for his wallet again, and drops another two hundred dollars on the table. "Let's go."

Terrence lifts himself unsteadily from the table and walks toward the exit.

"Have a wonderful night!" the hostess calls out.

Terrence's hand is shaking as he waves goodbye.

Cold air nips my cheeks, but I'm comfortably wrapped in Salvatore's coat. Davide hasn't pulled the car around yet, but Salvatore seems to know where we're going.

"Over here," Salvatore says, pointing toward a dark alley on the side of the restaurant.

Terrence straightens his back. He looks just like I remember, pale skin and sandy hair. His navy coat only makes his beige, washed-out features stand out more starkly.

"I'd like to stay where there are witnesses," Terrence says, his eyes darting around wildly before landing on a family of four streaming into Nahash.

Salvatore shrugs. "Do you know who I am?"

Some of the bravado seeps out of Terrence's stance. His shoulders cave in. "You're the... Mafia," he whispers.

"And you still thought it'd be a good idea to show your face tonight? To take pictures of me and ruin my wife's dinner?"

I can't keep my eyes off Salvatore. He's so calm and unruffled. This could be the hundredth time he's had to give this speech. His high cheekbones and prominent nose cut a striking, fierce expression in the half-light of the street lamps.

"I'm going to send those pictures to the police!" Terrence hisses. "I'm going to show them the criminal who's hacking my company. I *knew* you guys were responsible, and I'm not going to stop until you see justice!"

Salvatore laughs, cold and cutting. He shoves his hands into his pockets and peers down at the smaller man. "Justice? Where was the justice for those warehouse workers in Biên Hòa?"

Terrence's eyes go wide as dinner plates. "W-what? H-h-how did you?"

"Do you remember how many people were trapped in that fire, Terrence Kinney?"

"I don't know what you're talking about!"

"One hundred and twelve. Do you remember how many were children? Thirty-four. And who got that email discussing unsafe conditions a week before the fire broke out?"

Terrence's eyes well up. He wipes the back of his hand across his face.

I stare. When did this happen? I had access to all of Terrence's emails, and I would've remembered something like *this*. Did he hide it?

"That's right. *You* did. And you said you didn't give a shit so long as your quotas were met." Salvatore leans in, his face bright and hungry. "And then you covered it up and moved operations to another warehouse one block away. Where's their justice?"

"That wasn't my fault," Terrence whispers. "I... I wasn't there. I didn't mean..."

Salvatore laughs and claps his hand on Terrence's shoulder. "Of course, it was your fault. But maybe you're still not understanding. Like how Cynthia didn't understand why you left her with that kid of yours and no child support. She can afford hearing aids on a teacher's salary, right? And who else is gonna give money to those strippers at Hattie's?"

Tears stream down Terrence's face. He glances at me, and Salvatore slaps his cheek in warning. The sound is brief but jarring. Terrence's eyes snap back to Salvatore.

"You don't look at my wife," Salvatore says, and for the first time, a hint of anger steeps into his voice. "Not when you're not fit to lick the bottom of her shoe. Tell you what, Terrence. If this were any other night, I'd take you to that back alley and give you the *justice* you deserve, but my wife's hungry, and I want to take her home to eat. So I'll leave you with a warning. If I *ever* see your worthless face again, it'll be the last time. And you're gonna stop spreading these harmful lies about your made-up shadow organizations. If someone *is* stealing money from that company of yours, then that sounds like justice to me, don't you think?"

Terrence nods, sobbing openly. "I'm sorry... please don't tell Cynthia..."

Salvatore drops his hand from Terrence's face with a sound of disgust and wipes it against his pants. "You're a real piece of shit, Terrence Kenney. Give me your phone —*unlocked*—and get the fuck out of my face."

Terrence scrambles for his phone and types in the password, all zeros, before thrusting it into Salvatore's hands and stumbling away. Salvatore flicks through Terrence's phone until he finds the photos of us and deletes them. He lets the phone drop to the concrete and crushes it underfoot.

"Well," Salvatore says, swiveling all of that intensity to me like a floodlight. "I hope that didn't ruin your appetite too much."

"Is it true? All those things you told him?" His coat feels like a warm, heavy embrace and an impenetrable suit of armor at the same time. I lean toward him.

"That's not even the worst of it. I'll bleed that bastard dry and let his ex-wife pick over the bones. She'll have a lawyer offer to come work for her pro bono soon enough."

"Sal," I start, but I can't finish with the lump in my throat. I stand up on my toes and crush my mouth to his. His hands brace me against him.

This cold, ruthless, *tender* man is all mine.

25

MARISOL

SOMETHING'S OFF with this strip club.

I freeze the video and peer closer at the redhead on Junior's lap. *Thud, thud.*

I recognize her nails. Lime-green acrylics designed to look like cute little kiwi fruit. The video clip from the night before shows a woman with blue hair sitting on Junior's lap. *Thud, thud, thud.* Same acrylics.

I lean back in my chair, searching for any video footage with those green nails and splitting them off to different monitors. It's the same woman. Different wigs and wildly different outfits... even different tattoos. What could this mean?

Thud, thud, thud, thud, thud.

I swivel in my chair. "Like I said the first twenty times, I can't work while you're pacing around like that."

Dom doesn't look up from his book, and he doesn't stop from treading a furrow into the carpet. "Like *I* said. Not gonna happen."

I rub my face into my palms and exhale hard. It's been over a month since the dinner with Grant, and whenever

Salvatore and I aren't working, we've been fucking or sleeping. It's been bliss. He left early this evening to have dinner with Senator Balast, and I stayed back to scroll through a mountain of footage of Junior without Salvatore standing over my shoulder. He needs to stay focused on Rekhson. If he knew how many of my nightmares and shadowed corners I see Junior in... well, I don't want him to get distracted.

Just like how Dom's distracting me. He's been pacing through the room, flicking pens against Salvatore's desk, or launching Buck's toys against the walls for hours, and it's driving me nuts. Compared to my calm, motionless husband, Dom's a tornado of movement and sound. And apparently, he's not allowed to leave me alone. Which is fucking great.

"Why don't you help me with this?" I say in a kindergarten-teacher tone.

"Why don't you get fucked?" Dom asks. He slows to a halt and looks up at me. "Uh... sorry."

I've been playing video games for years and some of those twelve-year-olds can be wildly creative. At this point, "getting fucked" barely registers as a curse.

I raise an eyebrow. "Are you gonna take a look at this or not?"

Dom chucks his book onto Salvatore's desk, earning a death glare from Buck who was napping in the nearby chair.

"Your cat's an asshole."

"Yeah, I know."

Dom comes to stand behind me, tucking his hands into his pockets. Now that he's finally still, I can focus long enough to scrub through the strip club footage for more shots of Kiwi Nails.

"What do you notice?" I ask, as I drop more images of Kiwi into my spare monitors.

"Is that a trick question?"

I freeze, my mouse on Kiwi shoving her bare ass into some guy's face. "What *else* do you notice?"

Dom laughs.

Once I've collected enough shots of Kiwi and her different clients—and she must be popular because there are a lot—I start grouping the clients together as best I can.

"Do you recognize any of these guys?"

Dom leans forward, squinting at the monitor. Whereas Salvatore's built like a panther, all lean muscle and quiet confidence, Dom's a bear. Tall, massive, and hairy. Probably has an industrial-sized shower drain.

"Him," Dom says, pointing to a man with a full-sleeve tattoo of a snarling dog. "That's Mad Dog Colin. Crazy bastard. Turi's caught him sniffing around Barbara's warehouses recently. I bet they're using that stripper to communicate. Nice work."

I roll my eyes. "Gee, thanks."

"Can you find all the men this woman's talked to for the past month?"

"I could..." I point to Salvatore's chair. "If you can sit still for more than a few minutes."

"I'll see what I can do."

Several hours later, he's asleep in Salvatore's chair, and I have my data.

I swipe a stack of sticky notes off my desk and lob them at Dom, expecting them to bounce off his belly, but at the last minute, he jerks up and catches them with more speed and grace than I'd expect from such a big man. He groans as he stretches long, dropping the notes onto Salvatore's desk.

"What the hell was that for?" he mutters.

"I'm done."

Scratching at his beard, Dom lumbers over to inspect my findings.

"So these are the woman's top five clients for the past month. Junior, Mad Dog, and these three guys. Do you recognize them?"

Dom leans in and squints. "All but one. See what Worm says about him. The other two are part of the Irish mob. I'd bet my left nu—kidney... that they're planning something. I'll have a talk with Gavin. He's Mad Dog's brother and the only sane one in the whole damn lot."

"I was thinking..." I say slowly. Dom crosses his arms and gives me a bemused look. "What if we sent someone to talk to the woman? See what she says."

"Junior'll sniff out we're tracking him. You willing to risk her life and the man we send?"

I hesitate, glancing back at the monitors. Dom bellows a laugh. "You're fucking ruthless, you know that? Sal's got a weird taste in women."

"Meaning what? Grown adults?"

For a beat, we stare at each other.

Then Dom smiles, and it's a cruel-looking thing. "I don't know what you *think* you know, but I'm not looking for judgment from the woman who'll let anyone get slaughtered if it means she gets to keep her pet capo."

What I *think* I know is that Salvatore told me Dom's always been especially protective of Annetta, Serafina's twin, who was sent off to be married at eighteen to a capo in Florida a few years ago. Whatever Dom's relationship to her, I can't imagine loving someone and letting them go like that.

"I wouldn't let anyone hurt Sal if I had a say in it. And if we don't take Junior down, Annetta's sister is gonna be his new stepmom. Fifth time's the try, I guess."

Dom laughs, low and dark as he leans down to face me. "Serafina's still got a few months before the wedding. A lot can happen between now and then. But since you know everything, why don't I send Davide over to that strip club? Let's see what happens."

"Deal."

A FEW DAYS LATER, I make the final adjustments on my website as Buck supervises me from the end of my desk.

Dom's been sweet-talking Caruso, an unsmiling, traditional capo, for weeks, warming him to the possibilities of Salvatore's resources at his fingertips. Caruso agreed, in the vaguest terms, to throw his weight behind Salvatore if we could cut off the head of "that Russian bastard's second-rate gambling operation", so I've spent every waking moment designing a fake website for the Golden Apple Casino, the business baby of Caruso's oldest enemy, as our first act of good faith. The moment this goes live, I'll redirect the flow of virtual traffic from the real casino to my imposter site, taking down the Golden Apple for a couple of days and harvesting all their sweet, sweet customer data while they go on a wild goose chase to recover their stolen domain name. Once Caruso's onboard, Dom thinks the other old-guard capos will be easier to sway.

I'm crossing my fingers that they won't all need a massive cyber-sabotage operation to convince—I don't know how many I can pull off on my own, and the rest of Worm's team is stretched thin. For weeks, Worm and Genghis Con have been sifting through mountains of data for anything they can use on Salvatores's dad Ottavio while dropTable does the same with District Attorney Rekhson.

In strip clubs and cigar shops, Dom and the rest of his

men are bribing and threatening the other capos to join Salvatore's cause.

No one's said it out loud, but we're all thinking the same thing: Salvatore's preparing his contingency plans. Rekhson, the Commission, or Aldo could retaliate at any moment, so he needs the Chicago capos at his side.

If this doesn't all go perfectly, he's going to start a war.

As for my own plan B, once I discovered the encrypted phone network CryptTalk was *already* infected with malware by Dutch police, Worm and Salvatore green-lit the operation of a Luporini phone manufacturer and network carrier. When—and not *if*—the police build enough of a case against CryptTalk's criminal customers, they'll hamstring everyone's communications at once—everyone, except the Family's. Once everything comes to light, Salvatore will look like a hero.

Or, if Salvatore needs a nuclear option, a little nudge to the police will set things in motion early, throwing even the Family into a complete network blackout for weeks, if not months.

After I brought this forward, Salvatore fucked me reverently for hours, hissing praise in my ear the entire time.

The memory makes me glance his way.

He stands with his arms crossed, his fourth cup of espresso hooked on a long finger. The intense frown darkening his face suggests disappointment with the whole cluster of monitors in front of him. Every few minutes, he stirs to change an image or two.

Worm's mentioned several times that he's never seen Salvatore under this much stress. I can see the effects on everyone else. Dom's been a walking powder keg, yelling at all the men and stomping into the house with blood on his knuckles. Davide's a nervous wreck. Giordana snaps at everyone who crosses her path. Camillo and Nola are constantly whispering to each other in the kitchen. But Salvatore seems unaffected.

His phone rings on his desk, and he answers with a tap.

Speaking in rushed Italian, a man's voice pipes into the room.

Salvatore adjusts several of his monitors until they land on the interior of the Capitol—scenery I'm becoming intimately familiar with. He listens passively for the most part, only asking the other man a few brief questions until he catches me watching and crooks a finger in my direction.

I should get back to work, I think, even as an invisible string tugs me forward.

Once I'm standing before him, he reaches out to run his fingers through my hair.

I've learned how much he loves to touch my hair. How much he loves to rub his face into my breasts and knead my belly and grip my thighs. He worships my softness.

I turn my face to kiss the inside of his forearm, and he pauses, waiting patiently until I've lifted my lips from his skin.

He treats every single touch from me like the most precious gift.

Desire flares to life inside me, sharp and unbearable. I've been told and shown in a hundred different ways these past few weeks that if Salvatore messes up what he's doing, we're all fucked. But the only worry I feel is a sort of aching desperation to steal more kisses and affection before the timer runs out.

I give Salvatore a sly smile and drop to my knees at his feet.

He smiles back, but he doesn't adjust his belt and doesn't stop stroking my hair as I kneel before him.

"Allora, cosa farai adesso?" Salvatore asks in his rich Italian, his eyes fixed on me.

The other man bursts into a long response, but whatever Salvatore said wasn't to him. He's talking to me.

I touch the warm metal of his belt buckle, my forearm brushing against his rising erection, but he stops me with a firm hand to my wrist.

He takes a step back to his chair, sits, and pats his upper thigh. So he wants to play this game instead?

I rise to straddle his lap, but before I can kiss him, he twists me so my back is to his front and traps my head against his shoulder, baring my throat. With his free hand, he touches me—stroking down my hair, collaring my neck, rubbing and cupping each breast, seeking every inch of softness on his way down. He finds my clit over my cotton shorts and rubs in tight circles.

I jut my hips into his hands as my face burns. A few nights ago, he made me spread my legs on the bed and show him how I got myself off. Then he made me come three more times as he mastered the technique. Heat builds with every strum of his talented fingers.

He shoves his hand inside the waistband of my shorts, and when he touches the wetness gathered in my panties, his entire body tenses under mine.

"Ho avuto un imprevisto. Continueremo questo più tardi."

Without waiting for a response, Salvatore reaches over to hang up. Abruptly, he shoves me forward onto the plush carpet, softening the fall at the last second with his arm wrapped around my waist so I float onto my hands and knees. I barely have time to grasp what's happening before he wrenches my shorts down and plunges into me.

I jerk forward, almost head-butting the floor, but he's

still got me. He cups a handful of my breast and ruts into me with harsh thrusts.

I cry out in delighted surprise, my clit throbbing with need, and Salvatore laughs.

"You shouldn't have spent all day tempting me if you didn't want to get fucked like an animal, passerotta."

He completely pulls out of me and spanks me hard before shoving back in again. Pleasure tears through me as I squeal and buck under him. He wrenches me up against him, gripping my jaw in his hand, and hisses in my ear, "I've been under a lot of stress, Marisol. I won't be held accountable for my actions while you let everyone see your cunt through those tiny shorts. Is that what you want, you little tease? You want to push your husband to the edge?"

"Sir, I'm... I'm gonna come," is all I can get out before Salvatore twists my nipple, and I whimper.

His cruel laugh is low and rich in my ear. "You were made for me, passerotta. You were made for my pleasure."

"Yes... s-sir."

Salvatore bites into my shoulder like a beast, setting off a hot and dirty orgasm that rips through me like a tornado. He crushes my body into his, and then he's coming too, the faint pulses inside me setting off aftershocks of pleasure.

We catch our breath in the otherwise silent room. Salvatore eases me onto the carpet where I lie like a rag doll.

"Stay there. I'll be right back."

His footsteps fade away to the connected bathroom, and after a minute, he returns. I jolt at the sensation of a warm, wet washcloth between my legs, but Salvatore soothes me with a *shh* and a hand down my spine. He kisses the spot he bit, and once I'm clean, he gathers me into his arms and sits us both on his computer chair.

We watch the monitors for a while as I bask under a golden sunbeam of contentment.

When he reaches for his espresso again, some of my awareness returns.

"What was that call about?" I ask. I glance through the monitors showing the Capitol.

"We bribed an intern in Rekhson's office to convince her to drop the case she's building against Aldo."

"And it didn't work?"

Salvatore kisses my shoulder. "How'd you guess?"

"You don't want me to give you blow jobs when you're upset."

Salvatore stills for a moment, considering this. "I don't want to be too harsh with you and have you not be able to clearly tell me to stop."

That's... kind of sweet? In either case, I certainly won't say no to the pleasant soreness of his angry fucks. "I trust you. I know you wouldn't hurt me."

He doesn't answer and instead hugs me closer against him. His cock gives a valiant stirring underneath me.

"Are you gonna plant another intern in her office?"

He sighs. "No. I'll leave her alone for a while. Not make it so obvious she's getting under our skin. But time isn't on our side. She has a charity gala coming up next week—I'll donate an obscene amount of money and talk to her then. Maybe she'll pick up it's better to be friends than enemies."

"Am I going with you?"

He hesitates. "If you want to. You're doing important work. I don't want to interrupt it just so you can be on my arm." He rubs his face into my neck and palms one of my breasts. "I won't lie, though, the thought is very tempting. I wonder what I could get away with while there's a crowd of people nearby."

I nearly scoff at the idea that I'm doing "important work", considering I've been fucking around with logos of cartoon apples for the past hour.

"I'd love to come," I say, before a wet blanket settles over my excitement. "I'll need a nice dress though, right?"

"I have a personal shopper. She'll take care of it," Salvatore says. He nips at my ear. "You can thank me on your knees later."

"Sounds like I should be thanking your personal shopper," I laugh.

He growls and pins me to him. "Over my dead body."

26

SALVATORE

IF I DON'T STOP, I'm going to rub a damn hole through her wrist.

I release Marisol's arm, but after a few seconds, my hand inevitably drifts to her waist. I'm not a superstitious man, but I can't stop from touching her like she's my personal rabbit's foot. She raises her dark eyes to me and smiles, sweet and sincere, though I've seen how quickly it can darken into something wicked. Her garnet off-the-shoulder gown hints at her true nature.

Below us, politicians and donors trickle into the industrial loft in singles and pairs before gravitating to the cloth-covered cocktail tables and buffet. I had a few cameras installed months ago when this event was booked, nearly out of force of habit rather than practicality, and I wonder if I'll fish anything useful from the footage. The old-school jazz singer crooning through the DJ's speakers makes general audio recording pointless. Camillo, Eduardo, and Dom, dressed in black suits and ties, are largely lost to the crowd, although I know they'll be hovering near the exits.

This is the type of easy, rewarding event to take a newer

made man like Davide, but Dom's already sent him out to a strip club this evening. Marisol hadn't mentioned anything to me about her findings or her request to Dom, but I'm content to see it played out. Dom wouldn't have obeyed her unless he thought the idea had merit.

Not that he's been a great help lately. Serafina's been like a little sister to him for years, and each day brings her closer to Aldo's bedroom and Junior's periphery. Dom's over at the Barbaras' every chance he gets, keeping an eye on the family and slowly poisoning Barbara against Aldo. It's a long shot. Barbara's been Aldo's righthand man for decades. He'll sooner cut Dom out like a tumor before he turns on his own don. But, Dom's always been close to his family. If anyone stands a chance, it's Dom.

Normally, I'm not afraid to take risks—it's all part of the job. But I'm on fucking edge tonight, and it's no mystery why.

The poison and the cure's right here with me, lockpicks stuffed in her bra, peering intently over the handrails at the supposedly hidden location for my third downstairs camera.

She performed for me in the shower again before we got ready for the gala. I lasted half as long as the first time before tearing open the glass door and storming in after her. She'd just laughed.

She's always laughing or teasing me, a bright northern star in the heavens of a black, storm-tossed sea.

I tuck a lock of her hair behind her ear, and her hair's so thick it jumps back into place. She stops her slow cataloging of my *hidden* cameras and turns to me, the corner of her mouth tilting upward.

"It won't taste as good if you let it go warm," I say, nodding to the flute of champagne she's been swirling for the past twenty minutes.

She holds it aloft with a sly grin. "Want it?"

"I don't drink."

"Because of your mom?"

"Yes. But you can still drink."

"But you hate it when I do, don't you?" Her grin widens. And she doesn't say it, but I can hear her. *Gotcha.*

With anyone else, the lie would be easy enough. *I couldn't care less.* But Marisol's a pearler. Once she senses a payout, she'll pry and dig and gouge until she harvests another gleaming pearl of information. We're the same like that.

There's no point in hiding something from her, so I don't try.

"I do."

She sets the champagne on the little table behind her. "I prefer soda anyway."

That's the other reason I don't hide from her. She accepts it all. Every raw, twisted, blackened, stinking, defenseless part of me. It's like she wants to catalog my every atom so she knows exactly where she needs to apply tender affection.

If she's doing it to manipulate me, I don't care.

She could point me like a gun in any direction, and I'd serve her without question.

If she doesn't tell me soon that she loves me back, I'll go insane.

I cup her face in my hand. Her face brightens. She loves this game. I think she loves it more, knowing how much it tortures me. "Have I told you tonight that I love you?"

"Not in the past five minutes."

I lean down to kiss a path from her cheek to her neck. "In that case, I am furiously, desperately in love with you, Marisol."

Her breath hitches, and she leans in close enough that her breasts and belly curve against me. All the stress and frustration melt out of me at her touch, although it's a small relief when an aching hunger comes flooding into their place.

"And I love... this new dress."

I wrench her against me to whisper in her ear, "I thought I taught you what happens when you tease me."

"I thought you knew I'm a terrible student." Her free hand skates along my forearm and squeezes. I brush a thumb along her nipple, and she melts further. "Someone's going to see us."

It's not a complaint. My little daredevil wife's instigating me. I can feel her smile against my chest.

Downstairs, Dom catches my eye as a laughing, dark-haired socialite in a green dress hangs off his arm. He dips his head to his right and then turns back to his date.

District Attorney Rekhson's at the foot of the stairs, nodding attentively to a fat old donor. We still have a little time.

I crane over Marisol and splay my hand along her lower back. She shivers when my lips touch her ear. "If the student hasn't learned, the teacher hasn't taught. I think what you need is a more advanced demonstration. Maybe I'll have to lean you over these handrails and thrust into your sweet cunt until you say what I want to hear. You could use some hints from the crowd."

Marisol tucks her burning-hot face into my shoulder and clutches my suit jacket.

"Tell me to stop, passerotta." I pause and then grin. "Would you prefer I stalk you into a dark corner of this room and make my men stand guard while I finger you to completion? Maybe you can get on your hands and knees and make all the dirty old men here green with envy that *my* wife is the most beautiful, most talented woman here."

Rekhson's close-by, practiced laugh cuts through my fantasy.

"Lucky break. We were about to play Truth or Dare," I say. I grab Marisol's hand to pull her along, but she jerks me to a stop like a dog on a leash.

"I just need a moment." She takes a few deep breaths with a dreamy smile. I avert my eyes to give myself the chance to will my erection back down. "Okay. Ready."

Once Rekhson stations herself along the rails with her husband, watching the crowd below just like Marisol and I were moments ago, we approach.

"Marjorie Rekhson," I call out. Rekhson looks up with a photo-perfect smile, trying to place my face. "What a pleasure it is to finally meet you in person."

She relaxes a little and smiles back at me. "Lovely to meet you...?"

"Salvatore Luporini," I say, and her smile turns poisonous. "And this is my wife, Marisol Luporini."

Judging by the angry fire in Rekhson's eyes, she recognizes my name. Good. That'll make the next part go much more smoothly.

Marisol steps toward Mr. Rekhson. "What a beautiful event. Who picked out the location?"

Mr. Rekhson, looking like an overgrown cherub with his chubby face, curly blonde hair, and baby blue bowtie, launches into a practiced speech about how difficult it was to secure this local, but well worth it given the number in attendance and for such an important cause, didn't she think?

"Let's grab a drink," I say to Rekhson. She glances back

at her husband with a hint of concern and then turns back to me and nods, determined.

We walk a little ways away to a small table where a waiter's serving champagne and both grab a glass. Rekhson holds hers at waist height but doesn't take a sip. Neither do I.

"How's the fundraiser going?" I ask. "I know how difficult it can be to get support for some of these events. Especially when they're pet projects like this one."

"Yes... well, thank you for such a *generous* donation," Rekhson says. She looks a little at war with herself and finally sips from the champagne. "I have to admit, I was surprised to see the Luporini Foundation making such a large donation to the charity for victims of *gang* violence."

I smile. My gaze wanders back to Marisol who's nodding as Mr. Rekhson speaks animatedly. In my side vision, Mrs. Rekhson eyes me like she'd love to lunge forward and rip out my jugular with her teeth.

"Mr. Luporini was very invested in the success of your predecessor, Harrison. He helped Harrison do a lot of good for the city. He'd be very interested in helping you do the same."

Rekhson narrows her eyes, smile still pasted on. "Good for the city? Like passing the bill to *lighten* sentencing for gangsters?"

"Prisons can encourage recidivism. Mr. Luporini believes in the use of community hours, which give back to the city instead of punishing a single individual."

"Those individuals rarely got to contribute to their communities when Harrison miscategorized so many essential files."

"Digitalization is very important in today's day and age. Something funding can help promote."

"His lack of enforcement of antitrust laws—"

"Mr. Luporini is a firm supporter of healthy business practices and competition. I'm sure if you and your husband accepted his invitation to dinner, he'd be able to discuss those topics with you at length." I pause. "We could meet Friday night. Donatella's? Your two lovely daughters and their families would be more than welcome to join."

Friday nights are Rekhson's special date nights with her husband. Usually at Donatella's.

Rekhson's smile finally falls, but instead of fear, it exposes a look of steely composure, which is a bad fucking sign for me. "Is that supposed to be a threat?"

"Of course not," I say evenly. "There's nothing Mr. Luporini believes in more than the sanctity and importance of family. That's part of why this event is so near and dear to his heart. You should accept the dinner invitation, Ms. Rekhson. Mr. Luporini can do a lot of good for you and your city."

Rekhson sets her champagne down on a nearby table and turns to me, eyes glinting. "Please thank your boss for his generous donation. He can let his accountant know it can be written off as a charity donation. And also to let his accountant know he should be recording *all* of his income streams."

"My boss won't be too happy to hear this, District Attorney Rekhson," I say quietly. In my peripherals, Marisol glances over at me. "I highly suggest you reconsider. We'll be at Donatella's this Friday at six. I hope to see you there."

"I don't dine with criminals, Mr. Luporini." Rekhson gives me one last look and joins her husband, whispering in his ear as she pulls him toward the stairs.

Well, that went about as well as I'd expected.

A dull roar sounds at the edges of my hearing.

I could just shoot her now. There's a big crowd—maybe it'd cover the crime.

I track the Rekhsons until Marisol's close enough to touch my elbow. Although her look is questioning, she doesn't ask how it went. My little hacker knows better than to voice her thoughts out loud in a public place.

I drink in her bright, curious face, in contrast with the deep, mature red of her dress, and something in me calms— no, not calms. The tension just flows in a different direction.

"Have I told you how much I love you?" I ask. I'm going to get my wife home and have her ride my face until I can't think.

She breaks into an unsure smile, but she plays along. "Not recently."

"Come along. I think it's best if I *show* you."

MARISOL TRACKS some invisible point on the ceiling as her chest heaves up and down.

"Sal," she says languidly. Her eyes are glazed over with bliss as she turns to look at me. "That was amazing."

What's amazing is that in two months' timeframe, I've made almost no progress in keeping my wife's eyes in her head and the both of us in one piece. I haven't talked to Marisol about it yet, but I've been marking out a few locations for safe houses in case this all goes to shit. If we can't handle this in a few weeks, I'll either have to stage a coup or take Marisol and run, leaving all of my staff and men here to suffer Aldo's—and Junior's—rage.

I roll over Marisol, caging her on the bed in my arms.

She gives me a lazy smile that has my dick swelling, though I'll need more time to go again. That's fine. I'll get her ready with my fingers.

She jerks when I scrap the pad of my thumb against her clit.

"So sensitive," I tease.

"That's what happens when you come three times in a row," she says, but her hips rock into my hand, and her hands brush over my chest. "What happens next?"

"I'm going to rub you until you're right on the edge of another orgasm, and if you come too quickly, I'm going to spank you and make you start over. Then I want you to keep holding off until I've filled you up."

She exhales, her cheeks flushed and eyes bright. "I-I meant with Rekhson."

My hand jerks over her clit. For a moment, I pause, staring into her face. Then I drop my hand lower to push two fingers against her entrance, sliding into her wet heat up to the second knuckle. She squirms underneath me.

"New plan," I say. "I'm going to see how many fingers I can fit into you until you come."

Knock, knock.

"Turi, get dressed. You'll wanna see this," Dom calls through the door. I jerk my fingers out from inside her.

"What's going on?" she whispers, eyes wide.

"I don't know," I say, tasting bitterness. I should know exactly what's going on, but I've been avoiding my work for the past two hours by feasting on my wife. I kiss her and push myself off the bed. "I'll be back soon. Don't move."

Dom's halfway down the hall when I slip out of the bedroom a few minutes later. He spins, and the look on his face drops a lead weight in my stomach.

"It's Davide. In the kitchen," he says. "Mad Dog got him."

The weight turns into molten rock, bubbling and burning through my veins. Everything Mad Dog touches turns to shit. If he's hurt one of my men, we're going to war with the Irish—and I can't fucking afford another conflict right now.

We turn the corner to the kitchen to find Davide waiting on a bar stool, looking fifteen years old in his dove grey sweater. Rust-colored splotches stain the fabric near his neck and a long strip of white gauze wraps around his head.

It covers his eye.

Dr. Macaluso pops up from behind the counter with a bottle of white wine. On the other side of the bar, Giordana's in a fluffy pink robe and slippers. She must be exhausted this late at night, but she's still got plenty of energy to glare daggers at Dr. Macaluso over her cup of tea.

"What happened?" I ask in a low voice, biting back the overwhelming urge to shout.

Davide meets my gaze with his one good eye—blue and a little glassy, likely from pain meds—before glancing at Dom.

"I sent him to Lucky Stars," Dom says. "Found out there was a stripper there who dances for Junior, Mad Dog, Mattie, and Feisty. But Davide barely got a chance to talk to the girl before Mad Dog and Feisty came into the club. They took Davide to the back alley and cut his face up. Left him there to bleed out. He managed to call Macaluso, and they came here straight after. Doc says he won't be able to see out of that eye again."

"And the girl?"

"Gone. Worm's looking for her."

"Cams in the alley?"

"No."

I exhale on a count of three. I want to throw myself at the kitchen bar and break every glass and plate there and strangle Macaluso for being so *fucking* drunk all the time, but that's not what my men need from me right now. They need a cool head. A leader.

I clap a hand on Davide's shoulder. "You did good. Go home and get some rest."

Davide looks up at me. When the damage to his eye heals, he won't have a baby face anymore. "I want to stay. I want to work."

"You want revenge, and I promise you'll get it, but it won't come overnight. Now, you need to rest. You call me if there's any other detail you remember, even if you think it's not important. When Macaluso says you're clear, you and I, we'll make a plan to get back at those bastards."

He's disappointed but nods anyway. He knows I'm right, even if I'm being a fucking hypocrite by telling him to rest. He shouldn't have made the mistake of coming back here. If he really wanted revenge, he would've stayed out until he got it.

"Dom, can you take Davide home?"

"Sure, boss."

I glance at Macaluso with his half-empty bottle of wine. "And Macaluso too."

Dom grunts.

"Give me that," Giordana says, swiping the bottle from the doctor.

I turn and make my way back upstairs.

Marisol's wide awake, dressed in one of my t-shirts and eating the rest of the gummy worms from my lockbox of her things.

"What's going on?" she asks, setting the empty candy bag on her nightstand.

I sit on the edge of the bed and take my time to properly fold my shoes, socks, pants, and shirt as I fill her in. Only once I've finished, do I look up at her. Her dark eyes are wide, and her hands are a fidgety mess on her lap.

"I have something to tell you," she says in a near-whisper.

She needs to be punished.

She needs to learn not to send my men out like pawns. Any other man in my employ would be out on the street right now, helping to hunt down Mad Dog and Fiesty.

But instead, I smooth my fingers over hers and pull her into me until she's completely wrapped in my arms.

She starts to object, but I shush her gently. "You're not ever going to keep me in the dark again, are you?"

She lays her head against my chest. "It wasn't a secret. You were watching."

I stroke her long, soft tresses, now mine to touch as I please and not pixels on a screen. "I can't catch everything. So next time, you'll tell me."

"Okay."

I sigh against her head, staring at the dark shadows in the corner of my room. "I'm doing everything I can to trap Junior and keep you safe."

That's what she'd been looking for, wasn't it? An opportunity to catch Junior. I let him live, and now I'm letting him haunt her.

"It's not enough," she says in a small voice.

"I took his eye."

"It's not enough." Her nails dig into my back as she forms two tight fists.

She's right.

I kiss the top of her head and hold her in the darkness.

27

SALVATORE

MY HAND SHAKES as I bring a cup of espresso to my mouth, droplets splattering onto my t-shirt collar. Sloppy.

Common sense would say to stop drinking the caffeine.

But I have forty days left and nothing to show for it.

Before the dinner with Rekhson, I had men driving past her house, getting coffee at her favorite cafe, and sitting in the waiting area of her husband's pharmacy. All to remind her of the very real threat I hold behind my back while I offer her friendship. She didn't show up at Donatella's.

After, Dom knocked on her door at night and, with his sharp-toothed smile, asked if she'd be interested in going to see her favorite opera with Aldo.

She tried slamming the door in Dom's face, but he pushed through to finish their chat. Again, she said no. Now she has a police chaperone with her, her husband, and her daughters' families at all times.

Worm has a few leads on my dad, but nothing so damning that we could strongarm him into vouching for us with the Commission. It'll need to be ironclad to make that good-for-nothing bastard help us. If I was on fire, I doubt he'd bother to spit.

I rake a hand through my hair and change the images in front of me to Aldo's house and Junior's strip club Lucky Stars.

It's unlikely I'll get an extension of time—Junior's been in Aldo's ear for two months, telling him how I broke omertà for taking his eye and asking him what kind of father he is to let this happen.

I shove my shaking hands in my pockets and turn toward Marisol's desk.

A set of pink headphones on, she has her feet tucked under her ass as she leans forward to squint at one of her monitors. She finished the Golden Apple website yesterday and has already thrown herself into her next assignment, assembling a botnet to attack the casino again.

We've been arguing more. I haven't blamed her or punished her for her part in sending Davide to lose his eye, but she's paying penance for it all the same. She falls asleep at her desk more often than not. It's a struggle to get her to do her rehab exercises or to eat anything other than candy.

On some level, I knew she'd be like this—like me. Loyal. Hard-working. Obsessive. So when I took her and placed her in this world, I thought I would know best how to protect her from those traits, but I can't seem to purge the poison fast enough.

I don't want her to suffer for any reason, least of all an honest mistake. Dom and I approved sending Davide too. It was a risk, and it didn't pay off, but Marisol seems intent on resting the world on her shoulders.

That's supposed to be my job.

The door beeps.

Marisol yanks off her headphones, snapping her head toward the newcomer like she's bracing to be slapped.

Dom waltzs in, stretching out his shoulders and rubbing the back of his neck.

"How'd it go?" Marisol asks as she scrambles to her feet. The DNS attack she'd been working on for a month was finally put into play last night, but her website crashed too early. Dom left to do what he could with Caruso to spin the outage situation into gold. Another failure, in her eyes.

I woke up to an empty bed this afternoon and found my little hacker at her desk, destroying the end of a ballpoint pen with her teeth. Even exhaustion is alluring on her, the dark circles under her eyes making her look hypnotic and tragic. In lieu of breakfast, I took her belly-up on her desk while her breasts jiggled in my palms.

She made me like this.

I made her like this.

"He wasn't happy at first," Dom says somberly, and then his face splits into a wolfish grin. "But when I explained to him crashing the website meant all those customers lost trust in good ol' Golden Apple, he came around. He wants you to go ahead with the bot attack."

"Botnet," Marisol and I correct at the same time. She glances toward me and hides a smirk.

Dom groans. "Fucking *nerds*. Yeah, I'll just pat my own back later. Turi, you ready to go?"

"Grab some lunch. We'll be down in a bit."

"We?" Dom asks, eyebrow cocked.

"Boss's orders. He just texted me."

Dom gives me a meaningful look but leaves the room without a word.

Marisol tracks my movement with her dark eyes as I

draw near. In another life, she would've compelled sailors to wreckage with those eyes. Fuck, in this life too.

"I told you, you have nothing to worry about." I stroke the length of her ponytail, willing my hand to be steady.

"And I told *you*, letting the entire database crash was a brain-dead mistake. I should've known better."

Marisol purses her lips together in that prim expression she makes when she's upset. I force a smile down. She's too cute like this.

I already talked to Worm. The fake website she built for Caruso crashed in the scant few hours she slept. She lost the data for thousands of customers, and in that time, the real Golden Casino got their act together and rerouted their customers back to the correct website. Worm said it was a rookie mistake, but that what she did in such a small amount of time, with barely any input from him, was still incredibly impressive. He showed her how she could correct her error next time and privately mentioned to me that she'd be teaching him new things within the year.

"Dom fixed it. Caruso's happy. That's a success, passerotta."

Marisol scowls. "No *passerotta*. What would you say to me if I were a regular person on your team, and I did this?"

I kiss her temple. God, she smells good. Feminine, soothing, and almost saccharine from the candy she hides in her desk. Even an innocent kiss makes my cock swell. If we survive this, I'm seriously considering splitting my desk with her so that she can work from my lap all day long. I'd never get a thing done, but it'd be bliss.

"I'd tell them they're new and that I expect them to make mistakes."

Marisol shoves me off. "Oh, really? Mr. Send-Camillo-to-the-Woods-for-Days? I'm serious, Salvatore. What would you tell me?"

Salvatore. She *is* serious.

I think for a moment. "I'd tell them that there's no room for mistakes in my organization. And the next time they make a rookie mistake like that, I'll have Dom the Butcher cut off one of their toes."

Marisol's eyes go wide, almost comically so, as she processes this.

"Don't be scared. I wouldn't ever let someone touch you. Especially your toes."

She doesn't smile. "No, it's okay... I needed to hear that. I'll do better next time."

"I'll do better next time...?"

Now a small smirk tugs at her lips, and her face loses a bit of its gauntness. "I'll do better next time, *sir*."

My cock jerks at that. "Good girl," I purr, lowering myself to rub my face into her neck. She gasps underneath me. I wish I could live buried in her hair like this forever.

"Are you ready to go?" I murmur against her earlobe before straightening. Her eyes flick to my erection. "We have to leave soon," I add reluctantly.

With a sigh, she casts around the piles of sticky notes, snacks, and little TV show figurines on her desk. She spots her phone and shoves it into a small purse before standing. I can't help but stare. Her heels, long skirt, and sweater are a complete one-eighty from her usual soft shorts and over-sized tee. I almost forgot how distracting her tits are when they're not hidden in the equivalent of a cotton sack—not that her outfit today is much of an improvement to her regular clothes. Anything she wears is just an obstacle to her being naked.

"Ready," she says, holding out her hand. "Who do you think is gonna win?"

I take her hand in mine as we walk out. In my grey wool suit, we're a matching pair today. "The Cardinals. Aldo's got a lot of money riding on the Cubs losing. And I didn't think you liked sports."

"God, no," Marisol laughs, and fuck, it's good to hear that sound. "The only reason I even know who the Cubs are is because Calvin was a huge fan... did Aldo rig it?"

"He tends to win his bets."

"Oh." A beat. "How does he do that?"

I chuckle. "I'll tell you. But you need to eat your whole lunch first."

She gives me a calculated look. "What if I scrounge up a bag of chips and figure it out on my own instead?"

I place my hand flat against her lower back and guide her toward the kitchen, ignoring her slight resistance. "Then you also won't get to hear about the time I fed a man to a lion."

"It's a good one," Dom chimes in as I tow her to the kitchen bar where a few other people are eating.

Marisol considers me for a long moment like she's contemplating cracking my head open and picking through my thoughts without permission anyway. When that fails, she sits gracefully on the bar stool and swipes a piece of cold cut off her plate. "Alright, let's hear it."

A LITTLE WHILE LATER, Dom's driving while I hold Marisol's back to my front. Her breathing is even and slow as she watches out the window with a sleepy expression. After she ordered me to install car dividers, this is the only place she'll fall asleep without being fucked to exhaustion first. And touching her like this is the closest thing I get to relaxation. A couple of days ago, I scheduled a car ride just so she could get some sleep, and I could have a moment of internal peace. When she woke up, she just laughed at my trick and plunged back into her work in the watchtower.

I lean back to rest my head, letting my eyes fall closed.

I'm not surprised Aldo invited Marisol to the game today. He wants to show me that I'm still his tool, his man. That when he asks, I'll bring my most precious possession to him and thank him for sparing her. But the fact that he's testing his hold over me like this means he's starting to sweat too.

Rekhson's redoubled her efforts to nail down Aldo. For as many men as I have spying on her and whittling down that fragile sense of safety she's still clutching onto, she's got just as many snooping around Aldo's businesses, probing for weak points.

With Barabara's financial genius of a son, none of those idiots Rekhson employs will be able to pin a thing on us. And the Family's good at keeping their mouths shut—most of them anyway. But we can slip up in other ways. In an organization as big as ours, no defense is airtight.

Aldo's right to worry. And if he's finally sniffed out that I've been working to curry favor with the other capos, he might do something reckless today.

Crushed between my back and the leather car seat, my gun's heavy with dark intent. Aldo's not the type of man to carry out his own hits, but I don't like surprises.

I've confirmed again and again that Junior's still at Lucky Stars—he's taunting us by returning there after that business with Davide—and Worm's on high alert to report back if the bastard so much as sneezes.

My hold on Marisol tightens. She sighs and burrows deeper into my arms.

Aldo and Junior might see her as a new vulnerability to exploit, and maybe that's true. But she's also a whetstone, honing my focus and my ambition into a keen blade. If they think I'm a soft mark and try to move against me, they'll find I'm more dangerous than ever.

Dom's already in a mood as he drops us off at the private entrance to the stadium before leaving to find parking. Aldo ordered him to join too. I think he gets off on courting Serafina in front of her dad and her more-or-less adopted brother.

If we get through this, I'll have to do something about their wedding.

As we walk into the stadium, the weight of all the people on the other side of the brick wall squeezes my lungs. I'm like a spider with its silk tweaked in every direction at once. When the crowd bursts into a cheer, I snap Marisol to my side out of reflex.

She glances up at me with a soft expression. "You want to hear about the first time I tinkered with a system?"

"Yes." She wants to distract me. It's sweet.

We pause in front of the elevators. A bright red light counts down from six.

Marisol leans in so the cluster of half-drunk young men next to us can't hear. I position myself between her and them.

"I got my growth spurt in eighth grade and with it"—she motions to her generous breasts—"so freshman year of high school, someone made a MySpace account called 'Marisol is a Slut' with a bunch of pictures of me. I found out who it was—Erin Wilder—and reported her to the principal."

"That's all you did?"

Her smile's a sharp little thing. "I also sent out emails to her entire list of friends and family about what she'd been doing and reported her for CP. Her parents divorced, and she moved schools before the year ended."

I pull her in close and kiss the top of her head. "That's my girl."

The weight on my chest lightens somewhat.

She puts on her most doe-eyed, innocent expression as we pass through the door to the executive suite. My brave little liar.

The luxury suite at Wrigley Field is a small room with a bar and a huge window along one wall that opens up to the field. Aldo, in a perfectly fitted royal blue suit, mixes himself an old-fashioned as we enter. Next to him, poised like a mannequin in a skin-tight black dress and tall heels, is Serafina. She watches him with a far-away expression and a fixed smile. Barbara, seated in front of the window, doesn't bother to stand, simply waving his hand in greeting.

"Turi!" Drink forgotten, Aldo opens his arms wide and brings me into a hug as soon as we enter. "And the lovely Mrs. Luporini!"

Aldo kisses the air next to Marisol's cheek, and I have to crush the surge of anger that follows.

"You making my boy happy?" he asks her, his hands on her shoulders.

She offers Aldo a sweet smile that I imagine got her out of lots of speeding tickets. "I certainly hope so."

Aldo grins, oblivious to me shoving my shaking hands in my pockets. He tugs Serafina to his side. "This is my beautiful fiancée, Serafina Luporini."

Aldo's always favored petite women, and Serafina's no exception, but this is the first time I've seen a woman at his side who dares to wear heels that put her a few inches above him. I've met her at plenty of Family events in the past—only in flip-flops. Is this a little rebellion of hers? Maybe she's not as meek as she seems.

"Lovely to meet you, Marisol," Serafina says in an elegant voice. "Hi, Turi. Could I get you two a drink?"

Marisol nods with a bright smile, and they walk off to the bar. Aldo stares after his fiancée with a hungry expression.

"So I talked with her," I start, but Aldo waves me off, his attention lingering on Serafina's ass before turning to me.

"Turi, always so serious. It's bad for your heart. Let it wait until we watch the game a little." Aldo swipes his drink off the bar and returns to the seats in front of the stadium windows. After a moment, Serafina joins him with a nearly full-to-the-brim glass of wine. She takes a long draw. She's so young to be drinking. It tugs at some underdeveloped part of my heart.

Marisol fills her cup with orange juice and leads me to our seats. She offers some to me with a tiny smirk. I take a sip. *Huh.* No alcohol. I take another sip and intertwine her fingers in mine.

In the fourth inning, Dom joins us, says his hellos, and leans against the bar. I watch the game for a bit before taking my phone out to send off emails and texts. Worm set us up with new security measures that delete our messages every twenty-four hours instead of every week, so I have to make sure I'm on top of everything. He asked me for permission to buy a new data center in Canada last month so we could make our own cell phone network. I need to check with him on its progress, because losing messages every day's a real pain in the ass.

By the seventh inning, Aldo leans toward me while Serafina and Marisol refill their drinks.

"How'd she take it?" he asks. Finally, we're getting to Rekhson.

"Not well. She said to check your income streams with your accountant."

Aldo whistles low and frowns. "And your dad?"

"I'll call him this week."

Aldo raises an eyebrow. "I'm starting to think you might need more motivation, Turi. Why's this taking so long?"

I don't have an answer for him. I don't like to move until I have everything in order, but Aldo's forcing me to rush. "I'm very motivated," I answer stiffly, staring straight ahead.

"That's the thing, Turi, I ain't seeing it. Rekhson's gonna try RICOing me this month. You know that?"

Of course, I do. I'm the one who gave the report to Barbara to pass to Aldo, but I don't say shit.

"If I gotta leave the States for a while, I'm not gonna be able to keep Junior on a leash, capisce?"

If Junior gets anywhere near Marisol, I'll kill him. Aldo and the Commission will put me at the top of their hit lists. We'll go into exile.

But Aldo doesn't really want me gone. I might be the only one who can get Rekhson off his ass and get him out of this scot-free. If he leaves the country, he won't come back, not for a long while. For now, we need each other.

"Understood, boss."

"You got till the end of the month. I need results." He faces forward, shoving a handful of popcorn into his mouth.

I squeeze my phone with one hand and shove the other in my pocket before the tremors give me away.

Twenty days to the end of the month.

My time just got cut in half.

"Maybe have that new wife of yours help you out?" he

says, without taking his eyes off the game. "Since she's so talented."

I have to work to unclench my jaw. "That's not her area of expertise."

"She better learn, or she's not going to be long for this family."

Aldo's expression is hard. I've only ever seen that look directed at men who fuck up, usually right before they're whacked.

"He's like a woman, bitching at me every day about her," he continues, mouth twisting in distaste. "I don't like my boys fighting over pussy. It's not good for the business. You should just pass her on to Junior. I'll find you the sweetest virgin to warm your bed after."

Rage bubbles in my gut. "I'll speak with my dad. Your problem will be handled. Maybe get Junior one of those virgins you're talking about."

He exhales and settles back in his seat, giving me a weak smile.

"You know how he is. Dog with a bone." He pats my hand, and for the first time in my life, it doesn't give me a sense of fondness or security. I want to take his old, weak fingers and break them one by one. "I'll do what I can, Turi, but Junior's a big boy. He's gonna make his own decisions."

This was fine when Junior decided to poison Kasey Boyle a few years ago or kill that cop. Aldo always cleaned up after his son, so I wasn't about to lose sleep over it.

But now Junior's slavering after *my* wife.

The next time he looks at her, I'll carve out his other eye.

Aldo's older and more tired than I've ever seen him. He's only in his sixties, but he looks eighty. He's losing his edge. Does he know I've been talking to the other capos? I haven't overheard any talk about it on my mics.

I glance past Aldo to Barbara. Barbara might be slipping too. He hasn't warned Aldo about what I'm doing—or he might not be such a loyal consigliere after all.

Serafina comes over and sits next to Aldo, breaking my line of sight to her dad. She stares forward but her mouth is pinched shut. I look back. Marisol approaches with an *oh shit* look. Dom's fuming. His arms are crossed, and he's glowering at the back of Serafina's head. Guess he pissed her off. Just because I didn't bug this room, doesn't mean someone else didn't. I don't care what he said to her, but he better keep it together, because I can't manage any more fuckups right now.

When the game ends and the Cubs lose—against their sworn enemy the Cardinals no less—Aldo shoots up with a bright expression and claps his hands together.

"Nothing like a good game to get the blood pumping," he says. "Some of the players are coming up here to sign my jersey. You guys want stuff signed?"

I grimace. Players mean publicity. "No thanks, boss. We've got stuff to handle at home."

WHEN DOM KILLS the engine in front of the house that night, Marisol's already asleep on my lap. I gather her into my arms and take her to our bedroom. She stirs a little as I undress her, but not enough to fully wake. When she settles back into my arms in bed, I stare at the ceiling and listen to her breathing, wishing I could build a fortress around her and never let her leave.

I knew this was coming.

There are no good options. Not when I have my wife to think about. I can't risk her life even more than I already have.

Even though it feels wrong down to my bones, I should have left her alone. I should've threatened her when she first started blocking our systems and been done with it.

I turn toward her, and she worms deeper into my chest.

I have to fix this.

I kiss the top of her head before easing myself out from under her. My heart pounds as I step into the bathroom and shut the steel door behind me.

I pull out my phone.

This is a stupid fucking idea. I should wait. I don't even know what I'm going to say.

I glance at myself in the mirror. Christ, I look like shit. My eyes are hollow from lack of sleep, my hair is disheveled, and even though I've been hounding after Marisol to eat, I can't force myself to swallow more than a few bites.

I should crawl back into bed and fold myself into her.

Instead, I press the call button, and the phone rings.

Ring, ring.

Blood rushes in my ears. Fix this. Fix this.

Ring, ring.

He's not even going to pick up. We haven't spoken in almost twenty years.

Ring—

"Who's calling me?"

My hands shake so badly that I have to set the phone down on the bathroom counter with the speaker on.

Ottavio Matassa. Unofficial head of the five New York families and all of Cosa Nostra. My deadbeat, piece of shit father.

Fear and rage shoot through me. I suck in a silent breath before answering, "Salvatore."

Ottavio pauses, the silence stretching on for so long that I have to check that the call hasn't ended.

"I didn't expect you to call." He's got gravel in his voice that wasn't there twenty-some years ago.

"I have a favor to ask. Sir." The second to last time I forgot to call my father *sir*, he backhanded me so hard my teeth felt loose after. I did it once more, and he hit Mom instead. I never made that mistake again.

"I haven't seen or spoken to my son in twenty-six years, and the first thing he does is ask for a fucking favor?" His tone stays calm and steady. I've seen him saw off a man's hand without raising his voice.

My heart beats against my chest like a wild animal trapped in a cage.

I bite back a hundred other responses.

"Aldo's being hunted—"

"I don't want to fucking hear it, Turi. Thirty years and you haven't figured out how to fix your fuckups like a man. You still have to ask papà to fix it for you. What've they been teaching you down in Chicago?"

Marisol's lotion is on the counter. I grab it and squeeze so hard that all the lotion shoots out in a single fire hydrant stream. Cherry blossom perfumes the air.

I take a breath. "I'll make it worth your while. Still trying to get that luxury brand deal with the Chinese?"

Ottavio pauses. "We're not doing this over the phone. Come see me. Father to son, the last of the Matassas. Just like old times. Tomorrow."

"My na—" I snap my mouth closed. I can't lash out right now. Marisol needs me to be calm and cool.

Ottavio knows my name is Luporini, after Mom's maiden name. I haven't been a Matassa in a long time.

He's trying to fuck with me, to test how badly I need this favor.

I swallow my *useless* pride and anger. "Where are we meeting?"

"Villa Fresco at seven. You heard of it?"

One of the elite social clubs in New York. Yeah, I've heard of it. I wonder if he knows I've been inside before.

"Yes. Sir."

"See you then, son."

I hang up.

I take several minutes, breathing deeply in and out and gripping the counter so hard that the marble groans underneath me.

I meet my own gaze in the mirror.

Keep it together.

This is a good thing, I remind myself. The first crumb of progress in two months.

But it feels like my tongue is coated with poison.

I send out a text to my pilot to have him prepare the plane. The flight should take two hours. I have some time before I need to leave.

After a moment's hesitation, I send out another text.

> Can you make a flight to Germany in the next few days?

I need a plan B for when everything goes to shit. A quick and easy way to send Marisol off to a safe house to lay low while she waits for me... or to start her new life without me.

I stride back to the room where my wife lies sleeping under the covers. She stirs a little.

"Sal?" Her voice is thick with sleep.

I kick off my clothes and reach into the side table for lube. I squirt it onto my slowly hardening cock before reaching between her legs to push her underwear to the side.

Marisol smiles up at me, her eyes barely opening. "You needed me—"

I sink halfway into her with one brutal stroke. Her eyes fly open, arms wrapping around my neck.

I squeeze her jaw and kiss her.

"You're safe," I tell her in between each thrust. "Do you understand me? No one will ever take you from me."

Marisol moans and lifts her hips, seeking friction. I push the rest of the way in. "I'm all yours, Sal. I'm not going anywhere," she whispers.

"You beautiful, perfect, wicked creature," I growl into her ear.

Marisol bucks up, and her pussy grips me in a vice. "Sal!"

"That's right, bella, come for me." Her pussy grips me to the point of pain, and I groan as I thrust once more into her and flood her insides with what feels like a fucking river of cum.

I hug her tightly against me, refusing to pull out for a long time.

She'll ask me about this tomorrow, but for now, she strokes my back without a word and kisses me gently until we fall asleep in each other's arms.

28

SALVATORE

NEW YORK'S not as cold as I remember.

I peel off my gloves and shove them in my coat pocket as I walk up to the entrance of Villa Fresco alone. Just like at Aldo's house, I leave my gun in the car.

Don't bring a weapon when you're asking for a favor.

Technically, my other item isn't a weapon, but it weighs in my coat pocket with the same purpose.

A spineless purpose.

Dad was right. I shouldn't be here on my knees, crawling to him for a favor. I should be dragging him back to my basement to fulfill my promise to my mom. He has to suffer for all the fucked up shit he's done to us over the years.

But I promised Marisol too. I promised her I'd protect and provide for her.

Even when she's pissed at me.

She saw the texts to my pilot this morning and said only one thing to me before I left for New York:

"You're not ever going to keep me in the dark, are you?"

I haven't apologized. I hadn't been planning on hiding

my safehouse plans from her or lying to her, but I'm not above either if it means keeping her safe, and I won't apologize for the lengths I'll go to keep her safe. She has to know there's nothing I wouldn't do for her.

I step to the side of the building, which reeks of a charming blend of cigarette smoke and piss, for one last look at her.

The camera feed to the interior of my watchtower shows Dom reading a book at my desk in a complete waste of his time, but he's the only one on my staff I trust to watch her. I have a suspicion that I have a rat problem in my ranks—it'd explain how Junior was able to track Marisol and how Davide was caught so quickly in that strip club, but I'm not interested in sowing discord among my men right now, so it's another problem that gets put aside for later.

Marisol's desk looks like it got hit with a floral grenade. Blush pink roses spill over every inch of free space, pressing against Marisol like a crowd of overeager suitors. Giordana was a little too gleeful to deliver the roses to the watchtower, but for once, I'm glad for her meddling.

Marisol leans toward one of her monitors, squinting, and then she gives the middle finger to the camera over her shoulder. She's mad, but she's still at home. She's not running away. I pocket my phone. Maybe she'll like the delivery of locks and candy that should arrive in the next couple of hours.

I enter Villa Fresco.

The entire front lobby area is gilded in a garish burnished yellow that attempts to suggest wealth but comes across like a visual scream. What isn't coated in dingy gold is paved with old marble or draped in curtains the color of spoiled milk. Fat cherubs and naked women with big tits chase each other through clouds spanning the length of the ceiling. Far off, the faint notes of piano music slowly die off as they strain to reach me.

Sharp clicks head in my direction.

A woman with dark hair scraped back into a long pony-tail and wearing a tight white dress approaches me with an empty smile.

"Mr. Matassa?"

I don't give any sign of acknowledgment. My name is Luporini.

The woman isn't bothered. "Follow me, please."

She leads me up two flights of stairs and past several rooms of expensive-looking people eating, gambling, and flirting around red satin tables.

Meet your enemy in a public place so they're less likely to shoot.

Ottavio will probably be disappointed I didn't bring a gun.

When we turn to the room my dad's sitting in, my composure and scheming are stripped away. I'm eight again, walking toward my father and praying he hurts me and not the woman beside me.

We pass the round tables, each with a flickering lamp and faces I vaguely recognize from Ottavio's ranks until we stop before him.

He sits alone, drinking a glass of wine and wearing a thoughtful expression that makes me want to spill out all my sins and hope that he'll have mercy.

The woman stops to fill my glass with wine—Pinot Grigio, Mom's favorite—and then slides onto my father's lap, draping her elegant arms around his shoulders.

"Sit," Ottavio says to me in a quiet command that brokers no discussion.

I sit.

"Drink."

And just like that, the spell is broken. I meet Ottavio's eyes, amber like mine, but lined with crow's feet. "I don't drink."

Ottavio takes a long drought from his cup and passes it to the woman. She holds it aloft and stares forward like an expensive statue. She looks a little like my mom.

"I heard you were sober now. You always were a momma's boy," Ottavio says with a note of refined disgust. "And now you have a new woman to play lapdog for. Marisol, is it?"

Anger sweeps through me at the implied threat, but I'm acutely aware of all the eyes in the room on us. I can't afford to let him affect me.

"That's right."

Ottavio drinks from his glass again. "I'd like to meet her. When will she start giving you heirs?"

Deep breaths.

"We aren't having them."

He raises an eyebrow. "That's a mistake. You're the oldest boy in the family. You need an heir, and she's what? Thirty-two? You don't have much time left."

I know he's prodding at her to get a rise out of me, but understanding that doesn't mean it's not working. My fingers itch to check on her in the watchtower. I need to get back to her.

"Do you know why I'm here today?" I ask.

A waitress brings by two steaming plates of stuffed calamari.

My stomach roils, and Ottavio allows himself a small smile.

Matteo always used to gag when this was served. He'd slip a roll or two to Mom's terrier under the dinner table.

When Dad found out, he woke us up out of bed in the middle of the night and made Matteo shoot the dog.

"Don't ever skirt your responsibilities."

That was the last time I saw Matteo cry. He was seven.

"Eat," Ottavio says.

Fuck you, I think bitterly. My hand clenches over my thigh and grazes the box in my coat pocket. I run my thumb over it before calmly picking up a fork and knife.

"I have a contact in China that I'd like to put you in touch with," I say after a few bites. There's no water at the table, only the wine.

If the woman on Ottavio's lap is uncomfortable, she doesn't show it. She browses her phone without reacting to the conversation. I wonder how much he's paying her to sit there.

"I don't give a fuck about the Chinese," he says.

My knife twitches.

That's not what Worm told me. He said Ottavio's been trying to get a deal to import fake luxury clothes brands for months now, but hasn't been able to get them to agree to his terms. I paid a lot of fucking money for Ottavio to decide he doesn't care about this anymore.

"Is that all you came to the table with?" Ottavio asks. He dissects me with a look. "You think I'll convince the other four families to let you and that don of yours break omertà for a discount on purses? Why did you even come here if that's the best you can do? I thought I raised you better, Salvatore. Raised you to be strong and cunning. But you've grown soft in Chicago, crying over your mom and hiding under your uncle's skirt. Come back to New York. Work with me again. I'll remind you to be a conqueror, not a fucking beggar."

Ottavio watches me with a quiet expression of triumph on his face. He roughly kisses the woman on his lap, whispers something in her ear I don't strain to hear, and sends her off. More than a few tables around us have dropped into silence.

Lowering my head, I pull out my phone and send out a text before I resume eating.

After a few moments, Ottavio barks out a laugh. "I'll take that as a yes then."

"What about Marisol?" I ask, sawing into my calamari.

"She's really got you by the balls, doesn't she? You can bring her. She can be your mistress, but you'll have to marry into one of the other families to make this work. You'll need heirs, of course."

I wipe my mouth and hands with a napkin and then take my time to fold it twice before setting it neatly on the table next to my full glass of wine. A waitress walks past, and I flag her down.

"Water, please."

She assents wordlessly and returns a moment later with a full glass.

"Thank you."

I savor a drink. I set my glass back down.

A few low murmurs around the room announce the moment.

"That's not going to work," I say. I reach for my jammer and flick it on before placing it on top of the table. A sense of ease blankets over me.

Ottavio's eyes flick to the black box onto the table and then around the room where the grumbling grows louder.

"I have a different proposal for you. How would you like to be partners?"

Ottavio drags his attention back to me. Someone's shouting in Italian behind me.

"What're you offering?"

I pull my gift out of my coat and rest it on the table next to my jammer.

"A cell phone?" he scoffs.

His woman clicks toward him and leans down to whisper in his ear. His eyes widen, and he shoves his hand in his pocket to pull out his phone.

The screen faces away from me, but I know what it says:

Government entities have illegally seized our domain.
Your data has been compromised.
Your phone is clearing itself of all local data. Remove SIM
card and physically dispose of phone.

"What's this?" Ottavio says, swiveling his phone toward me.

"Dutch police officers are raiding the servers for CryptTalk."

Behind me, chairs scrape as men scramble out of the room to toss their phones.

Ottavio glances at my new cell phone on the table. "You thought you could be the next phone network? And you compromised the entire Family for it. Heads are gonna roll for this, Turi."

"They would, if the feds could get access to our data. A week ago, I had all the data for our entire organization set to be completely overwritten every twenty-four hours. The police have been preparing for this raid for a long time with no one the wiser, but instead of getting access to months of our organization's data, the most they'd get is a day. Except, I also had that set to clear within minutes of a forceful entry."

I don't mention the rest. That every last detail of this was Marisol's proposal from her very first assignment.

Ottavio turns his old cell phone over in his hand before tossing it on the table.

"How many of these new phones you got?"

"Hundreds. Thousands in another week. A lot of people are gonna need new phones, and we'll be the only major provider in the market."

"What do you want?"

"Rekhson has to go. I want a guarantee the Commission won't come after me."

"That's a big ask, Turi."

"I know."

Ottavio takes a swig of his drink. When he sets it down, he nods. "I want a seventy-thirty split in profits. And I want New York to get their phones first."

"A batch will be delivered in the next ten hours."

"I'll reach out to you in the next couple of weeks to discuss marriages. Dom or Barbara's son."

Dom will be pissed.

"Deal."

A smile flickers over Ottavio's face. He takes his new cell phone off the table. After a beat, he takes the jammer too. "Enjoy your flight, son. I'll see you and the wife for Christmas."

"Enjoy your meal."

As I stride away, I pass a group of waiters huddled together as they glance covertly around the room that's been entirely cleared of its patrons.

. . .

In my car, the first thing I do is check on Marisol. She looks up at the camera with a raised eyebrow and a small smile. A heavy-looking pile of locks sits at the end of her desk. She pulls her hand out of the bag of gummy worms I'd sent her.

I call the encrypted phone I left in the file cabinet under her desk.

Marisol startles when she hears the ringing sound and tugs open drawers until she finds the phone.

Her voice pours into my ear, "How'd it go?"

I take my time to answer, savoring the way those three words make me feel focused and borderline drunk at the same time. "It went well. All thanks to my genius wife."

"Oh, yeah?" she says, "I'd love to meet her sometime. I can't imagine who'd be fool enough to steal the heart of Salvatore Luporini."

"She's no fool. She's *very* clever."

"Mm-hmm."

"And gorgeous."

"Mm-hmm."

"And so forgiving."

"That's not what I heard. I heard she's vindictive and stubborn."

"Don't forget impulsive."

"Almost did."

I scrub my hand across my jaw to hide my smile. She makes me feel like a kid on Christmas morning.

"I'll see you very soon. Make your way to the bed by the time I get back. I'll be hungry."

Marisol twirls her hair around one finger as she laughs. "Calamari didn't fill you up?"

How did she—?

I shake my head. God, I can't wait to get back to this

woman. "There's only one thing that satisfies my hunger, and it's between your legs. I love you, wife."

"And I love... all these new locks you sent me."

"Keep tempting me and you won't like the outcome," I growl.

Marisol laughs again, all bubbles and sunshine. "Oh, I think I will. See you soon."

Click.

I've never driven through traffic faster in my life.

29

MARISOL

I WAKE up in the darkness to Salvatore shaking my arm.

"Sal?" My mind rushes to catch up. Some of the phones came in late last evening by a harried-looking delivery driver, and we started distribution. I must've fallen asleep at my desk. "Did you take me to bed? When did you get back?"

I push myself up, but Salvatore gently eases me back down. "You should go back to sleep. You're pushing yourself too hard."

I scoff, remembering I'm still pissed at him for hiding that safehouse conversation. "That's rich coming—"

"Turi!" Dom's voice calls from inside the house.

I flick on the bedside lamp, and my breath hitches. Salvatore's dressed, with a bulk around his chest that suggests a bulletproof vest. Panic swells inside me.

"What's going on?" My voice sounds shrill. Scared.

Salvatore kisses my forehead. "I got back an hour ago. I have to go. Fighting's broken out in the shipping district, and someone set Barbara's warehouse on fire. The Irish are hitting us hard, and I need to go help."

"What?" This has Junior written all over it. "How did they contact you?"

"One of my men called me. He spoke in code. Mad Dog's using the blackout to hit us while we're down."

"*Mo!*" Dom's voice sounds closer.

Salvatore inhales sharply, but his voice stays soft for me. "I have to go. Do you remember how to get to Worm's club?"

"What?"

"Do you?"

"Yes."

"That's your safe house. If anything happens, and I'm hurt, you go there, and Worm's instructed to take care of you." Salvatore brings my hand to his mouth and kisses my palm. "You're a very tempting target. You can't let anyone take you."

I reach under Salvatore's pillow where he keeps his gun, and my fingers brush over the cool metal.

He smiles in the gentle light. "Good. Go through the escape tunnel. There's a car at the end. Use it. Giordana and Nola are here in the kitchen, along with Camillo. Eduardo and Davide are walking the perimeter outside. Don't trust anyone but Dom or Giordana, understand?"

"*Turi!*" Dom calls again. With his own bulletproof vest, he fills up the doorway as he glares at us. He throws his hands up in exasperation. "For fuck's sake!"

"Coming!" Salvatore barks over his shoulder. Then quietly to me, "Don't open the door to anyone. Don't trust anyone. Don't leave until you have to."

He hesitates and repeats more slowly, "Don't leave."

I nod. "I won't."

"I love you." Salvatore crushes his mouth to mine. I fling my hands around his neck and hold him against me, savoring every moment of his mouth pressed against mine, but he tears himself away too soon. He strides out of the room, nearly crashing into Dom. They start speaking rapid-fire Italian, and after a few moments, the house's front door slams shut.

For a long time, the only sound is my heartbeat thundering in my ears. Even though I've still never shot one, I pull Salvatore's gun into my clammy grasp.

My phone says it's two in the morning. Did Salvatore sleep at all? He's walking into a war zone, running off of caffeine and adrenaline.

After several minutes of watching the bedroom door while dread claws up my throat, I decide I'm going to get ready. I don't know for what yet, but I can't sit here any longer in this room. I pad out of Salvatore's bedroom to my old bedroom, still stuffed with boxes of my clothes. The rest of the house is silent as a crypt. Everyone must be bunkering down, resting in the calm before the storm. I can practically see Giordana now, eyes closed as she sips her tea while Nola and Camillo hold each other's hands across the table. Davide, looking broken and ragged with his black eyepatch as he patrols the grounds.

I pick out a pair of jeans and a t-shirt and toss them onto the bed.

I dial the shower to its coldest setting.

While the freezing water pelts my face, I make a plan. I'm going to get dressed and head to the watchtower. It'll be safe and, more importantly, I can search for any of Salvatore's cameras in the area and provide some kind of surveillance support.

If Mad Dog's doing this, Junior's involved somehow. Maybe I can prove that in some way. Finally pin down what a traitorous bastard he is.

I step out of the shower, sliding a dry towel around my

hair with shaking, frigid fingers, and notice that my outfit's been changed. Has Giordana been by? Why would she change my jeans into a white summer dress?

I approach the bed, reaching out to graze the fabric, when something cool and sharp presses against the back of my neck.

"Mari, what a pleasure is it to meet again."

Fuck.

"Junior."

A thousand questions race through my mind. How the *fuck* did he get here? Did someone let him in? Is this a trap for Salvatore?

Salvatore.

Has he done something to Salvatore?

"Get dressed."

My phone's on the side table. If I can reach it, I can call Salvatore—even though the knife pressed against the back of my neck warns me not to. The blade trails to one side, flaring pain along its path. *It was a light touch*, I tell my racing heart. I can still get to my phone.

"Don't bother with the phone," Junior says. "I'd rather this be just between us. Why don't you get dressed now?"

"Could you turn around?" I ask as I pick up the dress. I've seen him naked through the cameras dozens of times, though I don't think he knows that.

"No."

His tone is still relaxed, and I'm not dead yet, so I take a deep breath and let my towel drop. Junior whistles, and I grit my teeth as I yank on underwear.

"I didn't get it at first, why Salvatore lost his damn mind over you. You look like every other fat nerd. But I see it now. It's the tits. I get it."

Salvatore, where are you?

Probably miles away in the middle of a firefight. Dead maybe, bleeding out before some strange man comes to pick up his body to dump into Lake Michigan.

I can't think about that right now. My hands shake as I clip on my bra and slip the dress over my head, anticipating a vicious stab from behind at any second. I reach for the dress's zipper, but Junior bats my hands away.

"Let me."

He smells like blood and gasoline. Bile burns my throat. When he's finished, I turn to face him, rocking back a step toward my nightstand.

He's not wearing an eyepatch.

His eye is... less horrific than I'd imagined. Even weeks later, faint yellow bruises linger on his skin, but the rest is healed. His eyelid droops over the empty socket, allowing the smallest glimpse of the red flesh underneath.

He gives me a sinister grin.

My gaze lights on the knife in his right hand, and he waves it at me. Conchetta's chef knife. He's dressed in dirty jeans and a black hoodie with a spray of dark liquid across the front. Blood.

"Giordana was not happy about me taking this, but I shut her up. And Nola. And Camillo."

He's bluffing.

"Don't believe me?" Junior puts on a woman's voice and screams, "Camillo! Help! He's raping me and cutting me up into a thousand itty bitty pieces!"

The answering silence wraps around my throat like a noose.

I might have a chance if I run, but I won't be able to grab my phone at the same time. I'll just have to find one later. I can't be stuck in here with him. I inch toward the door.

Junior shows me his teeth again, brilliantly white and perfectly spaced.

"Thinking you're gonna fly off, little birdie? I wouldn't do that if I were you. You're safest with me."

I sway a little closer to the door.

"Don't say I didn't warn you." Junior sniffs and rubs his missing eye socket. "Hurt like a bitch when that husband of yours tore my damn eye out. You gonna say sorry about that?"

I don't feel bad for him. I wish I'd asked Salvatore to take his other eye too. I've seen Junior do lots of horrific things. He deserved it.

His gaze hardens. He wants an answer, now, but it's a trap. I lie, and he cuts me with his knife. I tell the truth, and he cuts me with his knife.

"You kidnapped me. You were going to pull out my eye." I'm close enough to the door now that I can touch the frame. I'm not fooling Junior, though—he's tracking my every movement.

Does he *want* me to run?

He scoffs. "I was only going to take your finger. Salvatore knew you'd have to pay some price. You know that's why he let you drive off? So I could scoop you up, and he could play hero. He gets his little dick warmer *and* an excuse to come after me. I thought you were supposed to be smart. He's been using you from the start so he can take my position as underboss and work his way up to don."

I barely register what Junior's saying. I'm too focused on positioning myself as subtly as I can. I'll throw myself into the hallway and try to slam the door shut behind me. Then I'll make it to the tunnel or the back door.

Except, Junior hasn't moved to stop me the entire time I've been creating distance between us.

What am I missing?

Junior sits on the bed and crosses his feet at the ankles. He lays the knife flat across his lap and chuckles.

Bait or not, this is my chance. I dart out of the room and immediately stumble forward, pinwheeling into the wall and clawing at the crown molding to support my weight.

My feet are *cut.*

Junior's lined the hallway with broken glass.

30

MARISOL

I CHOKE BACK A SCREAM. My feet feel like they've been sliced to ribbons, but I don't dare check.

Run, run, run!

I have to keep moving. I hunt for the widest gap between the shards of glass and aim for it. It's like pressing the ball of my foot into searing hot coals.

Junior steps behind me, his boots crunching over the glass, and shoves me against the wall. I bounce off and nearly fall, but catch myself at the last moment, tottering on my toes.

There's no relief. All I can feel is white-hot pain.

I glance back and close my eyes just as quickly. I'm leaving behind bloody footprints with every step. Fifteen steps and I'll be at the end of the hallway. The plan hasn't changed.

Maybe I can throw myself down the stairs faster than Junior can run—but then I'll have a broken arm to go along with everything else. And I still don't know how he got in—someone might be ready to grab me at the bottom of the stairs.

Why the fuck didn't I make Salvatore take both eyes? *Don't think about him.* Where is he? Did Junior set a trap for him too? *Focus.*

"Where you headed, Mari baby?"

I grit my teeth as I shuffle forward. Twelve more steps.

"You know that little battle Turi's going to? Wanna guess who started it?"

A tear scalds my cheek. I have to survive this. If he hurt Salvatore, and I die, he'll get away with this. I have to survive, and I have to warn Salvatore.

"Any guesses? Come on, don't be boring."

Don't be boring. "Conchetta?" I guess, hoping he'll laugh.

After a pause, he does, and it's a cruel, jagged sound. "The cook? I wouldn't put it past the old bitch. Don't let the sweeties fool you, she's done time just like the rest of us. No. You have two more guesses, or I'm cutting your Achilles tendon."

Six more steps. I can't afford a wrong answer, although I want him to stay entertained enough not to lash out. "You."

"Ding, ding! It *was* me. The puppet master, pulling all the strings from behind the scenes. It wasn't even that hard. Turns out anyone can start a turf war with some can-do attitude, elbow grease, and a little network blackout. You plan that, Mari? Wanted to make yourself look good so Papà wouldn't want to give you to me?"

Two more horrible, painful steps. Junior's taking his time to follow, zig-zagging behind me.

"Did Turi tell you what he did to the Columbians after Matteo died?"

A plan forms in the back of my mind, but I don't think about it too clearly. I don't want him to pluck the hope out of my brain just to crush it.

"He went completely nuts. Slaughtered them all in a few

nights. Rumor has it, he was covered head to toe in blood after. That's who you sleep with at night?"

I crouch and lean over to pinch the largest glass shard and pull it out of my foot. Both feet are bloody, pulpy messes. My stomach roils, and I swallow a sob.

"Hoping to change teams?" Junior says with a laugh, and then I hear the clink of his belt buckle. I just need him a little closer.

More glass dusts the floor ahead of me, but I'm through the worst of it at least. Salvatore's doorway is just out of reach.

"God, Turi would hate that wouldn't he?"

I grit my teeth. I hope I live long enough to see what my husband will do to him.

As I tend to my feet, Junior takes another step forward and leans down to whisper something especially horrible.

Perfect. I curl as if I'm going to remove more glass but instead, I grab the edge of the hallway runner. With all my strength, I wrench it upward, launching shards of glass into his face.

"You *fucking* bitch!"

I lurch into Salvatore's room and slam the door shut behind me. I hope I got his good eye.

Salvatore's gun is on the bed, but the steel door of the bathroom is just a little further ahead.

I hobble to the bathroom. *Almost there.*

As I pass, I fling the floor mirror and a lamp to the ground, hoping something slows Junior down. He wrenches the door open, and his boot connects heavily with the mirror as he stumbles over it, shattering the glass.

My fingertips graze the steel door and with every ounce of force I can summon, I slam it closed.

A second later, Junior pounds on the other side of the

door, screaming, "You fucking bitch! I'll fucking kill you, a farti fottere! Sei un cazzo di puttana! Muori male!"

Every curse is audible. I double- and triple-check that the bathroom door's locked, even though it should automatically lock when shut.

Turning away from Junior's fury, I swing open a cabinet door and flick on the display monitor inside.

Through the camera in Salvatore's bedroom, I watch Junior pace the room like a caged animal. He screams and hurls himself around in a fit of rage, kicking down the nearest nightstand and stomping on it until the wood splinters beneath him.

I still when he finds the gun I left on the bed.

Bang! Bang! Bang!

He's already flung it to the ground by the time I realize he tried shooting into the bathroom. I skate my fingers along my body shakily. I'm whole. The room's bulletproof. A weak laugh escapes my mouth.

Something scrapes along the floor outside.

I glance toward the monitor to watch with morbid fascination as Junior drags a heavy wooden dresser against the bathroom door, sealing me inside. Then he takes his knife and whirls to score deep cuts into the mattress. The chandelier is next. It falls with a horrible crash.

I turn away.

While Junior occupies himself with the remaining furniture, I scour the bathroom for something to staunch the bleeding. I drop to my knees and search underneath the sink where Salvatore had pulled out medicine for my lip.

I find a first aid kit, some rations and water, a gun, and —*oh, thank God*—an old flip phone. My heart pounds in my ears as I pop the battery back in and pray it turns on.

The screen flashes blue and loads.

I clap a hand over my mouth to keep from screaming in relief and joy.

I hope Salvatore takes his time with him.

The contacts list is empty, but I still remember Salvatore's phone number from my road trip. I dial it.

The call fails immediately, and hope drives out of me like a punch to the gut.

That was his old phone number. I have no fucking idea what his new one is.

"You have got to be kidding me." I search around the applications to find where Salvatore's number might be hidden, but it's fruitless. And *my* phone's light years away in my bedroom.

I crush the heels of my palms against my eyes and try not to cry. Of course, I didn't memorize his new number, because I'm a huge fucking idiot.

My head snaps up when I hear silence on the other side of the door, and I startle at Junior's too-close face. His breath fogs the lens, so near it's as if he can reach through to me.

"Gotcha," he says. He plucks the camera, then the feed is cut, leaving me without any knowledge of what's going on outside. Silence. The hairs on the back of my neck rise.

For a long pause, nothing happens. Pain throbs in my feet, growing with intensity. I ease myself on top of the bathtub counter with a groan and set myself to pulling out the glass piece by piece with tweezers I find in one of the drawers. The biggest shards go first, rinsing away under running tap water from the faucet. My fingers tremble from too much adrenaline, and I have to stop several times to flex my hand, exhale, and try again.

I catch a glimpse of myself in the mirror. Blood stains

the back of my neck—although when I touch a finger to the skin, it's not bleeding aggressively. Small miracles. My wet hair and bloody hands make me look like a vengeful ghost.

I smile. Maybe I am.

BANG!

I scream and jerk for the gun as something pounds on the door.

He can't get me. I'm safe in here.

I clutch my gun with shaking hands. I hope the staff got out. I hope he didn't kill them all or hurt them. I can't name them even in my head, or I'm going to break down.

After several long, heart-pounding moments, I return to my feet. It becomes impossible to find any more glass splinters in the blood and raw flesh, so I do my best to work by touch. I let myself cry, smearing my tears against my shoulders when my vision grows too blurry.

I make a plan. The computer monitor is bright blue, but it shows the time at least—a little after three. I'm going to bandage my feet. I have water, a gun, and a phone. Maybe Junior doesn't know about the gun. I could take him by surprise.

Hurry, Salvatore.

I spend the next few minutes in silence while I work.

Then the lights flick off, plunging me into darkness.

Junior cut the power.

Panic seizes me. I squeeze my hands against my knees in the dark as the running faucet hushes next to me. I turn it off and strain my ears. The only sound is my own pounding heartbeat.

The monitor is still on, showing a tiny square of blue light. After my eyes adjust, I realize I can make my way around the bathroom. It must be connected to a different source of power, although now that Junior's cut the feed, it's just a glorified clock.

A wave of emotion threatens to tow me under, and I catch myself on the tub at the last minute. I force myself to breathe. One thing at a time. I grab a roll of gauze from the first aid kit and wrap each foot several times to fashion shoes, freezing to listen whenever I hear a whisper outside the door.

After I finish, I ease myself down onto the bathroom floor before letting out a sharp hiss of pain. Okay, I definitely missed a few spots. A lot of spots. I crumble to my knees and suck in a breath. The hard part's over. I can do the rest.

I slide the gun to the toilet, then do the same with the rations and the water. Crawling on hands and knees, I make my way over so I can pull myself up to sit on the lid.

"What's the plan?" I ask the bathroom trash can. It doesn't reply.

I desperately wish I had my phone in here and not Salvatore's. I could do a lot with *my* phone. But with this ancient piece of crap Salvatore left me? It can't even access the internet. Maybe I can use it as a projectile.

I don't need to be told not to call 911. Even if they could help us, it's far more likely they'd see the address and send someone in the Outfits's pocket. And I have no idea if that'd be Salvatore's or Aldo's pocket. I could be making things a lot worse.

I shiver and wrap my arms around myself. Without the heat running, the bathroom's getting chilly.

Who the fuck knows what else Junior's doing out there? If he gets to the staff, he's going to torture them to get to the codes. He'll torture them regardless.

Tears well in my eyes. Maybe he's cutting up Nola right now while he makes Camillo watch.

Then I remember Junior's smell. Blood and gasoline.

Gasoline.

"Fuck, fuck, *fuck!*"

I suck down one of the water bottles before taking the rest of the gauze and bandages to add more padding to my shitty shoes. I can't stay. He pushed the dresser to the other side of the door to trap me in here. He's going to light the house on fire.

I crawl to the bathroom door and use the handle to drag myself up. My reflection makes eye contact with me in the mirror.

"You wanna go instead of me?" I ask her. The bitch is silent.

I pull the handle down, inhale sharply, and throw myself against the door.

Pain explodes through my shoulder and feet. I bounce off the steel door and crash against the bathroom counter.

"Ow..."

My vision blurs with tears. Okay, that door's not moving.

I make my way back to the toilet and sit on the lid. When I unlatch the safety, the gun settles more deeply into my hands.

I think.

The staff knows where I am. And even if they're all dead, Worm should have *some* notification set up. The house couldn't burn that quickly. Salvatore will know where I am. If he's still alive.

I never told him I love him.

I was going to. I just... I liked teasing him by not saying it, and he *did* lock me in a basement, and he'd had such a long head start to loving me first, that I wanted to wait longer before I said it back. And... I was scared. What if I said it, and it broke him out of whatever spell that made him so drawn to me?

I twist the wedding ring on my finger. Would I feel it if he died, like a jerk of an invisible string around my heart? Or will he leave like Kristin, gone in a blink?

Grant never found out I stayed with his mom's dead body for an entire day, wailing over her until the police came to her door on a noise complaint and took her away.

If my husband's dead, I'll find his body too and lay next to it every night until I've made every soul who's ever done him wrong suffer. I'll whisper to him every night all the ways I loved him.

The throbbing pain in my feet worsens as the minutes crawl by. My ass aches from sitting on the toilet seat lid, so after a while, I shift to the floor. I dig through the rations until I find a chocolate protein bar that tastes like the blade of a dusty computer fan.

Somehow, this isn't where I thought my life would end up.

I thought I'd be Grant's not-so-happy little wife. Instead, I ended up with a man like Salvatore. Whose existence puts my life in danger. Who never leaves me alone or gives me a single moment of privacy. Who makes me exercise and eat food that isn't just candy. Who forced me to marry him.

I never told him I loved him.

The power kicks on, and I startle. I must've dozed off in the darkness. I freeze, glancing at the camera monitor. It's six a.m.

A rustling sound outside the bathroom sends me scrambling back to the wall.

With shaking hands, I raise the gun and point.

Junior found the door code. I have one chance to get this

right. I flick off the safety. Outside, the dresser scrapes along the floor with urgency.

Beep. Beep. Beep. Beep. Beep. Beep.

The bathroom door unlatches, and I inhale and exhale with control.

One chance.

31

SALVATORE

"Marisol?" I call out before I poke my head around the corner. I know there's a gun inside, and I'm not trying to get my head blown off. The thought that Junior might still be in there with her, hurting her, drowns me in terror.

Dom stands behind me with his gun out.

"Sal!"

Frantic scrambling comes from the other side before Marisol opens the door. I rush past her to do a quick sweep of the bathroom as she bursts into a jumble of speech, "Sal, Junior came while you were gone—he came after me—I don't know what he did with the others. He destroyed your bedroom, and he turned off the power. He has a knife, but—I-I don't know if he has a gun."

"My men are sweeping the house now. There's no sign of him," I say. "Camillo's being rushed to Dr. Macaluso now. Nola and Giordana are shaken up, but they're fine. What happened to you, passerotta?"

Her white dress is smeared with blood, and her feet are completely covered in gauze. She's sitting on the edge of the bathroom counter—that was the sound I heard—she was shuffling along the counter on her ass. After seeing the glass outside, it doesn't take a genius to guess what that piece of shit bastard put her through. Burning, suffocating fury rises in my throat.

Distantly, I hear my men calling out, "Cessato pericolo!" throughout the house. *All clear.*

A corrosive shame burns through my lungs. I didn't protect her. I didn't kill Junior. I let this happen to her.

"Dom," I say numbly. "What's the ETA on Dr. Macaluso?"

"Hours, Turi. He can't come by until this evening at least. And the new doctor's still out in the field."

"I'm taking Marisol to the hospital."

Dom and Marisol both start speaking at the same time.

"She's stable. She can wait until the doctor comes by."

"Are you going to get in trouble? I can wait, Sal. I got most of the glass out."

I got most of the glass out. Thunderous rage buzzes in my ears. I sweep Marisol into my arms.

"Sal!" she shouts. "Don't you dare! Set me down right now!"

Dom watches me warily from the doorway as I stop before him. He'd win in a fight. But not if I shoot him first.

"Dom, is he going to get in trouble if he takes me to the hospital?" she asks.

Dom rubs his jaw with the hand that isn't in a sling. "I'm not sure. It's a risk, especially after tonight's events. It's ill-advisable... but you'll need a radiograph to detect all the glass. So the hospital might be your best bet in either case."

Marisol tilts her beautiful face toward me. "Leave me here, Sal. I can wait for the doctor. It's not an emergency. I'm okay."

A maelstrom of emotion roils through me. Only once

have I felt like this, and I swore I never would again. I can barely breathe.

"Ritirati," I tell Dom. *Stand down.*

Dom steps to the side without a word. I'll deal with whatever complaints he has later. I stride toward the door, stop, and then wade back through the wreckage of my bedroom to my closet to pull a clean shirt and a coat off my coat hangers. I don't want a civilian giving me a second look while we're at the hospital, and I don't want Marisol getting cold.

"Sal." Marisol sounds exasperated. "You can help me take the shards out. Just wait for the doctor."

"I can take the shards out, but you risk infection if they stay or if Macaluso misses something. And we don't know if Junior's poisoned the glass."

"What if you get in trouble?" she asks.

"I'm always in trouble, passerotta."

I'M DRIVING BACK from the hospital in broad daylight when my phone rings.

I glance toward Marisol. Her eyes are glassy with exhaustion and pain as she stares straight ahead. She wouldn't take the painkillers no matter what I threatened. The doctor gave her thirty-two stitches. Her gaze drifts to me, and she quirks that wicked smile I love so much—but instead of reassuring me, it drops my stomach into icy depths.

I answer my phone.

Worm chimes in through the speaker, "Guess who's in the hospital right now?"

"*Worm,*" I growl. I'm not in the mood for games.

"Rekhson. *Someone* gave Two-Fingers the green light,

and he shot her and her husband. They're at Northwestern right now where the husband's getting surgery for a bullet to the lung. But check this, Ms. Rekhson? She's doing just fine. Bullet grazed her."

Marisol and I share a look.

"Where's Two-Fingers now?"

Worm laughs, and the clicking sound of a keyboard is faintly audible. "Wouldn't you know it? He's missing."

Fucking great.

"I want this under wraps until we have more information."

Worm hisses. "Sooo, about that. Aldo already knows. Junior went home and told him. They're driving over to Barbara's now."

I squeeze the steering wheel until my arms feel like they're going to burst. "Who do I have that's closest?"

"Davide, but he's a half hour away. And there's no need, because they're coming straight to you. They all think Rekhson's about to kick the bucket, so Aldo wants to congratulate you on a job well done."

After Davide's eye was destroyed, he's been cycling closer and closer to Junior, looking for his revenge. He might get it tonight.

"Let me know when they move," I say.

"Will do, boss." Worm hangs up.

Junior's doing his damnedest to keep me on my toes, but tonight, we'll be ready for him. I told him the next time I saw him, I'd kill him, and it's time to finally make good on that promise. Anticipation crackles through, then deadens the second I glance over at Marisol.

I dial Dom's number next.

"Your cousin does drywall—have him take a look... Hey,

boss," Dom says. He's still neck-deep in assessing all the damage Junior did to the house.

"I want you to message my pilot and have him get his plane ready," I say in Italian. I can practically feel Marisol's gaze burning into the side of my face. She sits upright like a cat who's spotted a bird.

Dom switches to Italian as well. "What am I telling him?"

I relay what Worm told me. "I want every man at their station. Have the house staff cover up what they can of Junior's mess downstairs and send them home after. I'm bringing my wife home, and then I want you to take her to the pilot. I've already worked out the details. There's a safe house in Germany. Talk to Worm. I want you to go with her and stay with her until this all gets settled."

Dom pauses for a long time while my heartbeat thunders in my ears. Marisol whispers my name, but I don't look at her.

"You're telling me Junior's coming right now, and you want to send me off—" Dom starts.

"You're the only man I trust for the job." I lower my voice, speaking quickly. We're only a few minutes from the house now.

He exhales. "You said they're coming to celebrate? Will Serafina be there?"

"I don't know. Most likely."

"Alright. I'll take Marisol. But promise me Serafina will be okay. And... promise me you won't let her marry Aldo. She's just a girl, Turi."

Dom the Butcher, savior of child brides. "I promise."

"I'll go have Giordana help me pack her stuff."

"We'll be there in a few seconds."

I resist the urge to take a breath or to signal in any way

what I have planned. She's going to be furious, but she'll live.

Dom curses and hangs up.

"What was that about?" Marisol asks, her voice laced with suspicion.

"I'm sending you to a safe house while Junior visits." Technically not a lie, but it still burns the same. I focus hard on the road in front of me as it fractures into my driveway.

I'm going to kill Junior tonight. And that casts everything else into uncertainty. If Aldo or the Commission retaliate or, hell, any of the other capos, Marisol's a prime target. I'll send her to live in the middle of a fortress in Antarctica before I let any of those bastards touch her again.

"Where is it?" she asks.

Dom's already waiting at the front door. As we pull up, Giordana passes him a big black suitcase that he carries toward one of my SUVs. I didn't give him enough time to get a beater.

"The safe house, Sal. Where is it?"

I can tell her the truth. It's not like she can run or fight now. "It's in Germany."

Dom approaches her side of the vehicle. Marisol locks the car and clutches her seatbelt.

"I'm not going to fucking Germany. I'm staying here. With you."

I wave Dom off. We don't have much time, but I can spare a little for this. He shrugs and walks back to his car.

I start to take her hand in mine, but she tears it away. When she gets mad like this, her sweet face sharpens into something lethal—even with her fleece pajamas and matching slippers that say "Chicago!" from the hospital gift shop and her hair pulled back into a messy bun. She looks exhausted and beautiful. She's been everything I could've dreamed of.

"You can't walk," I say. "Can't shoot. You'll be a sitting duck. You know what I told Junior. Next time I see him, I'm going to kill him. There's going to be an aftermath for this, and I want you as far away as possible."

Her gaze darts to Dom and then back to me, narrowing. "I want to stay here with you."

Even as that fills me with affection, I shake my head. I wish she'd let me touch her before she leaves. "You can't. It's too dangerous."

"You said I could set the terms. I'm staying."

Words I've never regretted more in my life.

"And you can..." I agree, "up to the point you reject common sense."

Her eyes flare. "You think it's 'common sense' for me to escape the country at the slightest hint of a problem, but I say I'm at much higher risk being so far away from you. We've been trying to pin Junior down for months—unsuccessfully—and *now* Worm overhears his plans? That doesn't strike you as suspicious? Junior orchestrated that fight with the Irish, knowing you'd throw yourself at it, and then he came here, and he cut me up. You weren't there, Sal. I thought I was going to die. I thought *you* were dead." Her eyes fill with tears. I touch her cheek and memorize the feel of her, softer than any rose. She leans into my palm even as she shakes her head. "I'm never going through that again. Either we go together, or we stay together."

"You know I can't do that. If I go, all of the people who depend on me will suffer. I won't be able to provide for you. We'll be hunted the rest of our lives. I need you somewhere safe so I can focus and finish this all out. It won't take long—a few months, a year at most."

She twists her face out of my hand. "Have you even found out how Junior tracked me to that hotel?"

Shame burns through my chest. I've searched and had Worm do the same, but we've had to prioritize everything else lately. Another fucking failure to add to the list.

"I think we might have a rat." It's my only theory, for all the good it does. The wider the net, the bigger the holes. I track everyone all the time, but that doesn't mean people don't know how to evade me. Junior's escaped me plenty of times.

She scoffs, shaking her head with a bitter smile. "A rat? That's the best you got? It could have been one of the dozen trackers you put on me, or someone trailing me, but really, you have no idea and neither do I. Junior could use the same resource to find me again, and then how'll you 'focus and finish this out' while he's sending you little sawed-off pieces of me? Let me stay. I can help you."

The image she's painting fills me with rage. And no small part of terror. My hand twitches against the center console.

"How would you help?" I ask with scorn. "By getting caught? Getting my men's eye taken? Making a website that crashes in the first few hours? I found you before he... before that... that *fucking* piece of shit hurt you the first time, and you *barely* escaped the second time. How many times do we have to get lucky before you realize this is a bad fucking idea? I'm not going to keep you here just so I can have someone to warm my bed. I've made my decision, Marisol. If I have to drug you and drop you on a plane to the middle of fucking nowhere, I will."

Her mouth drops open while I talk. Silent tears stream down her face—I've fucked up. I can't stop fucking up.

She has to know I'd never let anyone touch her. That there's nothing I wouldn't do for her.

She angrily swipes the back of her hand across her face. "Is that what I am to you? Just some dumb damsel in distress you have to keep from falling into someone else's hands? An idiot you let play pretend on the computer? If you just needed a warm hole to fuck, you should've paid a prostitute and left me home. What *you* did, taking me and making me feel special until the chips are down and your true feelings come out, that's fucked up."

She takes a shuddering breath and meets my gaze with her angry, tear-filled eyes.

"You don't mean it," she says in a near-whisper. I don't know if the words are aimed at me or her.

A fist crushes my heart. I'm hurting her.

Then I sit up in a flash of complete clarity.

This is what I want. She has to let me go so she'll leave. I need her gone. I need her safe.

"I mean every word," I say, leaning in until I'm crowding her in her seat. She turns her face from me, but I capture her jaw in my fingers and point her toward me. Her dark eyes are already so full of anger. I swallow back the poison in my throat and arrange my expression into one of utter contempt. "I took you because I wanted to see if I could. And now that I'm *this* close to finally taking over the Family, I'm done with you. I want you out of the house and out of my life, but I fucked myself because I let you know too much. You just couldn't help yourself from prying into places you weren't welcome. So now you're going to take that plane and lay low until I decide I need my dick sucked again, or I'll have Dom take you to the basement and shoot you in the back of the head."

An angry sound tears out of her mouth as she cries, and something hot and sick settles low in my stomach.

"*Fuck you*," she pronounces with absolute conviction.

She wipes her arm across her face and struggles with her seatbelt before launching herself out of the car and slamming the door shut.

I sit for a moment, letting the silence roar in my ears. I did the right thing. I need her gone, and if she isn't going to listen to reason, she'll listen to lies. It'll be better this way. If I die, she won't mourn me, but if I live, she'll be alive for me to beg forgiveness.

Dom's boots crunch across the gravel to her side. I can barely stand to look. My stomach churns—when was the last time I ate? Slept? Will I ever see my wife again?

Dom bends down to help her up, and a poisonous jealousy swells in my chest. That's still my job.

I step out of the car.

Marisol's already standing, wavering on her sliced feet, clutching onto Dom's arm for support. When she meets my eyes over the hood of the car, wrath flashes across her face like a strike of lightning. She throws herself off Dom and scrabbles at the car, pouring her weight into her wrists, and stumbling toward me like a broken, fallen goddess.

"Stop," I demand, striding over to her, stopping just before touching her. I harden my face into stone. She can't pierce me.

She lifts herself to her full height and jabs a finger hard into my chest, looking wild and beautiful and furious. "We are *not* fucking done with this conversation. And I don't *ever* want to hear you say such stupid shit to me again *in my life*, do you understand? You are *not* putting me anywhere near a plane, because if you do, I will break out and come back to you, and I will *ruin* you!" She pulls off her wedding ring with a few tugs and throws it at my chest where it bounces into the gravel. "You can give that back to me when I've decided you've apologized enough. *We* don't ever hide secrets or keep the other in the dark, remember? That cuts both ways. Now, I'm going into the house to take a shower, and then I'm going to get dressed for dinner because we are a team, Salvatore Luporini. *I* brought Caruso over to your side, *I* proved Mad Dog was conspiring with Junior, and it was *my* cell phone proposal that you used to bring the entire fucking Commission to heel. You *do* need me, and you will sooner get rid of your fucking *liver* than you will me. Do. You. Understand."

She can't stay. She has to leave.

This is what I asked for.

I coveted her, and I stole her because I thought I had finally found a woman who was loyal enough and strong enough to stand at my side and wicked enough to enjoy it.

Something in my chest cracks open, raw and charged with vulnerability, and the truth of it all seizes me with a cold horror.

I have to succeed.

There's no other option. I have to finish this, and I have to keep Marisol safe and at my side because even though she still hasn't said the words, no other woman in the world will love me as much as she does, and because she's right, no one will fight to keep her safe like I will.

I'm better off trapping a tsunami in a bottle than I am forcing my wife to do something she doesn't want to.

I am a wretched fucking fool.

I drop to my knees heavily. "Marisol..." I say, voice thick.

"I don't want to hear it. You have a lot to think about before you apologize to me." Her voice is harsh, but she laces a gentle hand through my hair. I shiver at the faint touch. "Don't *ever* say anything like that to me again."

I nod and press my forehead to her belly.

"I'm so—"

"I know," she cuts in softly. "And I can't wait to see how you make up for this."

She leans forward and cups my face in her hands, peering down at me.

My beautiful, brave Marisol. The one true love of my life.

She might look exhausted, but she's strong. As strong as I knew she'd be, even from the start.

"We are going to get through this," she whispers, and I nod into her palms. She drops her hands away and throws Dom a withering look. "Help me into the house."

"Yes, boss." Dom wraps an arm around her waist and guides her inside.

I stay there on my knees for a long time, collecting my thoughts and dragging them into some semblance of order. Then I search through the gravel for Marisol's wedding ring and follow her inside.

32

MARISOL

By the time dinner comes, we're as ready as we'll ever be. Salvatore sits next to me, holding his phone out so we can watch Aldo drive up to the house.

Dom greets Aldo, Junior, Barbara, and Serafina as they step out of the vehicle. From the video, I can't tell what Junior or Aldo are planning. Neither make any sudden movements toward their guns. Aldo's holding a bottle of red wine.

Eight of Salvatore's men are stationed around the house.

Giordana's the only member of the kitchen staff that's still here. She demanded to stay so Junior would see she's not scared after he threatened her and carved into Camillo's face yesterday. If Salvatore doesn't pull the trigger tonight, I'm fairly certain Giordana will fish out a gun and do the job herself.

Maybe I'll have her shoot Salvatore too.

I should be focused on seeing my would-be murderer again, but I can't stop thinking about what Salvatore told me. That he thought he could get rid of me. If we get through this, I'm going to carve my name into his chest with a knife.

He reaches over to touch my hand, but I wrench it out of his grasp.

"Marisol—"

"Don't."

His arm flexes as he grips his chair arm instead, and his jaw clenches. His visible suffering eases a tiny bit of my anger.

We watch through his phone as the guests enter our house.

I touch the gun strapped to my thigh. I'm wearing a maxi dress with a full skirt and an ugly pair of sneakers that Salvatore demanded I wear. It looks ridiculous, but the shoes are more forgiving to my stitches than any other pair I own. I bound my hair up with three of my lockpicks, stuffing them into a bun. It makes me feel better just to have them on me, and Salvatore nodded approvingly when he saw what I was doing. If we'd had more time, I'm sure he would've strapped knives and grenades to my chest.

He slides his phone in his pocket as everyone enters the room. I know he has to be nervous and frustrated, but the expression on his face is neutral—bored, even. It calms me a little.

"Turi, what happened to the place?" Aldo asks jovially. He sweeps in, kisses my cheek, and hugs Salvatore, who stands to greet him. He sits next to Salvatore and pours himself a glass of wine. Serafina and Barbara sit next to me, and Dom floats to stand behind them. Junior seats himself at the other head of the table, throwing me a smile. My heart pounds, but I meet his gaze.

"Training exercise gone wrong," Salvatore says evenly. Most of Junior's mess is still visible throughout the house, but it's not a problem. Everything's getting put on the table tonight.

Junior hides a smirk but says nothing. I note the red scratches from the glass I slung into his face with immense pleasure, though I'm disappointed it didn't seem to hit his good eye. He's wearing an eyepatch and an all-black suit like a cartoon villain. He licks his lips when his glance returns to me.

Under the table, Salvatore and I reach for each other's hand at the same time and squeeze. I'll make him pay for what he said later, but tonight, we're a united front.

Giordana brings in everyone's plates as Aldo talks. When she sets Junior's food down, the food's all been charred beyond recognition. Junior throws a malicious look at her. Aldo doesn't seem to notice.

Salvatore rubs his thumb over the back of my hand. I offer him a small smile and bite back a laugh at the way his mouth goes slack with relief.

"*Great* job with our little problem, Turi. I'll be honest—and don't take this the wrong way—I half-expected you not to go through with it. I gotta say, though, I never should've doubted. You always get the job done." Aldo digs into his plate, and after a beat, looks up. "Everyone, eat! Don't let this food go to waste."

Aldo seems determined to pretend everything is fine, but there's no way he doesn't notice Junior and Salvatore staring daggers at each other across the table.

Serafina pushes her food around, periodically bringing the tiniest possible bite to her mouth while her dad Barbara works through his plate methodically. She's wearing all-black, and she looks... different somehow. She dabs at the corner of one teary eye with a napkin.

What's going on there?

Once Aldo's done, he slides his plate away and sighs contentedly. "Delicious as usual. I gotta admit, your chef knows how to cook the old-fashioned way."

"I'll pass along the compliment," Salvatore says dryly.

"Let's go check out your bar in the kitchen. I want to talk shop. Let the ladies catch up."

Salvatore and Junior stand simultaneously, eyeing each other without blinking. Salvatore traces his hand along my arm.

"I'll be back soon," he says, in a voice just for my ears.

They follow Aldo and Barbara out of the room. Through some unspoken command, Dom stays behind with Serafina and me.

Serafina's shoulders slump forward, and she chokes out a sob. Dom watches her with a pained expression.

I'm itching to see what's going on outside the room.

"I... uh, need to go to the bathroom," I say.

"No," Dom says, without even looking at me. "Stay here."

Serafina spins around to face him. "Dom."

I glance between the two of them.

"It's okay," he says to her in a soft voice. Then to me in a dickish voice, "You need to stay here until Turi says otherwise."

I hesitate. "I need... to check my phone," I say lamely.

Dom nods. "You want to watch the cams? Go ahead."

I glance at Serafina pointedly, who's taking in everything with wide eyes. Dom looks down at her. "She's good. She can see too."

I don't know if I completely trust her, but I don't have time to stall. "Fine." I whip out my phone and cycle through the cameras while Dom brings Serafina to stand behind me and watch.

There. The kitchen. Aldo's drinking another glass of

wine and gesturing between Salvatore and Junior who are glaring at each other from either end of the kitchen bar. Barbara slumps forward on a stool, looking half-asleep. I turn the volume up just enough so we can hear what they're saying.

"...the Commission's going to be pretty fucking pissed once our phones come back online and they hear word of this," Aldo says, "and I have a couple of thoughts on that. Don't think I don't know about what's going on between the two of you."

"Do you?" Salvatore asks evenly.

"You two couldn't have made dinner more awkward. I don't like to see my boys fighting. You were never this bad before that girl of yours came into the picture, you know that? So, I got a proposition. Salvatore, Junior's agreed to step down as underboss. Says he doesn't want it, right, Junior?"

"That's right, Papà." Why the fuck is Junior smiling at this news?

"Right. So, Turi, I want you as the new underboss. And together, I got big plans. While the cell phones are offline, we're going to take down your old man."

Behind me, Serafina whispers to Dom, "He's talking about killing Ottavio?"

Dom mutters something in Italian and drags his hand over his jaw.

"...talked to a few of the heads, and they're not too happy with your dad. They don't like the way he thinks of himself as the capo di tutti capi, and they're willing to look the other way if it means Ottavio's taken care of. So here's my offer, Turi. Get rid of that girl. She's done some good work, but she's nothing but trouble for the family. She's tearing you and Junior apart. Junior's gonna take care of her, bring her to a nice farm to spend her days, capice? I'm gonna make you underboss and then, to really sweeten the deal, we're gonna kill that dad of yours."

There's no way Salvatore would say yes to this. He loves me.

"How will you kill Ottavio?" Salvatore asks. *Why is he stalling? Just shoot Junior already.*

"I got a man on the inside. But I need a little help from all your cameras to see when the best time would be. I planned to do this later, but with the cell phones out, this is gonna be our best chance. We can finally make good on your oath to your mom. Give the bastard what he's got coming to him. And we get ourselves a seat at the table. I'm not gonna be boss forever, Turi. I want to retire in the next five years. Take Serafina somewhere sunny"—Serafina makes a choked noise behind me—"and spend the rest of my days relaxing on a beach. You have what it takes to lead this family. Make Junior your right hand. He's a good boy, Turi, just like Matteo was. He just don't got the head for business like you do. But he can do the stuff no one else wants to do, isn't that right, Junior?"

Junior's nasty grin widens. "Yes, Papà."

"You agree to this, Turi, and Ottavio's dead tomorrow."

I wait for Salvatore to pull out his gun and shoot both of them in the face. But he doesn't. He's *considering* this. I clench my jaw. Is he serious? Was this whole relationship a lie? Or is he just willing to trade me in as a pawn if it means he gets to kill his awful dad and be the next don? Why did I throw my fucking wedding ring at him?

I steady my breathing. No, I'm freaking out. He's lulling them into a false sense of security, and then he's going to shoot Junior.

"What do you think, Turi?" Aldo asks.

Salvatore measures Aldo, and I see his hand rise to his waist, mostly hidden by the kitchen counter. Junior echoes the same movement on the other side. Salvatore stops and so does Junior.

"I think we have ourselves a deal."

My heart plummets. What's the plan here? There's no way he gives me up like this. *You got him the position. You were always a pawn. Something disposable.*

I'm trying to trust Salvatore here, but it's flying in the face of logic. Junior's words float back to me. *"He's been using you from the start so he can take my position as underboss and work his way up to don."*

Aldo grins and claps Salvatore on the shoulder. "I knew you'd make the right call." He jerks his head toward the kitchen doors. "Junior, you wanna go grab her?"

Junior launches up from his stool.

"Hold on," Salvatore says calmly. "There're a few more things I want to discuss."

"So she can go run out the back door?" Junior sneers.

"Barbara, can you escort Marisol to the basement?" Salvatore says. "She'll be safe there until we're finished."

Barbara eases up from his stool with a grunt and shambles out of the room.

I turn the camera app off. I have to get out of here.

I start to lift from my chair, but Dom's hand lands heavily on my shoulder.

"Dom!" Serafina says. "Don't!"

She wraps her thin hands around his forearm and pulls to no effect. A sense of panic rises in me. Dom's the rat.

"Trust Turi. He has a plan," Dom says. He holds Serafina at arm's length with his other hand.

"His plan is to sacrifice Marisol," she hisses. "Let her go!"

When Barbara comes around the corner, he doesn't

show even a flicker of surprise at the scene playing out in front of him.

"Dom," Barbara says sharply. "Take Serafina home. Now."

Without hesitation, Dom hauls Serafina up and carries her out of the room while she screams at the two of them.

For a long moment, Barbara watches me with a bored expression. He doesn't give a shit if I live or die. "You gonna be smart about this?"

I touch the gun under my dress. Barbara has his own gun and will probably shoot me before I've even gotten the safety off. I ease myself up, and he nods. When I wince at the pressure on my feet, he meets me in the center of the room and takes my arm in his like a man taking his granddaughter out on a stroll.

We pass Camillo on the way. He's got a new set of stitches on his face. He gives me a wide-eyed look but says nothing. He doesn't stop Barbara.

My face prickles with shame. *I'm such a fucking idiot.*

"So that's all it takes then? A chance at his dad?" I mutter.

Barbara guides me to the basement door.

"Keypad, huh?" he says, half to himself. Then to me, "Like I said Marisol, be fucking *smart* about this."

He gives me a long look and understanding clicks. He hasn't taken my phone or my gun. He mentioned the keypad. He... *wants* me to escape?

"We're gonna be in the kitchen for a long time," he says and ushers me into the basement. "So get comfortable."

The heavy door shuts with a soft click.

I'm left in total darkness. The silence and the absence of light swallow me whole as though I've been dropped into the center of a freezing lake. I fumble for my phone, sucking in a deep breath once the light from the screen flickers on.

What the fuck was Barbara trying to tell me? If he wanted me to escape, he could've given me a better hint of how to do it. Junior will see the basement door from the kitchen the moment I open it, and that's not to mention the rest of the guards around the house.

Camillo's just outside. Will he let me escape or follow his boss's implicit orders? If I try to leave through the tunnels, who does Salvatore have stationed there? Will they be a rat too?

I have to tell Salvatore about Dom.

I chew on my lip as I open the camera app back open.

Barbara's already back in the kitchen, accepting a top-off of wine from Aldo.

"—he's not gonna bite!" Junior's saying. He's making erratic movements with his hands, but he's still rooted to the same spot on the kitchen floor.

God, I wish there was a second exit from the basement.

"Why don't you tell *Papà* why I'm not biting?" Salvatore says. Even now, his voice is calm and low. *My husband's got a plan. He's in control. I have to trust him.* Junior glares daggers at him across the kitchen bar.

"What's he talking about?" Aldo asks. He glances at Barbara who shrugs and sips his wine.

"I'm talking about you coming to my house—"

"*Don't*," Junior utters.

"And assaulting my staff and my wife. Except you failed, didn't you? She won that little encounter."

A flush of heat rushes through me. *Yeah, I fucking did.* I grin in the darkness.

"What the fuck is he talking about?" Aldo shouts.

"Not for long, Turi," Junior grits out. "Cause she's mine now, yeah? And I'm gonna finish what I started."

Salvatore whips his gun out at the same time Junior does.

"*BOYS!*" Aldo screams. "Put the *fucking* guns down *now*! That's a direct fucking order!"

Do I go?

Junior will still see me, but maybe it'll distract him and allow Salvatore a clean shot.

Except he has a clean shot now, so why isn't he taking it?

"I'm not going to do that," Salvatore says. "It's time to put him down, Aldo. Your son's a fucking menace. I've been loyal to you. I've made you money. I don't run around like a rabid dog all day. We're family, Uncle."

"Kill him, Papà!" Junior screams.

Aldo looks between them, his hand pulled back on his waistband. Understanding dawns. Salvatore's giving Aldo the chance to side with him. To kill his own son or to let him be killed.

Aldo takes a deep breath, lifts his gun from its holster... and levels it at Salvatore. "Put the gun down, Turi. Last chance."

Now.

I flip to the app for the basement door and key in my code with trembling fingers. The door clicks open, and I shove through in time to hear Junior's wild laughter.

The noise sends a shiver down my spine. I glance at the kitchen as I hurry in the opposite direction—Junior turns toward me with a look of shock in his good eye.

BANG.

I run past Camillo, feeling a stitch pop open in my foot as I lunge for the next door only a few feet away. Camillo's arm shoots out and grabs me. We meet each other's eyes. My old guard. Without a word, he squeezes my arm, nods, and then draws out his gun and dashes to the kitchen.

I wrench the door to the tunnel wide open and fly down the ladder, screaming through gritted teeth when I land hard on my feet.

The tunnel's short. I just need to get to the end, start the car on the other side, and *pray* I can reach the road.

BANG. BANG.

The concrete around me swallows up some of the sound, but not enough. *Please be okay, Sal.* I jerk my dress up and pull out the gun. It's warm and clunky in my hand.

I scurry down the path, jumping at every sound I hear outside. Adrenaline's shooting through my veins, smothering the pain in my feet. *Move past the bend, and you're home free.* I'm going to get to the car and call Worm, and he'll know who to contact.

A man appears before me.

I scream and stop short.

"Davide!" My heart's pounding so fast it could explode at any moment. "Davide, they're shooting upstairs. Dom's a rat. Please, you have to go help Sal!"

Light flickers behind me, and a door slams distantly.

A look of concern on his face, Davide lays a hand on my shoulder and pulls me behind him. "Sal's got men with him upstairs. He'll be fine," he says.

Junior emerges from around the bend, gripping a bloody shoulder.

"Turi's dead."

I raise my gun, flick the safety off, and shoot.

Pain explodes in my hand, and my ears burst into ringing. Davide throws me to the ground, and I land hard on my hip. *Fuck...* I think he broke my hip. My thumb stings, and it's bloody for some reason.

Did I shoot myself? I wonder wildly.

No, I was holding the gun wrong, and the metal clipped my hand.

Shoes enter my line of vision. I look up. Junior looms over me, laughing as if he's completely lost his fucking mind. His voice is barely audible, drowned out by the ringing in my ears.

I scramble back, gasping at the pain in my hip, but he stomps on my ankle, grinding bone into the concrete floor.

"—dumb bitch," I catch him saying. "Did you think... really work? You missed. Why he would waste so much time on an outsider defies reason. I was going to really draw this out for Turi's sake, just to teach him a lesson. Maybe send him a new body part every few days. But now I think I'm just going to burn you alive and dump you on the Boughan brothers' doorstep as a little lesson for fucking up. Davide, grab her."

Gun! Where's my gun?

Davide—*Davide's the rat*—lowers and goes to grab my arm with a gentle touch, but I roll away from him.

With a sneer, Junior shoves Davide aside and drops down on top of me. He digs rough fingers under my skirt as I scream and flail against him. Another laugh bubbles out of him while I fling my useless arms against him.

"Don't worry—you're not so lucky. Just making sure there's no more surprises down here. We'll have more time back at my place for the rest. And you know what, since I'm so *fucking* nice, I'll still let you pick on the way there. Which am I taking first, Mari, a finger or an eye?"

I'm gasping for air with the weight of him on my chest.

"Sir," Davide says nervously. "We have to go."

My lockpicks. If I can pull one out of my hair, maybe I can stab his good eye.

He'll take that gun and shoot you.
He'll strangle you.
He'll burn you alive.

A crafty look crosses Junior's face. "You think you're gonna be brave, passerotta? That's what he calls you, doesn't he? You got another gun under here?"

I can't cry—*I can't cry*—I won't be able to see if I cry.

Time slows as Junior digs his hand through my skirts, and I reach my hand up to my hair where my lockpicks are. I'll have one chance to get this right.

"Junior!" Aldo screams.

Boom.

Junior freezes, his eye darting to the side. Cold dread squeezes my heart—did Salvatore get shot? Junior must be thinking along the same lines because his face crumples in. I wrap my fingers around a pick.

"Papà?"

I wrench forward and stab Junior in his good eye. Resistance—then *pop* like a grape bursting.

Junior reels back, screaming as he clutches his face, and I'm bucking, thrashing underneath him to try to throw him off. Junior wrenches the pick out with a choked groan. His face is a horrible nightmare of blood. I gag. He swings his hand at me blindly but Davide launches his body off of me with a sharp kick.

I don't hesitate to roll to the side and scramble to my knees.

Davide wrestles with the gun in Junior's hands.

"Run, Mari!" Davide grunts.

Before I turn, two more figures appear in the tunnel.

Salvatore and Camillo both have blood on their shirts and faces. Salvatore's gaze crashes into mine.

My beautiful, calm husband is *furious*.

"Camillo, get her out of here, *NOW!*" Salvatore roars, and it makes every cell in my body freeze cold.

Salvatore kicks the gun out of Davide and Juniors' joined hands. They scream out. Camillo rushes forward, clutching his thigh.

"Don't look back," he says once he's within earshot. He ushers me to the exit and up the ladder.

I barely feel the pain as I push my body up. On the last rung, I glance back and see Salvatore with a mask of savage rage, choking the life out of Junior.

Once the cool evening air touches my face, I choke out a sob.

No, I can't. I can't lose it yet. I step to the side for Camillo and scan the trees for a car.

There.

It's a little, beat-up tin can nearly buried in the overgrowth of the forest, but I've never seen anything so perfect.

"Junior's reinforcements are at the door. We gotta go right now," Camillo says and guides me forward. Like he's summoned them, gunfire crackles from the front of the house.

Camillo limps to the driver's side and shoves branches out of the way before wrenching the door open. I'm not far behind and once inside, another wave of emotion crashes through me. I heave in a deep breath before bursting into tears.

After two attempts, the car starts.

Camillo doesn't exhale a sigh of relief until we've reached the city outskirts.

33

MARISOL

"Can you stop that?" I demand.

Camillo rakes a hand through his hair. "Stop what?"

"Stop clicking that pen. You're driving me nuts."

Camillo lobs the pen to the side of the couch. Great, *now* all I can hear is the distant *thump* of the club past the walls of Worm's room. How does he deal with this?

"Can we go back yet?" I ask.

Camillo shrugs. He's too fucking relaxed, and it's pissing me off.

"Yeah, let me check," Worm chimes in. "Nope, no news since three minutes ago when you last asked."

He's lucky. He has his entire computer set up to occupy him.

Dr. Macaluso came by an hour after we arrived to check on Camillo and me, but after he left, we've all been stuck in radio silence for the past two days.

I trust Salvatore.

But I need to do *something*. Worm's couch can't take any more of my destruction, and even Camillo's getting snippy.

Worm's got a bathroom and shower here, and his friend

Jocelyn brought me some clothes. But I'm tired of sleeping on the couch and looking at Camillo's and Worm's stupid faces.

And I miss my husband.

I made Worm show me the video of what happened in the kitchen while I was underneath the tunnel.

Once Salvatore shot Junior in the arm, it was an all-out firefight. All four men dove behind the kitchen bar and table.

Junior fired off several shots before running after me. He shot Camillo in the leg and dove into the escape tunnel.

Without backup, Salvatore's men swarmed Aldo like wasps.

It was over once Aldo saw he was overpowered. He held his hands up, one of them crimson, and tried talking to Salvatore, but Salvatore was already running toward the tunnel.

In the kitchen, Aldo didn't get much out before Barbara shot him in the chest.

"Junior!" Aldo screamed out before Barbara shot him again.

Then Barbara spoke so quietly, it took Worm several rewinds to catch what he said.

"That's for my daughter."

The next clip Worm showed me was of Salvatore and the rest of his men dragging Junior, Davide, and Aldo's bodies to the basement while his men made short work of Junior's reinforcements.

Worm said he didn't have access to the camera in the basement, but the way he held my gaze just a little too long made me think he was lying.

I glance at the clock. Camillo's casually watching a soccer game on his phone. He's like a fucking human Xanax.

I pull a particularly satisfying thread from the couch with an audible rip.

"Will you *stop* that!" Worm shouts.

"Text Giordana!" I yell back.

"I already have a hundred fucking times! I'm not going— oh shit."

I perk up.

Worm comes out from behind his desk, staring at his phone screen. "Dom says he and Barbara have spoken with the other capos. They held a vote. Sally's the new don."

"That's good news, right?" I ask, because Worm sounds like his grandma just died.

"He says you should come see Sally right now. Says he's bad. Real bad."

I stand up suddenly and wince at the pain in my feet, sinking back down. "Are you still sure Dom isn't a rat?"

Worm rolls his eyes. "Yeah, for the hundredth time. Dom won't even wipe his ass without a thumbs-up from Sally. He was following orders."

I'm still unconvinced, but I'll deal with it later. "So what do you mean, Sal's *bad*?"

Worm glances at Camillo uneasily. "It means he's lost control. He won't talk to anyone, and he won't eat. Dom wants to see if you can break him out of it."

I look between the two of them. It means I'm going to meet *il Diavolo*.

Worm offers me his arm. "Come on. We better not wait."

An hour later, a sense of unease fills me as I step through the doors to my home. Giordana and Dom wait for me by the entrance with solemn expressions.

Nola sprints from the kitchen and crashes into Camillo's

arms. He staggers back, speaking to her in Italian while she sobs and covers his face in kisses. Worm makes a sound of disgust next to me.

Dom and I consider each other for a long moment. He gave me to Barbara back in the dining room, and he doesn't look the least bit guilty about it.

"He's in the basement," Dom finally says, breaking our staring contest.

As we pass through the house, movement catches my eye. It's Dr. Macaluso slumped over the kitchen counter. A bottle of whiskey sits just past his fingertips.

"What's he doing here?" I ask, feeling my heart drop to my belly.

Dom glances over to the doctor. "He's here to keep him alive."

I don't ask what he means. I take a deep breath and key in my door code to the basement.

Dom helps me forward, and we lock ourselves inside.

The smell is what hits me first—caustic and metallic. Then the scent of meat, cooked and sickening in the way it makes my mouth water. I hold my breath, but it doesn't help. I can feel the poisoned air seeping into my pores.

There are three chairs in the room.

Davide sits in one. He could be sleeping, if it weren't for the bullet hole in the middle of his forehead. I swallow back the emotion swelling in my throat. *He was a rat*, I tell myself, but I can't help but think of my midnight guard playing sodoku in the hallway and the man who saved me from Junior in the tunnel.

A second body is wrapped in a black trash bag against one wall of the room. Aldo.

The third man is unrecognizable. He's naked, strapped to a chair. I don't focus on him for too long, because the split-second image of raw human muscle and bone has my belly churning and saliva pooling in the back of my mouth.

I focus on the only man standing upright.

Salvatore.

He towers over the body in the chair. His hands are completely coated with blood up to the elbow—the viscous red so dark it's nearly black. He holds a small, thin knife in one hand and with the other, shoves back a lock of hair from his face before steading himself on the arm of the chair. He's tired.

"Salvatore," Dom says.

Salvatore whirls—the raw emotion on his face makes me stagger back, glad for Dom's presence behind me.

The whites of his eyes are visible, and his teeth are bared. Blood streaks up his temples like war paint. He takes a step toward Dom first and then seems to focus on me. His shoulders sink as some clarity seeps back into his eyes. His lips press together, and he flicks his gaze back to Dom.

"Why did you bring her here?" he croaks in an unused voice.

"You need to kill him, Turi. We don't have time for this. The men need orders, and we still have to do damage control."

"When he's suffered enough, I'll stop."

The man in the chair behind Salvatore groans, and I realize two things in a heart-stopping moment: it's Junior, and he's *still alive*.

Salvatore grins, and it's a cruel, menacing thing.

I understand now. *The Devil.*

How many men saw his face smiling down at them before dying in hellish misery?

And of all the people, it was Junior who warned me.

"That's who you sleep with at night?"

"Send for Dr. Macaluso," Salvatore says, turning.

I hold a hand out to Dom to stop him and step forward to Salvatore, gritting my teeth through the pain in my feet. "Sal, listen to Dom. It's time to stop."

Salvatore freezes. His gaze zeroes in on me like a jungle cat sizing up its prey. He sees me—really sees me for the first time—and his hands fall to his side like a puppet whose strings have been cut.

Fear tingles down my neck and spine, but I push it aside. I take two more steps forward and gently slide the knife out of his hand. I set it on a tray next to Junior, and then I turn back to Salvatore and touch his chest.

"It's time to stop."

I rub a hand up his neck to cup his cheek. He leans into the touch, eyes shuttering closed.

"I can't, passerotta. They hurt you."

I pull his head down, this machine of a man, designed for suffering and pain, who still softens at my touch and bows his head for me. I press a tender kiss to his lips. They're cracked and dry.

"It's all done now. It's time to let them go," I whisper.

After a moment, Salvatore raises his hands to brush against my hips and kisses me back weakly.

"I love you," he whispers. "I'll never let anyone touch you again."

Tears brim in my eyes. "I know. I love you too."

Salvatore inhales sharply, crushes me against him, and kisses me. He stinks of blood and he's ice-cold, but I don't care. I hold him against me tightly.

Junior groans.

Salvatore stiffens and turns from me. With brutal efficiency, he takes the knife and slits the throat of the Chicago Outfit underboss. After, he gathers me up into his arms. His first step is faltering. I clutch the back of his shirt, worried we'll fall, but after a few more steps, he regains his usual grace and strides out of the room.

The rest of the household watches us cautiously from a distance. I barely spare them a thought. I'm too focused on biting back the desire to call Salvatore's name or touch his cheek as he glides through the house with the detached familiarity of a sleepwalker. Once we're inside our bedroom with the door shut, he stops. He looks lost.

"I have to get clean," he murmurs.

"Let's go to the bath," I offer.

I guide him through setting me on the edge of the tub so he can undress himself and sit inside. Avoiding the bandage wrapped around his shoulder, I wash him gently with warm water.

I know I shouldn't feel sympathy for him. For what he did.

But with each stroke wiping away the blood and flesh and gristle from my husband's face and hands, I remember he did it all for me.

And instead of feeling upset, I'm *proud*.

"You did good," I murmur as I rinse conditioner out of his hair.

Salvatore blinks several times. He focuses on me as he captures my wrist with his hand. We both sit still for a moment, the air thickening with humidity from the running faucet. The washcloth in my hand is stained pink.

"I'm... sorry," Salvatore says in his calm, velvet voice. His touch on my wrist is feather-light. "I'm sorry I dragged you into all of this. I never should've taken you just so I could let you get hurt. I failed you."

I try to hold it in. I really do.

But I laugh.

Salvatore's eyebrows shoot up.

"Sal, I spent my whole life hiding who I was—craving excitement and challenge and love and thinking I couldn't have them all at the same time. Then you came into my life and you... you *understood* me. Better than anyone else in my life. Better than I understood myself. And even though you're way too tidy and a bossy control freak, and I'm *still* pissed at you... you're my other half. You didn't take me—you reunited two pieces of the same twisted, shriveled heart, and I'm so *fucking* glad you did. Don't be scared I'll break. And don't be scared to lose me. You are never, ever getting rid of me."

As I talk, his expression lightens, like a sunrise, from confusion to admiration.

"Does this mean you'll take your ring back?" he asks, glancing hopefully toward his pants on the bathroom floor.

I laugh. Loudly. "No. But murdering Junior for me was a very good start."

Despite himself, a smile ghosts over his mouth.

"My bloodthirsty little wife," he murmurs.

He takes the rag from me and finishes scrubbing himself down. When he's done, he gives me a look that has me rising from the edge of the tub.

"Don't do it," I warn. "I'm serious."

Salvatore lifts himself, water streaming from his body in rivulets. He looms over me. Before I can take a single step back, he snatches me into his arms and carries me to the bed.

"You're all wet!" I scream as I fight to roll away from him.

He lowers me onto the bed.

I eye him. "Don't you do it, Salvatore Luporini. You're dripping wet."

The corners of his mouth twitch as he lowers his wet body on top of me.

"Sal!"

He takes my jaw in his hand and steals my breath with a kiss.

"You really need to sleep," I mutter against his mouth. "They said you haven't slept for two days—"

"What I need," Salvatore says as he shoves my leggings down to my ankles and notches himself at my entrance. "Is to hear my wife say it again."

"That you're a... *oh*... b-bossy control freak?" He pushes into me, torturously slow. He nips at my neck before soothing the sting with a kiss.

"Not that."

"That your tidiness borders on compulsion?"

Out. In. Out. Salvatore pushes so deep inside me that I'm crawling up the bed for relief, but he seizes my hips and pins me down.

"You can take it," he says. "Can't you, passerotta?"

Heat blooms across my face. I remember how much I like what a compulsive, bossy control freak he is.

"Y-yes. Yes, sir."

Another slow joining.

"That's my girl. Tell me again you love me. How you love all of *this*."

"I l-love you," I stammer as he picks up the pace. "I love getting to work right... *oh*, right next to you. I love how you watch me. How you take care of me in *every* way."

His thumb finds my clit, and suddenly, all the built-up pressure spikes up. He buries his face in my neck and groans. "Tell me you're mine. Please, Marisol."

"I'm yours, Sal. I'm not going anywhere. Ever. I'm all yours."

"I'll spend the rest of my life earning a place at your side." He shudders and clutches me against him. "I love you."

I love you. I love you. I love you.

The pressure under my skin swells and swells until a wave of emotion crests and breaks over me, dragging me underneath its massive weight. I gasp and drive my nails into Salvatore's back, fighting hard to keep my body from being torn apart. Then his strong hands hold me against him, and I hear him groan *Marisol* into my ear.

And I recognize the sound.

It's *devotion.*

I stop fighting and simply let myself be swept away by the ecstasy.

Afterward, he holds me close on the bed and whispers gentle praise into my ear until we both drift off into a heavy sleep.

34

SALVATORE

IN THE END, they all come to pay their respects. I mark each face in the crowd as the priest drones on.

Aldo Luporini was a loving father.

A devoted family man.

A man who didn't shy away from the difficult choices.

In peace may he come to rest, amen.

Caruso walks up the stone steps and bows low to kiss the ring on my finger.

"To a long reign," he says.

We embrace roughly, and he turns to Marisol. Not nearly enough time's passed for her to wear those tall, black heels, but she said she didn't want anyone looking down on her today. And I won't deny her what she wants.

Caruso turns to Dom and Barbara, my new underboss and consigliere, and offers them his respects.

They didn't have to be here today. During the cell phone outage, Serafina's twin sister Annetta was hit in a car crash. Barbara took it in stride. He's no stranger to grief after all the years in the business, even for a daughter.

But when Dom found out, he was devastated.

He's thrown himself into work for the past couple of weeks, snuffing out minor rebellions as they rise, but after today, I'm forcing him to go to the woods to be alone. If he doesn't take time for himself, he's going to self-combust.

He could've skipped the funeral. But he couldn't miss his own wedding earlier this morning. Barbara himself coordinated the match between his one remaining daughter and Dom.

We all knew Dom loved Annetta. Maybe he'll find solace in Serafina.

Dom's new wife is at home, rightfully grieving, but the rest of the family—all eleven Chicago capos, and their soldiers, wives, cousins, sons, daughters, and grandmas are all here to pay their respects.

Davide's mom—who Junior threatened for months to force Davide to turn rat—sits in the front row, dabbing at her eyes with a tissue. She thinks Junior killed her son, and I haven't corrected that belief. For the rest of her life, she'll be financially taken care of, and everyone here will know her son was a hero.

The whole family is crammed into rows and rows of pews below us, pretending to watch the priest, but stealing glances at us every chance they get. The unhappy ones are smart enough to keep it off their faces—not that it really matters when I'm slowly tearing through their last shreds of privacy. If they can't be bought or cowed, it's just a matter of time before they'll be silenced.

Gavin Boughan, head of the Irish Mafia, steps forward. He's not much older than me but today, his normally stern face is lined with grief and exhaustion. After the warehouse fiasco, he let me know the men from that incident had been dealt with, and that he wouldn't seek retribution for his brother's death. I haven't decided if I believe him yet. Mad

Dog Colin and Junior were two wild assholes who did as they pleased, and Chicago is better off without them, but Gavin still loved his fuckup brother. Time heals all wounds, but I suspect this one will fester.

"My condolences," Gavin says, extending a hand.

Faces blur into the background as soon as they've offered their sympathy. Today's not a day to sniff out my enemies or measure loyalty, though I can't entirely suppress the instinctual sorting going on in the back of my mind. Today's about showing the type of leader I'll be—present, capable, aloof, and above all, a Family man.

Marisol leans in to kiss Aunt Francesca, and as she turns to me, her smile slices through my brooding like a ray of sunlight. When I was in that basement, all I could think about was returning the pain and insult done to her a thousandfold, but now that she's with me and she's safe, I want to lounge at her feet and bask in her glow.

"Let's go home," I murmur into her ear. Aldo's was the last of a long line of funerals. It's time to take my wife to our bedroom and seal ourselves inside.

She nods with a knowing smile.

As we weave through the throng of people, two men step out. I slow, threading my arm around Marisol's waist and folding her into my side.

Ottavio Matassa stands before us, dressed in a black, bespoke suit. A tall, young man with a buzz cut, wearing a white *blouse,* and slouching with both hands tucked into his dark pants meets my gaze with casual defiance. He's got the same amber eyes as our dad.

Ottavio's gaze touches Marisol, and my attention snaps to him, but I force my body to stay relaxed. I can be calm. The last man that touched her disintegrated into a vat of hydrochloric acid.

I wait for Ottavio to speak first, a practice long ingrained from childhood, although I already know why he's here and what he wants.

"Marisol," he says. One day, I'm going to cut that fucking tongue out and make him choke on it. I haven't forgotten my vow to Mom. "You're the woman who so charmed my son."

Marisol presses against my side, but she meets Ottavio's challenge with an easy smile. "That's right."

Ottavio's upper lip twitches. His gaze ticks to Marisol's empty ring finger.

Her ring burns in my pocket like a hot coal. She still hasn't let me put it back on her despite countless gifts and apologies. I think she's waiting for me to fall to my knees and beg. Maybe I'll try that tonight.

"The boys aren't pleased with how you handled things," Ottavio says. The teenager on his right smirks.

Ottavio waits so I can offer an excuse or an apology.

He must know that Rekhson is alive and well. After Marisol brought me out of the basement, I paid a visit to Rekhson and her husband in the hospital, prepared to threaten her to keep her in line, but she only held her husband's hand on his hospital bed and asked if the bastards responsible had paid for what they'd done. Two-Fingers was already dead for obeying Junior's orders over my own. And with Junior in an unmarked grave and Aldo's body prepared to follow, I told Rekhson the truth. They had. She'd simply nodded. Turns out we're more alike than we thought. We're having dinner with her and her husband next week.

The Commission could have my head for killing my don and underboss without permission, but the fact that Ottavio's here and not a stranger with a knife tells me what I need to know. He's already resolved this. He was probably giddy—or in his case, lightly amused—with the knowledge that the man who helped steal his wife and sons away was dead. He doesn't care to punish me. He wants a favor.

I wait.

"You don't go over their heads when you want something handled," Ottavio continues, undeterred, as if he had ordered me into silence. "We've turned a blind eye to Chicago for too long, and now you're too big and unstable to have your own sovereignty."

The boy next to Ottavio looks as if he's tuned out this speech, instead lazily watching the guests mill around us.

"What're you suggesting?" I ask, knowing I'm playing into Ottavio's hands and not caring. I don't want Marisol out in public any longer. She should be locked away in my watchtower or with me in bed.

"A merging. Nico here needs to learn the ropes. Take him in and teach him how things are done here. Find him a wife. In a couple of years, he'll come back to New York as my heir."

I look at the toddler in front of me. "How old are you?" I ask.

The infant responds, "What's it to you—"

"He's twenty-six," Ottavio cuts in. "Old enough to take some responsibility for the family business."

I continue to stare at Nico. He raises an insolent eyebrow. He's got yellow bruising around his temple and a cut on his lip, probably a gift from Dad.

"Your wife won't bear you children," Ottavio reminds me. "And you already married off Dom. Without consulting me. This is the first step in making amends for what you did."

"My wife—" I start, but Marisol squeezes my arm.

"We'll take him," she says.

Ottavio narrows his eyes at this exchange while Nico's grin turns smug. I don't think I've ever seen a more slappable face.

"We'll take him," I echo.

"I'll send him to you after the new year," Ottavio says. "And Turi? My condolences."

I can't get Marisol out of that fucking church fast enough.

The moment we're in the car, just the two of us, I turn toward her. A burst of euphoria buzzes through me, hot and electric.

"What do you think about a beach trip, passerotta?"

Marisol smiles, eyes sparkling. "I think we still have a lot of work to do, don't we?"

I take her hand in mine as I start driving a little too fast through the streets. "There's always work to do. I want to take my wife to the beach."

"Won't it be cold?"

"I can build us a fire."

She laughs. "I think I'd like to see you build a fire."

Her laugh soothes something deep inside me. Despite all our struggles, my Marisol is here, alive and happy.

Safe. Strong.

At my side.

Delirious need rushes over me. "Lean your chair back."

She does as she's asked, watching me with a wicked little grin. "Why's that?"

I lean over and slip my hand between her legs. "Because I want my wife to be nice and ready to be fucked by the time we get home."

There's no sweeter sound to my ears than her soft moan.

EPILOGUE

MARISOL

"Don't be nervous," Salvatore says gently.

"I'm not nervous," I lie, and he laughs. The damn man can read me like a book.

I reach out my hand, and the second it brushes against warm fur, tears prick my eyes.

"How does it feel?"

"So soft," I whisper.

"Stroke. Like this."

He places his hand over mine and glides it down Buck's back. My orange cat's little spine arches up to meet my palm, and he starts honest-to-God *purring*.

"Sal." My throat is thick with emotion.

"I know, passerotta. I know."

Buck hasn't let me touch him like this since Kristin died. And even when she was alive, he'd barely let me scratch his head before he ran off.

I get one more pet in before Buck lashes out and bites me. He launches off Salvatore's lap and scurries to his palace.

Salvatore observes me carefully. "Are you okay?"

I hold my bitten hand to my chest, tears crowding my vision. "Yes," I say. "That was amazing. Thank you so much."

Salvatore sighs with relief and pulls me onto his lap. We've been working for weeks to get Buck comfortable enough to let me pet him, and this was the longest he's ever tolerated. My chest expands with happiness. All thanks to my husband.

"Does this mean you'll take your ring back?" he asks hopefully, making me bite back laughter.

We've been working non-stop since he's taken the helm of the Chicago Mafia. I thought with the threat of Junior gone, things would slow down, but we've barely had a chance to sit together like this. When we meet each other in bed at night, it's with a desperate flurry of kisses and sex before we fall asleep for a few hours in each other's arms. Even so, Salvatore's found time to bring me little gifts: my favorite gummy worms, new locks, the entire set of figurines from Demon Blaster, a jar of gourmet peanut butter when I got my period. A jar of crappy, generic peanut butter when he noticed I wasn't eating the fancy stuff with my usual enthusiasm.

And no more secrets. I show him everything I'm working on, and he whispers all of the Family business into my ear at night while I trace shapes over his chest. He told me about Junior confessing to double-crossing Matteo while they were in the basement. And about his vow to kill his dad. Instead of trying to hide it to protect me, he asked for my help—and I said *yes*. We're partners, in everything.

I drop my gaze to my empty ring hand. In truth, I've missed my ring every second after I threw it at him. And even though he hasn't said a word about it, I think he's guessed as much.

He's been penitent and patient.

He killed Junior for me.

He does everything for me.

"Yes, Sal. I want my ring back."

With almost startling speed, he fishes the ring out of his pocket and slips it back onto my finger.

"A little exc—" I start, but he swallows the next word with a hard kiss. His arms flex against my back as he folds me into him.

When he pulls away, he drops his forehead to mine. "I love you, Marisol." His thumb catches my ring as it brushes against the back of my hand.

"I know," I say and smile. "And I love you more."

If love's a competition, I'll win that too. And for once, it's okay, because my husband *loves* to watch me win.

He groans and drops his mouth to my neck to suck and nip at the skin.

I surrender completely to him for a few delicious moments before pulling away. "I still have to pack."

This is the first week we've had a little breathing room. I finally accepted Salvatore's offer to take us to the crystal blue beaches of Favignana while Worm, Dom, and Barbara handle our workload here. When we get back, Nico will move into the house, but thoughts of dealing with Salvatore's half-brother are getting packed into a box and shoved to the side. For now, all of my energy is going into stuffing myself with Italian sights and foods. And a certain Italian man.

"Pack what?" Salvatore says as he continues his descent down my neck. "You'll be naked the whole time."

"But what about Grant and Calvin?"

It was Salvatore's idea to fly out Grant, Calvin, and their families with us. I'd grown up with both boys, and we all shared a love for Kristin, even if I loved her the most. She'd want us to be on good terms. We could try again, for her sake. They'll all visit for three days and then fly back while Salvatore and I spend another week at the resort he rented out.

"Fine. You can pack one dress," he says before tugging my breast out of my bra and stuffing as much as he can into his mouth.

I moan and melt underneath him.

FAVIGNANA IS EVEN MORE stunning than the pictures. The view of the rocky coasts and neon blue waters stretches out endlessly from our room. Overhead, seagulls glide and dip with the salty winds. It feels like I've passed through a storm and arrived exactly where I was meant to be.

Salvatore comes up behind me on the banister and circles his arms around my waist, his bare chest brushing against my naked back. We've been making up for a lot of lost time since we've gotten here.

Grant and Calvin will touch down on the island today with Lilah and Calvin's wife and kids. I'm excited to see my nephews and the rest of my family. Grant called ahead of time with Lilah to apologize for his cheating. He'd waited so that I could apologize for my "cheating" as well, but I'd said nothing. Seeing as how Salvatore had his head buried between my legs at the time, Grant was lucky the conversation lasted longer than thirty seconds. Grant had been fired from Snap Close, but "it was okay because he'd gotten a fantastic job at Black Shield Security with great benefits". I'd smiled on the phone. Somewhere, I know Kristin is proud of me. That woman didn't have an ounce of hate in her heart for anyone. She can rest easy knowing all her children are happy and taken care of.

And I *am* happy—happier than I've ever been in my life. I have someone who makes me feel special with every gesture and every glance.

I'm still terrified. I don't think that'll ever go away, but whenever I think of any of the hundred different ways I could lose him, I remind myself I have him now. And that I don't give up easily.

As if echoing my thoughts, his arms flex possessively around me.

"What are you thinking about?" I ask.

"I'm trying to decide if I'll tie you to the bed or add another lock to the door. I don't feel like sharing you quite yet."

"Why don't you try both and see how long it takes me to get out?"

Salvatore nips at my ear. "How about a game? Which do you think will happen faster? That you escape or that I catch you?"

The familiar threads of arousal and challenge wind through me. I twist in his arms and rise on my toes to capture his mouth with mine. He's strong and sure under my touch as he deepens the kiss. I pull away to drink in the sight of the dangerous man who owns my heart and soul. His amber eyes stay fixed on me, never wavering. I trace my hand along the little sparrow—*la passerotta*—tattooed over his heart, and I know, I own him too. Salvatore wraps his hand over mine.

I smile. "Let's find out."

ABOUT THE AUTHOR

Eve Ciric writes mafia romances with heartbeat-raising action and panty-melting dirty talk that will have you staying up late just to see what happens next.

She lives with her two black cats on the East Coast between the mountains and the sea. She loves running outside, practicing Spanish, baking slightly undercooked chocolate chip cookies, and HUGE... cups of coffee.

Stick around and sign up to the newsletter to see what goes on behind the scenes, fan art, bonus short stories, and more.

www.eveciric.com

Printed in Great Britain
by Amazon